James Holland was born in Salisbury, Wiltshire, and studied history at Durham University. A member of the British Commission for Military History and the Guild of Battlefield Guides, he also regularly contributes reviews and articles in national newspapers and magazines.

He is the author of four historical works – *Fortress Malta*; *Together We Stand*; *Heroes* and, most recently, *Italy's Sorrow* – and four wartime novels. His many interviews with veterans of the Second World War are available at the Imperial War Museum and are also archived on www.secondworldwarforum.com.

D1136481

THE ODIN MISSION

JAMES HOLLAND

CORGI BOOKS

TRANSWORLD PUBLISHERS
61–63 Uxbridge Road, London W5 5SA
A Random House Group Company
www.rbooks.co.uk

THE ODIN MISSION
A CORGI BOOK: 9780552157360

First published in Great Britain
in 2008 by Bantam Press
an imprint of Transworld Publishers
Corgi edition published 2009

Addresses for Random House Group Ltd companies outside the UK
can be found at: www.randomhouse.co.uk
The Random House Group Ltd Reg. No. 954009

The Random House Group Limited supports The Forest Stewardship
Council (FSC), the leading international forest certification organisation. All
our titles that are printed on Greenpeace approved FSC certified paper carry
the FSC logo. Our paper procurement policy can be found at
www.rbooks.co.uk/environment

Typeset in 11/14.5pt Caslon 540 by
Falcon Oast Graphic Art Ltd.
Printed in the UK by CPI Cox & Wyman, Reading, RG1 8EX.

2 4 6 8 10 9 7 5 3

For TCN

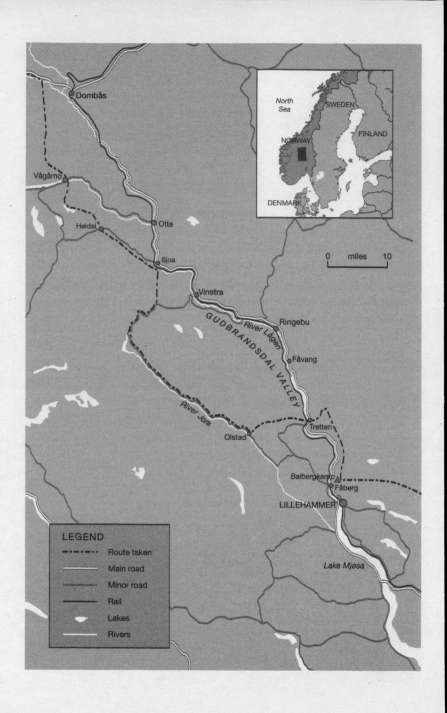

Dombås

North
Sea

SWEDEN

NORWAY

FINLAND

DENMARK

Vågåmo

Heidal

Otta

Sjoa

0   miles   10

Vinstra

GUDBRANDSDAL VALLEY

River Lågen

Ringebu

Fåvang

River Jora

Olstad

Tretten

Balbergkamp

Fåberg

LILLEHAMMER

LEGEND

- - - - -   Route taken

————   Main road

————   Minor road

————   Rail

⬦   Lakes

————   Rivers

Lake Mjøsa

1

Thursday, 18 April 1940. The German invasion of Norway was nine days old, but in that time the small Norwegian village of Økset had seen little sign of the disaster that faced their peace-loving nation – a few aircraft overhead, that had been all. Indeed, Stig Andvard had listened to the unfolding news on his wireless with a feeling of mounting unreality. Swastikas now flew over the capital, Oslo, over Kristiansand, Stavanger, Bergen, Trondheim and Narvik, the coastal ports that provided the life-blood of the country. The King and Government had fled – God only knew where to, but His Majesty's voice could still be heard crackling over the airwaves. A number of lads from the village had responded to the general mobilization and had hurried off to Elverum to join their army units, and had since disappeared into that other world where the war was taking place. Where were they now? Still fighting, or prisoners of the Germans? Norwegian resistance in the south was crumbling, that much was obvious, but to the north, British troops had landed at Namsos and the Royal Navy had sunk a number of German warships.

And yet could these cataclysmic events really be happening? It all seemed so far away. On his farm, Stig still had his pigs to feed, his cows to milk, and his sheep to watch. He had still drunk beer with Torkjel Haugen and Jon Kolden in the bar the past two Wednesdays, just as they always had. Life had continued during those nine days with the same unwavering regularity as it had for as long as Stig could remember.

In the valley, patches of grey grass were beginning to emerge through the snow, but the landscape was still monochrome, as it often was in April. Spring: a curious time of year, when the days were long and light, with barely more than three hours of darkness, but the ground remained stuck in winter, as though it had yet to catch up with the sun.

That morning, however, as Stig had dropped in the slops to the pigs, he heard a distant, dull thud from the south, followed by further muffled crumps. 'Elverum,' he muttered to himself, then stomped inside to find his wife. 'Guns,' he said to her. 'From Elverum.'

Agnes put her hands to her mouth. 'My God,' she said. 'Do you think they'll come here?'

Stig shrugged. 'It's only a little village,' he said. 'What do the Germans want with a place like this?'

'Oh, Stig, what are we going to do?'

'Try to keep calm.' He knew it was hardly a helpful comment, but in truth he had no idea what they should do. Their farm was the first house to the south of the village, more than half a kilometre from the next. He wondered whether he should walk into the village and see what everyone else was planning, then dismissed the idea. What would anyone else know? He glanced briefly at Agnes and could see that she was looking to him for guidance. Angry at his lack of decisiveness, he banged the kitchen table with his fist, then, avoiding her eye further, headed back out into the yard, where the sound of detonations and explosions from the south was becoming louder and more persistent.

What to do for the best? Stay, or pack up the truck and head north? He went over to the shed and opened the bonnet, checked the oil and fuel levels, and that the plugs and points were clean. At one moment, he glanced up towards the house and saw his wife staring at him from the kitchen window, her brows knitted together. Slamming the bonnet down harder than he might otherwise have done, he sighed, kicked at the watery mud on the ground and strode back across the yard to the farmhouse, into the kitchen, sat down at the table and drummed his fingers on the ageing pine.

'Stig, I'm frightened,' said Agnes, after a few moments' silence. 'I'm going to fetch Anton.'

Stig nodded. Their second son was still at school in the village. 'Yes, I think you should,' he told her. But then, as she was taking off her apron, he added, 'We'll stay put. Stick together. They won't want anything with us. Why would they want to do anything to us?' Agnes looked at him and then left, a brief brush of her hand on his shoulder as she passed him. Stig cursed under his breath, annoyed with himself for betraying the uncertainty he knew his wife had recognized.

For two more hours, Stig tried to keep busy and to pretend that all would be well, but he had read reports of the fighting in Poland. The newspapers had printed pictures of burning villages, of towns shrouded in smoke. Polish resistance had been brushed aside and he hated to think what had happened to the people there. Agnes returned with Anton, and Nils, their elder son, came back from the wood where he had been sawing the pines they had felled the previous day. 'Stay with your mother,' Stig told him. 'I want all of you to stay near the house.'

At lunch, they sat around the kitchen table, saying and eating little. Stig toyed with his soup. His stomach felt heavy and nauseous and eventually he pushed the bowl away and went out again, into the barn where he hoped the banging of his hammer as he repaired some of the woodwork would deafen the sound of battle eight miles to the south.

It was Anton who fetched him early in the afternoon. 'Henrik's here, Papa,' he said, 'with some men.'

They were standing round the range in the kitchen when Stig entered – five of them – holding their hands to the warmth of the iron.

'Henrik,' said Stig.

'Forgive the intrusion,' his cousin said, clasping his hand firmly, 'but I'm afraid we need your help.'

'Of course.' Stig looked at the other four men. All, like Henrik Larsen, wore the grey-blue serge greatcoats of the Norwegian Army, with their double row of buttons and red piping round the collar and cuffs. Their large green canvas haversacks were piled in the corner, along with their rifles. One of the men stepped forward. There was a gold band around the kepi he clutched in his left hand.

'Forgive us,' he said. 'I am Colonel Peder Gulbrand of His Majesty the King's Guard. We urgently need to head north, but unfortunately our car broke down some kilometres to the south.' He was, Stig guessed, in his early forties; a strong face, lined round the edges of his eyes and mouth, and clean apart from a two-day growth of beard. The colonel looked exhausted, though – they all did. Stig glanced at them again. A lieutenant of perhaps thirty, and another younger officer, like Henrik. The fifth man was older, with round spectacles and a dark moustache flecked with grey. Stig noticed he was not wearing a tunic under his greatcoat, like the others, but a rollneck sweater and wool jacket. Nor was he wearing uniform trousers. Colonel Gulbrand followed Stig's gaze, and said hastily, 'I wish I could say more, but please believe me when I tell you our mission is a vital one and undertaken at the direct request of King Håkon.'

Stig nodded. 'You've come from Elverum?'

'This morning, yes.'

'We've heard the guns.'

'The town will be in German hands by evening.' Colonel Gulbrand looked at Stig, then at his watch.

'I've a truck out the back,' Stig told him. 'You take it. I checked it this morning. The tank is full and I've some spare cans of petrol you can have. It's old but has never let me down yet.'

'I can't thank you enough,' replied the colonel. He looked as though he was about to say something more, then stopped.

'Have you time for something to eat?' Stig asked him. 'You look tired, if you don't mind me saying so. We've got some mutton soup and bread—'

'Colonel?' said Larsen.

'All right,' said Gulbrand. 'God knows we could all do with something inside us.'

Agnes had already put the soup and a coffee pot on the range. 'Nils, go and get the fuel from the shed and put it into the truck.'

Nils hurried out and Stig ushered the men to sit down. As they did so, Colonel Gulbrand said, 'I think you were intending to use the truck yourself.'

'I had thought about it, but no,' said Stig. 'I decided we must stay.'

Colonel Gulbrand smiled. 'Even so, I appreciate what you're doing. It's a big sacrifice.'

'Not as big as the one you're making,' said Stig. 'We must all do what we can.' He turned to his cousin. 'Where're Else and little Helena? Are they safe?'

Larsen nodded. 'In Oslo still. I hope so. You can imagine, it's been difficult . . .'

The soup had barely been set on the table when Nils rushed breathlessly into the kitchen, his eyes wide. 'The Germans are coming!' he exclaimed, pointing wildly towards the road.

The men scraped back their chairs and stood up. 'How far?' Gulbrand asked him.

'Half a kilometre,' Nils replied, 'maybe a little more. Two trucks full of men and a car out front.'

'Quick,' said Gulbrand, 'to the truck.' The men grabbed their packs and rifles, but at the door Stig said,

'I don't think you'll make it. They're too close. Let me hide you. Perhaps they'll go on through the village. Then you can head back to the bridge.'

Gulbrand peered through the window, glanced at his men and nodded at Stig. 'All right. Quick.'

Stig led them through the house and out of the back, away from the road, across a patch of packed snow to the ground floor of the barn, where the cows still sheltered. The animals shuffled and snorted nervously at the sudden intrusion, but the men made their way through the heavy, warm bodies and up a dusty ladder to the floor above. The upper deck of the barn was filled at one end with a stack of hay. 'Get under that,' Stig told them. 'I'll smooth it over afterwards.' The men did as they were bidden just as the sound of the trucks reached the barn from the road. As Stig covered the men and looked anxiously around him for any sign of their presence, he heard muffled shouts in German and felt his heart quicken. He hurried down the ladder, pushed through the cows and stepped out into the yard once more. Not more than forty metres away, by the road, several German troops were clambering out of a grey-painted Opel truck and running over to an officer who stood a little way from his staff car. The remainder – some thirty troops in all, Stig guessed – waited in the two lorries, the tips of their rifles pointed menacingly skyward. Stig felt his heart lurch, then froze as he heard the officer call out to him.

'You!' shouted the German. 'Come here!'

Stig walked towards him, praying Agnes and the boys had cleared away the bowls and mugs and any sign of the five men. The officer stared at him, watching his every step until Stig stopped a few yards away.

'Who lives here?' the German asked, in fluent Norwegian.

'Myself and my family. My wife and two boys.' Stig looked at the implacable face. The man had a pistol by his side and behind him six men were armed with rifles. The officer's pistol was pointed directly at Stig's stomach. 'We're looking for soldiers,' said the officer. 'Have you seen any Norwegian troops?'

Stig shook his head. He felt a bead of sweat run down his back.

'We've had reports that troops were seen heading this way. You can show me around. If you're telling the truth you have nothing to fear. The house first, I think.'

Stig led the way, his heart thumping, to the back. He felt his hand close round the metal latch, briefly closed his eyes, then opened the door. The officer brushed past him, glanced around, then ordered his men to start their search.

'Where are your family?' he asked.

'Probably in the kitchen. It's where I left them.'

'What do you mean?'

'After lunch,' Stig said quickly.

The officer studied him, eyes boring into him. 'You seem nervous,' the German said to him.

'We're not used to having troops here. You're the first Germans I've seen. All these weapons . . .' He let the sentence trail.

The officer eyed him again. 'Continue the guided tour.'

Stig led him to the kitchen where Agnes and the two boys stood anxiously at the far side of the table. Glancing around quickly to see that they had removed all evidence of their guests, Stig walked over and stood beside his family, waiting. The officer peered into a tall cupboard, then found the door to the cellar. He shouted to his men, who were evidently checking upstairs, the sound of heavy feet and the moving of furniture clunking loudly through the timber boards. Two appeared soon after, ducking their helmeted heads as they entered the low-beamed kitchen, then disappeared into the cellar. They found nothing.

'Outside now,' the officer said, and Stig looked anxiously at his wife and sons, then followed.

'I've a couple of sheds and a main barn,' said Stig. 'Nothing more.'

'You have a truck,' said the German. 'A Ford truck. We might need that.'

Stig's heart sank, but the officer was now looking at the barn. A stone and earth ramp led from the yard to the height of the first floor, and a wooden bridge linked the ramp to two large doors at the front. Underneath the bridge stood an old cart.

'Can you open those doors?' the officer asked him.

'Only from the inside at the moment,' Stig explained. 'There's a wooden bolt across them.' Instead he led them to the door at the side on the ground floor.

Above, Henrik Larsen had his face pressed to the floor-boards. There was the tiniest crack and through it he could see Stig leading the German troops into the barn.

15

He, too, could feel his heart pounding, so hard that he feared its movement would disturb some of the dry dust and give away their position. A cow bellowed, then another, as the soldiers roughly pushed them aside.

'And what have you got up there?' the German officer was asking Stig.

'A few stores. The remnants of last year's hay,' Stig replied.

Larsen watched as the officer pushed his way through the cows and stared up at the floorboards above, so that it seemed to him that the German was staring straight at him from under his peaked field cap with its curious flower embroidered on the side. Dark eyes, square face and thin lips. Larsen tensed as he watched the officer carefully unfasten his holster cover and remove his pistol. And by God he felt hot under the hay, still in his shirt, thick tunic and greatcoat. He could feel the sweat running down either side of his face and he worried suddenly that a bead of it, rather than the dust, would drip through the rafters. Fighting off a desperate urge to wipe his brow, he remained still, hardly daring to blink or even breathe. Stig, he could see, was terrified: his eyes were darting from one man to another, and he swallowed repeatedly. *Come on, Stig,* he thought, *don't go and get yourself killed.* As a boy, Larsen had always looked up to his older cousin. *And now this.*

The other soldiers were also looking upwards, their rifles at the ready, as the officer began slowly, purposefully, climbing the rungs on the ladder. Larsen watched him, until all he could see were the German's boots and then, moments later, he heard the man clamber out onto the floorboards beside them. His footsteps trod carefully towards the two doors at the end. There was a clatter as he moved something out of his way, and then he was walking back again towards the pile of hay. Larsen froze once more, then heard movement in the hay to his left. Closing his eyes, he heard the German cock his pistol. An earth-shattering crack jolted him as a shot rang out. But instead of feeling any searing pain or hearing the cry of a comrade, he was aware of the German officer laughing. 'You have one less rat in your barn,' the German called out to Stig.

After that the Germans left, but it was not until the trucks and the car had moved on towards the main part of the village and Stig had crept back up the ladder that any of them dared speak.

'They're searching the rest of the village,' Stig told them, in a loud whisper, and one by one they stood up, dusted themselves down and pulled the wisps of hay from their collars and hair. 'They won't be able to see you – there's a bend in the road between us, the church and the rest of the houses.'

Colonel Gulbrand clasped Stig's hands again. 'Thank you,' he said. 'I shall make sure the King hears of what you have done for us.'

Stig smiled, his earlier terror receding. Extreme relief, mixed with a surge of adrenalin, gave him an almost exultant feeling. 'Head back a couple of hundred metres, then cross the bridge over the Glåma,' he told Gulbrand. 'The road along the valley leads north-west and it's clear of snow.'

The men hurried out of the barn to the open shed where the truck stood. Throwing their packs into the back first, the younger guardsmen clambered in while Gulbrand and the curious bespectacled man jumped into the cab. The engine started immediately. Stig looked up at Larsen. 'Good luck,' he said. 'One day you can come back and tell me all about it.'

'Stig, thank you,' Larsen replied. 'Take good care of yourself. Look after your family.'

'I will.'

Larsen gripped the wooden stock of his rifle with one hand and clenched the side of the truck with the other as they cautiously rumbled across the yard, then turned out onto the road. As Stig had assured them, there was no sign of the Germans. Larsen glanced back to the farmhouse one last time and saw his cousin wave, then step back into the house.

Gulbrand turned the truck across the bridge, then right onto the valley road. On the other side of the wide Glåma river the village of Økset drifted into view between the trees on the river's edge. Larsen could see, as the others could, the German trucks by the church, and a dull ache churned once more in his belly. Surely, he thought, they would be spotted. He could almost feel German field glasses trained on them.

A sickening feeling washed over him as it dawned on him with sudden clarity that his cousin would be in trouble. He couldn't believe he had been so stupid. Why had it not occurred to him at the time? Of course the Germans would return to the farm, find the truck gone and put two and two together. *Jesus*, he thought. *What have I done?*

Sitting opposite him, Lieutenant Nielssen grinned. He had taken off his cloth field cap so that his fair hair was blown across his forehead. 'What are the odds on when our friends in the Luftwaffe will appear?'

'For Christ's sake,' muttered Stunde. He was the youngest of them, only recently promoted to lieutenant.

'Two to one says it'll be less than an hour.'

In fact, it was half that time. They had not driven more than a dozen miles when two Messerschmitt 110s were bearing down on them. No sooner had Larsen seen two dots rapidly transform into wasp-like planes than rows of bullets spat up lumps of soil behind them before catching up with the pick-up, smashing one of the headlights from the front wings and puncturing the bonnet. In seconds the aircraft were past, the two dark crosses on each wingtip vivid against their pale, oil-streaked undersides. They watched the two fighters roar onwards, then bank and turn.

'Christ, look at the bonnet!' yelled Stunde. Larsen stood up and peered over the cab at the huge tear from which steam was hissing.

Gulbrand pulled the truck into the side of the road. 'Out, out, quick!' he shouted.

Grabbing their rucksacks, they leapt out and ran into the dense pine forest that rose high above the valley. This time Larsen heard the clatter of machine-gun bullets before the roar of the aircrafts' twin engines. Pressing his head into the snow he felt an explosion followed by a surge of bright heat as the truck exploded in a ball of flame. Shards of glass and metal rained through the trees, and branches crackled as those closest to the inferno caught fire. Larsen glanced at the colonel and saw him almost smothering the civilian, Hening Sandvold.

'Anyone hurt?' called Gulbrand. Miraculously, no one was. 'Good. Let's get away from here.' He pulled out a map. 'We'll climb up into the mountains, then cut across and join a road here.' He pointed.

Larsen hauled himself up beside the colonel. Drops of melting snow from the pines were falling around them. 'You knew they'd come back for Stig.'

'It was inevitable,' he said. 'I'm sorry. He's a strong man, though. I'm sure he'll come through.'

Larsen smiled weakly, then continued scrambling up into the mountains.

But Stig Andvard was already dead. As Colonel Gulbrand had known all along – and Larsen and his cousin had realized too late – the Germans had seen the truck speeding along the far side of the valley with five men aboard. When they returned to the farm and found the pick-up gone, Hauptmann Wolf Zellner, in his fury at being duped by a mere farmer, had taken out his pistol and shot Stig in the head. As Larsen scrabbled up out of the snow, Agnes lay over her prostrate husband, wailing with grief while a pool of blood spread in an ever-widening circle across the packed ice next to the empty shed.

More than two hundred and fifty miles away, as the crow flies, a British Royal Navy light cruiser steamed across the North Sea towards the Norwegian coast. There was a moderate swell and grey clouds overhead, conditions enough to ensure that HMS *Pericles* pitched and rolled with gusto as she carved her way through the grey-green sea. For the majority of the infantrymen being given passage – and whose stomachs were used to a steadier footing – this movement was too much. Below decks, soldiers lay in their bunks, pallid and groaning. A few played cards or smoked, but despite the smell of tobacco and oil, the stench of vomit was overwhelming.

It was why one soldier was on the main deck. An experienced sailor compared with most of the novices on board, he'd had no seasickness and, now that the rain had stopped, had stepped out into the bracing North Sea air.

Leaning against the railings to the port side of the forward six-inch gun turret, he watched the bow pitching into the sea, arcs of white spray pluming into the air. The wind brought tiny droplets of seawater across the decks, and he found the thin spray refreshing against his face.

He stood a little over six foot tall, with broad shoulders and dark skin from years of being baked in a hot sun, and bolstered during the past week in Scotland by unusually warm, sunny weather. Dark brown hair and brows accentuated his pale blue eyes, from which spread the lines of crow's feet. His nose was narrow but slightly askew, broken several times over the years. Otherwise his face was clean-shaven and as yet largely unlined – although he was still only twenty-four, his demeanour and the overall impression he gave were those of someone several years older.

Sergeant Jack Tanner glanced casually at a passing

seaman, then shuffled his shoulders. The thick serge still felt unfamiliar after years of wearing cotton drill, and the unlined collar made his neck itch, but he was not one of those mourning the demise of the old service dress, with its long tunic and leggings. The RSM had been broken-hearted, but that was because he had known no other uniform and because he liked his men to look immaculate on the parade ground – all polished boots and shiny brass buttons, service caps down over the eyes. Looking smart was all very well, but Tanner had come to learn that practicality was more important when trying to kill the enemy, which was why he approved of the new khaki battle dress, with its short blouse and high-backed trousers, so completely different from anything that had come before, and which had not yet reached either India or the Middle East. Indeed, the battalion had only been issued with the new pattern a few weeks before.

Three cream chevrons on either arm marked his rank, while above, in a gentle curve at the top of the sleeve, was a black tab with 'Yorks Rangers' written in green. It was a regimental marking idiosyncratic to all three battalions of the King's Own Yorkshire Rangers, and a distinction the sergeant still felt proud to wear after eight years. The Rangers had had a long history, having fought from Africa to Asia to the Americas in numerous battles and campaigns as far back as Blenheim, and Tanner was glad to be part of that. It gave him a sense of purpose and belonging.

Even so, when he thought of the regiment, it was the 2nd Battalion – the one with which he had served since joining up eight years before. He had assumed that once

22

his leave was over, he would be returning to Palestine, where the 2nd Battalion was still based, but instead he had been told that the 5th Battalion needed experienced men and had been packed off to Leeds to join them instead.

At the time he had been distraught to leave behind so many good friends, not to mention the way of life he had come to know so well, but it was also a matter of pride, and Jack Tanner was a proud man. The 5th Battalion were not regulars but Territorials and, as everyone knew, were barely more than poorly trained part-timers.

In the six weeks he had been with them, he had not seen much to alter that view. Most of the men in his platoon were decent enough lads, but the majority were undernourished and from impoverished families living in the industrial cities of Leeds and Bradford. They lacked the stamina and fitness he was used to with the regulars. Few of them could fire thirty rounds a minute with anything approaching a decent aim. Parade-ground drill, route marches and a few exercises on the moors was the limit of their experience. Lieutenant Dingwall, his platoon commander, had been a solicitor from Ripon before the war, and although he was harmless enough he could barely read a map, let alone fell a man from five hundred yards. Tanner knew the subaltern inspired little confidence in his men, yet now they were heading off to war, and it was Tanner's job to keep them alive and help to make them into an effective fighting unit.

Tanner sighed and looked out at the ships of their small force steaming with *Pericles*. No more than two hundred yards away the transport ship, *Sirius*, carried the battalion's artillery, motor transport and much of their ammunition and other equipment. He would have liked to know whose idea it had been to put so much of their equipment onto one ship. 'Bloody idiots,' he muttered, then pushed his tin helmet to the back of his head and leant forward to gaze down at the sea racing past.

In fact, he had begun to doubt whether anyone in the entire army, let alone 148th Brigade, had much idea about what they were doing. Since leaving Leeds and arriving at Rosyth, they had boarded three different ships, loading and unloading their equipment on each occasion. Confusion and chaos had ensued. Kit had been lost and mixed up with that of the Sherwood Foresters and Leicesters, who were also part of the brigade, while once, they had even set sail before turning and heading back to port. Nobody seemed to know why. All the men had been grumbling and it had been universally agreed that the top brass needed their heads examining. This was no way to fight a war.

After disembarking the second time, they had marched eleven miles to a makeshift camp outside Dumfermline where they had remained an entire week, carrying out a few route marches but little firing practice or battle training: most of their ammunition and equipment was still lying somewhere on Rosyth docks. Even when they had finally set sail early the previous morning, the battalion had been horribly mixed up: two companies and HQ Company on *Pericles*, and one each on the other two cruisers, along with the Foresters and Leicesters. Worst of all, no attempt seemed to have been made to split up their heavy equipment. Tanner gazed at *Sirius* and wondered again whose idea it had been to put all their transport and guns on one thin-skinned, poorly armed transport ship. 'Bloody hell,' he said again, shaking his head.

'You all right, Sarge?' Corporal Sykes was standing beside him, cupping his hands with his back turned as he tried to light a cigarette.

'Yes, thanks, Stan. Not so much of a croaker now?'

'Think I'll pull through. Better for being out here at any rate. Christ, the smell down there. Bloody terrible.'

'Why do you think I'm standing out here?' Tanner grinned. 'You've got to eat something before you set sail. Do that and you'll be fine.'

The ship pitched again, causing a larger plume of spray to splash over the prow. Both men instinctively turned their backs but then, out of the corner of his eye, Tanner spotted a trail of white rushing across the surface towards *Sirius*.

'Sweet Jesus!' he said, shaking Sykes's shoulder. 'That's a bloody torpedo. Look!'

At the same moment, the ship's klaxon rang out, there was shouting across the decks and the crew rushed to their battle stations. Across the two-hundred-yard stretch of water, the men on board *Sirius* had also seen the missile, their frantic shouts of alarm carrying over the grey sea. Both Tanner and Sykes watched in silence as the torpedo reached the vessel. A split-second pause, then a deafening explosion. A huge tower of water erupted into the sky, followed moments later by a second detonation. Suddenly the ship was engulfed in flames and thick, oily black smoke. The *Pericles* began to turn

25

away rapidly, tilting hard to avoid the U-boat that must still be lurking below. The two destroyers escorting the convoy went back towards the stricken *Sirius*, depth charges popping from their sides only to explode moments later in great eruptions of water.

Tanner and Sykes ran to the stern as *Pericles* began to turn again. They lost their footing as the ship lilted, but grabbed the railings and watched as *Sirius* groaned in agony. She was now dead in the water. Men screamed, shouted and hurled themselves into the ice-cold sea. Then, with a haunting wail of tearing metal, *Sirius* split in two. The stern went under first, sliding beneath the waves, but the prow took longer, the bow pointing almost vertically into the sky before gently sinking out of view. It had taken a little under four minutes.

'Jesus, Sarge,' said Sykes, at length. One of the anti-aircraft cruisers had come alongside where *Sirius* had been moments before and was picking up survivors. 'Would you bloody believe it? How are we expected to fight the bloody Jerries now?'

Tanner rubbed his brow. 'I don't know, Stan. I really don't know.'

2

A Dornier roared overhead, the second within a few minutes, and so startlingly low that Tanner ducked involuntarily. It was huge and, Tanner thought, menacing with its wide wings, black crosses and swastikas. It was unnerving to think that German aircrew were just a hundred feet above him, and hurtling ever further behind Allied lines.

'Cocky bastards,' he said, turning to Private Hepworth.

'When are we going to get some aircraft, Sarge?' Hepworth asked. 'I don't think I've seen a single one of ours since we got here.'

'God knows,' replied Tanner. 'But these bloody jokers seem to be able to do what they bloody like. I mean, for Christ's sake, how low was that one? I'm surprised he hasn't taken a chimney with him.' He shook his head. 'They must be able to see our every damn move.' He opened the door of the truck and jumped into the cab, Hepworth following. 'Now,' he said, to himself as much as to Hepworth, 'let's try to get this thing started.' It was

French, a dark blue Renault, standing in a yard behind a butcher's shop in Lillehammer. He found the choke and the ignition switch, turned it clockwise, then located a starter button in the footwell. Pressing it down with his boot, he was relieved to hear the engine turn over and wheeze into life. As it did so, the dials on the dashboard flickered. A quarter of a tank of fuel. It was better than nothing.

Tanner ground the gear-stick into reverse, and was inching back when he became aware of a middle-aged man running towards him, waving his hands angrily.

'We'd better get out of here, Sarge,' said Hepworth. 'I don't think Granddad's too happy about us nicking his truck.'

Tanner thrust the gear-stick into first, and began to move out of the yard.

'Hey! That is my truck,' the man shouted in English. 'What do you think you are doing?'

'Sorry,' Tanner yelled back, 'but I'm requisitioning it. We need it to help defend your country.' He sped past the incredulous man, through the archway and out into the street. 'Poor bastard.'

'If we hadn't taken it the Jerries would have done, Sarge,' said Hepworth.

'We should have our own damned trucks, rather than having to cart around taking transport off Norwegians. It's bloody chaos here, Hep. Absolute bloody chaos.'

Not that it showed on the streets of Lillehammer that Monday morning, 22 April. Barely a soul stirred as Tanner drove through the deserted town to a warehouse next to the railway station. There, two platoons from

B Company and a working party of Sherwood Foresters had been unloading stores since shortly after midnight. Most of these had now been taken out of the warehouse, but large piles were still strewn along the platform and in the yard, waiting to be taken away.

As Tanner came to a halt the quartermaster, Captain Webb, strode over to him. A squat man in his late thirties with a ruddy complexion and a large brown moustache, he called, 'Ah, there you are, Sergeant. At last! Where the bloody hell have you been?'

'We were as quick as we could be, sir. There're not many trucks about, though.'

'Any fuel?'

'Just over a quarter of a tank. We could start taking cars, perhaps.'

The quartermaster sighed.

'Better than nothing, sir,' Tanner added. 'And it's more transport.'

'Let's get this loaded first. The sooner we can get it going, the sooner it can come back for another trip.'

Another German aircraft thundered over. 'Bastards!' shouted Captain Webb, shaking his fist.

Tanner called over some men and they began loading the truck with boxes of ammunition, grenades and a number of two-inch mortars. When it was full, Webb despatched it, and Tanner took the opportunity to sit down for a moment on a wooden crate of number 36 grenades until another lorry returned. He blew on his hands and rubbed them together. It was cold but not freezing, not in Lillehammer. He was exhausted. Neither he nor any of the men had slept more than a few hours since they'd landed nearly four days before.

Orders, counter-orders and confusion had dogged them every step of the way. He supposed that someone somewhere knew what the hell was going on, but if they did, it certainly hadn't percolated down the ranks. Trondheim, they had been told on the voyage over: they were going to head north to Trondheim. Instead they had halted, been sent south, then further south. And every time they had moved, battalions had become more and more mixed up, equipment had had to be loaded and unloaded. No one seemed to have the faintest idea what they had or where it was.

He lit a cigarette, and rubbed his eyes. He was gripped by a sense of impending doom, that they had come to this cold, mountainous country, still white with snow, completely unprepared. Christ, what a disaster the sinking of *Sirius* had been. Trucks, armoured cars, ammunition, guns, mortars, rations – not to mention their kit bags – all now lay at the bottom of the North Sea. Three infantry battalions were fighting the enemy with nearly half their equipment gone. It wasn't a problem the enemy appeared to share.

Sykes was walking towards him. 'All right, Corporal?' he asked.

Sykes yawned and stretched. 'If I had a bit of grub and a kip I might be.'

'Here,' said Tanner, offering him a smoke, 'take a pew for a minute.'

'Cheers, Sarge,' said Sykes, sitting down beside him on a box of Bren magazines. 'Fiasco this, isn't it?'

'Too right.' It was now nearly thirty-six hours since

they had reached Lillehammer station. Tanner winced as he thought of their arrival. As a sergeant, he had travelled on one of only two coaches, but the rest had been forced to endure the slow, winding journey in closed goods wagons. Exhausted men had stumbled off the train, and loaded with the kit of their full marching order they had begun banging into one another. For a while they had stood on the platform wearing dazed expressions, stamping their feet against the cold and blowing on their hands. What pained him most, though, was seeing Brigadier Morgan, commander of 148th Brigade, and the Norwegian commander, General Ruge, watching. With a stiff, high-collared blue-green tunic, pantaloons and black cavalry boots, Ruge had looked like a relic from the Great War, but while there had been no doubt of his military bearing, his disappointment at seeing such a tired, poorly equipped bunch of troops stagger with bewilderment from the train had been obvious. 'Christ,' Tanner muttered now. It had been humiliating.

'What, Sarge?'

'Oh, nothing. I'm just wondering what the hell we're playing at here.'

Sykes shrugged.

'I mean, for God's sake, the entire battalion's mixed up and no one knows what the hell is going on except that we're getting a pasting. Why on earth we ever bothered trying to help the Norwegians, I really don't know. Did you see them last night?'

'Not exactly inspiring, Sarge.'

'That's an understatement. I saw one machine-gun team, but otherwise I didn't see a single man carrying

31

anything bigger than a rifle.' And as the Norwegians had trudged back, so the Rangers' C Company had been sent forward to reinforce A Company to the south of Lillehammer. Tanner had watched them head off towards the fray. Aircraft, like black insects, had swirled over the lake to the south. Smoke had pitched into the sky. Explosions, some muffled, some sharp, had resounded up the valley. By the time dusk finally began to fall, the remains of A Company had been streaming back to Lillehammer too. Apparently, the newly arrived C Company had tried to hold the line as A Company withdrew, but since then news had been scarce. With no radios, each company had been depending on civilian telephone lines; they had now been cut.

As darkness had fallen, the sounds of battle had died down. A sense of defeat had hung heavy over the town. Sure enough, just after midnight, Hepworth, the platoon runner, had reached the warehouse with news from Battalion Headquarters. General Ruge had ordered a general withdrawal to a position a mile north of Lillehammer. The stores that Tanner and the rest of Four Platoon had spent an entire day unloading were to be moved to the new position with all urgency.

That had been nine hours ago, and still piles of boxes lay stacked in front of the warehouse and along the platform. Sykes flicked his cigarette clear of them, then said, 'Better see where the rest of the boys are,' and stood up and walked off.

Tanner rubbed his eyes again. Lillehammer lay perched on the lower slopes overlooking Lake Mjøsa. It was a small town – Tanner guessed the population was probably no more than a few thousand – and like every other town and village he had seen so far, the houses were mostly made of wood and brightly painted. It was one way of cheering up the drab two-tone landscape, he supposed. It was another grey day, but above the high, steep outcrop known as the Balberg, there was a patch of blue. Smoke still rose into the sky from the south and Tanner peered up again at the town, prettily snug against the mountain, and wondered how long it would stay that way once the Luftwaffe were bombing the place. Stretching away above, the mountains were covered with snow-clad pines. The whole country, it seemed, was the same: deep U-shaped valleys, wide rivers and mountains. He had fought in mountains before, in the North West Frontier between India and Afghanistan, but those had been quite different: jagged, dry and dusty. Here, everything seemed so much closer: the report of a gun could be heard reverberating across the valley, while the roar of aero-engines seemed to suck in all the air around them, blocking out any other noise.

Another German aircraft thundered over, then banked in a wide arc across the northern end of the lake. Tanner tried to remember his aircraft recognition chart – a Junkers, he was sure of it. A Junkers 88. Like all the German aircraft he had seen so far, this had twin engines, but the Dorniers had had twin tail fins and more rounded wings, like those of the larger Heinkel 111s. The wings on this one were more aquiline and it had a bulbous head that made it seem oddly out of proportion.

Hepworth brought over a mug of tea. 'There you go, Sarge,' he said, and stood holding it out while the Junkers banked round the far side of the lake. 'Feels like they're toying with us, don't it?'

'Recce planes, Hep,' said Tanner. 'They're making sure they have a damn good look before they start up again.'

'Probably can't believe it's so easy.'

'Defeatist talk, Private? Don't let Mr Dingwall hear you speak in such a way.' Tanner grinned at him, then took a sip of his tea. 'Great char, this, Hep. Good on you.'

A civilian car pulled into the yard outside the warehouse and Lieutenant Dingwall stepped out. A young thin-faced man in his mid-twenties, he strode over to Tanner. His face was ashen.

'Hepworth, go and find Captain Webb,' he said, then turned to Tanner and, in a conspiratorial tone, said, 'Grim news, I'm afraid. Looks like most of D Company's had it. The Norwegians had promised transport to get them out, but apparently it never showed up. We're hoping most are PoWs, but we've had no contact from Company HQ since the early hours and Jerry's only just south of the town. The colonel's beside himself. Looks like a company of Leicesters have been overrun too.' Tanner nodded. 'Amazing to think I was talking to Captain Kirby only last night,' Lieutenant Dingwall continued. 'And poor old Richie – I mean, Lieutenant Richardson. I was at school with him, you know. We joined up the same day. Hard to believe. Hope to Christ he's all right.'

'I'm sure he will be, sir.'

'Are you? Yes, you're probably right. Probably a prisoner. I'm sure they treat their prisoners fairly. They're signed up to the Geneva Convention and everything, aren't they? But, my God, you can hardly believe it, can you? We watched them march off last night, and they've gone – a whole bloody company, devoured . . .'

'Best not to think too much about it, sir,' said Tanner.

'No . . . no, you're quite right, Tanner.' He bit his lip and then his eyes glanced from Tanner's breast pocket.

Tanner followed his gaze and realized the lieutenant was studying the tiny ribbon, blue, white and red stripes, of his Military Medal above the left breast pocket of his battle blouse. He quickly buttoned his leather jerkin.

Dingwall looked embarrassed. 'Sorry, Sergeant,' he said, and swallowed hard. Then, smiling weakly, he added, 'Our turn to face the Germans soon.'

'You'll be fine, sir,' said Tanner. He wanted to give his platoon commander some reassurance but it was a difficult line to tread; it wasn't his place to undermine the man's authority. Yet he could see the fear in Mr Dingwall's eyes and it was important the lieutenant did not show it to the men. Nonetheless it was natural that he should feel apprehensive. If Tanner was honest, the tell-tale nausea in his stomach and the constriction in his throat were troubling him now. He tried to remind himself it was the anticipation of battle that was the worst; once the fighting began, adrenalin took over. Even so, the Germans were brushing them aside as though they were little more than toy soldiers. The enemy had control of the skies and, he'd heard, had tanks, armoured cars and large amounts of artillery; 148 Brigade had none of those things, and neither, it seemed, did the Norwegians. So how the hell were they supposed to stop them? He understood now what it must have been like to be a Mohmand warrior, armed only with muskets and swords against British rifles, artillery and Vickers machineguns. *Christ*, he thought. *What the hell are we doing here?*

Tanner looked to the south and noticed Lieutenant Dingwall follow his gaze.

'When do you think the bastards will attack?' the subaltern asked.

'Shouldn't think it'll be long.'

'What about all these stores? We've not cleared half of them.'

'We'll have to leave them, sir. Might be worth mentioning to Captain Webb that we should think about blowing it up, sir. Don't want Jerry to get his mitts on it.'

'I'll do that right away, Sergeant, thank you.'

Tanner followed the subaltern as he strode toward Captain Webb. However, just as Lieutenant Dingwall began speaking with the quartermaster, two lorries arrived back for another load.

'Jerry's not here yet,' Captain Webb told him, 'and so, for the moment, we'll do no such thing. Let's get your men busy, Lieutenant, and load up these trucks pronto.'

Tanner groaned to himself. *The bloody fool*, he thought.

Half an hour later, with the trucks despatched and the working party of Foresters already gone, he broached the matter with Lieutenant Dingwall again. 'Sir, I really think we need to get this place wired and move out. The Jerries could be here any moment.'

'Yes, all right, Sergeant,' Lieutenant Dingwall snapped. He paused, then said, 'Well, surely you've got other things to do, Tanner,' and strode off.

He had not gone ten paces, however, when there was a brief roar of aero-engines followed by whistling and a series of colossal explosions. Seconds later two more aircraft hurtled over, flying at no more than a few hundred feet off the ground.

Tanner immediately fell flat on the ground but turned his face to see a stick of bombs falling, thankfully wide of the yard but still terrifyingly close. As the bombs exploded, with an ear-shattering din, he felt the air around him sucked away before he was lifted clean off the ground by the blast and smacked back down again. He gasped, the wind knocked out of him. The air seemed full of debris and he closed his eyes as stones, grit, shards of wood and glass rained down around him. Choking dust and smoke shrouded the yard and warehouse. He pulled his handkerchief from his pocket, dampened it with water from his bottle, then clamped it to his mouth and staggered to his feet. Christ, the Germans would blow up the stores for them at this rate.

'Number Four Platoon,' he shouted, 'to me!' Men stumbled towards him, including, he was pleased to see, Lieutenant Dingwall. 'Right, lads,' said Tanner. 'Get your kit. Make sure you've got everything attached to your webbing, that your rifles are loaded, then grab as much ammunition as you can easily carry. It's time we got the hell out of here.' Wide-eyed and silent, the men did as he asked. He turned to Lieutenant Dingwall. 'I hope that's all right, sir. I'm assuming that since Jerry's started his assault we should hurry back to the new lines.'

Lieutenant Dingwall nodded.

By the warehouse, Captain Webb was also barking

orders for them to retreat. 'Everyone fall back!' he shouted. German guns had opened fire too. Shells were now thumping into the southern parts of the town. 'Leave everything!' yelled the quartermaster. Tanner saw him hurrying to the civilian car the lieutenant had been driving earlier with the regimental quartermaster sergeant.

'Goddamn it,' said Tanner, as he grabbed his own rifle and kit. Two shells hurtled overhead, whooshing through the air like a speeding train, before exploding some several hundred yards to the north.

'All right, men!' shouted Lieutenant Dingwall. 'Let's move.'

Tanner hurried to his platoon commander. 'Sir, I'll follow you out.' Lieutenant Dingwall swung his arm above his head, then down below his shoulder, signalling to the men to run from the yard.

Tanner stood back. 'Move it!' he shouted. 'Come on, get going!' Spotting Hepworth, he grabbed him, and said, 'Not you. I need you to help me with something.'

More shells whistled overhead. Hepworth looked distraught. 'But, Sarge, the Jerries'll be here.'

'We won't be long. Now, follow me,' he snapped. Tanner was fuming – with Captain Webb for not thinking ahead and for cutting and running before the others, but also with the lieutenant for not pressing the quarter-master hard enough. As a result, they were leaving the stores in too much haste and risking letting a mass of valuable war matériel fall into the enemy's hands – weapons and ammunition that any advancing force would gladly use against them.

They ran to the side of the warehouse. There, out of sight of the yard and platform and partially covered by overgrown bushes, they saw a small shed.

'What's this place, Sarge?' asked Hepworth. 'Can't say I'd noticed it before.'

'That'll teach you to have a proper scout round in future, won't it?'

Hepworth was not alone, however, certainly, no one else had thought to use it. But Tanner had, the previous day, and as dusk had fallen, he had quietly, without being spotted in the darkening night, moved half a dozen four-gallon tins of petrol there. He had also taken the opportunity to discard some of his kit and replace it with a number of items carefully put aside during the day's unloading. His gas-mask had been taken out and instead he had filled the respirator bag with a tin of detonators and two five-pound packs of Nobel's gelignite. From his large backpack, he had taken out several other items of kit. His hairbrushes and canvas shoes had been pulled out with barely a thought, but abandoning his greatcoat had been a harder decision. However, he had kept his thick, serge-lined leather jerkin, which would keep him warm and also allowed him to have his arms free; he had always hated them to feel restricted ever since he had begun shooting as a boy. Anyway, he reckoned he could always find another greatcoat if necessary. He filled the pack with a number of cartridges of Polar dynamite, a round tin of safety fuse, half a dozen hand grenades, ten rounds of Bren-gun tracer bullets, and as many clips of rifle rounds as would fit.

'Leave your pack and rifle here for the moment,'

he told Hepworth now, 'and help me with these cans.'

'What are we doing with them, Sarge?' Hepworth asked, as he pulled the large green canvas pack off his back.

'Just grab that fuel and do as I say, Hep. Come on, iggery.'

'Iggery, Sarge?'

'Yes, Private, iggery – it means get a bloody move on.'

They ran back to the yard. Tanner pulled out his seventeen-inch sword bayonet and stabbed the top of the flimsy tins, while Hepworth returned to the shed for the rest of the fuel. The sergeant then poured the petrol liberally over the remaining stores. When Hepworth returned, they finished their task. A dozen Heinkels thundered overhead, no longer concerned with the station but with the new front line. Small-arms fire from the Allied lines two miles ahead could faintly be heard, followed by a dull ripple of explosions. Suddenly there was a clatter and squeaking from the buildings to the south of the station yard.

'Tanks,' said Tanner. 'Quick! To the shed.' They sprinted back, Tanner putting on his jerkin, then heaving his respirator bag and pack onto his shoulders. They were heavier than he'd imagined, and he cursed to himself. Slinging his trusted Enfield on his back, he said, 'Right, let's go. Follow me, Hep.'

As they ran round the front of the warehouse, the sound of tank tracks grew louder. Then, from the side of a house, the front of a German tank swung into view. The two men ran on, until Tanner slid into a ditch by the far side of the yard.

'You'd better be quick, Sarge,' said Hep, his face taut with fear.

Tanner said nothing. Instead his shaking hands struggled to pull out a single .303 tracer round and push it into the breach of his rifle. German troops were now moving up round the sides of the tank, half crouching in long, field-grey coats and their distinctive coal-scuttle helmets. *So, face to face with Germans at last*, he thought.

One of the enemy troops shouted and, with his rifle, pointed to the stacks of boxes.

'Sarge!' hissed Hepworth.

'Wait, Hep, wait,' whispered Tanner. He watched as a dozen or more German troops ran across the yard towards the stores. He pressed the wooden stock of the rifle against his cheek, gripped the wood surrounding the barrel with his left hand, and felt his finger press against the metal trigger. Just over a hundred and fifty yards. Closing one eye, he aimed at a box of gelignite he had doused heavily with petrol and upended to make it stand out. Holding his breath, he squeezed the trigger.

The flash of the tracer round streaked across the yard and struck the wooden box. Immediately an explosion ripped the air, sheets of flame burst out and engulfed the largest stack of stores, followed in succession by a second, third and fourth explosion as the fireball engulfed the yard. The first half-dozen Germans were caught in the inferno, and Tanner saw three more catch fire amid screams of shock and pain.

'Run!' shouted Tanner. 'Run, Hep!' Then the two were scrambling to their feet, minds closed to what was going on behind them, concentrating on sprinting northwards for all they were worth, away from the yard and warehouse to safety.

Above the din of further explosions, the rattle and whizz of bullets detonating, Tanner was aware of a cannon shell whooshing past him only a few feet away and punching a hole through a wooden building up ahead. A few seconds later, machine-gun bullets fizzed over their heads. He and Hepworth dropped to the ground a few yards short of the bridge over the Mesna river. Tanner rolled over, unslung his rifle and pulled it into his shoulder. A little over three hundred yards, he reckoned. He could see the black-jacketed tank commander's head sticking out of the turret; he was now firing the machine-gun towards them. Tanner pulled back the bolt and fired. The man's head jerked backwards. When it righted itself, half his face had gone and the machine-gun was silent. He yelled at Hepworth to start running again. More soldiers were crouching by the tank. Tanner pulled back the bolt again and, without moving his face from the stock, hit a second man. *Two.* Pull back the bolt, fire. *Three.* Again. *Four.* This time he only clipped a soldier. Back came the bolt. *Five. Six. Seven.* Three rounds left. *That'll do.*

He turned and ran, ten yards, twenty, thirty – over the bridge and away from the inferno, away from the startled enemy. Ahead, the road turned, still running parallel to the railway but, he knew, out of sight of the yard. A bullet fizzed past his ear. He could see Hepworth had already made it. Another bullet zipped by, and another, and then he was safe, for a moment at any rate, out of sight of the enemy.

Hepworth was up ahead, slowing now, and Tanner paused, hands on his hips, leaning backwards, gasping for breath. Now that he had momentarily stopped, he felt his pack cutting into his shoulders. Bending double to relieve the weight, he grimaced, then began running again, albeit more slowly. Behind him, vast clouds of pitch-black smoke rolled into the sky.

Tanner drew level with Hepworth, who grinned. 'Some explosion, that one, Sarge. I reckon there's a few Jerries there who won't be bothering us no more.' He watched as Tanner pressed another clip of bullets into his magazine. 'Shoot a few of the buggers, did you, Sarge? Did you get that tank man?'

'Less of the chit-chat, Hep,' said Tanner. 'Let's concentrate on catching up with the others and getting out of here in one piece.'

They were nearing the edge of the town. A few frightened civilians were peering from their houses, but the streets were still empty. He had hoped to come across a car, a motorbike or even bicycles, but there had been nothing and no time in which to look more thoroughly. The houses thinned and then they were in the open, running along a cleared road, patchy snow at either side and yellowed grass showing through. Of the rest of the platoon there was no sign. How much of a head start had they had? he wondered. Fifteen minutes? No wonder he couldn't see them.

'How much further, Sarge?' gasped Hepworth.

'A mile. Not much more.' Tanner could see the mass of the Balberg strutting imperiously above them. German field guns continued booming behind them. They could

43

see the dark shells as they hurtled across the sky and exploded among the Allied positions, the sound of the detonation always arriving a moment after the flash. 'Keep going, Hep,' urged Tanner. 'Soon be there.'

Then, behind them, they heard the sound of gears grinding and the chugging drone of vehicles. Turning, they saw a column of trucks emerging from Lillehammer some half a mile away. Tanner's heart sank. Coming round a bend in the open road he could see at least half a dozen, filled with troops, each pulling an anti-tank gun.

'What are we going to do now, Sarge?' said Hepworth. 'We'll never be able to stop them.' Hepworth was a small lad, barely nineteen, his face pale and his brows knotted in despair. Tanner eyed him, then glanced around. The land was open, but about fifty yards ahead, a short way back from the road, there was a farmhouse.

'Keep calm, Hep,' he said. 'First we're going to head to that house where we can get a bit of cover.'

'And then what, Sarge?'

'If you asked a few less questions, Hep, I might be able to think a bit more clearly,' Tanner snapped. He was trying to weigh up a couple of options in his mind. 'Bloody hell,' he mumbled, as he tried to catch his breath. 'What a mess.' No matter what he decided, the reality was that he and Hepworth were now caught between the new Allied lines and the vanguard of the German attack. He had a good mind to floor Captain Webb if and when he ever saw him again.

3

Tanner noticed that a large barn extended out at right angles from the house. *Good*, he thought, grateful for whatever cover he could get. The twitch of a curtain showed the place was still occupied, but it appeared that the owners preferred not to show themselves. He crouched beside the stone ramp that led up to the barn's first floor and opened the haversack slung behind his left hip. He felt inside, pulled out an old piece of oily cloth and carefully unwrapped it.

'What's that, Sarge?' asked Hepworth, crouching beside him.

'It's a telescopic sight,' said Tanner. 'An Aldis.' It had once belonged to his father, and Tanner had carried it with him throughout his army career. Most gunsmiths could modify the Enfield rifle easily enough by milling and fitting two scope mounts and pads to the action body – alterations that were sufficiently discreet to enable a platoon sergeant to have his rifle adapted without his superiors noticing. Consequently, having joined the 5th

Battalion in Leeds, he had wasted no time in taking his newly issued SMLE No. 1 Mk III rifle to a gunsmith in the Royal Armoury to have it adapted and his scope sighted. It was a good scope and his father had sworn by it; certainly Tanner had found that on the rare occasions he had used it, the Aldis had never lost its zero.

'There's someone in the house,' said Tanner. 'Go and find out whether they've got any transport.'

Hepworth hurried up to the front door.

Screwing the scope into place, Tanner stood behind the ramp leading up to the barn and, using it as a rest, peered through the sight. The column was now about seven hundred yards away, and his sight zeroed at four hundred. He had found that allowing a foot's drop for every fifty yards beyond the zero usually did the trick, but this was going to be a long shot even with the scope; as it was, he could only just see the driver of the lead vehicle. Tanner reminded himself that all he needed to do was delay the column, cause a bit of confusion. He lowered his aim to the bottom of the truck, then lifted it again by, he guessed, about six foot. The truck was moving slowly – under fifteen miles per hour, he reckoned – and almost directly towards him. Half exhaling as he pulled back the bolt, he held his breath and squeezed the trigger.

The truck lurched and ploughed off the road, so that the vehicle immediately behind quickly emerged around it. This time Tanner aimed at the indistinct figure of the driver, then made a generous adjustment for the bullet's falling trajectory, and fired again. The man was hit – Tanner could see him thrown backwards. 'Damn,' he mouthed, pulled back the bolt again and fired once more. This time he saw the driver punched back in his seat, then slump forward. The man next to him grabbed at the steering-wheel, but it was too late and the truck struck the first, which came to a halt spread across the width of the road. Men were pouring out of the vehicles now and taking cover. Tanner smiled to himself with satisfaction, then turned towards the front of the farm, where Hepworth was still banging on the door.

'What the hell are you playing at?' shouted Tanner.

'They're not answering,' said Hepworth.

'For God's sake, Hepworth,' snarled Tanner. 'Forget 'em. Don't waste bloody time on niceties. A quick dekko in the barns and sheds. We need to get out of here – fast.'

There were several ageing carts in a barn but two bicycles in one of the sheds adjoining the house. One had a flat tyre and was covered with dust and cobwebs, but the two infantrymen grabbed them. 'Right, let's go,' said Tanner. 'Come on, quick.'

German artillery shells were whistling overhead with greater regularity now, bombarding the Allied positions just half a mile ahead. Tanner wove back and forth across the road, hoping to make himself a more elusive target should the Germans attempt to fire at them. His flat rear wheel was sliding badly, but he managed to keep his balance. Hepworth, making faster progress, repeatedly looked back until Tanner urged him to press on. Suddenly he became aware of an eerie silence – no birds singing, no blast of shells exploding. In the next moment there came a faint whirr and Tanner yelled at Hepworth, then flung down his bicycle and leapt into the snow by the side of the road, just as a stream of bullets spat up a line along the road followed by four Messerschmitt 110s thundering over.

He stood up and saw them strafing the Allies ahead, then shouted to Hepworth. To his relief, the private got up, dusted off the snow, hitched his rifle onto his shoulder and waved.

Soon after, they reached the Allied forward positions, waved in through the hastily prepared roadblock by a corporal from the Sherwood Foresters.

'Where're our lot?' Tanner asked.

'Behind. Two hundred yards, on the right of the road under the Balberkamp.'

A subaltern approached Tanner. 'Anyone behind you, Sergeant?'

'Only a column of enemy infantry.'

'How many?'

'Hard to say, sir. I counted at least a dozen trucks. They were all towing guns – about the size of our two-pounders, I reckon. And they've got tanks.'

'Good God,' muttered the lieutenant. 'You'd better report to HQ right away.'

'Yes, sir. Where is it, sir?'

'It's the only brick building around, a few hundred yards behind by the road. And it's a Joint HQ for all three battalions. The bastards have been dropping incendiaries to smoke them out, so follow the line of charred houses.'

Another shell hurtled over and they fell flat on the ground again. It exploded seventy yards further on, the noise deafening as the report echoed off the imposing Balberkamp. Tanner thanked the officer and then, with Hepworth, hurried forward. Men were still trying frantically to dig holes in the thin soil, officers and NCOs were shouting orders, while others were hastily laying down wire and building makeshift sangars. The early-afternoon air was still, heavy with the smell of cordite and smoke.

They found Joint HQ easily. One house nearby was still burning, thick smoke rising into the sky, another was burnt to the ground, while a third had a collapsed roof. A number of pines were still crackling with flames, their blackened branches bare of needles.

Outside, several civilian cars were parked haphazardly in the mud and slush. Tanner recognized one as the vehicle in which Captain Webb had made good his escape. In the yard beside the house there were a number of foldaway tables on which stood a line of field telephones, lines of cable extending across the snow. Evidently at least one was suffering from a break in the line as an exasperated Leicesters officer was cursing his inability to get through to his men. Runners reached the house as others headed through the trees towards the company positions.

'You stay out here, Hep,' said Tanner, pushing his way through the throng of clerks and other headquarters staff. His boots squelched on the mud. It was not cold, but the sky was overcast and grey and the snow was melting. Drips ran off the edge of the roof and from the branches of the trees. Indeed, Tanner now felt hot after his exertions, and he wiped the sweat from his forehead before he stepped inside HQ.

There was pandemonium. The house smelt musty, of coffee, sweat and damp clothes. In a room off the hallway, a number of men, including Norwegians, were peering at a map. Another Leicesters officer brushed past him, then Tanner spotted Lieutenant Wrightson, the battalion intelligence officer, sitting on the corner of a table in a room at the end of the hallway. Tanner knocked lightly on the open door.

Wrightson looked up. 'Yes?'

'I've been told to report to Battalion CO, sir, regarding what I've seen of enemy troop movements.'

Wrightson disappeared to fetch Colonel Chisholm.

A few moments later the colonel appeared with Captain Webb. 'Tanner, what the bloody hell are you doing here?' asked Webb. 'Shouldn't you be with the rest of your platoon?'

'All right, Captain, that will do,' said Colonel Chisholm. He was a tall man in his mid-forties, with a trim moustache above his lip and dark eyes. A North Yorkshire landowner and Member of Parliament, he, too, was new to war. 'What have you got for me, Sergeant?'

'I think Private Hepworth and I were the last out of Lillehammer, sir. We saw a tank entering the station with a number of accompanying troops, then a long column of motorized infantry deploying out of the town. The lead trucks had guns attached to the back. Only small ones, though. Anti-tank guns, I should say.'

The colonel ran his hand through his hair as Tanner spoke, then chewed one of his fingernails. 'How many tanks do you think they've got?'

'Hard to say, sir. There was one entering the station

50

yard and another not far behind, but I heard the tracks of others as we were heading out of the town.'

'Good God,' muttered Chisholm. 'And now they'll have taken our stores. Damn it, Webb, why the hell didn't you blow them first?'

'There wasn't time, sir,' said Webb, defiantly. 'We were loading until the last minute, trying to salvage as much as we could, and then Jerry was upon us.'

Tanner shifted his feet. 'Excuse me, sir, but Private Hepworth and I managed to destroy the stores.'

'What the devil are you talking about, Tanner?' said Webb.

'We poured petrol over them, sir, and blew them up.'

'Oh, really? And what were the enemy doing while this was happening, Sergeant?'

'Getting burnt and shot, sir.'

Colonel Chisholm smiled. 'Good man, Tanner. Well, that's something at least.' He squinted at his watch. 'All right, Sergeant, you'd better hurry back to your position. I think you'll have a chance to get a few more rounds off before long.' The colonel strode past him, presumably to inform his fellow battalion commanders, but as Tanner was about to leave, Webb grabbed his arm.

'I don't appreciate being humiliated like that,' he hissed.

Tanner clenched his fist. He had a strong desire to hit Webb, knock him to the floor, but instead he glowered at the man, yanked his arm free, then left the room. Outside, Hepworth was waiting for him. 'Come on,' growled Tanner. 'Let's go.'

They left the road to head through the trees and across

the thinning snow. It was still in the woodland, and Tanner paused briefly to light cigarettes for himself and Hepworth. He passed one to the private and breathed in the smell of tobacco mixed with burning pinewood. A brief release of tension spread through him. Somewhere they heard the chatter of Bren light machine-guns, and a moment later another Junkers roared over, its twin engines louder than ever in their close surroundings. A split second later came the whistle of falling incendiaries, and once again Tanner and Hepworth flung themselves face down into the snow. A deafening ripple of explosions erupted a short distance behind them and the ground shuddered. Shards of shrapnel and splinters of wood pattered nearby, followed by the crackle of burning branches.

Lifting himself to his feet once more, Tanner saw his crumpled cigarette in the snow. 'Bugger it!' He glanced across at Hepworth.

'I reckon it's dangerous being near you, Sarge,' said the private, as he brushed snow from his battle dress.

'You're alive, aren't you?'

'Yes, but only just. Look, Sarge, my hands are shaking.' He held them out to show Tanner. 'I don't think I'm cut out for war.'

Tanner could not help smiling. 'Another beadie will sort you out,' he said, pulling out his packet of cigarettes again. A moment before he had thought to save his last precious few, but now his resolve was weakening. In truth, he needed a good smoke himself. 'Just don't go telling the rest of the lads or they'll think I've gone soft,' he said.

They found B Company soon after, strung out between the trees on the lower, more gentle slopes at the foot of the Balberkamp, next to a company of Norwegian troops. Men were attempting to dig in here too, hacking away at the shallow soil with their short spades, building sangars from stone, bits of wood, and anything else that could be salvaged. Shells continued to whistle over at intervals, but were landing further towards the road so the men were no longer bothering even to duck, let alone fall flat on the ground.

Number Four Platoon held the end of the line. Each of the three sections was trying to make their own defences – a sangar of sorts for the Bren team and whatever holes in the ground they could manage. Tanner was in despair. Nothing he had seen since reaching their lines had convinced him they had the remotest chance of holding off the enemy, and the efforts of his own platoon, only recently arrived at the position, were the worst of them all. What good were a few stones and a hole barely deep enough to lie flat in against tanks, guns and especially aircraft? What was it the brass knew that he didn't? Perhaps reinforcements were on their way. Perhaps the RAF. Perhaps another shipment of transport and guns had already docked and was driving towards them. He sighed, pushed his helmet to the back of his head and looked around for Lieutenant Dingwall.

The subaltern had seen him first, however, and strode over from his newly sited platoon headquarters between two close-together pine trees. 'There you are, Tanner. You took your bloody time. If I'd known you were going to be so long I'd never have let you take Hepworth – I've had to use Calder as my runner instead. Where the devil have you been?'

'I'm sorry, Mr Dingwall,' said Tanner. 'We got a bit held up and then I was ordered to report to Joint HQ.'

'Well, all right, but I need you here now. We've got a lot to do on these defences, so get digging.'

'What about reinforcements, sir?'

'Some Norwegian troops have joined us.'

'I saw them, but with all respect, they're not going to manage much, are they? They've got less equipment than us and most of them have only been in uniform a fortnight. Where's the heavy stuff? Have you heard anything, sir?'

Dingwall shook his head. 'Apparently there's another company of Leicesters on its way – they got left behind somehow at Rosyth, but Captain Cartwright heard from the IO that another supply ship's gone down.'

'For God's sake!' Tanner was exasperated.

'Rather you didn't spread that about, though, all right?' added the lieutenant, in a lower voice.

'My God, sir,' said Tanner, 'this is madness. What the hell are we going to achieve?'

'Keep your voice down, Sergeant,' said Dingwall, sharply. 'We're playing for time. Trying to keep the enemy at bay and help the Norwegians.'

'Then why not keep them at bay a hundred miles back towards Åndalsnes? We've got a hundred-and-fifty-mile supply line here, with no guns to speak of, no bloody tanks, no trucks, and one piddling railway line that Jerry will knock out in no time if he hasn't already. And look at the men, sir. They're exhausted. When did we last have some proper grub? It's insanity.'

'We've got to do what we can, Sergeant,' said Dingwall. 'Captain Cartwright has been promised that hot food will be issued tonight. In the meantime, we must make do with what limited battle rations we've still got.'

Tanner knew there was no chance of any hot meal that day – how would it reach them? Captain Cartwright had been fobbed off, of course he had, but there was no point in saying any more to the lieutenant. He'd said his piece, got it off his chest, only it hadn't made him feel any better. Rather, a new wave of weariness spread over him.

'I'd like you to take over the end of the line and make sure our defences are up to scratch,' said Lieutenant Dingwall.

Tanner saluted, and wandered through the trees until he found Corporal Sykes and his section.

'Afternoon, Sarge,' said Sykes, cheerfully.

Tanner was pleased to see that Sykes had made the most of a large rock and a pine tree for positioning the Bren. Other, smaller, rocks had been brought over, and branches carefully placed so that the machine-gun was almost entirely hidden from forward view. 'Good work, Stan,' he said, as he eased off his pack and haversack.

Sykes grinned. 'Try digging, though, Sarge. It's flippin' 'ard rock they 'ave 'ere.' Sykes put down his entrenching tool and stood up. From his battle blouse he pulled out some chocolate, broke it in two and offered half to Tanner. 'Superior stuff this, Sarge.'

'Thanks. I'm starving. Just what I need. Where d'you get it?'

Sykes tapped his nose. 'Trade secrets . . . Well,

actually, I got it from some Norwegian bloke in Lillehammer. Said he'd rather give it to us than have it stolen by Nazis.'

Tanner smiled. 'Makes for better tiffin than hard tack, that's for sure.' He liked Sykes. Of slight build and with short, mousy hair slicked to his skull with brilliantine, he was, as Tanner had discovered, far stronger than he looked. Sykes was sharp too – always ready with a quick reply – and he was the only man other than himself in the company who hadn't come from Yorkshire. Rather, he was a Londoner, from Deptford, as he had proudly admitted the first time they had met. Tanner had sensed an unspoken affinity between them, in part because he regarded himself and Sykes as outsiders. Every time Tanner opened his mouth, he revealed the soft remnants of a West Country burr that had not left him even after so many years away. Sykes's South London accent was even more marked among the thick Yorkshire tones of the other rankers.

He took out his spade and was about to start helping Sykes and the other men in the section when a Messerschmitt 110 pounded overhead, strafing their positions. There was no need to tell anyone what to do: they all hurled themselves flat on the ground as bullets kicked up gouts of earth and snow, shards of stone, and snicked through branches above. Tanner heard a bullet ricochet from the rock beside him and a tiny sliver of stone nicked the back of his hand.

It was over in a trice and, cursing, Tanner got to his feet once more. His hand was bleeding. 'This is a bloody Goddamn joke!' he said. Angrily, he picked up his spade and hacked at the ground behind Sykes's Bren post. As the corporal had warned, the spade cut through a few inches of soil, then hit rock. Repeatedly, he tried to find an area where the soil might be deeper, but every time it was the same. Rock.

'Who gave us these poxy spades anyway?' he barked at Sykes. 'Bloody useless, they are. What was wrong with the old pick-and-mattock tool we used to have? I wouldn't want one of these at the bloody seaside, let alone in the middle of sodding Norway.' He dug in the spade and the wooden handle snapped. With a curse, he flung what was left of it behind him.

'Who threw that?' snapped a voice behind them.

Tanner and Sykes swung round to see a platoon of strange troops approaching through the trees. Leading them, and striding towards Tanner, was the man who had spoken. 'Who threw that spade handle?' he said again.

Ah, thought Tanner, catching the accent. *French*. 'I did,' he said.

The man walked up to him in silence. He was shorter than the sergeant by several inches, with a narrow, dark face and an aquiline nose. 'Isn't it customary to salute an officer, Sergeant?' Tanner slowly brought his hand to his brow. 'And stand to attention!' said the Frenchman, sharply. 'No wonder you British are making such hard work of this war. No discipline, no training.'

Tanner fumed.

'Well?' continued the Frenchman. 'What have you to say for yourself?'

Tanner paused, then said slowly, 'I apologize, sir. I hadn't appreciated there were French troops in the vicinity.'

'Well, now you know, Sergeant. There are – one company of the Sixième Bataillon Chasseurs Alpins, part of General Béthouart's Brigade Haute-Montagne. We have been sent here because you British have no élite forces capable of fighting in the mountains. So – you no longer need to worry about your flanks. When *les Allemands* attack, you can take comfort from the fact that we shall be above you, watching guard.' He pointed up towards the Balberkamp, then repeated the line in French to his men with a knowing smile. They laughed.

'Where are the rest of the company, sir?' Tanner asked.

'You don't need to know such things, Sergeant.'

'Only I'm not sure one platoon will be able to do much to save us. The mountain's a big place. Furthermore, you've only got rifles. Jerry's got machine-guns and artillery and, even better, he's got aircraft. Lots of aircraft. But I appreciate your help, sir. I really do.' It was now the turn of British troops to laugh.

'Who is your superior officer, Sergeant?' the Frenchman asked curtly.

'Lieutenant Dingwall, sir. He's just over there.' Tanner pointed. 'Only a hundred yards or so. Shall I take you, sir?'

The Frenchman bristled. 'I don't like insolence, Sergeant. Not from my men or any others. You've not heard the last of this.' He barked some orders. Then, with a last glare at Tanner, he continued on his way with his men.

It was by now nearly three o'clock on Monday, 22 April. The shelling had noticeably intensified, as had the number of enemy aircraft flying overhead, but there was still no sign of enemy troops to the front of them.

Tanner was soon ordered back to Platoon HQ to cover the absence of Lieutenant Dingwall, who had been summoned to see the B Company commander, Captain Cartwright. When Dingwall returned, he was flushed, his expression grim. 'It looks like we might be outflanked,' he told Tanner. 'There have been reports of German mountain troops climbing round the Balberkamp. The CO wants me to send a fighting patrol to watch out for them and, if possible, hold them off.'

'What about the Frogs? There was a platoon of mountain troops heading that way.'

'Well, yes, but Captain Cartwright wants some of our own troops up there.' He paused. 'I say, you haven't got a cigarette, have you, Sergeant?' He patted his pockets. 'I seem to be out.'

Tanner sighed inwardly, and handed over his Woodbines. 'I've three left, sir. Be my guest. Think I'll have one too.' The whine of a shell, followed by another in quick succession, whooshed overhead, the echo resounding through the valley. Dingwall flinched, but both men remained standing. The shells exploded some distance behind them. Tanner handed the lieutenant his matches and watched as Dingwall lit his cigarette, fingers shaking.

'About that fighting patrol, sir,' said Tanner, as he exhaled a curling cloud of blue-grey smoke.

'Yes. I want you to take it, Sergeant.'

'Two sections?'

'Not that many. Fourteen. One section and three

others, not including yourself. I've been told to keep at least two whole sections here.'

Fourteen men, thought Tanner. *Jesus.* It wasn't a lot. He drew on his cigarette again, then said, 'I'd like to take Sykes's section, sir, if I may. Shall I take the other three from Platoon HQ?'

'Yes. I'll keep the mortar team here. You can have Hepworth, Garraby and Kershaw.'

Tanner took another drag of his cigarette, then flicked it away. 'Right, sir. Better get going.'

'Just have a look around up there, all right? If you see anything, only open fire if you really think you can hold them up. I need you all back here in the platoon . . . Look, I think we both know we won't be staying here very long. If for any reason we have to move out, it'll be along the valley, and I'm only guessing, I'm afraid, but you might be able to make some ground across here where the river loops westwards, then back towards Tretten. Here.' He gave Tanner a hand-drawn map. 'It's the best I can do, I'm afraid. Another thing we're short of – decent maps.'

'Thank you, sir.'

Dingwall held out his hand. 'Good luck, Sergeant.'

'And you, sir.'

The lieutenant hesitated again, then looked at the ribbon on Tanner's chest. 'I – I've been meaning to ask. Your MM. What were you given it for?'

Tanner shrugged bashfully. 'Oh, you know how it is with gongs, sir,' he said, then realized that, of course, the lieutenant had no idea. He kicked at the ground. 'It was during the Loe Agra campaign a few years back. On the

North West Frontier. Those jokers weren't as well armed as the Germans, but they were vicious buggers all the same. Had rifles but bloody great swords and all sorts as well. Those *wazirs* would slice your belly open without a second thought, give them half a chance.'

'It must have taught you a lot, Sergeant.'

Tanner nodded. 'I suppose so, sir.'

'I envy you that experience. I'm sure it's the best training there is. Oh, and I heard about what you did today,' he added. 'You want to watch it, Tanner. They'll be giving you another bit of ribbon if you're not careful.'

Ten minutes later, Tanner and his patrol were on their way, climbing through the snow and trees round the north-west side of the Balberkamp. The slopes were steep and the men soon gasped for breath. Lack of sleep and food hardly helped. Nor did the weight of their equipment. Tanner had insisted that each man repack his kit, as he had done himself the night before. He had ordered them to discard any non-essentials and replace them with extra rounds of .303 and Bren ammunition. Gas masks were put to one side, as were items of personal kit. As Tanner pointed out, there were large differences between what had been drummed in to them during peacetime and what was practical in war. Most wore their greatcoats so that their large packs could be left behind, but Tanner carried his, full of rounds and explosives, with his haversack on his hip. He had with him around sixty pounds of kit.

The men had grumbled, and they grumbled again now as they forced their way up the mountainside, but Tanner knew it was not his job to be popular. His task was to lead by example and to inspire trust. Being a tough bastard was what mattered, not making friends. The ribbon on his tunic helped, and he was glad of it because it marked him out, giving him an automatic degree of authority and respect. It had made his life easier since he had joined the battalion. Now, though, he was about to be properly tested. Battle was about to be joined. His mouth felt dry and cloying as it always did before a fight. Earlier, at the station yard, he'd hardly had time to think, but now, in expectation of the German attack, he felt on edge and irritable, his mood worsened by his run-ins with Captain Webb and the Frenchman.

He wondered what they would find up on the slopes. In his own mind, it seemed rather pointless for the Germans to try to outflank their position from the mountains when they could attack head-on with artillery and armour and achieve the same result; the Allies would not be standing firm for long, of that he was sure. But there were always rumours in war – some turned out to be true, many more proved false. He supposed it was the commander's job to decide which was worth taking seriously. At any rate, someone had considered the threat of an attack by enemy mountain troops to be real enough.

No matter, he and his fourteen men were now cut adrift from the rest of the platoon and, indeed, the entire company and battalion. His gut instinct was that they would not be rejoining them for some time. He had no radio link, only a hand-drawn map, and no easy route back to the valley. His only means of signalling Lieutenant Dingwall was a Very pistol and three flares, only to be fired if they spotted significant numbers of German troops. But the lieutenant had no way of contacting him: if the battalion was overrun, he could not let Tanner know. And if they fell back, there was no guarantee that Tanner would be able to get as far as Tretten before the Allies had passed through.

Two of the Bren group stopped, exhaustion written across their faces.

'Come on, you idle sods,' Tanner chided.

'Give them a break, Sarge,' said Lance Corporal Erwood, the Bren group leader.

'Stop grumbling and get on with it,' said Tanner. 'Here, give me that.' He took the Bren off Saxby, clasping it by the wooden grip on the barrel. The machine-gun was certainly heavy, but he knew they needed to reach the open plateau at the top of the mountain as soon as possible, and that if he allowed them to stop now, they would only have to stop again.

Several Junkers thundered down the valley, and from where Tanner stood it seemed as though he were looking down on them. All the men halted, as bombs dropped from the planes directly over B Company's positions. First the whistle of falling iron and explosives; then the spurts of flame and clouds of smoke, earth, wood and stone mushrooming across the entire position. A moment later, the report, cracking and echoing off the mountainside.

'All right, let's move,' said Tanner. The knot tightened in his stomach. He almost wished he could meet some Germans now. It would take his mind off things.

4

In a large room on the top floor of the Bristol Hotel in Oslo, three men sat round a small, low table. Although it was afternoon and the sky outside for the most part clear, the room was quite dark where they sat. In the far corner away from the windows a lamp cast a circle of amber light towards the ceiling, but it remained a room of shadows.

It was also a room of refined good taste, part of the largest suite in the hotel, requisitioned by the newly arrived Reichskommissar. The carpet was finely woven, the shallow wainscoting painted a flawless cream. The furniture was elegant, a mixture of French and Scandinavian, while the paintings on the wall spoke of an idyllic rural Europe several hundred years before. Admittedly the Reichskommissar had only arrived that morning, but nothing about the room suggested it was inhabited by the most powerful German in Norway: there were no flags, no busts or pictures of Hitler, no army of staff scurrying in and out.

Reichsamtsleiter Hans-Wilhelm Scheidt glanced at the new Reichskommissar, then turned to the person sitting next to him. As he did so, he felt mounting contempt. The man was a mess. Tiny globules of sweat had broken out on his forehead, and aware of this – subconsciously or otherwise – the Norwegian was periodically running his hand over it, smoothing the sweep of his sandy hair at the same time. A sweat-laced strand of hair slid loose repeatedly, until another swipe of his hand smoothed it back again. His face, Scheidt reflected, was pudgy, the nose rounded, but the lips were narrow and his eyes darted from side to side as he spoke, rather than steadfastly eyeing the Reichskommissar. The suit he wore was ill-fitting and, Scheidt noticed, there was a stain on the sleeve near the left cuff. Nor was the tie tight against the collar: Scheidt could see the button peeping out from behind the knot.

And the drivel coming from his mouth! Scheidt had heard it over and over again during the past week: how he, Vidkun Quisling, had long been a true friend of Germany; that he was the head of the only Norwegian political party that could govern Norway effectively; that the new Administrative Council appointed by Ambassador Bräuer consisted of vacillating incompetents who could not be trusted; and that while it was true that his National Party enjoyed only minority support throughout Norway, that was sure to change. Norway was a peace-loving nation; the fighting had to stop. He could help deliver peace and ensure Norway remained a fervent friend and ally of Germany. The Führer himself had singled him out. As founder and long-standing leader of the National Party, he could govern Norway now and in the years to come.

That was the gist, at any rate, not that Quisling was a man to say something in one sentence when given the opportunity for a long-winded rant. To make matters worse, as the man spoke, spittle collected at the side of his mouth. What was the Reichskommissar making of him? Scheidt wondered, and glanced again at the compact, slimly built man sitting opposite.

The contrast could not have been greater. Josef Terboven was immaculate. It was indeed warm in the room, but there was not even the hint of a sheen on his smooth forehead. The fair hair was combed back perfectly from a pointed widow's peak. The gold-framed round spectacles sat neatly on his nose, while his narrow eyes watched the Norwegian with piercing intent. His double-breasted black suit revealed no insignia of rank, but was beautifully tailored and fitted its wearer like a second skin. The shoes were polished to glass, the shirt cuffs starched white cotton. Terboven exuded confidence, command and control. It was a Party rule that Scheidt had learnt well: look superior, feel superior. It was why he himself had spent so much at one of Berlin's finest tailors; it was why he took such trouble over his personal grooming. For all Quisling's professed admiration of Germany and all things German, sartorial pride was one lesson he had failed to grasp.

Scheidt recrossed his legs, his Louis XIV chair creaking gently. A large lacquered walnut desk stood by the large window, an art-deco drinks cabinet in the corner beside it. Even Terboven's choice of the Bristol made an important statement: it was not necessarily the best hotel in Oslo in which to make his temporary base, but certainly the most stylish.

Terboven raised a hand. 'Stop, please, Herr Quisling. For a moment.' He closed his eyes briefly, as though in deep thought, then opened them again and said, 'Another drink?' He signalled to an aide as Quisling nodded.

Another mistake, thought Scheidt, watching the man pour the Norwegian another whisky as Terboven placed a hand over the top of his own tumbler. 'No, not for me,' he said. Scheidt also knew to refuse.

'All you say may be true, Herr Quisling,' said the Reichskommissar, 'but what about the King – who, it must be said, has shown nothing but contempt for your political ambitions?'

Scheidt smiled to himself at this flagrant criticism of the man sitting next to him.

Quisling shifted in his chair. 'The King fears his position, his authority,' he said. 'It is why he must be captured and brought back to Oslo. I'm sure with a little coercion he can be persuaded to co-operate. For the greater good of Norway.'

Terboven put his hands together as though in prayer and rubbed his chin. 'Hm. It probably won't surprise you, Herr Quisling, to know that I'm no admirer of the King – or any royalty, for that matter. Neither, it should be said, is the Führer.'

'The King must be captured,' said Quisling. 'The Norwegians love him. We voted for him in 1905 when we split from Sweden and since that time he has proved a diligent and extraordinarily popular monarch. He must return to Oslo. Once in the Royal Palace and publicly supporting the National Party, Norway will be the friend and partner Germany wants – indeed needs, Herr Reichskommissar. But so long as King Håkon remains at large, his colours tied to the British mast, there will always be Norwegian resistance to Germany. You must – *must* – find him. Not only that, Herr Reichskommissar, it is imperative you also find the nation's bullion and the Crown Jewels. The King and the former government took them when they fled the capital. So long as the King has money and funds, he will be able to feed resistance. Without them, his task will be that much more difficult.'

He took a gulp of whisky, then leant forward and said, 'My dear Terboven, I really cannot stress enough the importance of capturing the King – before it is too late.'

'He and Prince Olaf are reported to be on the coast now,' said Scheidt. 'At Molde.'

'Thank you, I have read the reports,' said Terboven. He turned back to Quisling. 'Yes, well, thank you, Herr Quisling. We will speak again, but now, if you don't mind, I will bid you good night. As you can imagine, there is much to be done, not least a battle to be won.'

He stood up, signalled Scheidt to remain, and led Quisling to the door. Scheidt watched him shake the Norwegian's hand. It had been a masterly performance: Terboven had shown himself to be well informed yet had listened to the Norwegian; he had been cool and authoritative, but gracious too. He was, Scheidt realized, a formidable opponent.

And right now he was an opponent. It was how it

worked in the Party as Scheidt had learnt early in his career. Climbing the ladder was about jockeying for position, backing the right horse, and outmanoeuvring potential rivals. So far it had worked: he had patrons high up in Berlin and had been given the backing to groom Quisling – backing that had come with the Führer's personal support for the Norwegian. Two weeks before, on the eve of the German invasion, Scheidt had believed everything was in place, and that nothing could go wrong. Quisling would be the new prime minister in name, but as Scheidt had known all along, the Norwegian was far too indecisive and lacked the charisma to be anything more than a German puppet. Scheidt would pull his strings.

But Ambassador Bräuer had lost his nerve and messed everything up. How that fool could have expected the King to roll over, Scheidt still struggled to understand. The days that had followed the invasion had required resolve and cool nerve, but Bräuer had panicked, sacking Quisling as prime minister and bringing in the ludicrously ineffective Administrative Council in the false hope that this would satisfy the King. It had achieved no such thing. And in doing so, he had committed the biggest mistake of all: he had angered the Führer and been recalled to Berlin, his political career finished.

Scheidt knew that he himself was hanging by a thread, but he had not crawled up the Party hierarchy without learning two other golden rules: to trust no one, and always to keep something up one's sleeve. Terboven was in Norway with far-ranging powers – powers that Scheidt could not hope to undermine. However, in this new regime there was still a part for him to perform – an important one, if he played his hand correctly.

With Quisling gone, the new Reichskommissar wandered over to the window and looked out over the city. 'Not an impressive man,' said Terboven, 'and yet, as his political adviser, you pushed for him to remain as prime minister.'

Scheidt remained seated. 'I never viewed him as anything more than a malleable stooge,' he said, after a moment's pause. 'What one has to remember is that Quisling, for all his obvious failings, has unwavering loyalty to Germany, as the Führer clearly recognizes. He is, you know, a devout Christian and a highly regarded academic. He passionately *believes*, Herr Reichskommissar. This is what Bräuer failed to appreciate. Quisling lacks resolve and charisma, but his assessment was right. The Administrative Council is a disaster. Devious and not to be trusted.'

'They sound like perfect Party members.' A thin smile. Terboven came back to his chair opposite Scheidt. 'And what about the King? Is he right about him? Should we worry, or should we simply announce the abolition of the monarchy?'

'In my opinion,' said Scheidt, carefully, 'he is right.'

'And about the bullion and jewels?'

'Resistance needs funding. So yes.' Scheidt shifted in his seat. Was this the time to reveal his hand? Timing was everything, yet Terboven's implacable face was so hard to judge.

'There's something more, isn't there, Herr Scheidt?'

He smiled again. 'It's all right. Feel free to speak frankly.'

By God he's good, thought Scheidt. 'The bullion and Crown Jewels are not with the King,' he said at length.

'Go on.'

'There are more than fifty tons of gold. I'm afraid we've lost track of it – we were not quick enough off the mark when the Norwegian government fled Oslo. It's been hidden, I'm certain, but they have to move it in bulk because if they try to split it up it will never be brought back together. Too many people will have to become involved and they cannot risk that.' He shrugged. 'People will steal it – that's human nature. I have no doubt that at some point an attempt will be made to smuggle it out of the country – but we will catch them. We have complete mastery of the skies and the Norwegians cannot hope to move fifty tons of gold without being spotted.'

'You sound very confident.'

'Fifty tons would require a special train or a convoy of trucks to move it. Of course we will find it. It's just a matter of time. And patience.' Terboven had not taken his eyes from his. 'Some of the important Crown Jewels, however, are with a small group of the King's Royal Guard led by a certain Colonel Peder Gulbrand, and we have been tracking them more closely. We lost them a few days ago, but have now located them again.'

'And why are these men not accompanying the King?'

'They were. I saw them with Bräuer on the tenth of April at Elverum. But they *came back* to Oslo.'

'Surely not to get the jewels?'

'No. To collect a man.'

'Who?'

'Someone more valuable than gold,' said Scheidt. He saw Terboven blink then watched as the Reichskommissar removed his spectacles and carefully cleaned them with a silk handkerchief. A chink at last, he thought.

'Are you going to tell me who this man is?' said Terboven, slowly. It was couched as a question, but it might as well have been a direct order.

'We're not yet certain of his name,' Scheidt lied, 'but what he knows is literally worth liquid gold.'

Terboven offered Scheidt a cigarette from a silver case, then took one himself. The aide hurried over with a lighter and for a moment the Reichskommissar's face was partly hidden in pirouetting smoke. 'Leave us a moment, please,' he told the aide. When the two men were alone, Terboven said, 'Don't try to play games with me, Herr Scheidt.'

Scheidt took a deep breath. He could feel a line of sweat running down his back. His heart thumped. *Keep calm*, he told himself. 'Herr Reichskommissar,' he said slowly, 'you and I both know how precarious intelligence can be. I ask you now to trust me to deliver this man, and to believe me when I say that when I do so, we will have the eternal thanks of the Führer.'

Terboven drew on his cigarette, then tipped back his head and exhaled. 'And what measures are you taking to capture him?'

'It is in hand, Herr Reichskommissar.'

'I could have you arrested and tortured, you know.'

'Yes,' said Scheidt, 'and then you lose the source too.'

'You have thought of everything, Herr Scheidt.'

'I think so.'

Terboven stubbed out his cigarette half smoked and stood up. 'Very well. I shall give you a week. And I hope very much for your sake that you can deliver on all counts – the man, the information and the jewels. A week, Herr Scheidt, that is all. Clear?'

'Perfectly, Herr Reichskommissar.'

Scheidt felt the tight grip of the Reichskommissar's hand and the narrow eyes boring into his, then he was out of the room, walking down the corridor and being escorted into the lift. *My God*, he thought, *a week. But I must be able to find him*. How hard could it be? For God's sake, didn't he have them cornered already? He just prayed his hand was as good as he hoped.

After a steep climb through thick pines and birch, having passed numerous false summits, Sergeant Jack Tanner and his patrol had reached the mountain plateau some two thousand feet above the valley. Here, the air was noticeably colder, but so long as the sun shone through the gauze of thin cloud, Tanner knew they had nothing to fear from the temperature. More of a concern was the depth of the snow, which in places, where there was a hidden hollow or it had drifted, was waist deep or more. The difficulty was that these patches were hard to spot. Some of the men found themselves taking a step forward only to sink. It was exhausting and progress slowed. Then Sykes spotted what appeared to be a drover's track where the snow had been compacted quite recently so Tanner directed the men towards it. Although it was not on Lieutenant Dingwall's map, he guessed it ran over the Balberkamp to the south and along the lip of the valley sides to the north.

'All right, we'll head southwards for a bit,' he told them. It meant they could no longer spread out in the wide arrowhead formation he preferred, but he reasoned that it was best to able to move easily. Ordering Privates Bell and Chambers to walk ahead as scouts, he directed the rest to move in staggered threes at either side of the track, so that the entire group was spread out over almost a hundred yards.

The trees were thinner, and offered less cover, but Tanner was surprised by how much they could see. The plateau now rose only gently; the shallow summit of the Balberkamp was less than a mile ahead, while to the east, the land fell away again only to climb gradually once more. Tanner paused to scan the landscape around him. It was so still. Nothing stirred up there. He thought of home, his village in the south of Wiltshire. The birds were cacophonic at this time of year. And in India, even Palestine, they were always singing, with a multitude of other noises: insects, cattle, sheep, men shouting, the exotic wail of the *imam* calling the faithful to prayer. But here, high on the mountains of Norway, nothing. Just the occasional explosion down in the valley.

He could see no sign of the enemy. Lieutenant Dingwall had been unable to tell him whether German mountain troops would be wearing special snow uniforms, or even if they would be using skis. He was certainly conscious, however, of how ill-suited their own uniforms were to the task in hand. The new battle dress might have been created by clever ministry boffins, but it had not been designed for snow-covered mountain warfare. Tanner sighed. Everything about this campaign had been badly planned by the top brass, it seemed. Surely someone had thought about the conditions they were likely to face in Norway. And if so, why hadn't they organized white overalls and jackets? It was obvious they should have been given such kit. He circled as he walked, his trusted Enfield ready in his hands, and checked the line of men strung out along the rough track, all in khaki and some, like himself, in tan jerkins. It would offer camouflage of sorts if they were hiding behind trees, but against bright white snow, they stood out horribly, easy targets for an enemy trained to operate in such an environment.

Perhaps it wouldn't come to that. The mountain seemed so empty. They hadn't even seen the Chasseurs Alpins. He began to think the rumour of enemy mountain troops must have been just that; and although explosions and the sounds of battle continued from the valley, they were sporadic. He had no impression that their lines were about to be overrun. As he thought of this, his spirits rose. Perhaps they would rejoin the platoon, after all. There were even trees on the summit of the Balberkamp, albeit sparsely spread, and he now had it in mind to climb almost as far as the top of that out-crop of snowy rock. From there, using the trees as cover, they would have a far-reaching view. If any attack was coming, they would see it from there.

They were only a hundred yards from the summit

when Tanner caught the faint hum of an aircraft. So, too, did the others.

'D'you hear that, Sarge?' said Sykes, from behind him.

'It's heading into the valley.' But no sooner had he replied than from the Balberkamp a Messerschmitt appeared, immense and deadly, thundering directly ahead of them as if from nowhere, and flying so low it seemed almost close enough to touch. The noise of the engines tore apart the stillness of the mountain. Tanner yelled at his men to lie flat but it was too late. The twin-engined machine was spurting bullets and cannon shells from its nose, stabs of angry orange fire and lines of tracer hurtling towards them. Tanner felt shells and bullets ripping over his head and either side of him. Something pinged off his helmet, while another missile ripped across the top of his pack. His eyes closed, grimacing into the snow, he pressed his body to the ground, willing himself to flatten.

Two seconds, maybe three, that was all. The ugly machine was past. One of the men called out. Tanner got to his feet. It was Kershaw, one of the two men sent ahead as scouts.

'Christ, oh my God!' he shouted. He sat half upright in the snow staring down at something beside him.

'All right, calm down, Kershaw!' called Tanner. 'Is anyone else hit?' Now there was gunfire a short way to the north. The Messerschmitt was strafing someone or something else.

'Gordon's down, Sarge,' shouted Private McAllister.

Tanner turned to Sykes. 'You go to Gordon, I'll deal with Kershaw. And, lads, keep watching out. Come on!'

He hurried ahead, all the while keeping a watch on the Messerschmitt a mile or two to the north. Now he saw it turn and double back towards them. Tanner was about to yell another warning when the aircraft banked and swept out in a wide arc over the valley and disappeared south.

As he approached Kershaw he saw, with a heavy heart, a mess of dark red stark against the snow. A cannon shell had struck Keith Garraby squarely in the midriff, tearing him in half, so that his still-trousered and booted legs lay in the track, while his upper body had been hurled several yards and now lay upright against the trunk of a tree, the eyes still gazing out in disbelief. Kershaw sat rooted to the spot, ashen-faced, his friend's blood streaked across his face and greatcoat.

Tanner closed Garraby's eyes, then hastily collected the dead man's legs and guts, placing them beneath the rest of the body. The grim task complete, he offered Kershaw a hand. 'Come on,' he said. 'Up on your feet now. Let's get you away from here.' Kershaw did as he was told. Then, glancing back at his friend, he heaved and vomited.

Private Bell was beside Tanner. 'Best hurry, Sarge,' he said. 'Gordo's in a bad way.' He averted his eyes from Garraby. 'Sweet Mother of God,' he muttered. 'The bastards.'

Tanner ran back. Sykes was crouched over Private Draper, desperately pressing field dressings over two wounds in his chest and arm. 'All right, Gordo, you're going to be fine,' he was saying. 'Just hold on, son.'

'Give me some more dressings,' said Tanner, squatting beside him and pulling out his own packs of bandages from his trouser pockets. He opened Draper's jerkin, then tugged his sword bayonet clear of its sheath and deftly slit open the battle blouse, shirt and vest. Draper was pale, his eyes darting from side to side. 'I'm cold,' he mumbled, blood now running from his mouth. He was shivering, but beads of sweat lined his brow and upper lip. Silent tears ran down the side of his face. 'Help me,' he sputtered. 'Help me. I don't want to die.'

'You're going to be fine,' said Tanner, stuffing wadding into the bullet-hole in Draper's chest. 'Stan, press down here,' he said to Sykes. 'Quick – he can't feel a thing. He's in deep shock.' Several others were now gathered round him, peering at Draper's prostrate body. 'I thought I told you to keep watch,' growled Tanner. 'Stop bloody gawping and keep a lookout. Now!' He turned back to Draper. Blood still seeped through the mass of wadding and bandages. Draper's eyes were filled with fear and he was frothing at the mouth. 'Mother!' he gurgled. 'Mother!' He kicked. 'Easy, Gordo, easy. You're all right,' said Tanner. But, of course, he was not. Tanner and Sykes tried to steady him and then a sudden calm spread over Draper's face. The kicking stopped and his head dropped limply to one side.

'Goddamn it!' cursed Tanner, slamming a fist into the ground. He glanced at his watch. It was now nearly six o'clock in the evening. Standing up and scanning the mountains, he could still see no sign of any troops, enemy or otherwise. 'Stan, you stay here with three of your lads and bury Gordon and Keith.' Sykes nodded. 'The rest come with me.'

* * *

It was often hard for a pilot to hit a human target on the ground. Travelling at high speeds there was little time to aim, and although the mixture of MG17 7.92mm bullets and Oerlikon 20mm cannon shells poured out through the nose cone of the twin-engined Messerschmitt 110, there was no time to respond should the targets suddenly fling themselves out of the line of fire. Nor was there much chance to see the fruits of such an attack. The rule of strafing was simple: keep your finger on the firing buttons, then fly straight on out of harm's way as quickly as possible; it only took a lucky bullet and the plane could be in serious trouble, especially at such a low height.

Leutnant Franz Meidel was pleased with his efforts, though. Flying low along Lake Mjøsa, he had climbed due north using the bend in the lake as his marker. He had arrived south-east of the Balberkamp, then pulled back on the throttle so that he was travelling at two hundred miles per hour, and swooped north without being seen or heard. He had not been expecting to see a patrol of British troops but at just under a hundred feet off the ground he had seen their distinctive wide-rimmed helmets clearly. A three-second burst of fire had certainly knocked them over, and he was sure he had seen one man badly hit before the reeling figure had flashed out of sight beneath the aircraft.

Leutnant Meidel had flown on, spotting five men. There was so little time in which to assess who they were, but they carried rifles and looked – so far as he could tell – like Norwegian troops. He had opened fire on them too. Although he had been unable to see whether or not he had been successful, his rear-gunner told him he was certain at least one man had been hit. Meidel flew on, and since there were neither enemy aircraft nor anti-aircraft fire to worry about, and because the adrenalin coursing through him was making him feel bold, he had decided to turn and swoop back low over the tree-tops to examine his handiwork. Of the men there had been no sign, but he had spied a distinct trail of blood in the snow. *Good*, he thought. 'I think we can go home, Reike,' he said.

Although Sergeant Tanner had heard the second attack, it had not been his intention to investigate further. He guessed it had been made on the Frenchmen, in which case he hoped the German pilot had been successful. And, in any case, his orders were to look for German mountain troops preparing an outflanking manoeuvre, not get caught up in somebody else's trouble.

So, with nothing to report from the summit of the Balberkamp, he had told his still-shaken patrol they would head down to rejoin the rest of the company. They had retraced their steps and had cleared the lip so that they were looking down on the Rangers' positions, when Tanner realized something was wrong in the valley. Sykes had spotted it too.

'If the lads are still down there, Sarge,' Sykes said, behind his shoulder, 'why isn't there any sight or sound of gunfire? And why are the Jerry shells landing further to the north?'

'You're a mind-reader, Stan. Mind you, they were shelling behind our lines earlier, too.'

'And our positions at the same time. But it's quiet now. I reckon they've bloody scarpered.'

Tanner felt for his haversack on his hip, reached into it and pulled out the Aldis sight. With one hand he held the leather lens cap as a shield to avoid any light reflecting into the valley, while with the other he put it to his eye.

Sykes eyed the scope admiringly, then peered at the rifle now on Tanner's shoulder. 'You crafty sod, Sarge! You've had the fittings added. Blimey, I never noticed that.'

'Nor has anyone else,' said Tanner, still observing the valley. 'I can't see any sign of them. Jerry aircraft and Jerry shells have done for them, I think.'

'It was a bloody hopeless position in the first place, if you ask me,' said Sykes.

''Course it bloody was,' agreed Tanner. He replaced the cap and carefully put the scope back into his haversack. He felt in his pocket for his cigarettes, only to find he had already smoked the last one. 'Sod it,' he said, tossing away the empty packet. Lieutenant Dingwall had mentioned Tretten, some miles to the north, but in the snow, with almost no food and on the back of four days and nights of very little sleep, this would be tough on the men. They now looked at him expectantly.

'Sarge?' said Sykes.

A faint chatter of small arms could be heard further up the valley – it was the indication Tanner needed. 'We head north,' he said. 'We'll rejoin that track.' The men looked downhearted. 'Listen to me,' said Tanner. 'No one ever said this war would be easy, but unless you want to end up in some Jerry cooler, we've got to keep going. If you've any rations left, eat something now.'

Lack of food was his prime concern, and as they set off once more it played on his mind. When in action, with adrenalin pumping through the blood, hunger melted away, but as he well knew, there were always long intervals between. Hunger could torment a man, sap his energy, weaken his spirit. He had hoped they might be able to shoot a rabbit or some birds, but on this mountain he'd seen few of either. The lads were not grumbling yet; rather, they were quiet, most still stunned by the loss of Garraby and Draper. Tanner had to remind himself that those deaths had probably been the first his men had witnessed. The platoon was close; some had joined at the same time, but all had trained and headed off to war together. To lose good friends so violently was hard to take.

He wondered whether he should have said more. He could have told them that the first dead body was always the worst. That the brain becomes used to such sights and the loss of friends. And that too soon it was possible to put the death of even a close mate quickly to one side and carry on as though nothing had happened. It was strange how hardened one became. The moment for such words had passed, though. They would work it out soon enough.

From the valley below came the continued sounds of battle. More aircraft, more shelling and, occasionally, distant bursts of small arms. He pulled out Dingwall's map. Assuming the lieutenant had drawn it to scale, then Tanner reckoned they were nearing a bend in the Lågen river just south of a village the lieutenant had marked as

Øyer. He had been leading the patrol due north and certainly the fighting now sounded closer, which tallied with the eastward bend in the valley. But although the patrol appeared to be making progress, he knew they must still be behind the front line. A breather in the fighting, that was what he needed. The chance to catch up, get ahead of the German advance, and then they could rejoin the battalion.

His thoughts returned to his stomach. By God, he was hungry. Curse this bloody country, and curse the idiots who'd planned the campaign. Thoughts of food entered his head: a steaming game pie like his father used to make; curries he had eaten in Bombay; the baked apples Mrs Gulliver used to bring round sometimes on Sundays, covered with treacle and currants. He chided himself. *Stop thinking about it, you bloody fool.*

A raised hand from Sykes provided him with the distraction he needed. Tanner had sent the corporal and McAllister up ahead and the two were now squatting fifty yards in front. Warning the rest of the patrol to halt, Tanner moved in a crouch towards the two men. 'What is it?' he whispered, as he reached them.

'I'm not sure,' said Sykes. 'I thought I saw someone up ahead. Behind that rock.' He pointed to an outcrop, some fifteen foot high, emerging darkly from the snow next to a young pine some hundred yards ahead. Silently, Tanner signalled to the rest of the patrol to move forward, then holding his arm out flat and with his open hand facing the ground, waved downwards to make sure they, too, crouched as they came. The three men of the Bren group were the first to reach them. 'Dan, get ready with the

Bren,' he said, under his breath to Lance-Corporal Erwood. 'Mac,' he said softly to McAllister, 'you and I will move forward. Make a run for a tree, then cover me as I go to the next. Then I'll cover you. All right? Dan, you cover us with the Bren. The rest of you stay here, don't make a sound, and watch our backs.'

McAllister, clutching his rifle, took a deep breath, then set off, making for a tree no more than ten yards away. Tanner followed. Whoever was behind the rock – if anyone – made no attempt to move. They pushed forward again until, as Tanner was leading, he spotted a line of blood and several footprints in the snow. He beckoned McAllister to him and pointed to the trail. 'There's someone there, all right,' he whispered to McAllister.

'What do we do now, Sarge?'

'You wait here.'

Treading carefully, Tanner approached. Yards from the rock, he paused. From the other side he could hear voices, faint and indecipherable. Slinging his Enfield over his shoulder, he began to climb the rock. He had noticed that the top was reasonably level, and having deftly scaled the southern side, he crouched across the broad roof of the outcrop and unslung his rifle. Pulling back the bolt as quietly and carefully as he could, he peered over the edge.

There were three men, two of them soldiers in blue-grey Norwegian uniforms. On the right was a young officer, while on the left was a much older man who, although clad in a Norwegian army greatcoat, wore civilian clothes. In the middle, clutching his side, was another Norwegian army officer. A trail of blood followed him round the side of the rock to where he now sat propped against the dark stone.

'You look like you're in trouble,' said Tanner. The three men flinched and looked up, startled. 'Who are you?'

'I am Colonel Peder Gulbrand of His Majesty the King's Guard,' gasped the man in the middle.

5

Jack Tanner noticed another set of footprints leading away from the rock. 'Whose are those?' he asked.

'Lieutenant Larsen, also a member of His Majesty the King's Guard,' said the younger man, in heavily accented English. 'He has gone to find somewhere for us to hole up. Our colonel needs help.'

Tanner signalled to his men, then clambered down from the rock. 'Me and my men are from the 5th Battalion, the King's Own Yorkshire Rangers,' he told them. 'That makes us allies. I'm Sergeant Tanner.'

'And I am Lieutenant Nielssen,' replied the blond officer.

Tanner looked at the colonel. 'Is it bad?'

'A splinter in his side,' Nielssen told him. 'He's lost a lot of blood. We were attacked an hour ago. The stupid German missed us, but a shard of wood from a tree struck the colonel.'

'We saw the attack,' said Tanner, kneeling beside Gulbrand and pulling out another twin pack of field dressings. 'He was more successful firing at us. Two dead.'

'I'm sorry,' said Nielssen. Tanner was conscious of a tapping sound and turned to see the civilian clicking together two small stones. The man looked exhausted, with dark hollows around his spectacled eyes and an unkempt moustache and grey stubble around his lined face. Seeing Tanner's glance, he stopped tapping the stones, dropping them by his side into the snow.

'And who are you?' asked Tanner, as he tore open the cotton and ripped off the waterproof covering around each of the dressings.

'Someone we are escorting,' said Gulbrand hoarsely before the other could answer.

Tanner nodded. *You don't want to tell me. Fine.* It wasn't his business. 'Is the shard still inside?' he asked.

Gulbrand nodded. 'Yes.' He grimaced, then opened his coat and tunic. His shirt was almost entirely red and glistened stickily. With clenched teeth, he lifted it free. Tanner inspected the wound. The blood was bright crimson. The tip of the shard protruded from the colonel's side. Tanner rubbed his face. Tiredness. It was catching up with him again.

'What do you think?' asked Gulbrand, his English near flawless.

'That it's embedded in your liver, Colonel,' said Tanner.

'I think you're right.' He took a sudden sharp breath and winced.

'I can't pull it out,' said Tanner, still peering at the wound. 'Do that and you'll bleed to death in about ten minutes.'

'He needs a hospital,' said Lieutenant Nielssen, 'an operation, and soon.'

'Easier said than done, mate,' said Corporal Sykes, now standing over Tanner.

'What about Lillehammer?' said Nielssen. 'Two of your men could take him.'

'Two of our men?' said Sykes. 'Are you having a laugh? Even if they made it back down the mountain, they'd walk straight into Jerry hands. Lillehammer's fallen, if you hadn't already noticed.'

'I know – we saw earlier . . . But they would save the life of the colonel.'

'If you're so bloody keen, why don't you two take him?'

'Shut your trap, Stan,' growled Tanner. 'You're not helping.' He turned to Gulbrand. 'Colonel, it's a bad wound. I'm sorry. Your lieutenant's right. You need a hospital.' He delved into his haversack again and produced a small tube of gentian violet antiseptic ointment. 'I don't carry much first aid, but this should help prevent infection.' He gingerly pasted the cream over the wound, then placed the dressings over it. Gulbrand cried out, but Tanner took another packet from Sykes, tore it open and wrapped more bandages round the colonel's waist. 'Why can't your men take you to Lillehammer, Colonel?' he asked. 'The fighting's going to be over soon. Better to live and fight another day, eh?'

'They can't,' Gulbrand gasped. 'It's impossible.'

'Why?'

Gulbrand stared hard at him, but did not answer.

Instead he said, 'Tell me, Sergeant, what are you doing up here?'

Tanner told him, then added, 'But now we need to get a move on. The front's fallen back this afternoon. I'm damned if I'm going to let us get stranded.'

'We're holding you up. I'm sorry.'

'But you're natives, sir. We help you, you can help us. We desperately need a map, and someone who speaks Norwegian would be useful.' He noticed that the sounds of battle from the valley had quietened. An occasional aircraft, desultory shellfire, that was all. Had the Allies fallen back yet again? 'And what about you, sir?' he asked Gulbrand. 'Why are you up here?'

Gulbrand closed his eyes. 'It's a long story.'

Tanner was about to ask him more when Lieutenant Larsen appeared. He had found a *seter*, a mountain hut used by herdsmen and shepherds during the summer, not far away. It would offer them shelter.

'We'll help get you there,' said Tanner, 'but then my men and I must push on. Put your arm round my neck,' he told the colonel. He glanced once more at the strange civilian. The man was gazing out through the trees, seemingly in a world of his own. Tanner called over to Sykes. 'Here, Stan, give me a hand, will you?' They lifted Gulbrand. 'Can you walk?' Tanner asked.

'With your help, I'm sure.'

The civilian now awkwardly got to his feet and with enormous effort, slung his pack on to his back, and then staggered a pace or two, so that Tanner thought he might fall over backwards. 'Does he speak English?' Tanner asked Gulbrand, he was conscious he had not heard the man utter a word.

'Yes. Almost everyone does in Oslo and the coastal cities. It's only inland that you will struggle to be understood.'

Tanner turned to the man. 'Carry the colonel's pack, will you? Come on, we need all the help we can get.'

The man smiled sheepishly then pulled it on to his shoulder, faltering as he did so.

Reichsamtsleiter Hans-Wilhelm Scheidt sat at his desk in his rooms at the Continental Hotel, the black telephone receiver to his ear. Anger surged through him as he listened to Sturmbannführer Paul Kurz's latest report – rage fuelled, he knew, by his mounting fear of failure. Damn it, Terboven was not a man to mess with, and only a couple of hours after his meeting with the new Reichskommissar, Kurz was on the line telling him that the most important man in his life had narrowly missed getting a 20mm cannon shell through his guts.

'For God's sake, Kurz, that's the second time one of those flyboys has nearly killed him. We were fortunate he survived the last one. It might be third time lucky for those idiots and then where will we be? We need him *alive*, Kurz, not spread over some bastard mountain.'

'Calm down, Scheidt,' said Kurz, from his newly requisitioned office in Lillehammer. 'We've just heard. They got the colonel, and seriously too. Even if he doesn't die of his wound – and the odds are that he will – he's out of the picture, as far as they're concerned. Odin is as good as in our hands already.'

'Only if the Allies haven't got him before you reach him,' snarled Scheidt. 'Now, do what you're supposed to do, Kurz, and tell that idiot Geisler to stop his pilots attacking those men.'

Scheidt had heard the panic in his voice and so had Kurz. 'Don't try to tell me my job, Herr Scheidt.' Kurz told him flatly.

'Listen,' fumed Scheidt, 'you do your job and you won't hear me complaining. But if anything happens to Odin before we've had the chance to get the information from him neither you nor I will have a career, let alone a life. Now, you're the SD man here – start using your influence and get Geisler's boys to keep away from them.'

'Stop worrying,' said Kurz. 'We'll find them soon enough. They're not going to get very far up there.'

'That's just not good enough!' Scheidt exploded. 'For Christ's sake, so far you've let them slip through your hands once, and twice nearly had them shot to smithereens by the Luftwaffe. Don't tell me to calm down – tell me what you're doing to find Odin. What troops have you got for the operation? Tell me they're already tracking them down. Damn it, Sturmbannführer, why the hell am I having to ask you all this? Tell me something that gives me confidence – something that makes me believe you're actually trying to get to this man.'

'You politicians,' said Kurz, 'always the same. I'm sure it seems very straightforward to you from where you're sitting on your arse in Oslo, but up here Engelbrecht's division are facing the British and Norwegians – there's been heavy fighting all day. The SD don't have the authority to tell generals to hand over their troops for an operation they know nothing about.'

Scheidt pinched the bridge of his nose wearily. *Give me patience*. He'd always thought the Sicherheitsdienst were an unintelligent and idle lot. 'Then tell them Terboven orders it.'

There was a sigh at the other end of the line. 'Jesus, Scheidt, of course. That's exactly what I have done, but the entire Army is not at our beck and call. And you're forgetting that we only learnt of Odin's whereabouts this morning, and that's pretty vague – and it was only earlier today that Lillehammer fell. As it happens, I've got a company of reconnaissance troops from Dietl's Gebirgsjäger Division, and I've had to pull a lot of strings to get them. They're attached to Engelbrecht's division. They're setting off to hunt for them now.' He paused. 'And they'll get Odin because Gulbrand's out of the picture and those Norwegians aren't going to get far, up on that mountain. Tomorrow morning, Herr Reichsamtsleiter, we'll have an altogether more pleasant conversation.'

It was Scheidt's turn to sigh. 'Just get him, Kurz. Get men up into those mountains, find Odin and bring him to me in one piece.' He slammed down the telephone and slumped back in his chair. A cigarette and a drink, that was what he needed. He leant forward, opened a drawer in his desk and pulled out a bottle of cognac. Having poured himself a generous measure, he lit a cigarette. The smoke danced in front of him, curling towards the ceiling. The brandy stung his lips and tongue, then pleasurably burnt the back of his throat. *Argh, but that was good.*

He stood up, walked to the window and gazed out over the city. It seemed so quiet, so peaceful. Perhaps Kurz was right. Perhaps he *was* just sitting on his arse. Was there really any need to remain in Oslo for the rest of the month? Quisling's pride might have been wounded, but he was busy with his new role as Commissioner for Demobilization and, in any case, still had Hagelin, Aall and the other leading National Party members around him. Quisling, Scheidt realized, could do without him for a few days.

He drained his tumbler. Yes, damn it, he would get out of Oslo, head to Lillehammer and oversee the operation to capture Odin. That would shake up that idler Kurz. Scheidt smiled. Already, his mood was lightening.

Another aircraft overhead, higher this time and slightly away towards the valley. It hummed gutturally, then, as the pilot throttled back, the engines seemed to catch and change tone. No firing of guns, no bombs dropped; a reconnaissance aircraft, then. Tanner followed its route until it disappeared from sight. Had any of the crew spotted them? He couldn't know, but he felt as though he was being watched. It unnerved him.

And what the hell were these Norwegians doing up here? He had probed Gulbrand once more, but the colonel had been evasive. Sykes joined him as Tanner scanned all around with his scope.

'Got a spare beadie, Stan?' Tanner asked him.

Sykes tapped the packet out of his pocket. 'There's

something funny going on with these Vikings,' he said as he struck a match into his cupped hand. He passed a lit cigarette to Tanner. 'They look terrible and not just the colonel. They've been up here a fair few days. If it weren't for the fact that there're lots of Norwegians in the valley I'd say they're on the run from something.'

'The Bosches?' suggested Tanner, with a grin.

'Course from Jerry, but there's more to it than that. Why are they up here? What's more, who's that civvy geezer? Nah, I tell you, Sarge, there's something going on. Something they don't want to tell us.'

Tanner shrugged. 'Maybe. But right now I don't give a damn what they're doing up here as long as they can help us get back to the battalion.' He blew out some smoke. 'Stay out here a moment, Stan, and keep a dekko. I'm going to get one of those Norwegians and sort out a plan of action. We've wasted enough time already.'

Tanner went back into the *seter*, where most of the men now sat. The temperature had dropped noticeably and it was cold inside, despite the men now huddled there. The hut was small – perhaps twenty foot by fifteen – a simple wooden structure that had a musty smell of dust and damp pine. There was a door at the centre, and a window to the side from which the thick cobwebs had been removed.

Tanner sighed. Christ, he was tired. Tired and bloody starving. Several of his men were already asleep and they had only been there five minutes – Hepworth was squatting in the corner, his head falling forwards. Tanner stooped over Gulbrand. 'He's asleep,' said Larsen.

'Asleep or unconscious?' asked Tanner. As he said this

the colonel groaned. 'Asleep for now.' He stood up again. 'We've got to get him out of here somehow.'

Larsen nodded. He had a pale, lean face, with several days' growth of gingery beard. Like the others, he was exhausted, his eyes grey and hollow.

'Who's the most senior of you lot after the colonel?'

'I am,' said Larsen. 'I've been two years a lieutenant. Nielssen was only promoted last year.'

'Have you got a map?'

'Here.' He delved into his rucksack.

'Look, my corporal's outside. Do you mind if the three of us have a talk?' Larsen followed him out. 'It's after nine now,' said Tanner, blowing into his hands. He could see his breath on the chill evening air. 'It doesn't get dark until after eleven, so we've a couple more hours of daylight. We need to get a move on if we've any chance of catching up with the Allies. But we've got two big problems. First,' he said, to Larsen, 'Colonel Gulbrand. We're not going to get far if we take him with us.' Larsen nodded. 'Second,' continued Tanner, 'we've got a lot of exhausted men in there – or, rather, starving exhausted men – and I include myself.'

'And me an' all,' said Sykes.

'Yes,' said Larsen, 'it is the same for us.'

Tanner eyed him. 'Are you going to tell us what you're doing up here? You look like you've been on the go even longer than us.'

'I wish I could,' said Larsen. 'But please believe me that it is of vital importance. Vital importance.'

'All right, but I'm assuming you want to reach the Allies too?'

'Yes. Very much.'

'So, first we need to know where we are and find out what's going on down in the valley. And, second, we need food. I want to have a dekko, see how far Jerry's got and where our boys are.'

Sykes noticed Larsen's quizzical expression. 'I know, sir,' he said to the Norwegian. 'It took me a while to understand the sergeant's lingo. He means he wants to have a look.'

'I see,' said Larsen.

'And at the same time, we try to find some food. How far down do we have to go before we get to some farmhouses, sir?' he asked Larsen.

'Not so far. I think we are above Øyer.' Larsen opened the map and held it up. 'Look, this stream. I'm sure it is just ahead – you can see the ground falling away. If so, there are bound to be farms high above the village.'

'And from the contours, sir, it looks as though the valley sides are not as steep here as they were around Lillehammer. That'll make things easier.' Tanner looked at them both. 'In that case we should take the colonel. If there are farms below, as you say, we can leave him at one of them. They can get him into the village and then to Lillehammer. All right,' Tanner continued. 'I suggest you and I, sir, go on a recce. We'll take a couple of others with us – one of my lads and Lieutenant Nielssen. Between us we can carry the colonel. Stan, you stay here and look after the others. Make sure there's a guard at all times, but that'll give them a chance to get some kip. There's going to be a reasonable moon tonight, so I reckon we should rest up here until dark. Then, if things are quiet, we'll head down into the valley.'

'How will you carry the colonel?' asked Sykes.

'We find a couple of strong sticks and thread the arms of two greatcoats through them to make a stretcher.'

The colonel, however, woke as they tried to lift him on to the improvised stretcher and refused to be moved. 'No,' he said, through gritted teeth. 'I will not be handed over to the Germans. I cannot.'

'But you need to get to a hospital, sir,' said Larsen.

He glared at his lieutenant. 'No, Henrik.'

'Colonel,' Tanner added, 'the longer we leave you, the greater the chances are that you'll die before we can get you proper help.'

Gulbrand winced with pain again. 'No!' he hissed. 'Now, do as I say. Leave me.'

Tanner did as he was ordered. Whatever their reason for such secrecy was their affair; as long as they continued to help him and his men, it made no odds. He understood. He had secrets of his own; dark secrets he had never spoken about to a living soul since he had joined the Army as a sixteen-year-old boy soldier. In any case, he reasoned, their climb down the mountain would be easier without the colonel – and greater manoeuvrability meant the risk would be less. Wounded men, he reminded himself, were always a hindrance.

Tanner took Private McAllister, one of the riflemen in Sykes's section – he seemed less affected by the afternoon's events than the others. At any rate, he was still awake and appeared to have his wits about him. Nielssen accompanied Larsen, leaving the civilian with the colonel.

Progress was slow to begin with but, overlooking the steep ravine cut by the stream, they found the outline of a rough track that wound its way through the trees and off the slopes. The further they climbed down, the more the snow thinned until eventually the dark stone and grit of the track was revealed and the four men were able to walk freely. As the trees cleared, they crept forward to the bank at the side of the track. Spread beneath them was the snaking valley of the Lågen river, which resembled a winding lake. Nestling above the water's edge was the village of Øyer, the valley and the single railway line clearly visible. Beyond, isolated farms dotted the lower slopes on both sides of the river, and around them, marking clear breaks in the thick pine forests, were small fields – which would soon be full of rich grass for hay-making and grazing. Now, though, in the third week of April, the valley was like a photograph – black and white and shades of grey. Only the water of the Lågen, deeply, darkly, icily blue, offered colour.

Almost directly below there was a farmstead, and another beyond, a hundred yards further down. Tanner admired the now familiar design: the steep-pitched roof, the ornate wooden veranda, the barn with its stone ramp. A dog barked briefly, but otherwise it was as eerily still as it had been higher up on the mountain. Again, he could not hear the song of a single bird.

'It seems quiet enough,' said Larsen.

Tanner pulled out his scope. 'There's movement,' he said. Several Heinkels flew northwards along the valley, dropping their bombs a few miles north-west of the village. Clouds of smoke erupted on the lower slopes of the mountains and across the river. Intermittent artillery shells resounded around the same part of the valley. In the distance there were bursts of small arms.

'They're making some kind of stand up there,' said Tanner.

'What can you see?' asked Larsen.

'Not sure. Hard to tell, even with this. A few vehicles on the road in front of us, though. What look like several carts. I need to get closer.'

'Nielssen and I will try these farms,' said Larsen.

'All right,' said Tanner. 'McAllister and I will cover you. We'll be able to see if the coast is clear, then we'll head down a bit further.' Tanner looked at his watch. 'It's a quarter to ten. Meet back here in half an hour, no later. We need to get on our way. If the front really is only a few miles up the valley, we've a good chance of catching up tonight.'

Larsen nodded. 'Good luck, Sergeant.'

Tanner and McAllister watched the two Norwegians walk cautiously down the track towards the farm, their rifles slung over their shoulders and rucksacks still on their backs. Tanner heard McAllister's stomach grumble. 'My God, Mac,' he said. 'That's some racket your belly's making.'

'Sorry, Sarge,' said McAllister. He grinned at Tanner sheepishly. 'It's them Vikings heading off for food. It's got me going again.'

'Well, stop thinking about it. Concentrate on keeping a bead on them.'

Tanner had his own rifle out and aimed towards the farm. In silence now they watched the two men approach the house. Two dogs barked and ran towards them. Nielssen held out his hands and they approached, tails wagging at the friendly gesture. Larsen knocked on the door, which opened. A middle-aged man, with a grey moustache. Talking – an explanation. Then the two men were inside, the door closed behind them.

'Good,' said Tanner. 'Looks like we might get some grub. Come on, Mac, let's get going.'

They left the track and moved back into the trees. The forest was dense and dark. Melting snow dripped round them, but the ground, although steep in parts, was covered with no more than an inch or two and they were able to move easily, almost running in places. Skirting another farm, Tanner stopped by a clearing in the trees from which they could see the road, now no more than a few hundred yards ahead.

They were behind several pines to the side of the clearing, and Tanner knew they were well hidden, especially now that the light was fading. A column of men and horses pulling artillery pieces was working its way towards the village. Tanner peered through his scope. 'Damn it,' he hissed.

'Jerries?' whispered McAllister.

Tanner nodded, then turned towards the village. There were trucks, cars, other vehicles, and by the church, a huge tank, with a squat, thick-muzzled gun. Emerging from the village was a line of men, three or four wide. From their helmets and greatcoats, he knew they were British. 'Jesus,' he murmured.

'What is it, Sarge?'

'You don't want to know.' Several German infantrymen were walking beside them, rifles in hand. As they cleared the village and tramped slowly out on the valley road, they met the line of artillery. Tanner saw the Germans jeering, then strained his eyes to the front of the prisoners and realized with dismay that none other than Captain Cartwright and Lieutenant Dingwall were leading the column.

Poor sods. For the moment, though, he would keep it to himself. No point unduly worrying the others. 'Come on, Mac, we've seen enough. We need to get a move on.'

They found Nielssen and Larsen waiting for them by the track above the farm. Between them they had managed to get hold of some salted ham, a dozen eggs, some cheese and several loaves of bread. Larsen cut Tanner and McAllister some ham now and passed it to them. It was old, almost blue, and as salty as seawater, but to Tanner it tasted delicious. 'Here, have some bread too,' said Larsen, tearing off a chunk.

'Damn me, that's good.' Tanner grinned. His energy was returning.

'Did you ever have chocolate as a kid, Sarge?' McAllister asked him.

'Once or twice maybe. Why?'

'This tastes even better than that.'

Tanner laughed. 'I reckon you're still a bloody kid, Mac. How old are you?'

'Eighteen, Sarge. A fully grown man, I am.'

'And so, old enough to carry a rifle and go to fight a war,' added Larsen.

'Yes, sir,' said MacAllister. 'Although I admit this wasn't quite what I'd imagined.' Larsen sighed. 'Me neither, Private. Me neither.'

The sky was darker now and would be even more so once they were within the shelter of the dense wooded slopes. 'We should get going,' he said. 'Those are dark clouds. We could be in for some snow up here.'

By the time they were nearing the *seter*, the cloud lay low over the mountain. Snowflakes were falling.

'Bloody hell,' cursed Tanner. 'Of all the luck.'

'This is not good,' said Larsen.

'It might be all right in the valley,' added Nielssen, 'but up here . . .'

Tanner was pleased to see that the guard outside the *seter* was awake and alert. Hepworth asked him whether they had managed to find food and if the front had fallen back. 'Yes to both,' Tanner replied. Inside, most of the men slept, although they soon stirred with the arrival of the recce party. The two Norwegian officers passed round the food with, Tanner noticed, considerable fairness. Nielssen produced a Primus stove and a mess tin, then put on some water to boil. The men eagerly crowded round.

'I'm gasping for some tea,' said Kershaw, prompting an enthusiastic muttering of agreement from the others.

'Only coffee, I'm afraid,' said Nielssen.

'Perfect, sir,' said Sykes, quickly. 'Anything wet and hot will be pure nectar.'

Tanner went over and crouched down beside Gulbrand, then looked at the civilian still sitting next to him. He was curious about this fellow – what was a gaunt-faced, middle-aged man doing with these troops of the King's Guard? A politician or diplomat perhaps? He wanted to ask, but reminded himself that it was not his concern why these men were here or what they were doing; after all, he hated people nosing into his own business and saw no need to pry into theirs.

The man eyed him, then leaned over and dabbed the colonel's brow. 'It's not good,' he said. 'He's getting a fever.'

'That probably means his blood's infected.' Tanner opened Gulbrand's greatcoat once more.

The colonel stirred. 'Ah, you're back, Sergeant.'

Tanner continued to peel back his clothing. The smell as he lifted the tunic was overpowering. Gangrene was setting in. Probably septicaemia too. The antiseptic hadn't worked; Tanner had never really thought it would. That shard had probably taken soiled cotton and serge with it into Gulbrand's side and liver. A bit of gentian violet couldn't have performed the miracle the colonel needed.

'It's all right,' said Gulbrand. 'I know I'm going to die.' His voice was low and hoarse.

'I'm sorry, sir. If you'd let us take you down the mountain . . .'

'It would have made no difference. But that's not the point.' He gripped Tanner's arm. 'Tell me, Sergeant, can I depend on you?'

'To get your men to safety? I don't know, sir. We've a

103

few problems just at the minute. But you can depend on me to do my damnedest. I've no intention of getting myself killed or spending the rest of my life in some Jerry prison camp.'

Gulbrand released him, then turned to the civilian. 'Sandvold? Will you leave us alone a moment?' The man got up and walked to Nielssen. Gulbrand watched him, then said, 'We should be with the King. We are, after all, his bodyguard. I have been in His Majesty the King's Guard for nearly twenty years. My loyalty is total. The King knows that. It's why he chose me for this task.' Tanner listened without saying a word. 'The ninth of April was a terrible day,' Gulbrand said. 'A terrible day . . .'

The Germans had attacked Oslo. Everyone had been completely unprepared and it quickly became clear that the capital would fall. Prime Minister Nygaardsvold was persuaded by his government that they should leave Oslo and head north where they could continue to govern and manage the crisis away from German guns. The King was informed of the decision and immediately agreed that he and his son, Crown Prince Olav, should go with them. Shortly after, he called for Gulbrand. King Håkon wanted a dozen men to act as his bodyguard and for the rest of the Guard to follow to Hamar as quickly as possible. Gulbrand was to remain with the King, who entrusted to him a number of documents and jewels for safe-keeping. The King had made him swear to keep them about his person at all times.

The train for Hamar had left at seven that morning. 'Imagine what that was like,' said Gulbrand. 'To leave the capital. It felt as though we were running away. It was hard to bear.' But, in truth, they had had little choice. Norway was a peaceful country – a neutral country – and her armed forces were ill-equipped to deal with such an invasion. 'A mobilization order was announced that same morning,' Gulbrand told him, 'but it was too late. Far too late. Most of the men fighting in the valley here have had no training whatsoever. They've been given a uniform and a rifle and sent off to fight. Those serving in the standing Army will have had just eighty-four days' training. That's not even three months. We in the Guards, of course, train all the time, but even so, our equipment is poor so our training has been limited. All my men, Sergeant, can fire a rifle as well as anyone, but that's not enough to stop these bastards. We've got no tanks, no anti-tank weapons, no mines. We don't even have any hand grenades. Our field guns are old. We've got some machine-guns but few men have had any training on them. My God, there haven't even been enough uniforms. Half the men have been issued with 1914-pattern. So, you see, we had no choice but to leave Oslo.'

The train took them to Hamar, but by evening word reached them that German forces were on their way to capture them so they boarded another train for Elverum. Two days later a German delegation arrived, offering peace terms, which had been rejected. It was shortly after this that Gulbrand had been summoned by the King. His son, Prince Olav, had also been present, but otherwise they had been entirely alone. King Håkon had a task for Gulbrand. In the chaos of their departure from Oslo, they had left someone behind, a man named

Hening Sandvold. The King wanted Gulbrand to go back to Oslo and fetch him. 'I'm afraid I still cannot tell why he is so important,' said Gulbrand. 'I made a solemn vow to the King and Prince Olav and I am not prepared to break it. Not even now. But I will tell you this: if Sandvold fell into the hands of the Nazis, it could have catastrophic consequences, not only for Norway but for Great Britain and all of the free world too.'

Tanner looked over towards Sandvold, now standing by the door, a lost and wistful expression on his face. Whoever he was, whatever he did, it was clear he was a fish out of water up here in the mountains with these soldiers.

He turned back to Gulbrand. 'How did you get him then, sir?'

'By keeping it simple,' the colonel replied. 'The King told me to take whatever men I needed but I decided to take just three others: Larsen, Nielssen and Lieutenant Stunde.' He trusted them, and each had different skills. Stunde spoke fluent German, Nielssen was strong, an excellent athlete and experienced mountaineer. Larsen was clever and good at thinking on his feet. All were first-class shots. They had left their uniforms in Elverum and headed to Oslo. The city was calm, and although the sight of swastikas was hard to stomach, they were surprised by how few German troops were there. They found Sandvold easily enough and although he was initially reluctant to leave, when they showed him the King's personal letter to him, he eventually conceded. 'We all have to do things we wish we didn't have to.'

Getting back to Elverum had been more difficult.

They had driven whenever they could, stealing cars and ditching them whenever they drew near a roadblock. They had walked many miles too. When they eventually reached Elverum, the King and the Government had long since gone, but the monarch had warned him this might be so. His instructions had been to catch him up if he could, otherwise to find the British and get Sandvold safely across the sea to England.

Having retrieved their uniforms, and with the Germans never far behind, they had headed north from Elverum, had nearly been caught hiding in a barn and soon after shot at by aircraft. They had been forced to abandon their transport again and cross the mountains. It had been a difficult four-day journey. On the second day, Lieutenant Stunde had broken his leg. They couldn't carry him so had been forced to leave him. 'It was,' said Gulbrand, weakly, 'the worst decision I have ever had to make. We found a *seter*, and hoped someone would find him, but we knew there was little chance of that. Poor Roald. It would have been kinder to put a bullet in his head. So, you see, I couldn't ask Nielssen or Larsen to make an exception for me. And, in any case, I couldn't allow the enemy to catch me. What if I told them something when I was delirious?'

Gulbrand's teeth were chattering now. Beads of sweat ran down his face. His skin looked sallow, his eyes hollow, even in the dim light. 'I have entrusted Larsen and Nielssen with the jewels and papers, but what I ask of you now is of far greater importance. You must get Sandvold to safety somehow. To the coast and Britain.'

'All right,' said Tanner, 'you have my word. I'll try. But

why me? Why aren't you saying this to Larsen or Nielssen?'

Gulbrand coughed, which evidently caused him further agonies. Eventually he sank down again. 'They are officers, yes, second lieutenants, or *fenriks*, as we call them, but Nielssen should be a sergeant or less. The Norwegian Army did away with non-commissioned officers a few years ago. Now men train as NCOs for a couple of years, then spend a year as a sergeant before being promoted. Larsen is different, but he is not the leader you are. I've watched you, Sergeant. You are in command of these men, not Henrik Larsen. And I think you have more experience than the rest of us put together.' He smiled weakly. 'Yes, Sergeant Tanner, and you are already a decorated soldier.'

Tanner was embarrassed. 'Thank you, sir.'

'Don't thank me,' said Gulbrand. 'It is a thankless task I have given you. But you will have the eternal thanks of my king and country if you succeed, and I suspect your own as well.' He closed his eyes, grimaced, then said, 'One last thing. Trust no one. And kill Sandvold rather than let him fall into enemy hands. Kill him and destroy any papers he may be carrying. If the others try to stop you, kill them too. Do you think you can do that?'

'Yes,' said Tanner. 'One thing, though, sir. Do the Germans know about him? Are you being followed?'

Gulbrand gasped. 'I don't think so. Why would those planes have tried to kill us? Sandvold's no use to them dead. But they mustn't get him, d'you hear?' He gripped Tanner's sleeve. 'They mustn't get him.'

Tanner left Gulbrand. *What a mess*, he thought. *The*

108

whole bloody show. He thought of Captain Cartwright and Lieutenant Dingwall, prisoners now along with many others. He wondered if anything remained of the company; or even anything of the battalion. It was hard to accept. A damned stupid waste of lives. And now he had the extra burden of Hening Sandvold. He had no idea what was so special about him. A scientist, he supposed. What those boffins knew was beyond him; the world was changing so fast. He just hoped that in Sandvold's case it would be worth it.

It was after eleven and he stepped outside to find the snow falling heavily now. Christ, this was all he needed. He wanted to get going, move off this God-forsaken mountain, try to catch up with the Allies while they still had a chance. He prayed it was snowing in the valley too – at least then the front would be held up as they were.

'We can't move in this.' It was Sykes, taking his turn as sentry. 'Just in case you were thinking of it, Sarge.' Tanner said nothing, so Sykes added, 'They're only scrawny tykes. They're probably not as fit as you are, Sarge.'

Tanner breathed out heavily. 'Yes, all right, Stan. I've got the message.'

'Christ, it's dark out here,' Sykes said, banging his helmet against the side of the *seter* to knock off the snow. 'You were having a long chinwag with the colonel, Sarge.'

'We've got to take the Norwegians with us,' said Tanner. 'That civvy – he's special. A boffin or something. Anyway, we've got to get him to safety. Preferably back to Britain.'

'Where's the front?'

'Not at Øyer.'

Sykes tutted. *There's a surprise.* 'So where are our boys?'

In the hands of the Jerries, thought Tanner. 'Not so far. A few miles. It's so bloody frustrating. I just want to get going. Sodding Norwegians.'

'Well, we can't go anywhere in this,' said Sykes again.

'It's my only consolation.'

But it was at that moment that Sykes heard something moving between the trees not forty yards ahead. Then Tanner heard it too. Footsteps. In the faint glow of the snow they saw the dark shape of troops approaching.

6

Brigadier Harold de Reimer Morgan, commander of the British 148th Brigade – or what was left of it – placed his index finger on the map at a point roughly three miles west of Øyer where the river narrowed. 'Here,' he said. 'I'd like to say there are two companies of Leicesters but, in truth, it's a mixture of Leicesters, Foresters, Rangers and Norwegians. Let's call it a composite force of Allied troops.' His eyes stung with fatigue and from the dim light in the room. 'They've been bombed and strafed and the enemy has got his 5.9s trained on them, but they seem to have stout hearts and are doing their best. It's quiet now but, come the morning, they won't be able to hold on long. The rest of our force is here,' he added, pointing to the narrow gorge south of Tretten, a couple of miles further back along the winding valley. He stood up and smoothed back his hair. 'But I have to tell you, General, that without support, I cannot guarantee that we'll be able to hold Tretten for long.'

General Ruge studied the map in silence. The

building in Fåvang that he had made his latest head-quarters was the station house, a simple brick structure with a handful of rooms. Until the day before, his office had belonged to the station master, but although there was dust on the shelves and the floorboards were worn, it had an old leather-topped desk and a clock on the wall that proved to be an accurate timepiece, and there was room enough for the Norwegian Army commander and several staff officers.

Ruge ran a hand round the stiff collar of his tunic, stretched his neck, then sank back into his chair. 'Where is the extra company of Leicesters from Åndalsnes? Are they at Tretten?' he asked Brigadier Morgan.

'Yes, but without much kit, I'm afraid. Apparently there's a Bofors waiting to be moved down here from Åndalsnes, but as yet no one has found a way to get it here.' He was eyeing the general keenly. 'So we still don't have a single anti-aircraft gun.'

Ruge said nothing. Instead he banged his fist hard on the desk top. Frustration, anger.

'The Tretten gorge is a good natural defensive position,' Morgan continued, 'but I'm worried about our flanks. The enemy's mountain troops went round us successfully at the Balberkamp and I'm concerned they'll do so again. But I don't have enough men. I need to make a position here, to the east of Tretten village, otherwise—'

'Very well, Morgan, I take your point,' snapped Ruge. 'Beichmann,' he said, to the staff officer seated next to the desk, in English so that Morgan could understand, 'find Colonel Jansen. Order him to place his Dragoons there, and tell him he is now to fall under the direct command of Brigadier Morgan.'

'Sir.' Colonel Beichmann saluted and left the room.

General Ruge sighed wearily. 'What else can we do?'

'It would help the men greatly if they could have something to eat, sir. Most haven't had anything for more than thirty-six hours. We were promised that Norwegian troops would be bringing up rations this afternoon, but so far nothing has arrived. All we have is a store of dry rations left at Tretten station by the newly arrived Leicesters. It's not enough.'

'All right, Morgan, I'll look into it. The problem, as you know, is transport.' He chuckled mirthlessly. 'Just one of our many problems,' he added, holding up his hands – *what am I expected to do?* 'Just one of many.'

Brigadier Morgan left the general and drove back towards Tretten in a requisitioned Peugeot, squashed into the back seat next to Major Dornley, his Brigade-Major, their knees knocking together and elbows almost touching. It was cold, and he pulled up the collar of his coat so that the coarse wool scraped against his cheeks and ears. He was fifty-two, which, he reflected, was no great age to be a brigade commander during peace time, but too old in a time of war. He felt the cold more than he had in his younger days, and right now he felt more exhausted – mentally and physically – than he had ever done as a young man in the trenches.

Outside, light snow was falling, dusting the road ahead. Out of his left window, dark, dense forest ran away from the verge; to his right, he could see the smooth, almost black mass of the Lågen river, as wide as a lake; while above, dark and menacing, were the mountains. Magnificent, yes – but right now a snare, trapping and constraining his meagre forces. A funnel for the Luftwaffe and German gunners.

Morgan bit one of his nails.

'Are you all right, sir?' asked his Brigade-Major.

'I suppose so, Dornley, thank you for asking.' He clicked his tongue several times, then said, 'It's just bloody difficult trying to command a brigade when you've got someone like General Ruge breathing down your neck.'

'I thought you were getting along all right, sir,' said Dornley.

'Oh, we are – but that's not what I meant. He's a decent fellow and, I grant you, doing his best in very difficult circumstances. But the fact is, Dornley, General Ruge has only just been promoted from colonel, and is now ten days into the job of being C-in-C of a tiny tinpot army with no battlefield-command experience whatso-ever. A couple of weeks ago he was junior to me in rank, yet now we're subordinate to him. It's all rather absurd.'

'He's giving you a pretty free rein, though, isn't he, sir?'

'Now he's got us down here, you mean?' He bit his nail again, then stared out into the darkness, shaking his head. He sighed heavily and closed his eyes. 'I'm beginning to think I made the wrong call. We should be at Trondheim now. Instead, the brigade's being chewed up bit by bit in this damned deathtrap of a valley.'

'Sir, you had very little choice in the matter.'

'Really?' said Morgan.

'We had no word from London and, as the general pointed out, as commander of Norway's forces, every other Allied officer in the country had to come under his command. And his orders were to reinforce his troops here. I can't see what else you could have done.'

Morgan sighed again. 'It's good of you to say so, Dornley, but I rather think now that I might have made that decision too quickly.' He knocked his fist lightly against his chin. 'I do really. I should have waited longer for a response from London. I had no idea what state Ruge's forces were in and it's since become perfectly clear that he expected a damn sight more from us.' He shook his head. 'Christ, we must be a disappointment. I can see what he must have been thinking – that these chaps have been fighting all their lives, that they beat the Germans twenty years ago, that we'd be bristling with guns, aircraft, tanks and M/T. Instead, all we've been able to offer are three battalions of inexperienced territorial infantry, half of whom are already dead, wounded or taken prisoner.'

'But it's not your fault, sir, that we lost two supply ships.'

Morgan laughed with exasperation. 'It *is* my fault, Dornley, that I allowed myself to be persuaded by Ruge to move the brigade south. I should have waited for word from the War Office.' He knocked his fists together. 'For Christ's sake, we haven't got a single bloody anti-aircraft gun. Those Luftwaffe boys are laughing their heads off. Jerry artillery are firing their 5.9s over open sights in full view of us from as little as two thousand yards – and what can our chaps do about it? Not a damned thing, because we've got sod-all with which to reply.' He glanced at Dornley, but this time his Brigade-Major was quiet. *Perhaps I've said too much*, he thought.

In front, his driver was peering intently through the windscreen. Morgan was glad it was not himself driving through the night in these snowy conditions with only narrow slits for headlights. The windscreen wipers groaned as they swiped the snow from the glass.

He felt in his coat pocket and pulled out his pipe and tobacco pouch. Once filled, he lit it, inhaling the rich fumes and watching the dark orange glow reflected in the window. Much of their misfortune, he knew, could be blamed on the losses of *Sirius* and *Cedarbank* and problems of an over-extended line of communication. Even so, he had begun to accept, with an increasingly sickening feeling after three days of a fighting retreat, that in the Germans they were confronting a formidable enemy, both in tactics and strength. Overwhelming air support working hand in hand with the troops on the ground was a devastating combination – yet such tactics had barely been discussed back at Staff College. At least, he'd never heard anyone talk in such terms – and he'd been a bloody instructor, for God's sake. What had they all been thinking? In every respect the enemy seemed better prepared, better trained and better equipped. So, the mountains and conditions were unfamiliar to his men; but they were to the Germans too, yet they had trained mountain troops, ready to take advantage of such surroundings.

It was a bitter pill to swallow and his confidence in his country, and in the Army he had served loyally for so long, had been shaken. They had won the last war, and he had played his own small part in that, but it now occurred to him for the first time that perhaps Britain would not survive a second one. And although he tried to push such thoughts clear of his brain, they doggedly remained rooted there. Certainly, they could never hope to defeat Germany like this. Times had changed. War could no longer be fought without support from the air and without modern equipment. Norway was not a colonial outpost and neither was the enemy a rag-tag of troublesome tribesmen. Britain needed to catch up – and quickly. *I hope it's not too late.*

Tretten. He wondered whether Colonel Jansen and his promised Dragoons would materialize. Even if they did – presumably with their usual lack of arms and ammunition – he doubted that he could hold the position for more than a day. His only hope of extricating himself and his men from this mess was the arrival of 15th Brigade, which was expected to reach Åndalsnes within forty-eight hours. And with 15th Brigade came Major General Paget, who was to take over command of both. *Thank God*, he thought. Bernard Paget was an old friend and yet he was glad that he would soon be handing over the responsibility for this failure. His own task was no longer to defeat the Germans – he recognized that was an impossibility. Rather, it was to complete a successful fighting retreat, holding the Germans at bay for as long as possible with the loss of as few men as possible until he could hand over the reins to Paget.

He rubbed his stinging eyes. Even that would be a considerable challenge.

*　*　*

The figures stumbling through the thick snow towards Tanner and Sykes were so close there was no time to warn the others. Instead, heart pounding, Tanner whispered to Sykes to move to the side of the *seter* and to have a hand grenade ready. If it came to it, he hoped the explosion would not only kill or maim several of the foe, it would also produce a dazzlingly bright light that would temporarily blind them and produce confusion while he fired as many rounds as he could. That was the theory, anyway, but although he told himself that the element of surprise was a considerable advantage, he had no idea how many were advancing towards them – he simply could not see clearly enough. His body tensed. *It's fear of the unknown*, he told himself, as he slung his rifle from his shoulder and silently, carefully, pulled back the bolt. *Calm down.*

He could hear them more than he could see them, their footsteps in the snow, until several shapes, with rifles and packs, became clearer as they reached the hut.

'*Halt! Hände hoch!*' shouted Tanner. The men, startled, swivelled towards him.

'*Vous tous, vite faites ce qu'il vous dit!*' one of the men shouted.

Relief surged through Tanner. They were French. He laughed to himself as he approached, rifle still pointed at them.

'You are British?' said one of the Frenchmen.

'Too bloody right,' said Sykes, emerging from the other side of the *seter*. At the same moment, Larsen opened the door, as startled as the French troops.

'A patrol of Frenchmen, sir,' Tanner told him.

'How many?' Larsen asked, pulling out a small electric torch.

'How many are you?' Tanner asked them.

'*Sept* – seven. Myself and six men,' came the reply. The French commander stared at Tanner. 'You! The Tommy who likes to throw shovels at his allies.'

Tanner's heart sank. Christ, this was all he needed, some arrogant Frog to put a spanner in the works. But he was in no mood to pander to the man's jumped-up self-importance. 'The Chasseurs Alpins,' he said slowly, with no attempt at a French accent. 'I appreciate that you're élite forces, but since you've surrendered to me, perhaps you'd like to tell me who the bloody hell you are and what your men are doing up here?'

'How dare you speak to a superior officer like that? And how dare you suggest that I have surrendered to you?'

'But you did, sir,' said Tanner. 'I said, "Halt, hands up," and you put your hands in the air. That's the recognized way of surrendering. It's in the Geneva Convention.'

'Perhaps you could tell me your name,' Larsen suggested to the Frenchman. 'I am Henrik Larsen of His Majesty the King's Guard.'

The Frenchman turned to Larsen, his face tense with anger. 'And I am Lieutenant Xavier Chevannes of the Deuxième Compagnie de Fusiliers Voltigeurs, part of the Sixième Bataillon de Chasseurs Alpins. We were on a reconnoitring patrol after the British ordered a withdrawal to Øyer. But it seems our allies have fallen back yet again so we were stranded. When the snowstorm came we went looking for shelter.'

As Chevannes and his six men followed Larsen into the *seter*, Tanner placed a hand on Sykes's shoulder. 'Hold on a minute, Stan.'

'Who the bleedin' 'ell does 'e think 'e is?'

'A pain in the ruddy arse,' muttered Tanner.

'But, Sarge, be careful, hey? I enjoy seeing you make him look a right idiot as much as anyone, but he could make life tricky if we're not careful.'

'He's a bloody show-pony,' said Tanner, irritably. 'Anyway, we'll soon be shot of him and his sodding patrol. Haven't you noticed?'

'What, Sarge?'

'It's barely snowing any more. Look up there. What can you see?' He pointed to the sky.

'Stars, Sarge.'

'Exactly. So, let's get back in the hut, kick everyone awake and get the hell out of here. Leave those Frogs to get some kip. I'm sure they need it.'

Tanner and Sykes burst noisily into the *seter* and immediately began to shake awake the rest of their men. 'Come on, wakey-wakey,' said Sykes. 'Mac, Hep, come on, up you get.' The men yawned and stretched.

'Just what do you think you're doing, Sergeant?' said Chevannes. 'Is this how you always treat your men?'

'We're off,' Tanner said tersely. 'Time to go.'

'You'll do no such thing, Sergeant.' In the dark half-light, Chevannes glared up at him, almost daring Tanner to challenge him.

'You're not in command of my men, sir. I am. And,

furthermore, Colonel Gulbrand has ordered me to take Mr Sandvold here to the safety of the Allied lines. If I'm to do that, I need to get going while it's still dark and the Germans are getting their beauty sleep.'

Chevannes laughed. 'The colonel ordered you, did he? Tell me, Sergeant, why on earth would a Norwegian colonel order you – a mere sergeant – to such a task when two of his men, his fellow countrymen and officers senior in rank, are infinitely better placed to carry out that role?'

Tanner felt his anger rising. 'He ordered me not fifteen minutes ago. Ask him yourself.'

Chevannes' mouth curled into a barely suppressed smile. 'Yes, why don't we?' He moved towards the colonel and, crouching beside him, said, 'Colonel Gulbrand? Colonel, can you hear me?' The colonel's eyes were wide and staring, his face glistening with sweat. 'Colonel?'

Gulbrand gibbered, his words inaudible.

'Colonel!' said Chevannes again, then stood up slowly, and faced Tanner and the Norwegians. 'He's delirious with fever.'

Quickly Tanner knelt beside Gulbrand. 'Colonel! Colonel!' Gulbrand's eyes suddenly locked on his. With one hand he clutched Tanner's shoulder and began speaking in Norwegian, gabbling frantically, panic in his eyes. 'Colonel,' said Tanner again, 'it's me, Sergeant Tanner.'

'He thinks he is talking to the King,' said Larsen, quietly.

Tanner felt Gulbrand's grip loosen and with it his own grip on the situation. Anger and humiliation flushed

121

through him as he realized he had lost his fight with Chevannes. 'Colonel!' said Tanner again, searching desperately for life in Gulbrand's face. 'Come on, damn you!'

'Sarge.' It was Sykes, standing beside him. 'Sarge, he's gone.'

'Your corporal's right, Sergeant Tanner,' said Chevannes.

Tanner clenched his fist. By God, he wanted to knock the man down. Momentarily closing his eyes, he took a deep breath, then stood up once more.

'So,' said Chevannes, 'I am in command.'

'We still need to get going – and now,' said Tanner, with undisguised exasperation.

'We *need* rest.'

Give me strength, thought Tanner. 'Sir, we need to get to the Allied lines as quickly as possible. Half an hour before dark last night, the Germans were attacking a position only four or five miles west of here. My guess is that they're still there, and I'd put money on the rest of our forces being at Tretten. That's no more than six or seven miles. We can do that in three hours. The men can rest then.'

'Sergeant, it is still dark out there, the snow is deep, and although my men have proper mountain boots, yours do not, and none of us has either skis or snowshoes. It is freezing cold and my men – yours too – are exhausted. If we stumble out there now, we are asking for trouble.'

What was this madness? 'But we'll be in considerably worse trouble if we don't get to Tretten before the Germans.'

Chevannes smiled and scratched his chin thought-fully. 'You've obviously not been studying the German *modus operandi*, Sergeant.' He glanced at the Norwegians, then at his men, and chuckled. 'The German is an organized fellow, Sergeant, and has a plan that he likes to stick to. Let me enlighten you. Every morning at first light, reconnaissance planes are sent over. Later in the morning, their field guns start firing. At noon, the Luftwaffe arrives and bombs and strafes the position they are going to attack. The artillery firing increases and later in the afternoon, with our infantry nicely softened up, their infantry and armour move forward and attack. And he will do precisely the same tomorrow. So I tell you this – again. No, I order you, Sergeant.' The smirk had gone. 'We stay here now, rest, and leave in the morning. We will still be at Tretten before noon, well before your commander decides it is time to retreat once more.'

Tanner appealed to the Norwegians. 'You're surely not going to listen to this?' But as he said it, Nielssen avoided his eye and Larsen was unmoved. Some of his men were awake now, and he looked at them for support. No one spoke in his defence, but they wouldn't: it wasn't the place of privates and lance corporals to argue with officers. Their task was to obey orders, whether it be from their section leader, patrol leader or an officer.

'Sergeant,' said Larsen, his voice placatory, 'we have been on the run for more than a week and on these mountains for three days. We have lost Stunde and now our beloved colonel. Neither I nor Nielssen have had any sleep for two days. I believe Lieutenant Chevannes is right. We will, God willing, still make the Allied lines if

123

we rest here a while longer.' He nodded at Sandvold, huddled in the corner of the hut, his arms hugging his knees. 'He is still asleep. Leave him be a while longer.'

Tanner was defeated. 'Very well,' he muttered. He realized he was exhausted too. His limbs ached, his feet were sore, and he could no longer think clearly. 'We need to bury the colonel,' he said.

Chevannes spoke to two of his men, who went over to Gulbrand's body, lifted it and took it outside. Tanner slumped against the far wall next to Sykes, took out his gas cape, draped it over himself and closed his eyes.

'We'll all be better for the rest,' whispered Sykes.

'I don't give a damn,' muttered Tanner. 'We're soldiers and we're at war. Our task is to get back to our lines as quickly as possible and, according to Gulbrand, there's a hell of a lot at stake. If we fail because of that French bastard, I'll kill him.'

They were on their way by seven, with Gulbrand buried and their stomachs warmed with coffee. The sky above was blue and bright, the air cold and the snow deep. The landscape had changed. Golden early-morning light cast long, blue shadows. Snow twinkled brightly on the trees. Three of Chevannes' men were scouting ahead of the column, followed by the French lieutenant and the Norwegians, Tanner and his men trudging silently behind, like chastened schoolboys still in disgrace.

Snow crunched beneath their feet. Tanner clutched the canvas strap of his rifle and felt his pack weighing on his shoulders. The air was so still that his own breathing seemed to be amplified.

If he was honest, he felt better for the sleep, but his anger and frustration had not subsided. Neither was his mood improved when he realized the French and Norwegians were walking faster than his own men. He had promised himself he would keep Sandvold in sight at all times, but although he could still see him, the gap between his men and the Norwegians was increasing.

'Come on, lads,' he urged. 'Get a move on.'

'We're not so well dressed for a snowy stroll in the mountains as they are, Sarge,' said Sykes. 'Look at the clobber of those Froggies.'

It was true, and Tanner had eyed the Chasseurs Alpins' uniforms with envy. Each man had a thick sheep-skin jacket, or *canadienne*, as they called it, with a wide collar that could be turned up to warm the neck and cheeks. Underneath, they wore a waterproof khaki canvas anorak and a thick wool sweater, while their trousers were heavy-duty serge plus-fours. Stout studded mountain boots, made of sealskin, kept their feet warm and equally waterproof gaiters covered their ankles and shins. A dark blue beret, with snow goggles completed the outfit. Again, Tanner cursed the brass who had planned this expedition to Norway. The Germans had mountain troops, the French had mountain troops, why the hell didn't the British? Or, at least, why hadn't the bigwigs given the men kit designed for the job? Already, his feet were painfully cold; the leather of his boots was not waterproof now that the polish had largely worn off, while the soles were slippery in the snow. Nonetheless, the length of his stride gave him an advantage over his men, most of whom, he knew, were runts from the working-class slums of Leeds and Bradford. No wonder they were struggling to keep up.

And when, Tanner wondered, were they going to head back into the trees? Chevannes' men had led them round the top of the narrow ravine he had overlooked the previous evening, then round another, but Tanner remembered seeing no other such streams on Larsen's map.

'This is bloody ridiculous,' he muttered to Sykes. 'Why the hell are we slogging through this? I'm going to have a word with Chevannes.' He pushed on ahead and eventually caught up with the lieutenant.

'Ah, Sergeant,' said Chevannes, as Tanner drew alongside, 'your men seem to be struggling this morning. I hate to think how many we would have lost in the dark last night.'

'Why aren't we pushing further down towards the treeline?'

'We're taking the most direct route, Sergeant, so we can get to Tretten in good time.'

Tanner fought a renewed urge to knock Chevannes down. 'The most direct route, Lieutenant, is not the quickest,' he said. 'If we go along beneath the lip of the valley, the snow won't be so deep, and the trees will give us greater cover. Up here we stand out like sore thumbs.'

'Are you questioning my decisions again? Good God, Sergeant, your superior officers will hear something of this! Now, get back to your men and tell them to hurry. I do not want to hear another word.'

Tanner turned, then heard the now-familiar sound of

aero-engines and paused to scan the sky. A moment later he spotted the dark outline of a German aircraft, like an insect moving slowly in their direction from the south. Chevannes saw it too.

'Quick!' he shouted. 'Lie down!'

'Why, sir?' asked Tanner. 'I thought you said the Germans only send out recce planes in the morning.'

Chevannes glared at him. The Junkers flew over, a thousand feet or so above them, circled twice then flew west. Tanner, who had remained standing the entire time, watched Chevannes get to his feet and brush the snow off his jacket and beret. 'You were right, sir. A recce plane,' he said. 'I wonder how long it will take them to get that information back.'

'Go to your men, Sergeant!' Chevannes hissed.

Tanner glared back as he stood defiantly in the snow and waited for his men to catch up.

Soon after, the scouts changed direction, heading west towards the treeline. *At last*, thought Tanner. Perhaps now they'd make proper progress. And the sooner they got back to the Allied lines the better. Then they could be shot of the Norwegians and, more especially, of Chevannes and his bloody Chasseurs Alpins.

7

Reichsamtsleiter Hans-Wilhelm Scheidt reached Lillehammer shortly before noon, having driven the hundred miles without incident. Conscious that he would soon be among fighting men, he had been mindful to change out of his civilian suit and into the tan Party tunic instead. With his Amtsleiter tabs on the collar, Party badge on the right breast pocket and military belt, he felt more suitably attired, albeit less comfortable. Black trousers, knee-length boots and a high peaked cap completed the makeover.

He had managed to secure a brief audience with the Reichskommissar before leaving Oslo. Terboven had not been best pleased to have his breakfast interrupted but had given Scheidt the written authority to demand whatever assistance he required.

It was with this letter tucked into the inside of his tunic pocket that he strode past two SS policemen in Sturmbannführer Kurz's new headquarters, a comfortable townhouse that, until the day before, had been a lawyer's premises.

Kurz had brought with him a small staff of several junior officers and a number of clerks. For the most part, the room still looked like a lawyer's office, with book-shelves of legal case studies, and filing cabinets. A radio set and accompanying operator had been established in one room, but otherwise there was a temporary air about the place.

Kurz was on the telephone when Scheidt walked in. He was wearing the pale grey uniform of the Allgemeine-SS, rather than the plain clothes often favoured by Sicherheitdienst and Gestapo officers, and his long black boots were crossed on the desk in front of him while he gesticulated airily with one hand, a cigarette between his fingers. Seeing Scheidt, he swung his boots off the desk, raised a hand – *I'll only be a moment* – and hurriedly ended his conversation.

'Ah, Reichsamtsleiter Scheidt,' he said, with a broad smile. 'Here in person!'

'Have you got him?' Scheidt asked.

'Alas, no.' He stretched forward, tapped a cigarette from a paper packet and offered it to Scheidt. 'Cigarette? We might even be able to stretch to coffee. Or perhaps you'd care for something stronger after your drive. I take it you did drive here?'

Ignoring Kurz's small-talk, Scheidt said, 'So? Tell me. Are your mountain troops closing in?'

'My dear Scheidt,' said Kurz, the bad-tempered words of their previous conversation apparently a matter of the past, 'please, sit down.' He motioned to a chair in front of the desk. Scheidt did as he was told. How he disliked men like Kurz. Still young, and with the kind of arrogant insouciance Scheidt knew he had once perfected in himself but which he despised in others. Typical arsehole SD man. 'There was a heavy snowstorm last night,' Kurz continued, 'not so much down here in the valley but up on the mountains. A complete white-out. Not even mountain troops can operate in such conditions. But then again, Odin and his friends would not have got far either. Relax. We will get him.'

'And now?'

'We have reconnaissance aircraft looking for them.'

Someone knocked lightly on the door. 'Yes?' said Kurz.

'A Luftwaffe message just in, sir,' said a junior SD officer, passing Kurz a scribbled signal. Kurz took it, read it, smiled, then passed it to Scheidt. 'They've been spotted. And they've got some followers now – what looks like a British patrol. Most considerate of them. Much easier to find twenty men than three.' Kurz unrolled a map and spread it on the desk. 'Let me see,' he said. 'Yes, here they are. Heading for Tretten, by the look of it. The fools are crossing this high open ground here.' He chuckled. 'No cover, just deep snow.'

Impatiently Scheidt grabbed the map and turned it so that it was facing him. 'Where are the mountain troops now? They should be able to cut them off as they descend towards Tretten.'

'Exactly,' said Kurz, standing now and clapping his hands. 'You and I will go together to Engelbrecht's headquarters.' He picked up his cap and placed it on his head at a jaunty angle. Smirking, he opened the door and, with a flourish, ushered Scheidt out.

They took Kurz's car and drove through Lillehammer. A number of houses had been destroyed by bomb and battle damage; piles of stones, rubble and charred wood were evidence of the conflict that had taken place the previous day. They passed the station where the remains of a large warehouse still smoked and where debris littered the yard in front of it. At the far side, the blackened remains of a German tank still stood.

'My God, what happened here?' asked Scheidt.

'A British ammunition and supply dump,' Kurz told him. 'Unfortunately it was blown up by a couple of Tommies as our boys entered the yard.'

'I thought the enemy were rolling over?'

'Oh, they are. Of course, what do I know of military matters?' He turned to Scheidt and grinned. 'But I do know they've no guns and, it seems, no air force to speak of. Which is why I keep telling you you've nothing to worry about. The Tommies are beaten and so are the Norwegians. It's really not a question of *if* we catch Odin but *when*.'

As Kurz had promised, General Engelbrecht confirmed that he had a detachment of mountain troops ready for the task, and waved away Scheidt's attempt to show him Terboven's written instructions. They drove on to Øyer where they found troops preparing to attack the Allied lines at Tretten later that afternoon. By the church and along the main village street a number of horses were pulling artillery pieces, some standing still, their tails whisking away flies, while others slowly hauled howitzers and Pak 38 anti-tank guns through the village. There were trucks, too, and other vehicles – even one of the huge Panzer VI heavy tanks, the 'land battleships', that had been brought to Norway. As Kurz threaded his way through the milling soldiers and past the tank, it suddenly burst into life, a dark cloud of exhaust erupting from its rear. Scheidt started.

Kurz laughed. 'Don't worry, we'll soon be safely out of the battle zone.'

Scheidt ignored the comment; in any case, he was too absorbed in watching the activity – men, horses, machines: a German division on the move. Leaving the village, his gaze fell on two teams of six horses pulling a pair of 105mm field guns, the howitzers lurching forward with every stride of the animals. Alongside the gun carriages, solemn troops, grey greatcoats tightly buttoned, stared back at him. Some farm workers were in the fields nearby and Scheidt realized they were the first civilians he'd noticed since leaving Lillehammer.

A little further on, they reached a farmstead. Patchy fields spread up the slopes towards the treeline, and Scheidt gazed up the mountainside to the white-topped plateau beyond. He wondered whether Odin and his escort were up there, peering down at the activity in the valley. Kurz pulled into the farmyard, stopped by a timber barn and yanked on the handbrake with a loud grating sound. Mountain troops milled about, smoking and laughing. On the ramp of the large barn, a group of soldiers played cards, their packs and rifles stacked together. Another group stood round a small fire, evidently made from some old farm equipment, now burning warmly; a mess tin of coffee was brewing on it.

'Come on,' said Kurz, leading him into the farmhouse.

It was dark, but warm with another fire burning, this time the stove in the kitchen. Several junior officers stood up as they entered, but Kurz, with a casual flick of his hand, waved at them to sit down again. 'Where I can find Major von Poncets?' he asked.

A lieutenant showed them through to another room where clerks were tapping at coding machines and type-writers. Perched on a table, was Major von Poncets, commander of the 4th Battalion, 138th Mountain Regiment, talking animatedly with one of his staff officers.

'Sturmbannführer Kurz and Reichsamtsleiter Scheidt?' he said, sliding off the table and extending a hand. 'I was told you'd be coming.'

'You seem busy here, Major,' said Scheidt.

Von Poncets laughed. 'My men are going to be attacking the enemy lines at Tretten later. Fortunately the Tommies don't seem to have either mountain troops or aircraft, so outflanking their positions is proving easier than we'd hoped.'

'The men certainly seem in good heart,' said Scheidt.

'Of course,' von Poncets said. 'We're winning!' He clapped his hands together, then said, 'I've got some men for you from the Reconnaissance Battalion of the 6th Mountain Regiment.' He turned to one of his staff officers and asked him to fetch Hauptmann Zellner. 'He's commander of 1 Company and his men are here,' he said, turning back to Kurz and Scheidt. 'He'll be with us shortly.'

'And a company is how many?' Scheidt asked. 'A hundred?'

Von Poncets smiled. 'I take it you're not a military man, Herr Reichsamtsleiter.'

Scheidt noticed Kurz smirk. 'No,' he said. 'I wasn't quite old enough for the last war. I've been fortunate enough to serve the Reich in other ways.'

'And, of course, we need people like you,' said von Poncets, slapping him convivially on the arm. He added, 'No, Zellner's company is nearer two hundred, although I'm afraid I've told the battalion commander I need most of his men for the fight here. But one platoon of fifty or so should be more than enough and you do have a company commander to lead them. Don't forget these men are trained for operations in the mountains. As I said, the Tommies have no such troops, while the Norwegians – well, they haven't had any training at all.' He laughed. 'We're attacking again this afternoon with the outflanking manoeuvre following our initial assault, so unless these fellows reach Tretten within—' he consulted his watch '— the next hour, I would say they're as good as in the bag.'

'Aerial reconnaissance suggested that was likely,' added Kurz.

'Ah, here he is now,' said von Poncets, as a young officer entered the room and saluted crisply. He was dressed differently from the troops outside: although he wore the long grey trousers, puttees and studded brown ankle boots that marked out these units, over his field tunic he had on a thick green-grey cotton wind-jacket, into which was tucked a wool scarf, and a mountain cap, with an embroidered *Edelweiss* on the left side. A pair of tinted round lenses rested on the peak. Hauptmann Wolf Zellner stared ahead implacably.

134

'Stand easy, Zellner,' said von Poncets. 'I've told these gentlemen that you are taking just one of your platoons.'

'Yes, sir. The rest of the company, under Lieutenant Biermann, will be taking part in the attack on Tretten.'

'And you're sure that will be enough men?' Scheidt asked.

Zellner glanced at von Poncets. 'Yes, sir. I think that will be plenty. I don't wish to sound arrogant, Herr Reichsamtsleiter, but one platoon of my men will be more than enough for a few fugitives like these.'

'And the Reconnaissance Battalion is particularly well suited to high mountain operations,' added von Poncets, 'having trained extensively in the Bavarian Alps. Hauptmann Zellner has been fully briefed – but if there's anything else you'd like to add, Herr Reichsamtsleiter? Sturmbannführer?'

'I want to underline how important this man Odin is, Hauptmann,' said Scheidt. 'He could be of vital – and I mean vital – importance to Germany. He must be captured alive. Whether you kill the others or take them prisoner is of no consequence to me. But Odin I must see in person. You have his photograph?'

'Yes, sir,' Zellner replied. 'You can depend on me and my men, sir. We'll find him for you.'

Von Poncets had lit a cigar, and now a puff of smoke swirled lazily into the room. 'Good,' he said. 'Now, if you'll excuse me, gentlemen . . .' He smiled once more. 'I've a battle to win.'

Zellner saluted again, then left.

Outside, the sky was clouding over, but the air was still crisp and cold. His boots sounded loud, the metal studs clicking through the thin slick of mud caused by too many vehicles, carts and men trampling across it. He would have preferred to be taking part in the attack on Tretten, leading his company into battle, yet von Poncets, apparently, had insisted. Well, he now knew where that had come from – the politician, he was certain. But at least this mission gave him a chance for revenge. These were the men he'd so nearly caught five days ago north of Elverum. There had been no mention of anyone called 'Odin' then. All they had been told was that the Norwegians were carrying important documents and even Crown Jewels – but now he'd read the briefing sent by the SD and there could be no mistake. They were the same men. And this time he was not going to fail.

By noon the mixed column of British, Norwegian and French, twenty-two strong, was still some miles southeast of Tretten. Even though the French scouts had led them off the mountain plateau and into the treeline, the going had been tough. The stretch of the valley west of Øyer, before it snaked north into the Tretten gorge, was wider and the slopes gentler. Here, fields spread high above the wide Lågen river, and even where there was forest, it was far less dense than it had been. The high fields had forced them to stay well above the farmland, where the snow was deeper – not just because of the altitude but because the slopes were less precipitous and cover from the trees not so great. Even the Chasseurs Alpins struggled, the men frequently losing their footing, or taking a stride forward only to find themselves buried to their waists in drifts. Tanner had been forced to admit to himself that his claim that they would cover seven miles in three hours had been over-optimistic. Still, if he had been at fault in his calculations, he laid the blame for their slow progress with Chevannes. If they had left the *seter* when he had suggested, they would have had more than six hours' start.

It had been shortly after noon that the tell-tale sounds of battle had begun in the valley below. More aircraft had droned over, while the dull thud of artillery fire, although intermittent, had resounded ominously. The unwavering German battle plan Chevannes, it seemed, had judged that about right.

A little more than four hours later, they were nearing Tretten, the valley sides steeper once more. The wide farmland to the south had gone, the forest thickened and the snow thinned, and progress had improved. Below them, the shelling had increased, the medium howitzers booming more insistently now. The whistle of the missiles' flight could occasionally be heard, and the reports of the ensuing explosions echoed through the valley. A flight of bombers arrived, dropping their loads with a rip of detonations. Occasional small-arms chatter drifted to them on the afternoon breeze.

Chevannes called a halt. The men were exhausted, Tanner included. Once again, hunger was gnawing at him, as he knew it must be at the others. Their faces were drawn and blank with fatigue. Several of his men, Hepworth among them, fell asleep where they sat on rocks or against a tree stump.

Chevannes and Larsen consulted the map once more.

The Frenchman looked directly behind him to a peak marked as the Skjønsberg. 'We're no more than three kilometres from Tretten,' he said.

'Then we should start dropping into the valley,' said Tanner, who had walked over to join the impromptu conference. 'If we head slightly north-west, we can aim straight for Tretten. It'll be easier and quicker than if we continue north along the lip of the plateau.'

'What about the Germans?' said Larsen.

'They haven't started their infantry attack yet, have they? If we get a move on—'

'No,' said Chevannes, cutting him short. 'That's far too risky. We head due north, then cut down to the village. Two more minutes, then we get going.'

Tanner walked back to his men. 'Come on, lads,' he said. 'Nearly there now. Then this'll be over. One last effort, eh?' He shook Hepworth awake. 'Hep, come on, up you get.' Hepworth opened his eyes, nodded bleakly and stood up, stumbling backwards from the weight and awkward balance of his pack. 'Remind me never to go up a mountain again, Sarge,' he said.

Away to the left, Tanner spotted a clearing in the trees and what seemed like a rocky outcrop overlooking the valley. 'Stan, keep an eye on Sandvold, will you?'

'Where you goin', Sarge?'

'To have a quick look round. I'll catch you up.' He moved through the trees until he could see Tretten nestling just up the valley, then felt in his haversack and pulled out his scope. He squatted by a jutting rock and peered through the lens. A shell exploded near the village, the mass of smoke and debris mushrooming into the sky several seconds before any sound reached him. He looked south. Troops and vehicles were on the road, emerging round a bend in the gorge. He lowered his scope to clean the lens. Suddenly, movement caught his eye in the trees below to his left and he brought the scope back to his eye. Nothing. He scanned the trees, then there it was – men moving. A mass of German troops, just a few hundred yards below and no more than a quarter of a mile to the south.

'Bloody hell,' he muttered. 'We're bloody running out of time here.' He scrambled to his feet and soon caught up with the others, then strode on towards Lieutenant Chevannes.

'What is it, Sergeant?' The tone was impatient, weary.

'German troops, sir, on the slopes below, not far behind.'

'Who would have caught us out if we had done as you suggested.'

Tanner clenched his fist. Just one blow, he thought – that was all it would take to silence the man. 'No, sir,' he said slowly, 'because, as I explained at the time, it was a chance worth taking. The moment we saw them we would either have altered course or hurried onwards.'

'You can't ever admit it when you are wrong, can you, Sergeant Tanner? Your insolence is really wearing very thin. Do remember that you are speaking to a senior officer.'

'I don't give a damn,' said Tanner, his fury mounting. 'If we'd left last night when I said we should, we'd have been in Tretten by now.'

'I've had just about enough—'

'Please,' said Sandvold, speaking up for the first time. 'No more arguing. Let's just keep going. We still have a chance of reaching safety.'

Chevannes glared at Tanner. 'We must push on beyond the village. There is little we can do to stop the Germans outflanking Tretten now.'

Tanner thought of the gelignite and TNT in his pack. Actually, he realized, there was quite a lot they could do with a sackload of explosives and the twin advantage of height and steep, rocky slopes. Had it not been for Sandvold, he would have peeled his men away from Chevannes and had some fun. Instead he said, 'I'll tell my men to keep at it, sir,' then fell back towards Sykes and the others.

'What's going on, Sarge?' Sykes asked, as Tanner rejoined him.

'Jerries,' said Tanner. 'Down below.'

Sykes whistled softly. 'Cunning sods,' he said.

'Listen, we need to keep our wits about us,' Tanner told him. 'We don't want to get caught napping. We've got to watch our arses up here. Make sure we keep looking around.'

Sykes nodded, then repeated the sergeant's instructions to each of the men. Tanner walked on. He needed to think, but fatigue had settled over him, as though it was sucking out the remnant of energy he had left. *Come on*, he told himself. *Keep going. Think.* Gulbrand had said the Germans were not following them, but what if he had been wrong? The Norwegians had been strafed twice, nearly caught during a German search, and the reconnaissance planes must have spotted them that morning. Coincidence, perhaps, maybe these things had happened because there was a war on and they were near the fighting. Maybe the enemy didn't know about Sandvold but were aware that they were carrying something important. He rubbed his eyes and his brow. Tiredness was putting ideas into his head.

At least they were among the trees, rather than out in the open. The canopy provided by forest – the closeness of the environment, the sharpness of sound – was something he always found reassuring, even though these were high mountain forests of dark conifers, rather than the broadleaf woodland of southern Wiltshire. As a boy he had spent much of his time in woods, helping his father or on his own. He knew the smells of the changing seasons, the dry, cool shade of summer, the damp, earthy mustiness of winter. He knew the different songs of birds, from the nightingale to the wood warbler. From his father, he had learnt which mushrooms and fungi could be eaten and which would play havoc with your guts. He knew stoat from weasel, fox dung from badger, hawthorn from blackthorn.

He remembered taking a boy from the village one night to see the badger cubs; the other lad had been frightened of the dark and the night shadows; of strange beasts that might lurk. Tanner had been mystified – what was there to be scared about? – then angry when the boy had insisted on going home before they had got anywhere near the sett. 'It's the unknown that people are afraid of,' his father had told him. 'You and I have always roamed the woods. They're a second home to us.'

Home. What wouldn't he do to see it again – yet wasn't

the Army his home now? Certainly it had been all his adult life. Or, rather, the 2nd Battalion had been; but now, a little more than twelve hours since Chevannes and his men had stumbled on them, he felt new warmth for these Territorial lads of the 5th Battalion.

'Sarge! Sarge!'

Tanner was startled from his thoughts.

'You'd better come, Sarge. Looks like we're being followed,' Sykes gasped.

Adrenalin coursed through his blood and in an instant his mind cleared. He reached the end of their column where Riggs and Chambers were each crouched behind a pine, looking backwards, rifles ready.

'How far?' said Tanner, as he pulled out his scope once more.

'Couldn't say, Sarge,' said Riggs, 'but mebbe a third of a mile.'

Tanner peered through the scope. Yes, there they were, still some way off but climbing in their direction. He could see the lead men advancing through the pines. Silently he passed the scope to Sykes.

'They're wearing caps and goggles,' said Sykes.

'Mountain troops,' said Tanner. 'How many can you see now?'

'Hard to say. A platoon, is my guess. God knows whether there are more behind, though, Sarge. They can't really be after us, can they?'

Tanner shrugged, and put his scope into his trouser pocket. 'Right,' he said. 'Let's get out of here.' He hurried his men forward, Sykes chivvying them too, until they caught up with Chevannes and the Norwegians.

'*Mon dieu*,' muttered Chevannes, when Tanner told him what they had seen.

'We need to find out exactly how many there are,' said Tanner. His mind was alert once more, his heart thumping.

'Yes,' said Chevannes.

'I'll take Sykes here and two of my men and head back for a dekko,' Tanner continued. 'You keep going and we'll catch you up shortly.'

Chevannes nodded, his face taut.

Tanner hurried over to Lance Corporal Erwood, the Bren leader. 'Dan, I want you to take charge of the rest of the lads, and I need you to do one other thing. See that Norwegian civvy up ahead with the Frog officer?'

'Sarge.'

'Don't let him out of your sight.'

'Aye, Sarge. I won't.'

Tanner slapped him on the back. Then, collecting Chambers and Riggs, he briefly looked around. Although the valley sides were densely forested, especially along the east-facing slopes, up here, where it was more difficult for the loggers to fell and remove their timber, the pines and larch grew wildly, covering but not smothering the mountain. There were open patches too, and it was as the German troops crossed one that Tanner hoped to get a good look at their enemy.

He reckoned he wanted to be about four hundred yards away when he saw them – far enough for them to be out of effective range, but close enough for him to see them clearly through the scope.

'Sarge?' said Sykes. 'I don't like to hurry you or nothing but—'

'I know,' cut in Tanner, still peering at the snow and trees around him. He had spotted a small spur a short distance above and was trying to decide whether it would offer the view and cover they needed. For a brief moment he was paralysed by indecision, then said, 'Up there, quick, to that crest.'

They scrambled up and, as they crouched between two pines, Tanner was relieved to see they had a fine view down the undulating slopes of the valley sides.

'There they are,' hissed Sykes.

Tanner smiled as he watched the enemy troops reach the edge of the clearing, pause, spy the tracks in the snow, then continue forward. 'Start counting them, lads,' he said quietly, then screwed his scope onto the mounts on his rifle.

'You going to start firing, Sarge?' asked Chambers. He looked worried.

'Keep counting, Punter,' said Tanner, 'and if you've got a full magazine, take it from your rifle and hold on to it until I ask you to pass it to me.' He raised the rifle to his shoulder. Through the scope he could clearly see the first section of men. They were spread out in a loose single file and, Tanner was glad to see, their rifles were still slung over their backs. Behind the section leader was a machine-gunner, his weapon carried loosely on his shoulder. A further section of ten followed, and another beyond that. Tanner led his aim along the column. Where was the commander? Some of the men wore green-collared greatcoats, but most had on shorter, light olive jackets. All were wearing peaked field caps rather than helmets and had only small rucksacks on their backs. At that distance, even with the scope, it was hard to tell who was in charge.

'Thirty-nine, sir,' said Riggs.

'That's what I make it,' agreed Sykes.

'Fine,' said Tanner. 'You ready with that magazine, Punter?'

'Yes, Sarge,' said Chambers.

His father had taught Tanner a good trick for judging distance. The key was to be able to assess a hundred-yard stretch almost exactly. Do that, his father had assured him, and the next hundred yards and the hundred yards beyond that were easier to judge; it was a matter of understanding the naked eye's sense of perspective and increasingly reducing each ensuing hundred-yard stretch. He reckoned the leading troops were now at about four hundred yards. Then remembering that distance was easily overestimated when you were looking downwards, he aimed just a fraction low at the lead troop, exhaled gently and fired.

The man dropped immediately, and Tanner fired his next three shots while the startled troops looked around wildly and thought to flatten themselves on the ground. Even once they were prostrate on the snow, there were some easy targets as they lifted their heads to loosen their rifles, or crouched and ran for the cover of the trees. Tanner reckoned he had hit seven men with his first magazine. One man was crawling across the snow, vivid blood trailing behind him. Men were shouting. The first German rifle shot cracked through the mountainside, way off, but was followed by many more, bullets zipping through the trees above and below them.

'Give me that magazine,' said Tanner. His voice was steady, firm. He unclicked the first, drove the replacement into its place and fired again. Five shots and by then the machine-gunner of the second section was firing. The aim was wild, but the short, rapid bursts were well spread. Tanner fired twice more. Another burst from the machine-gun, and this time bullets fizzed close by. Riggs screamed.

'Sarge, we need to get out of here!' Sykes had grabbed Riggs, who was clutching the side of his head.

Tanner pulled back the bolt one last time and hit a man square in the chest. 'Come on, let's go. Is it serious?' he said to Sykes as they scrambled down from the spur.

'I've been hit in the head!' Riggs shouted, but he was still upright.

'Can you keep going?' Tanner said, grabbing Riggs's greatcoat and, with Sykes, propelling the lad forward.

'I think so,' he gasped.

Shots were still pinging through the trees, snapping branches and ricocheting off rocks, but most were fizzing harmlessly above their heads. A burr of intermittent machine-gun fire also cut through the mountain. 'Just keep going, lads. Run,' Tanner urged, as they rejoined their tracks to slide and stumble away from the enemy.

Only once the shots died out did they pause, bent double and gasping. Tanner put an arm round Riggs's shoulders. 'You're still alive, then?'

'I think I must be in shock, Sarge.'

'Let's have a look at you.' Blood covered the side of Riggs's face and neck. 'Under all this red stuff you look pretty intact,' said Tanner, as he clutched Riggs's head and peered intently at it. Then he spotted a gash at the side of his forehead and laughed. 'It's a bloody little nick! You've been grazed by a bullet or a splinter or something. But you'll live. You'll be fine.'

'It really hurts, though, Sarge.'

'Stop being such an old woman, Private,' said Sykes, pulling out a field-dressing pack.

'No, hang on a minute with that, Stan,' said Tanner. 'Bit of blood in the snow could be useful. Here, Harry, lean over a bit.' He pushed Riggs's head forward. 'Good thing about a cut on the head – lots of blood. That's it, drip there.'

'Bloody hell, Sarge, I'm draining away here!' Riggs was indignant.

'King and country, Riggs, think of that,' said Tanner. 'Right, now iggery. Let's get a move on back to the others and, Harry, if you could lean your head forward as we run, I'd be much obliged.' Sykes and Chambers grinned at him. Tanner slapped Riggs on the back. 'Well, done, Harry,' he said. 'You're a brave man – a very brave man.'

'How long do you reckon that'll hold them up, Sarge?' Sykes asked, as Tanner unslung his rifle, quickly unscrewed the scope and placed it back in his trouser pocket.

'Not long. But it'll make them more cautious, and that'll slow them. Those Jerries'll be a bit on edge now, too, and that's what we want. And, of course, there's a few less for us to worry about.'

'That was good shooting back there, Sarge,' said Chambers, as they hurried onwards, following the tracks in the snow.

'Thanks, Punter. A bit wild, I'm afraid but, dead or wounded, I reckon maybe ten won't be going any further today.'

'That was twenty shots in about half a minute.' Chambers was quite animated. 'I've never seen anyone fire so fast.'

'Really?' said Tanner. 'I don't know who's been teaching you to shoot, then. Any half-decent shot should be able to fire thirty well-aimed rounds a minute. If you've got someone at hand with spare magazines, it's not hard to fire forty a minute. Have you Territorial boys never been taught that?'

'No, Sarge,' admitted Chambers. 'We've done plenty of marksmanship but we've never timed ourselves.'

'Well, get practising, then.'

Pausing frequently to glance behind them, they hurried on, following the tracks of the rest of the column. Tanner conceded that Riggs now needed to staunch the flow of blood so they stopped to wrap a bandage round his head. Despite the hold-up, they had caught up with the others in half an hour. Ignoring the questions of his men, Tanner reported to Chevannes straight away. He told the Frenchman little, except to warn him that there were now about thirty men pursuing them.

'We must keep going,' said Chevannes.

'And watch our flanks,' added Tanner. 'They'll still be in better shape than us. They'll follow our tracks but they could probably outflank us and have us surrounded if we're not careful.'

'Thank you, Sergeant,' said Chevannes. 'I do realize that.'

148

It was just after six o'clock. Tanner guessed they must be level with Tretten, although he knew better than to ask Chevannes if he could have a look at the map. From the valley, guns and shells could be heard clearly. How much further was Chevannes going to take them before they cut down into the valley? They were so close; tantalizingly so. The sound of battle told him the Allies were still there. Another half-hour, and he reckoned they'd make it – thirty minutes, that was all. He also knew that their pursuers would be upon them sooner than that.

And then he heard the enemy mountain troops attacking from the flank. They all heard it – the increase in shelling, the intensity of small-arms fire, suddenly loud and echoing across the valley and up the mountain. Through the trees they could see Stukas wheeling and diving, their manic sirens screaming through the din of battle.

For a moment, no one said a word. No one needed to. After all, what was there to say? The Allied positions in Tretten were about to be overrun. How could it be otherwise with that weight of fire? All too soon they'd be back where they'd started, high on a mountain, without food or rest, out of reach of safety once more. Only now the enemy was stalking them.

Tanner tried desperately to think. Despair engulfed him. Despair, frustration and, above all, anger. *Think! think!* he told himself. Then ahead, through the trees, he saw something, and an idea entered his head.

It gave him a glimmer of hope.

8

Reichsamtsleiter Hans-Wilhelm Scheidt had returned to Lillehammer in a better mood than when he had walked into Kurz's office earlier that day. He had, he felt certain, been right to leave Oslo. Kurz was clearly unreliable. Despite the SD officer's words of assurance, Scheidt recognized in him a man who enjoyed the trappings of power and authority but who was consumed by idleness and complacency. *Thank God I'm here*, he told himself. Here in Lillehammer he could make sure people like Kurz got up off their lazy arses. He could chivvy Kurz and badger Army men like Engelbrecht. Keeping control was essential – he simply couldn't afford to allow others to let Odin slip from his grasp.

A room in a hotel not two minutes' walk from Kurz's office was the ideal place in which to make his temporary new base. The hotel owner had given in without a word when Scheidt had announced he was requisitioning the best room. Too frightened to refuse, Scheidt guessed, from the ashen expression on the man's face.

His room was dark and not a little shabby – far removed from the splendour of the Continental Hotel in Oslo. Indeed, up here in the central interior of the country it felt like a different world. The villages were small and sparsely populated; Lillehammer was more like a large village than a town. There were few metalled roads, and despite the single railway line, the entire area seemed little more than a vast expanse of mountain, water and forest – perhaps a good place to hide, but not for long. All too soon, the harsh conditions would flush out any man on the run.

Where was Sandvold? Perhaps already in the hands of the mountain troops. Scheidt had been impressed by both von Poncets and Hauptmann Zellner. Both had the kind of energy and determination that gave him confidence. The Wehrmacht, he reflected, might be rigid and rather narrow-minded, but they were straightforward to deal with – certainly a damn sight more so than the Allgemeine-SS.

Scheidt lit a cigarette and looked out of the dormer window of his room. In the streets below, Lillehammer was quiet, almost slothful, but some miles to the north, he could hear the dull thud and reverberation of battle. 'We're winning,' von Poncets had told him. Now Reichsamtsleiter Scheidt had to win his personal battle.

Despite Reichsamtsleiter Scheidt's mounting confidence, Hauptmann Wolf Zellner had not yet caught Odin.

Less than an hour earlier, however, when the tracks of about twenty men had been spotted in the snow, he had been convinced they had found the group they were looking for. With the thrill of the chase surging through him, he had given the order to proceed with all speed. Success, he had felt sure, was just round the corner. Soon, they would spot their quarry. Then they would inch forward and surround them. Footsore and weary, the Tommies would gladly surrender and Odin would be theirs. He had even played in his mind the scene at von Poncets' HQ, as he handed over the Norwegian. 'Odin, sir, as requested.'

But then they had been ambushed – which, most definitely, had not been part of his imaginary script. Eleven men, he'd lost. Eleven! Four were dead, and another five probably would be soon if he didn't get them off the mountain. Two were only lightly wounded and, of the more seriously hit, two would need to be carried. And that caused him another headache. He couldn't let the wounded – *his* men – bleed to death in the snow, but neither could he afford to leave any of the unharmed to tend them.

They had left one group from the platoon behind at the request of his Battalion CO, who had wanted them for the company's part in the outflanking operation at Tretten. At the time, he had agreed immediately, but he wished now he had those ten men. Under the canopy of pines, staring at the bright blood streaked across the snow, Zellner had quickly weighed his options. Common sense suggested he should return. He now had twenty-eight fully fit men, of which at least four would have to stay behind. That gave him only the slightest numerical advantage. To make matters worse, the enemy had proved they would not lie down quietly.

Zellner had pondered these factors for a few moments. He was twenty-four, an Austrian from Innsbruck, and had been with the 3rd Gebirgsjäger Division since Austrian and German unification following the Anschluss two years before, and with the Austrian 5th Gebirgsjäger Division before that. He had trained with unflinching dedication, proud not only to be part of such an obviously élite unit but of his own performance. He understood the importance of leading by example, and had been determined that he should be fitter than any of his men; that he should be a better mountaineer; and that his survival skills in sub-freezing conditions were second to none. In this he had succeeded and he had arrived in Norway confident that he and his men would be a match for any enemy troops they confronted.

So far, however, they had barely been tested. He had trained for years, waiting for the chance to fight and test himself in battle, yet as far as he could make out, the war in Norway had been won so far by the Luftwaffe and the gunners. As infantry, it seemed that their role was merely to mop up. It bothered him, too, that the only time he had been given a specific task – namely the capture of the Norwegian King's men a few days before – he had failed. Duped by a peasant farmer. The man had made a fool of him so Zellner had killed him.

Nagging doubts entered his head again. That had been clever shooting by the enemy. Two or more of them must have had sniper rifles and that in itself had surprised him. Indeed, the shooting had caught them completely off-guard, and had caused their first combat deaths since the beginning of the campaign. His men, every bit as confident as he had been before the shooting, were stunned, he could tell; good comrades were dead. Moreover, it had held them up, stopping them in their tracks.

With sudden clarity Zellner cast aside the doubts. Instinct told him that his enemy was not well armed, despite the sniper rifles. His men, however, still had three MG30 machine-guns. Furthermore, if the streams of British and Norwegian prisoners he had seen earlier that day were anything to go by, the enemy up ahead would be ill-equipped for mountain operations, short of sleep and food. His men, in contrast, were fit, healthy and, he was certain, a match for anyone. In any case, failure a second time would be too bitter a pill to swallow. They would go after those men and capture Odin. Then he would find the men with the sniper rifles and kill them.

Sergeant Tanner regarded the *seter* ahead. In appearance it was much like the one they had sheltered in the previous evening – a rough wooden hut perhaps fifteen feet long. It was slightly further up the mountain, in a clearing, and beyond it, a mountain stream ran from a narrow ravine above into a shallower one below. Across the brook, however, there were plenty of large stones, while yet more pines overlooked the shallow ravine above the *seter*.

'Do you see what I see, Stan?' Tanner said to Sykes.

'Another hut, Sarge,' said Sykes.

'Correct,' said Tanner. 'And a stream.' He rubbed

his chin. 'Nice place to set up a juicy ambush, I reckon.'

Sykes looked at him doubtfully. Like Chambers, he had been impressed by Tanner's cool-headed shooting earlier. Indeed, his respect for his sergeant had grown steadily, but he couldn't see how a run-down shack could be a good place for an ambush. In fact, he wasn't sure any kind of ambush was a good idea.

'Not sure about that, Sarge,' he said. 'Wouldn't it be better if we just hurried up a bit? Don't want to invite trouble, do we?'

'Of course not – but listen, Stan. Those buggers are going to catch us up soon enough, so we've got no choice but to stand and face them.' He spoke quickly, his eyes constantly darting to the trees behind them. 'I know they're Nazi bastards but they're not going to leave their wounded to die, are they? That means there'll probably be only twenty of them – maybe twenty-five at most. And if we're ready and waiting, we can beat them.' Sykes still seemed doubtful. 'Look, we all walk into the hut, then jump out the back and into the stream. No more footprints. By going up and down the stream we can get the men into position without Jerry seeing where we've gone. A few can clamber up on to that small cliff – it'll give a perfect line of fire. Others can go down the stream and hide behind trees and rocks.'

Sykes was smiling now.

'Jerry's going to see the tracks going into the hut and none coming out,' Tanner continued. 'And he'll see a bit of Riggs's blood. If he's not very clever he'll come forward – and we've got them in the bag. On the other hand, if he's got any sense he'll smell a rat. If it's Mr

Sandvold he's after, he's not going to risk spraying the hut with machine-gun fire, is he? Which means he's got to send some men forward to investigate.'

'And we shoot them.'

'I reckon so. Then he's got even fewer men, and he'll know we've got him covered. So he won't be able to move unless he goes backwards, or tries working round the sides. In any case, we'll still have him covered.' He looked back again. 'First we've got to persuade Chevannes, though. That stupid bugger won't listen to me. Maybe you should suggest it. He'll take it from you.'

To Tanner's surprise, Chevannes was receptive to the idea, as explained by Sykes. 'Yes, Corporal, I think there is something in what you say.' He turned to Tanner. 'You are lucky to have such a clever corporal, Sergeant. You could learn something from him, you know.'

The French lieutenant ordered the men to walk quickly to the *seter*, while Sykes and Tanner unwrapped the bandages from Riggs's head once more. The rifleman was indignant. 'If I faint from loss of blood, I'm blaming you, Sarge,' he said.

'Stop being such a baby, Riggs,' Tanner told him. 'You've got eight pints of the stuff. Losing a few spots won't make much difference.' With droplets of blood from Riggs's cut dripping and spreading in the snow, they followed the rest of the men into the hut. To his relief, there was a shuttered glassless window at the back, leading straight to the stream. Chevannes divided the men, posting his Chasseurs Alpins on top of the shallow cliff above the *seter*, and ordering Tanner to disperse his men

156

south of the hut. 'Sandvold, Nielssen, Larsen and I will take up positions over there,' he said, pointing to a rise in the ground below the ravine and further back from the stream. 'And no one will fire until I do so. You take my lead, you understand? Now, let us get into position – *vite*. We don't have much time.'

Chevannes' men clambered out first, followed by their officer and the Norwegians. As his own men were about to follow, Tanner stopped them. 'Listen, lads,' he said, 'make sure you position yourselves with decent cover, all right? Remember what you've been taught. Make sure your ammo's near to hand. Have your rifles ready. Use the trees and the larger rocks along the edge of the stream. And don't fire until Lieutenant Chevannes gives the order, all right? Once he fires the first shot, you can fire at will. You see any Jerry-wallahs, shoot the buggers.' They were frightened, but exhilarated, too, he knew. 'And, finally, make sure you don't leave any footprints until you're well clear of this basha. Don't you worry about getting wet feet because when we've got these bastards beat, we can pinch their boots. Now, off you go, quickly – but carefully.'

He patted them on the back as they squeezed out of the window, one by one, then noticed Sykes pulling at the straps of his pack.

Sykes caught his eye and grinned. 'We could always give him an even bigger 'eadache, Sarge.'

'What did you have in mind?'

Sykes winked, licked his thumb, then opened his haversack. 'I lifted a few bits of HE, didn't I?'

'You crafty begger!' said Tanner.

'Well, no point leaving it all at that train depot for Jerry, was there?'

Tanner smiled. 'No, Corporal. What do you think I'm carrying in these?' He pointed to his respirator satchel and pack.

Sykes chuckled. 'Bloody 'ell, Sarge, and there was me thinkin' I was the only sneaky bastard round 'ere.' He looked around conspiratorially, then said, 'In any case, I was thinking we could string something up to the door. Might give 'em a nasty shock.'

'Have we got time?' Tanner peered through a narrow slit in the timber along the wall by the door. 'Can't see them yet.' He had another look through his scope. Nothing, but he was certain it wouldn't be long.

Ignoring the sergeant's concerns, Sykes was already taking a length of safety fuse from a round metal tin in his haversack. 'It's good stuff, this,' he said. 'Perfectly strong enough for what we need.' He cut a short strip with his clasp knife, then tied one end round the latch on the door frame and threaded it through the handle. He took out a hand grenade, loosened the pin and tied the other end of the fuse, so that the grenade hung gently against the door.

For a moment neither man spoke. The hut smelt musty – damp wood and dust: probably unused since the previous summer. Tanner watched Sykes with mounting unease. 'I hope that pin's not going to slip out, Stan.'

'It'll need more pressure than the grenade's weight to pull it out.' He felt in his pack again. 'Now for a little extra something. A nice packet of Mr Nobel's finest, I think.' He produced a cardboard packet of gelignite and tied it to the door handle with more safety fuse.

'Bloody hell – careful, Stan!'

Sykes grinned. 'You know what your problem is? You worry too much.'

'Sod you, Corporal. I just don't want to be blown to smithereens.' Tanner watched Sykes put away his knife. 'Ready now?'

Sykes winked.

'Good. Let's get out of here, quick.'

Jumping into the stream, they clambered along the rocks, keeping an eye on the trees in the direction they had come and praying they wouldn't be spotted. The weight of his packs affected his balance, and Tanner slipped on a smooth rock. He cursed to himself as ice-cold water splashed up his trousers. Regaining his footing, he staggered on. Ahead he caught sight of Hepworth dashing from one tree to another. *Stop bloody moving about, Hep*, he thought. He could feel his pulse throbbing again; he wanted to run but the splashing of water would be too noisy, yet if the enemy arrived now he and Sykes would be sitting ducks. Fifteen yards ahead he spotted a pine close to the water's edge, leaning out awkwardly over the stream. *If we can just reach that*, he thought. The trunk would hide his tracks on the far side. 'Stan!' he whispered, and pointed urgently to the tree. Sykes nodded.

Reaching the tree first, the corporal clambered up out of the stream bed, holding out a hand for Tanner. A short distance away there was a small knoll between the trees, shallow, but offering good cover. The two men ran over to it. For a moment, Tanner lay on his back, looking up into the trees, breathing in the chill, crisp mountain air. In the valley below he could still hear the battle, but there was silence around them, save for water gurgling through the rocks on its journey down the slope.

Tanner rolled over, pulling his rifle to his chin. They were about sixty yards from the hut with a clear view towards it. Glancing around him he could see some of the men, thankfully now well hidden from the enemy behind rocks, trees and rises in the ground. Only a few yards away Lance Corporal Erwood and the Bren crew had their machine-gun ready.

A minute ticked by. Tanner wondered where the Germans were; perhaps the ambush hadn't been such a good idea. Maybe he should have kept his mouth shut. He glanced at his watch; he reckoned they now had at least a fifteen-minute advantage over the enemy. Perhaps they should have pushed on. Another minute passed. 'Come on, damn you,' he muttered. 'Where the bloody hell are you?'

'There, Sarge!' whispered Sykes. 'Look! See that Jerry dropping on to his knee?'

Tanner could see him clearly – perhaps eighty yards away. The man was studying the tracks in the snow that led to the *seter*. Tanner gripped the barrel of his rifle and felt his finger glide against the cool dark metal of the trigger. *About bloody time*, he thought.

Hauptmann Zellner saw the leading group commander stop, kneel, then signal back. Crouching, Zellner hurried forward.

'Tracks, sir,' said the sergeant, 'leading to the hut. And there's blood on the ground. Looks like at least one is wounded.'

Zellner took out his pistol. Clutching the grip was somehow reassuring. 'Well, there are certainly plenty of footprints here.' He lifted his arm and waved in a circular motion, the signal for his men to deploy into an open skirmish line. Two machine-gun teams hurried through the trees sixty yards either side of him, while the third fell in beside him. Without a word, the soldier carrying the MG30 lay down in the snow, prised apart the bipod, drew the stock into his shoulder, and pulled back the cock until it clicked into place. His partner crouched beside him with the spare ammunition, then unfastened the clip that held the two drum magazines together At the same time, the rest of the men had hastily taken up positions behind trees and on the ground and, with their rifles unslung, the *seter* was now covered. It had taken less than half a minute and Zellner felt proud of his men. They had confirmed what he already knew: that there could be few men better trained in the entire 3rd Gebirgsjäger Division. General Dietl himself would have been impressed.

'Do you think they're in there?' the sergeant asked.

Zellner was not sure. It seemed likely. After all, if they were not, where were they? These were the only tracks. He lifted his binoculars to his eyes and swept the ground ahead. He could see nothing out of the ordinary. But what if the hut was a trap? He bit at his thumbnail. Three machine-guns now covered it and were mutually supporting, while eighteen rifles were trained towards it.

In addition, his men each carried at least three stick grenades. It was a considerable amount of fire-power. Moreover, he had to do something. His mission was to capture Odin. He must act decisively.

'I'm going to tell them to surrender,' Zellner told his sergeant, 'and if they don't come out, I'll send you forward. What can they do? We've got them covered.'

Tanner had seen the German officer lift his binoculars and pressed his own head into the snow. He prayed that curiosity would not get the better of any of his young, inexperienced men and that they would, like him, keep themselves hidden. Seconds ticked by. Silence – no cry of alarm, no crack of a rifle. The enemy officer could not have seen them. Tanner breathed a sigh of relief.

'*Ergebt euch!*' he suddenly heard shouted out. '*Waffen neider!*'

'What's he goin' on about?' whispered Sykes.

'I think he wants us to show ourselves.'

'Surrender!' the German shouted in English. 'Come out with your hands up!'

'Told you,' whispered Tanner. Carefully he lifted his head. The German officer was ordering his men forward. Six soldiers, crouching, their rifles drawn to their shoulders and aimed at the hut, scampered across the open ground to the *seter*. Four stood at either side of the door, while the remaining two stood back a few yards, their rifles still aimed at the hut's entrance.

'The moment of truth, Sarge,' whispered Sykes.

One man had a silver bar on his upper left sleeve. Tanner guessed he was an NCO; at any rate, he now

162

walked to the door, listened a moment, turned briefly to the officer, then kicked hard.

The door swung open and Tanner's heart sank. 'Bollocks,' he muttered.

But then came a deafening crack and the hut erupted into a ball of angry orange flame. Even eighty yards away Tanner could feel the blast as the air was sucked towards the fireball, and a pulse throbbed through the ground. A shot rang out next to him. Dan Erwood's Bren began to chatter. Tanner could see the Germans were startled once again – so much so that, for a moment, they seemed frozen to the spot. As grit and flecks of bone and flesh fell round them, Tanner began firing. He saw one man go down and another fall prostrate in the snow. *Where's that Jerry officer?* He scanned the trees but already his view was clouded by smoke rolling across the clearing. Spurts of flame and tracer bullets glowed curiously through the haze, pinning down the rifle fire from beyond the stream. More tracer arced from the other end of the German line snapping branches and twigs. He heard one man cry out, then another.

'We've got to take out those MGs,' Tanner said to Sykes. 'They've got us covered but they're firing blind. Dan!' he called. 'Keep firing bursts, all right? I need you to cover me and Sykes.'

Lance Corporal Erwood raised his hand in acknowledgement. 'Good,' said Tanner, then turned to Sykes and pointed into the trees away and behind them. 'On three we're going to head back twenty yards over there where the ground slopes away, then use that drop in the land to get underneath the line of fire and work round their flank. OK?'

Sykes nodded.

Tanner took a deep breath. 'One, two, *three*!'

Bullets followed them like a swarm of bees, hissing over their heads and kicking up the snow around them, but although Tanner's body had tensed for the moment when one or more ripped into him, it appeared luck was with them. Suddenly the twenty yards had been crossed, the ground was falling away, and the bullets zapping clear into the wood above him. He stopped, crouched and, to his relief, saw that Sykes was beside him.

'Bloody hell!' gasped the corporal. 'That was a bit hot, Sarge!'

'Pretty warm,' agreed Tanner. 'Where are the rest of them?' He spotted Hepworth, Kershaw and Bell. Hepworth was lying flat on the ground, clutching his helmet to his head; Bell was taking occasional pot-shots then bracing himself against the rear-side of a thick pine. Kershaw was behind a rock by the stream, ducking every time a bullet whizzed past him. Then he saw McAllister, across the stream from Bell. Good, he thought. *That'll do*.

He picked up a lump of snow and hurled it at Hepworth, who saw him, and began to scurry over. Another snowball caught the attention of the other three. Short bursts of machine-gun fire still spat intermittently above their heads, while cracks of rifle fire rang out. 'We're going to take out those MGs,' said Tanner, to the five men now squatting beside him. 'We cross the stream out of the line of fire, move on sixty yards, then come round the back of them.' The boys looked tense; Hepworth, especially, was wide-eyed and ashen-faced. 'Come on, Hep,' he said. 'You know the drill. We work in pairs. Two forward, two pairs covering. Got enough ammo?'

Hepworth nodded.

Tanner patted his shoulder. 'We'll be fine. Let's go.'

Their bodies crouched low, they made it across the stream and pushed forward until the sound of firing was coming from behind them to the left. He hoped the enemy troops would be too busy with the fire coming from in front of them to have thought of an attack from behind. As he moved up the slope to the almost level ground above, he was glad to see his guess had been correct. Signalling to the others to follow, he pulled McAllister by the shoulder, then signalled for Hepworth to pair off with Sykes, Kershaw with Bell. 'Watch out for our own fire,' he warned.

He pulled out three grenades from his haversack, clipped them to his belt and briefly scanned ahead as a stray bullet whipped up the ground a few yards to his left. They were behind the far left of the German skirmish line. One of the machine-guns was just forty yards ahead, although hidden by trees, while the second was sixty yards to the right of the first. He could hear bursts from a third further away. His intention was to get within twenty yards of the first two and lob grenades at them. The danger would come if the gunners saw them first and turned their weapons on them.

'Sod it,' he muttered. Then, to his men: 'Forget the drill. Stan, you and Hepworth run towards that first MG and hurl a couple of grenades,' he whispered. 'Mac, you and I'll get the other. Bell, follow Sykes and Hep and cover them. Kershaw, you cover me and Mac. On three.'

He gripped the first grenade in his hand, counted down visually with his fingers, took a deep breath, then sprinted through the snow, praying the bullets would miss them once more. Thirty yards to go. A German rifleman was standing firing from behind a tree. Twenty-five yards. Three more riflemen and the second MG team. Twenty yards. Pull the pin from the grenade. *One, two, throw*. Aim good. A rifleman saw the grenade, looked round in horror, but it was too late. As it detonated, spraying the machine-gunners with shards of searing iron, they cried out and rolled. A second detonation came a split second later, just as Tanner brought his rifle to his shoulder once more, pulled back the bolt and fired, silencing the startled rifleman. Two more bullets fizzed above his head. Tanner ducked but, keeping his rifle tight into his chin, shouted, '*Hände hoch! Hände hoch!*'

He was only vaguely aware of McAllister standing a few yards from him, yelling the same instruction. To his amazement, several German troops dropped their rifles and slowly raised their arms. 'Where's the bloody officer?' shouted Tanner, then saw him, crouched by a tree, still clutching his pistol. "*Hände* bloody *hoch*, mate,' Tanner said to him, his rifle pointed at the enemy officer's heart.

Zellner dropped his pistol, his face flexing with anger. '*Waffen nieder!*' he shouted. '*Befehlen ist unter allen Umständen von der Englander zu leisten!*'

'Cease firing!' yelled out Tanner. A bullet pinged through the trees to his right. 'Bloody stop shooting. They've surrendered!' he shouted, as he stepped forward and picked up Zellner's pistol.

* * *

As the guns fell silent on the mountain above Tretten, the battle continued to rage in the valley below. The day had been every bit as difficult and depressing as Brigadier Morgan had suspected. It was nearly eight o'clock in the evening when he walked out of his makeshift office and stepped outside to smoke his pipe. He realized he'd not had any air all day, yet outside the house the sharp stench of cordite and burnt wood was so heavy he could feel it in his throat. He looked towards the river, but a heavy fog hung over the valley. Through the smoke, however, the sun was trying to break through; he could see it high in the sky, a hazy orange orb. Ahead, shrouded in fog, the battle boomed on. The ground shuddered.

After only a few puffs, he took his pipe from his mouth and tapped it against the heel of his boot. The brief break for a smoke had not been as calming as he'd hoped. He walked back inside, where clerks and the remaining brigade staff were still frantically passing on information and trying desperately to find answers to unanswerable questions.

In his office he sat at his desk and opened his small leatherbound diary. One day, he thought, he would write this up, 'How Not to Fight a War: Lessons from the Norwegian Campaign', and submit it to the War Office. 'The remnants of the three companies of Leicesters, Foresters and Rangers,' he scribbled, 'were attacked in the morning along their makeshift positions west of Øyer and soon fell back. Leicesters' company commander killed, and most of the officers in that mixed force now

167

reported missing.' Morgan's pencil hovered over the pale blue paper. *They had been fine men all,* he reflected. *A bloody waste.*

'By midday,' he continued, 'the usual array of aircraft appeared, bombing and strafing their lines.' And flying so low, too. Morgan had clearly seen the pilot of one Messerschmitt. The man's arrogance – sticking up two fingers to the soldiers below – had been hard to stomach. The German artillery had been in on the game too, systematically pasting the village. Most of the buildings in the small settlement were now destroyed, their timbers devoured by raging flames. 'By afternoon, a pall of grey smoke hung heavy over the valley. Spent most of the afternoon fending off desperate pleas for reinforcements and scratching my head, wondering how the devil I could possibly hold the enemy at bay until 15th Brigade joins us.'

Colonel Jansen's Dragoons had arrived, as Ruge had promised, and had been sent forward to bolster the forward positions in the gorge south of the village. 'Had I had just a few guns,' he scrawled, 'it might have been very different.' It was, after all, the kind of defensive position any commanding officer would normally only dream of. But the planes, the shelling and the enemy's armour were too much. What could a few machine-guns and rifles hope to achieve? It was like throwing snow at a stone wall. Indeed, Morgan had wondered, perhaps they should have tried chucking snowballs.

All afternoon he had fretted about a flank attack by German mountain troops. So, too, it seemed, had Colonel Chisholm, commander of the Yorks Rangers, who had been deployed on the far left of their lines on the low slopes above the village. Chisholm had pleaded for more men.

'Damn it, Colonel,' Morgan had told him, on one of the few field telephones that were working, 'I can't muster more men from thin air. Everything we have is thrown into the line. If the Germans try to outflank us, you must simply do your best.'

'And see my battalion destroyed?' Chisholm had fumed.

'Do you think I like leading lambs to the slaughter?' Morgan had asked him.

'Then, with respect, sir, order the retreat.'

But Morgan had been unable to do that. Not at four in the afternoon, just as his forward troops were engaging the advancing enemy. His task was to hold the Germans as long as he could; 15th Brigade was due to start arriving at Åndalsnes that evening so help was on its way but, as Ruge had reminded him at their meeting in the early hours of the morning, and as he had repeated on the telephone that day, checking German momentum and slowing their advance was crucial. They were playing for time – time that would allow 15th Brigade to arrive and deploy in strength. That meant every passing hour took on enormous importance. The problem was that soon he would have no brigade left with which to make any kind of stand, as Colonel Chisholm had painfully reminded him.

'Flank attack materialized shortly after 1800 hours,' he scribbled again. 'Ordered forward troops to fall back to the village.' In the mayhem of battle, with field-telephone lines cut and communication between units severely limited, these instructions had, inevitably, been too late. Indeed, half his staff had been sent forward to deliver messages, but had not been seen or heard of since. *What a mess*, he thought. *What a huge bloody mess*.

He closed his diary and went out to the hallway where he found Major Dornley. 'Latest news?'

Dornley looked grave. 'Enemy mountain troops have overrun the village from the east.'

'And the men fighting there?'

'Presumably captured. All lines are dead.'

Morgan steadied himself against the doorway and put a hand to his brow. 'God almighty,' he muttered. 'It's 2000 hours, we've got almost no brigade left and most of my staff are missing.'

Suddenly, above them, there was a loud drone of aircraft. Dornley and Morgan looked up as the wailing siren of Stuka dive-bombers shrieked overhead.

Both men fell flat on the ground, their hands over their heads. The whistle of bombs, followed by an ear-splitting explosion. Morgan felt himself lifted off the ground and pushed down again. With every boom and whoosh of detonating bombs, the house shuddered, the floor quaked and plaster fell from the ceiling. Morgan screwed his eyes shut. The percussion of the bombs pressed on his lungs.

Then the Stukas were gone, but as Morgan staggered to his feet and dusted himself down, he could hear artillery and small-arms still echoing through the valley. The sound was drawing closer. *My brigade*, he thought. *All those people*.

They could do no more. 'Dornley,' he said, 'order what survivors we have to block the roads, get the remaining trucks and vehicles loaded up and tell everyone to fall back.'

Dornley nodded.

Morgan hurried back into his office to collect his own case, his papers and few belongings. He could not turn and stand a few miles further up the valley this time because his brigade, as a fighting force, had ceased to exist. Rather, they would head for the village of Kvam, where General Ruge hoped they would meet Major General Paget's freshly arrived 15th Brigade. And it would take the Germans a while to get there, Morgan hoped, because Kvam was some distance away. Forty miles, to be precise.

9

Tanner put an arm to the nearest tree and rested his head against it. Now that the fight was over, the adrenalin surge that had kept him going evaporated as quickly as it had arrived. His legs ached, his hands were shaky, and his stomach was racked with hunger cramps. A pounding headache drummed in his skull, while his mouth was as dry as bone. Stiffly leaning down, he picked up some snow and put it into his mouth, the icy water striking the nerve ends in his teeth.

'Sarge,' said a voice.

Tanner looked round. Sykes was standing beside him. 'Three casualties, Sarge. Gibson's dead, Saxby and Riggs wounded.'

'Riggs again?' asked Tanner.

'Bullet through the shoulder. It's not hit his lung, but he needs help. The lads are patching him up now.'

'What about Saxby?'

'Shoulder as well. Should pull through. Neither'll be going far, though.'

Tanner put another handful of snow to his mouth. 'We'll have to think about what's best for the wounded. Better get Gibbo buried. And the Krauts. And Sandvold? Is the professor safe?'

'Yes, Sarge. Not a scratch.'

'Anyone else?'

'One of the Froggies bought it, and another was wounded, but that's it. Lieutenants Larsen and Nielssen are still good.'

'And bloody Chevannes?'

'Yes, Sarge,' said Sykes, with a wry smile. 'Nothing wrong with him.'

Tanner should have felt pleased. His plan had worked, Sandvold was safe, and the enemy threat was, for the moment, over. Yet despair overwhelmed him once more. It was half past eight in the evening and the sound of battle from the valley was noticeably lessening, receding into the distance by the minute, and with it their chance of freedom. They had been so close again – just a mile or two from the safety of their own lines. *Christ*, thought Tanner. How were they ever going to get out of this? Physically he was finished – they all were. Those last reserves of energy had been summoned by sheer will-power and the promise of reaching the Allies that evening. Now the finishing line had been cruelly moved, far out of reach. And then there was Chevannes. By God, Tanner hated the man: his arrogance, his stupidity, his woeful leadership the previous evening. It was Chevannes' fault they had failed today. Tanner had half a mind to shoot the bastard there and then.

'Sergeant! Sergeant Tanner!'

Chevannes. Tanner closed his eyes, quietly drummed his tightly clenched fist into the side of the tree, then faced the French lieutenant striding towards him.

'A good victory,' said the Frenchman, 'although you should not have blown the shelter without my permission.'

Tanner took a deep breath. 'It killed six men, sir, and gave us the chance to hit them hard before they had a moment to recover their balance.'

'Always answering back to everything I say,' Chevannes snapped. He paused a moment then said, 'We need to tie up these prisoners and bury the dead. See to it quickly, while I question their officer.'

Tanner said nothing, but walked away and called his men over. 'Well done, lads,' he said. 'You did well.' He looked into their faces, one by one. The youthfulness had gone. They had fought their first fight, had killed, had been touched by death and had survived. They had grown up, and he knew they were better soldiers for the experience.

He ordered six to fetch the dead, instructing them to line the bodies up by the stream, then strip them of usable clothing and kit. They were to cover them with snow and stones from the brook, and place the tin helmets strapped to their packs on top as a marker. 'Just take Gibbo's bunduck and ammunition,' he added. 'Leave him dressed.'

Burying the dead; a grim task. Few men died with a neat bullet hole through the heart; most did so with a profusion of blood, with chunks of their bodies ripped from them or their guts spewing from their bellies. It took time to get used to such sights, but there was no denying that most became inured to them quickly. War hardened the mind. *Probably the soul too*, Tanner thought.

He was sorry about Gibson – the third of his men to die. Gibson had been popular, a tough little Yorkshireman. *Bloody hell*, he thought.

He took McAllister and Hepworth to the prisoners who were being guarded by Chevannes' Chasseurs Alpins. The Germans were standing close together not far from the blackened crater where the hut had once been. Cordite hung in the air. The *seter* had gone but for a jumble of charred and still burning logs. Thick smoke rose into the air, a beacon for any passing aircraft. Tanner looked at his watch again. Just after half past eight. They needed to get a move on. 'Iggery, lads,' he said. 'Let's get into the woods.' He began pushing and shoving the prisoners and, with Hepworth, McAllister and the two Frenchmen's help, walked them past the mangled machine-gun crews being lined up on the ground by the stream and under the cover of thicker trees.

A hundred yards from the *seter*, he ordered them to stop. He turned one to face him, a youth with dark hair and a defiant glare. 'What's this?' Tanner asked, pointing to the flower embroidered on his sleeve. The same flower was on their field caps too.

'*Ein Edelweiss*,' the man replied. '*Wir sind der Gebirgsjägeren.*'

'It is the symbol of all Gebirgsjäger troops,' said another of the men, in heavily accented English. He looked slightly older, with pale grey eyes and pock-marked cheeks. 'We are mountain troops.'

175

'And your kit? Good, is it?' Tanner asked. He patted the younger man's pockets, felt the shape of a cigarette packet and took it out. 'Cheers,' he said, shook out a cigarette and lit it.

'Yes,' said the older man. 'We have the best kit of any fighting soldier in Norway.'

'Good,' said Tanner, 'because ours is pretty useless.' He pushed his way through the men, measuring his feet against theirs until he was standing beside a man of similar height and size. 'Yours look about right. I'll have those.' The man looked at him blankly, so Tanner mimed his demand. Reluctantly, the prisoner did as he was ordered. 'And you tell them,' said Tanner, turning back to the English-speaker, 'that I want all of you stripped. I want your jackets, tunics, boots and caps. And your goggles.' He took the pair from above the peak of the man nearest him and put them on.

'Isn't that against the Geneva Convention, Sarge?' asked McAllister. 'They could freeze to death.'

'Mac, do you want to survive this?' Tanner snapped.

'Yes, Sarge.'

'Then don't worry your head about things like that. And, no, I don't think it is against the Geneva Convention. Let's get on with it. And I want them to empty their packs too. Look for food, fags, ammunition, grenades – anything.'

'You can't do this to us,' said the English speaker.

'I can and I will,' said Tanner. 'Now, give me your pack and get undressed.' The man slowly slipped off his rucksack and passed it to Tanner, who emptied it on to the ground. To his delight there was some food – a chunk

176

of dark, dry bread and some cured sausage. The man had a small flask of schnapps too. Tanner ate hungrily, took a swig from the flask and felt the sweet, burning liquid soothe his throat. *Ah, that feels good.* He passed the flask and food to Hepworth, rolled up the tunic, cap and green-grey jacket, then strapped them to his pack. Finally, he exchanged his own boots and ankle gaiters for the German's dark brown ankle boots and puttees. 'Beautiful,' he said aloud. 'Bloody beautiful.' He threw his own to the prisoner whose boots he was now wearing. 'Here,' he said, 'have these.'

He went to help Sykes and the others, and found them laying stones and boulders on top of Gibson's grave. 'Take it in turns to get yourselves some kit from the prisoners,' he told them. 'Kershaw, hop it.'

'Nice boots, Sarge,' said Sykes.

Tanner smiled ruefully. 'Make sure you get a pair too, Stan. They're bloody marvellous, I'm telling you.'

'I have already.' He grinned, jerking a thumb towards a shoeless German corpse. 'Just haven't put 'em on yet.'

Tanner took out two cigarettes and gave one to the corporal.

'What do we do now, Sarge?' Sykes asked, as he exhaled a large cloud of smoke. He held his cigarette between finger and thumb, hovering in front of his mouth.

'We're too bloody late to get to Tretten.'

'I can hear. Or, rather, I can't.'

'We should have gone last night when I said.'

'No point agonizing over it, Sarge. It's done now.'

'Sodding French bastard.' Tanner kicked at the snow.

'I should have stood my ground.' He sighed. 'If I'm honest, Stan, we've got to find somewhere to rest. A farm or something. I need to think clearly and I can't right now.'

'Can't we just take our lads and scarper?' Sykes asked.

Tanner shook his head. 'I promised Gulbrand. It's not that, though – it's what he said. If this Sandvold really is as important as the colonel made out, we've got to get him out of here. I can't abandon him to Chevannes. I wouldn't trust him to get Sandvold to safety for all the money in the world.'

The minutes passed. The burial was completed, as was the reassignment of German kit. The prisoners, huddled together, stripped to their shirts and trousers, were shivering.

Eventually Chevannes reappeared with the German officer. 'Are you done, Sergeant?'

'Yes, sir.' Tanner turned to the German.

'Captain Zellner,' said Chevannes.

'*Heil Hitler*,' said Zellner.

'Don't you bloody *Heil Hitler* me, you Nazi bastard,' said Tanner, then asked Chevannes, 'What have you got out of him?'

'The captain refuses to say anything.'

Tanner was about to speak when Lieutenant Larsen appeared from across the stream.

'Wait,' he said, hurrying towards them. As he saw the German, his eyes widened. 'You!'

Zellner seemed surprised. 'Do I know you?'

'You were at the farm,' said Larsen. 'At Økset. North of Elverum.'

178

Zellner's eyes narrowed

'It was you,' said Larsen, jabbing his finger into Zellner's chest. 'You were looking for us. What did you do to the farmer?'

Zellner nodded – *yes, I remember now* – and glanced at Chevannes. 'Nothing,' he said. 'Nothing at all.'

'Liar!' said Larsen. He wiped his hand across his mouth, then punched Zellner hard in the stomach. The German doubled over and collapsed on to the ground.

'Lieutenant! My God, man, what do you think you are doing?' shouted Chevannes.

Larsen grabbed Zellner by the scruff of the neck, pulled him to his feet. Clasping the German's jaw in his hand, said, 'Tell me what you did!'

Zellner glared at him, his pale eyes wild with defiance.

'Lieutenant, that will do!' yelled Chevannes.

'He's lying!' shouted Larsen, face red with fury. 'I know he is! I want to know what he did to my cousin!'

Chevannes turned to Zellner. '*Capitaine*,' he said, 'can you give me your word as an officer that you did not harm Lieutenant Larsen's cousin?'

Zellner coughed, and ran his hand round his collar. 'Of course. I give you my word.'

'For pity's sake,' said Tanner. He put a hand on Larsen's shoulder. 'Leave it, sir.'

Larsen glared at Zellner. 'You lie.'

'Lieutenant! Enough!' said Chevannes. 'He has given you his word.'

Shaking his head, Larsen walked away.

'Sir,' said Tanner now, 'do you really think his say-so counts for anything? He's a bloody Nazi.'

'He may be, but he is still an officer,' the Frenchman replied. 'You may not understand what honour is, Sergeant Tanner, but I and my men most certainly do.'

'I don't believe this.' Tanner spun round and went to his men.

The German caught sight of his troops a short distance away, huddled in the trees, and spoke angrily to Chevannes, who turned sharply.

'Sergeant! Come back! What have you done to the prisoners?'

'Nothing. Just taken a few bits of clothing, weapons and so on.'

'They will die of cold if we leave them like that.'

'Then that's one less thing to worry about, isn't it, sir? Actually, sir,' Tanner continued, ignoring the lieutenant's barely disguised fury, 'I was wondering what you were thinking of doing with them.'

'Doing with them?'

'Yes, sir. We can't take them with us and we can't let them loose in case they make it back and tell their superiors about us – and, in particular our Norwegian friend. There is, of course, one way of getting them off our hands—'

'What are you saying, Sergeant? That we shoot them? My God—'

'No, of course not, sir. I was thinking we could try to find another hut and tie them up there. If they keep cosy they'll probably live. It's cold but it's not that cold. Or we could tie them up and leave them here.'

'Or you could behave honourably, Sergeant, and give them back their uniforms.'

Tanner's patience snapped. 'Christ, I've had just about enough of this,' he said angrily. 'We're miles behind the lines now – thanks entirely to you, sir – and all you seem to care about is sodding honour. This isn't bloody knights-in-shining-armour, this is war. It's nasty and bad things happen. I don't give a toss about upsetting these Jerries. I care about making sure my men survive and that we get back to our lines. Regardless of what you may or may not believe, I made a solemn promise to get Mr Sandvold to safety and I'm going to bloody well do it. But we're in a whole load of trouble and we need every bit of help we can get our hands on. These Jerry boots are a damn sight better than our own, and their kit will not only keep us warm but could give us a useful disguise, should it come to it. After this little fight our ammunition levels are down and the extra fire-power might come in bloody useful. If you think that's wrong, then you're an even bigger fool than I thought. Sir.'

Chevannes' cheek muscles were twitching and his lips moved as though he was about to answer. Instead, he merely barked orders that they were to get going and take the prisoners with them.

They set off in a column, the prisoners carrying Riggs and the wounded Frenchman on stretchers made from rifles and greatcoats, between Chevannes' and two of Tanner's men. Lieutenant Larsen was in front, keeping his distance from Zellner and the other prisoners. It was, Tanner guessed, still a few degrees above freezing, helped by the toneless grey cloud that covered the sky; he wondered whether it would snow again. The air was crisp, and although the light was fading, there was still a couple of hours' daylight ahead.

Every so often, Chevannes paused to scan the area with his binoculars, then they moved on again. Tanner wondered what the French lieutenant had decided. He wanted to suggest they talk to the Norwegians, find a farm in which to lie up for a while and make a properly considered plan. His men had endured so much over the past two days; he felt they had a right to know where they were heading now and how much longer they could expect to tramp through the snow.

They had been going for almost half an hour when Chevannes stopped again, peered through his binoculars, then told them to head up the mountain, out of the main treeline and towards the open plateau. The men groaned, but even with his naked eye, Tanner could see the *seter* through the trees above and smiled to himself. Perhaps Chevannes was starting to listen.

'Not another night in a God-forsaken bloody hut,' said Hepworth. 'Honestly, Sarge, I'm done for here.'

'You're all right, Hep,' said Tanner. 'I'm sure Mr Chevannes knows what he's doing.'

'You've changed your tune,' Sykes said, in a low voice.

'Only because it's what I told him we should do,' Tanner replied. 'We're going to ditch the prisoners in that basha up there.' He pointed to the wooden *seter* through the trees above.

'Kill 'em?'

'No, just tie 'em up. And I also suggested it might be a good idea to find a farm with food and somewhere half decent to rest for a while.'

'Too bloody right. Let's hope he listens to that too.'

On reaching the hut, Chevannes ordered the prisoners to be herded inside. He looked at Larsen. 'Let Tanner do it, Lieutenant,' he said. Larsen glared at Zellner, then walked a short way back down the slope.

Tanner pushed the prisoners inside. Using bootlaces and some of his and Sykes's fuse cable, they bound the men. As they were doing so, Tanner noticed that the German officer, Captain Zellner, still had his binoculars round his neck and his empty holster at his side.

'I'll take those,' said Tanner, lifting the Zeiss binoculars over Zellner's head and removing the holster and bullet pouches from his belt.

Zellner stared at him, then at his rifle, and noticed the scope mounts next to the breech. 'A sniper rifle,' he said in English. Tanner met his gaze. 'I'll not forget this, Tanner,' said Zellner. 'And next time I see you, I will kill you.'

'I'm sure you will.' He smiled. 'In the meantime, my apologies for what I'm about to do.' He drew his hand into a fist and rammed it into Zellner's temple. The German gasped and lost consciousness.

'Bloody 'ell, Sarge! Where d'you learn to do that?' asked Sykes.

'The Army can teach you a lot, Corporal,' Tanner replied, 'including how to box. Damned useful. I must say, I don't really like knocking someone out like that but he's a filthy piece of work and he threatened to kill me. And we don't want them following us too soon, do we?'

'No, course not.'

Tanner looked at Zellner carefully. 'Hit too hard and in the wrong place,' he told Sykes, 'and you can kill a man.

Too soft and you'll do very little damage at all. One blow, that's what you want. Short, sharp and very much to the point. He might not forget me, but he'll not want to remember the headache when he comes round.'

With the Germans tied and left in the *seter*, the men retraced their steps until they were back among the trees, clear of the plateau. Chevannes called a halt. 'We'll rest a moment,' he said.

Larsen walked over to Tanner. 'I'm sorry,' he said. 'I behaved badly . . . back there with that German.'

'No need to apologize, sir.'

'It was my fault,' he said. 'We stopped at my cousin's farm and took his truck. I didn't think at the time, but I should have done. It was obvious the Germans would come back and find it gone.'

'And you think they took your cousin?'

'I do not know. I had thought they might have killed him.' He shrugged. 'I am not sure now. Maybe he was telling the truth. I was angry – but more angry with myself.' He sighed. 'It has been preying on my mind, you see. I just wish I knew. I wish I could find out that he is all right.' He looked up at Tanner. 'Anyway, I wanted to explain.' He wiped his brow.

Tanner nodded. 'Thank you, sir,' he said, then moved a few steps and leant against a tree next to Sandvold. The Norwegian grimaced as he slipped off his rucksack. He was as white as a ghost, and Tanner realized that, despite his preoccupation with getting them all to safety, he had not thought about Sandvold's physical condition. He laid a hand on the man's shoulder. 'Are you all right?' he asked.

'I am tired, that is all,' he replied. 'I am forty-seven,

after all. You boys – you are all in the prime of youth. This has been a long trek for a man of my age.' He smiled weakly, then gasped and slumped against the tree. Tanner caught him, crouched, and rested Sandvold's head against his rucksack.

'My God, what has happened to him?' Larsen had hurried over and now stood beside them.

Nielssen joined them. 'Is he all right?' he asked, frowning.

Tanner felt for a pulse. 'He's passed out, that's all.' He took out the flask of schnapps and tipped it into Sandvold's mouth. The Norwegian spluttered, coughed and opened his eyes. 'I am sorry,' he said. 'What must you think of me?'

'It's all right,' said Tanner. 'Drink a bit more of this.' He gave Sandvold the flask, then stood up beside the two Norwegians. 'None of us can go much further tonight. We need to find somewhere to rest properly. Get some food – preferably hot.'

'But what about reaching the Allies?' asked Nielssen.

'They're not in Tretten any more. They've fallen back.' He sighed. 'We need a new plan.'

Larsen said, 'You are right, Sergeant. I know I could do with a proper rest. If we keep going like this, none of us will make it, let alone Professor Sandvold.'

Professor? Tanner looked down at him – the gaunt face, unkempt moustache, the dark rings and wrinkles round the eyes. Just what was this man's secret? He wondered whether he would ever know.

'I'll talk to Chevannes,' said Larsen.

'There are farmsteads along this side of the valley,'

185

added Nielssen. 'It's west-facing here so they will be quite high.'

'We must be careful,' said Tanner. 'With the Germans in the valley, it'll be hard to know who to trust. There'll be a lot at stake for the civilians.'

'I doubt we will find many pro-Germans up here, if that is what you mean,' said Nielssen.

Tanner yawned. 'I suppose there's risk with every move we make. It's a matter of balancing that risk. Right now, we need rest urgently. If that means we have to take our chance with some farmer, then so be it.'

'Hot food.' Nielssen smiled. 'I would risk a lot for that right now.'

It began to snow, only lightly, but Tanner was pleased to see the flakes drifting down from the blanket of grey above them. There was, of course, every chance that Zellner and his men would free themselves and get off the mountain, despite the strength of the fuse and the tightness with which he and Sykes had bound them. And then what? It wouldn't take them long to get down to the valley, where they would fetch help and begin to search the mountain once more. Had it been a cold, clear night, the enemy would have found their tracks with ease. They should have killed the prisoners, he reflected, but he knew he would have had no stomach for murdering men in cold blood, and neither would his men. War was cruel and hard, but there were still some lines that could not be crossed.

He tilted his face to the sky and felt the flakes land and dissolve. At least the snow would hide their tracks. That was something.

He now saw Sandvold lift himself to his feet, then reach back to the tree for support. 'Shall I get you a stick, Professor? Would that help?'

'Thank you, yes.'

Tanner picked up a fallen pine branch, cut off the loose twigs with his sword bayonet, than handed it to him.

'Thank you, Sergeant.' He straightened his back, grimaced, then said, 'You know, I never in my wildest dreams imagined anything like this.'

'Having to escape the Germans?'

'Yes, if you like, but Norway being at *war*. It's so incredible. We may have been Norsemen once, Sergeant Tanner, but that was a long, long time ago. We have forgotten how to fight. We are a peaceful nation – a nation that makes no claim on other land and wants no part in other people's arguments. All my life, Norway has been like this – a neutral country. While you were destroying each other twenty years ago, we Norwegians were getting on with our lives. And yet here we are, tramping across a mountain at dawn, praying we will not be captured and shot.' He shook his head. 'Do you have a family, Sergeant?' he asked suddenly.

'No,' Tanner replied. 'Only the Army.'

'A bachelor like me,' Sandvold smiled, 'wedded to your work. But I do have a mother still alive. At least, I pray she is. I was supposed to leave Oslo, you know,' he added, 'told to leave the moment the invasion began, but my mother would not come with me. She said she was too old to run away and that she was not sure she wanted to live if she could not stay in our home in Oslo. Well, it

187

has been her home for more than fifty years, so I suppose she had a point. I felt I could not leave her – my own mother, how could I? And then one day Colonel Gulbrand arrived with three men and suddenly the matter was no longer in my hands. My mother wept when I left. It is ridiculous, I know, but I am worried about her and I know she will be worried about me. And all because of my work – work that I thought would benefit Norway. Now I discover that what I know is so valuable that my own countrymen will kill me rather than let me fall into enemy hands.' He sighed again. 'There has been much time to think since I left Oslo – since I left my mother weeping at the door of the house. And if I am honest,' he chuckled mirthlessly, 'I have drawn few conclusions, except that everything I believed in and thought to be right seems to have been turned on its head. It is as though a kind of madness has descended. The war is like a plague or flood or some other biblical pestilence. It rips our world apart, bringing nothing but suffering and, it seems to me, achieving very little. I pray it will be over soon, but that seems unlikely, yes?'

'God only knows,' said Tanner.

'What am I trying to say to you, Sergeant? I am saying that I would be most grateful if you could get me to safety. I want to help my country, not become a martyr for her. And I also want to live for the sake of my mother, if that is not too sentimental.'

'Why are you asking me this?' asked Tanner. 'Lieutenant Chevannes is in charge. And there are two of your countrymen to guard you too.'

Sandvold smiled. 'Yes, I like your use of the word. It

makes me feel rather like a prisoner, which I suppose in a way I am. But I am saying this to you because I know what Colonel Gulbrand told you. Yes, I know. I left you and Gulbrand to talk, but I heard every word. And, as it happens, I agree with him. You are evidently a highly capable soldier, Sergeant. Even a pacifist like me can see that.'

'Thank you,' said Tanner quietly. 'Then you will have heard me give Gulbrand my word, which stands now as it did then. I can't promise anything, Professor, but I'll do my best.'

Whether it was what Tanner had said earlier, or the snow, or whether Chevannes had been persuaded by the Norwegians, the French lieutenant appeared to agree that they should find a farmstead in which to lie up and rest. They were now a couple of miles north of Tretten, beneath a peak known as the Vangsberget, and following the course of another shallow ravine. Now several hundred feet below the lip of the high plateau, they were walking through increasingly dense forest, so dark that the only glimpse of daylight came from above the mountain stream. They emerged along the top of a mountain pasture. The snow had stopped falling. At the far end of the field there was an old gate and beyond that a path, clearly well trodden.

Nielssen and Larsen led them along the track, which wound its way in a series of hairpin bends, then straightened out and ended at an old farmstead. It looked much like the others Tanner had seen, a large barn with a bright red tin roof and a stone ramp leading to the first floor, a cluster of other outbuildings and a main house of white clapperboard with a high pitched roof and carvings along the edges.

As they had the previous evening, the two Norwegian officers approached cautiously while the rest waited. The promise of warmth and food was intoxicating. Tanner watched Larsen and Nielssen reach the front, and heard a dog bark. His stomach churned with hunger.

Anxious minutes. Tanner could see the tension and exhaustion on the faces of every man. And there were the wounded to think of too – Riggs, Saxby and the French Chasseur. All three had shown stoic fortitude as they had been roughly carried over and down the mountain. The Frenchman had a bullet through the leg, but while none of the wounds were yet serious, Tanner was keenly aware they soon would be. His rudimentary antiseptic had not worked on Gulbrand and there was every chance it would fail these lads too. They needed proper help if they were to avoid gangrene and septicaemia – merciless killers both.

The valley was quiet. Tretten village, a short way to the south, was hidden from view, as were the road and railway below, but Tanner could see the river, now widening into a lake, and beyond, the densely forested valley sides.

A figure appeared at the door – Larsen – and beckoned them in. *Relief.*

'Bloody hooray,' grinned Sykes, who, with Hepworth, picked up the wounded Riggs. 'All right, Riggsy?' he said. 'Soon have you cleaned up, mate.'

Riggs smiled. 'Cheers, Corp,' he said.

A middle-aged man with greying hair, an unshaven chin and a large moustache stood anxiously by the doorway, his eyes darting from one man to another. He wore an old corduroy jacket, wool trousers and boots, and chewed one of his fingers as the men came towards him. Muttering to Larsen in Norwegian, he walked towards the large barn.

'Follow him,' said Larsen, 'including the wounded. He wants you all in there.'

The farmer scampered deftly up the stone ramp and opened one of the twin doors at the top, then swung his arm in a sweeping motion – *in you go* – until the men followed.

'The wounded need help right away,' Tanner told Larsen.

Larsen nodded. 'His wife and daughter are coming. They're bringing some bread and water first, then some hot water and bandages.'

The wounded had been set against one side of the barn, packs propping up their heads. They lay on the greatcoats that had been used as stretchers just a short while before. It was dark in there and dusty, the smell of dried hay and straw mixing with the stench of animal dung below. Tanner joined Sykes and eased off his packs. A burden released. He felt in his haversack for Zellner's pistol. It was a Walther, a neat semi-automatic that fitted comfortably in his hand. Loading it with a new clip of eight rounds, he put it into its holster. The men were quiet, too exhausted to speak. Tanner noticed that a Frenchman was already asleep on the straw, curled up, his rifle by his side.

So, too, was Sandvold. Beside him, Nielssen was looking through his rucksack. He saw Tanner watching him, then brought it closer to him and pulled the cord tight. Tanner wondered what he was hiding. Crown jewels and papers, or something more? What was the real story behind these Norwegians? He thought about Sandvold. He was curious – damned curious. What was that man's big secret? Had he invented some new terror weapon? It was hard to know what to think, but certainly the boffins had been busy over the past few years. The advances in aircraft, tanks and other war matériel was astonishing. They'd noticed the pace of change less in India and Palestine but he had found returning home that January quite an eye-opener: the world had moved on while he had been away. There had certainly been no Spitfires or even Hurricanes in the Middle East, let alone in India, yet suddenly there they were in Britain, completely different from anything Tanner had ever seen before. And so sleek and fast, rolling about the sky at more than three hundred miles an hour, a speed that had seemed impossible not so long ago. They made the old Bulldogs and Harts that Tanner had been used to seem horribly slow and outmoded. Even the bombers were now monoplanes, made entirely from stressed metal. And the size of them! It was still a wonder to Tanner that those beasts were able to leave the ground at all.

So perhaps that was what it was, Tanner thought. Sandvold had invented something that could be used as an earth-shattering weapon, one that would change the course of the war. And if that was the case, the sooner Britain got to use it the better, because here in Norway the Army was getting a pasting.

He lay back against his pack. The inside of the barn was much like any other, with its ageing beams, grain on the wooden floor, dust and distinctive smell. He closed his eyes, sighed, and thought of home and his childhood. They'd used to climb along the joists, he and the other lads on the estate; and once they were given a hiding for doing so. He could remember the sting of Mr Gulliver's belt even now.

Jack Tanner was dreaming, sleep a luxurious release, and then, all too quickly, he was being shaken. Voices. For a moment he was completely disoriented; he had forgotten where he was. Opening his eyes, sleep seeping away, he saw Sykes and next to him a young woman – a pretty girl with an oval face, pale eyes, dark eyebrows and straw-coloured hair.

'Sorry,' said Tanner, 'I must have fallen asleep.' He sat up, then checked that his rifle and haversack were still there. Suddenly aware that the girl had followed his gaze, he smiled sheepishly and said, 'An old habit.'

'This is Miss Rostad, Sarge,' said Sykes. 'She and 'er mother 'ave brought us some food an' water.'

'It's not much, I'm afraid, Sergeant,' she said, in fluent English, 'but until the chickens are cooked . . .' She passed him a bowl of soup and a piece of bread.

'Thank you,' said Tanner. The warm meaty stock soothed his throat. It tasted just about as good as anything he had ever eaten.

'It's about the wounded men,' she continued. 'My mother and I have done what we can, but I'm afraid that's very little. We have some first-aid equipment up here but not much. We've cleaned their wounds but they could easily become infected.'

'The bullet went clean through the Frenchie's thigh,' added Sykes, 'and through Sax's shoulder, but it's stuck somewhere inside poor old Riggsy.'

'How are they now?' asked Tanner.

'Asleep,' said Anna. 'We gave them some brandy. But they need a doctor.'

'In the valley,' said Tanner.

Anna nodded. 'We could take them down tomorrow, my father and I. We could put them in the cart.'

'I told her it's too risky,' said Sykes.

Tanner thought for a moment. 'Where would you take them? Tretten?'

'Yes. There's a doctor there.'

'The Germans would have surgeons too. You'd be questioned. What would you say?'

'That we found them. What else would the Germans expect us to do? If they stay here, they will probably die. If we take them into Tretten they at least have a chance.'

Tanner smiled. 'You're very brave – for what you've just said and for letting us stay here. And thank you – it's not right, involving civilians in such things. We soldiers, well, that's different. We're paid to go off and fight.'

Anna shrugged. 'I can't just watch the Germans swarm over our country and do nothing. Anyway, you have come to help us. It's the least we can do.' She looked at him wistfully. 'My brother, Jonny, is fighting somewhere. He was called up two weeks ago, so off he went to Lillehammer. We had a telegram from him in Narvik, but we have heard nothing since. He is my twin. I think he is

194

still alive but I cannot say for sure.' She wiped the corner of her eye. 'Really, it is too terrible.' She stood up.

Tanner grabbed his rifle and pushed himself up to his feet. 'Where are Larsen and Chevannes?' he asked Sykes.

'I think they're in the farmhouse,' Sykes replied.

'They are,' said Anna. 'They're talking with Father. I will take you to them.'

Anna led him out of the barn, across the yard and into the house. The three men were in the kitchen. It was getting dark and the shutters had been closed. An open fire, raised on a brick hearth, burnt gently in the corner of the room; to the side stood a bread oven and a blackened range. Soft pinewood smoke suffused the place, mingling with the smell of damp dog hair and tobacco. At the foot of the range lay two grey-muzzled canines, their coats drying slowly in the warmth. A large table stood in the centre of the room; Larsen, Chevannes and Anna's father were sitting round it. A lamp in the centre of the table flickered gently, lighting the men's faces.

'What do you want, Sergeant?' said Chevannes.

'To talk to you about what we're going to do,' Tanner replied.

'You're not an officer. It's up to us to make such plans and for you to carry out our orders. When we have decided what those are, we will tell you, as we will the others. Was there anything else?'

Tanner's expression was one of unconcealed anger. 'You might be the officer in charge here, sir,' he retorted, 'but I still have ten men to look after. That gives me a right to know what you're proposing, damn it.'

Larsen looked at Chevannes. 'He has a point.'

Chevannes sighed. 'You may stay and listen, Sergeant, but our decisions will be final. Understood?'

Anna's mother came into the kitchen. She looked much like her daughter, but older. Her eyes darted from one man to another, then she placed some more wood on the fire and glanced at the two chickens cooking in the range. The smell of hot fat wafted across the room. As she stood up again, Tanner could see the fear in her eyes. *But of course she's frightened*, he thought.

Larsen spread his map on the table and Erik Rostad pointed to where they now were. He spoke quietly with Larsen, as his wife put two bottles of beer on the table and brought over four glasses.

'There are mountain tracks that run along the valley,' Larsen explained to Chevannes and Tanner. 'It is not unusual to have snow still on the ground at this time of year although it has usually stopped falling by now. The snowfall of last night was not typical. Summer comes quickly here. In a week the snow could be gone from the valley, although not on the mountains.'

'We have to chance it and head north along here,' said Chevannes pointing to the map.

'We need roads,' said Tanner, 'a vehicle of some kind. If we try to walk it we'll never make it.'

'We nearly made it today,' said Larsen.

'But we didn't, did we? And we only had to cover six or seven miles. I've no idea how far the Allies have fallen back, but it's got to be some distance. At least to here – Fåvang – and that's, what? A dozen miles. Twenty kilometres. In any case, Brigade's lost so many men and we're so short of guns and M/T that there would be little point in making another stand just a few miles down the road. Those generals might want their heads examining but even they're not that stupid. But whatever distance they've retreated, we'll never be able to walk faster through the mountains than Jerry can through the valley. And he's got increasing amounts of M/T as well as horses.' There was silence for a moment. Tanner leant over the table. 'Here,' he said, 'what about this road? Look – it goes from Tretten, cuts over the mountains into this valley here. Jerry's not going to go down there because it's this valley that's the axis of his advance. If we can get over there and find ourselves some transport, we could overtake them. We could maybe get all the way to here – Otta – without seeing any Germans at all.'

Chevannes shook his head. 'Brilliant, Sergeant,' he said, smirking at the others, 'and just how do you think we can get past the Germans in the valley and across a three-hundred-metre-wide lake? And where exactly will we find a vehicle that will take us all?'

'We don't cross the lake. We cross at Tretten where the river is much narrower.'

'And the fact that the village will be full of Germans does not worry you?'

'We go at night, when it's dark. There's no moon tomorrow. Anyway, we've got German uniforms now. Of course it's a risk, but if we do as you suggest, we have no chance at all.'

'It's a preposterous idea.'

'There is a place you could cross,' said Anna. All eyes turned to her. 'Just north of the village, a few hundred metres before the bridge. There is a small spur that juts out into the river. The crossing is only about a hundred and fifty metres wide at that point and there is a wooden jetty. On the bank are several small row-boats.'

Good girl, thought Tanner. 'In any case,' he added, 'there's no reason why Tretten will be full of Germans. Some, maybe, but most will already have headed north.'

Anna spoke hurriedly to her father, who nodded. Then Larsen spoke to her in Norwegian. For a minute an argument ensued between Larsen, Anna and her father: Larsen, firm and emphatic, Anna increasingly animated and irate.

At length Chevannes said, 'What are you talking about?'

'She wants to come with us,' said Larsen. 'I told her it is out of the question.'

'But I know those mountains. I know the Jøra valley. My brother and I hiked all over the Oppland mountains last summer.' She looked imploringly at Chevannes, then Tanner. 'Please,' she said. 'I want to help.'

'What we have to do is far too dangerous for a woman,' said Chevannes, 'and especially for a pretty girl like yourself, Mademoiselle.'

Tanner groaned to himself, then said, 'But there's no doubting she'd be a great help. Listen to what she said. She knows these mountains – none of the rest of us do. Second, the fact that she's a woman might be an asset. The Germans would be less likely to suspect her.'

'And I speak German,' she added.

'Sir, please, listen to her,' said Tanner.

'She'll slow us down,' said Chevannes.

'I will not,' said Anna, defiant now.

Her mother spoke to her, but her father interjected angrily.

'Her father says she is twenty-two,' Larsen translated, 'and old enough to know her own mind. He also says he is proud of his daughter for wanting to help in the battle against these Nazi thugs.'

Chevannes sat quietly for a few moments, stroking his chin thoughtfully.

'Sir?' said Tanner.

The Frenchman picked up his dark blue beret, which had been on the table in front of him, and felt with his finger round the badge. 'I want to think about it. I am not at all convinced that we should even try to cross the valley, regardless of what you say, Sergeant. In any case, are you proposing that we stay here until tomorrow night?'

'If possible, yes. We might have to move elsewhere, but not too far from here. I don't see that we have any choice.'

'There is a cave in the forest above the farm,' said Anna. 'It is a secret place. We could show you in the morning.'

'And we need to move the wounded,' added Tanner. 'Anna and her father are proposing to take them in their cart to Tretten.'

'And hand them over to the enemy?' said Chevannes. He seemed appalled by the suggestion.

'They will die if they stay here,' said Anna. 'They need proper attention.'

'Sir?' said Tanner, again. Chevannes picked at his lip.

Come on, damn you, thought Tanner. *Make a decision.* 'Sir,' he said again, 'we need to make a plan.'

'Be quiet, Tanner!' Chevannes snapped. '*Mon dieu*, I need to think. Stop rushing me.'

'But what about the wounded?' Tanner insisted. 'You're the commander here. Mr Rostad and his daughter are willing to risk their lives to save them. Tell them what you want them to do.' He looked at the lieutenant with barely concealed contempt.

'Steady, Sergeant Tanner,' said Larsen. 'We are all exhausted.'

'Yes, we are,' snarled Tanner, 'but it's a simple enough decision.'

'All right, all right, damn you!' Chevannes ran his hands through his hair. 'Take the wounded men. In the morning.' He smiled weakly at Anna and her father, then said, 'Thank you, Mademoiselle, Monsieur.'

Larsen placed his hands flat on the table and said, 'Well, gentlemen, Miss, I think we should get some sleep now. The situation may seem simpler when we have rested.' He stood up and bade the family good night. Without a further word, Chevannes and Tanner followed him outside into the darkness.

The air was sharp and cold after the warmth of the kitchen. The sliver of moon was hidden behind the mountains, but despite the dark, Tanner could sense the looming immensity of their surroundings. Such a vast place. He looked towards the valley, a black cavity in front of him, and thought of the enemy below and the net they were casting inexorably over this land. *Christ*, he thought, *what chance have we got?* The responsibility, the huge barriers facing him at every turn, suddenly seemed too much. He wondered what the next day would bring, then chastised himself. *Don't think*, he told himself. *Sleep*.

10

Tanner had spent long enough in the Army to be able to sleep anywhere so, despite having only a thin layer of straw between him and the floor, he slept like the dead. When he awoke, it was nearly six in the morning. He blinked and scratched. *Lice*, he thought, or was it fleas from the barn? He hadn't washed properly since he'd arrived in Norway six days before. Six days! Not even a week. It felt like eternity.

He sat up and looked round the barn. Shafts of light shone through gaps in the roof, where suspended dust particles curled. One of the doors was also ajar, revealing a bright sliver of deep blue already bathed in sunshine. Gentle and not so gentle snores rose from some of the men, all of whom seemed to be still fast asleep. Next to him Sykes was sleeping peacefully, a contented smile on his face. Tanner grinned to himself.

It was only then that he noticed the wounded men were no longer there; neither was Lieutenant Larsen. Grabbing his rifle, he quietly left the barn, went out into the yard and crossed to the farmhouse. Anna and her mother were there, as was Larsen, drinking coffee. The smell of fresh bread and chicken filled the room.

'Good morning, Sergeant,' said Anna. 'You slept well?'

'Too well, thanks, Miss. Where are the wounded men?'

'We moved them in the night,' said Anna. 'They were in too much pain and crying out.'

'They were keeping some of the men awake,' added Larsen. 'I felt the first priority was to make sure the fit and healthy stayed that way.'

'Christ, I didn't hear a thing. And how are they now?'

'We gave them more brandy. Riggs is not good, though.'

Anna's mother passed him some bread and chicken and gave him a mug of coffee. *Ah, that's good*, he thought. How could something so simple taste so delicious? Sleep and food had made him feel a different man; his mind was clear and his limbs no longer ached.

'We need to post guards,' he said to Larsen, and then to Anna, 'When will you take the wounded into Tretten?'

'My father is tending the animals. Then we will go.'

'I'll come with you some of the way,' said Tanner, suddenly. He'd not thought of it before, but it now occurred to him that reconnaissance, however crude, would greatly improve their chances of success.

'Isn't that an unnecessary risk?' asked Larsen.

'We need someone to recce Tretten,' Tanner replied. He pushed back his chair, stood up, and took his rifle. 'Thank you for breakfast. I'll be outside. Call me when you want help with the wounded.'

Outside, the air seemed so still, and across the valley, the morning sun shone gold, casting long blue shadows over the mountains beyond. Behind him he could already hear melting snow dripping from the pines.

His mind was whirring now, thinking of the many possible scenarios that could unfold that day. They were now down to seventeen men, still a cumbersome number. He wondered whether Zellner and his men had escaped, whether Luftwaffe reconnaissance planes would spot them, if and when more German troops would be sent to search for them. And he wondered how he could best manage Chevannes. He was conscious that he had perhaps antagonized him too much the previous night, yet despite that he still felt certain that his plan to cross the valley was the right one. Getting back to the Allies would not be easy – far from it – and he knew their chance of success was slight. Even so, they had to give themselves the best possible opportunity. For Tanner it was a simple equation: if they continued north, they would fail; if they crossed the valley, they had a sliver of a chance. He had to persuade Chevannes of that.

He had let his men rest, mindful that they had endured much since their arrival in Norway, but now, at nearly half past six, it was time for them to be up and alert. Guards should be posted, weapons cleaned. Stomachs needed to be filled and the plan of action explained. Damn it, he thought, it must be made and agreed upon. He hurried back towards the barn as Larsen emerged from the house.

'Sergeant,' Larsen called to him.

'Are they ready to take the wounded now?' Tanner asked, walking over to meet him.

'Very soon, yes.'

'Have you seen Lieutenant Chevannes? Is he up?'

'Not yet.'

'Well, he should be. He's got fifteen men to command and one civilian to look after.'

Larsen offered Tanner a German cigarette, which the sergeant accepted. 'You know,' said Larsen, as he struck a match, 'you should try to patch things up with Chevannes.'

The comment surprised him. 'Have you, sir?' he replied, then immediately regretted it. He had sounded churlish, he knew.

'After yesterday, you mean? I don't blame him for that. I would probably have responded in the same way, had I been in his position. He had no personal reason to think ill of that German.'

'With respect, sir, his judgement is terrible. He makes bad decisions and he undermines my authority with my men.'

Larsen smiled. 'He is a proud man. He feels threatened by you – by your greater experience. None of us is very experienced in war. We are not experienced at all. No doubt he did well at St Cyr, but as we are all finding out, what is taught in peacetime bears little relation to what we discover in war. We are not warned, for example, about the sometimes very difficult decisions we are forced to make. Decisions that affect lives. Is it, I wonder, better that we save one life even though that might cause us to lose another?'

'That's the nature of command, sir,' said Tanner. 'Those difficult choices are part of the deal. We should have left the *seter* two nights ago when it stopped snowing. If we had we would be with the Allies by now.'

'And quite possibly prisoners-of-war.'

'But not Sandvold. He would have been whisked away to safety.' Tanner sighed. 'I know what I promised Gulbrand, and I'm sticking to that – not from a warped sense of honour but because of what he told me about the professor. If Sandvold is as important as the colonel made out, I have a duty – we all do – to see him safe. Then I have a duty to my men. If I keep quiet, Chevannes will lead us to disaster.'

'How can you be so sure? What if he's right? What if we head north instead?'

Tanner shook his head. 'Why are you saying this, sir?'

'Because I am not sure I know what to do.'

'Listen, sir, there's no road this side – other than that in the valley – for more than twenty miles and that leads away from the coast. Then there is nothing for a further fifty miles or more. Think about our progress these past days. We have neither the time nor the strength to catch up with the Allies. Our only chance is by finding transport and using roads as much as we possibly can. That means we have to cross the valley.'

'Yes,' said Larsen. 'You are probably right. But it feels as though we are heading into the lion's den, and I have my duty too: to the King and the mission he entrusted to us. Sandvold cannot be taken by the enemy.'

'He won't be,' said Tanner grimly. 'I won't let that happen.' He flicked away his cigarette. 'Perhaps, sir, you should talk to Chevannes. He's more likely to listen to you than me. And it would be useful to have Anna Rostad with us too. It's about survival, not about honour and decorum.'

Larsen smiled. 'All right, Sergeant. Yes, I will do that.'

Tanner nodded, then turned towards the barn.

'And, Sergeant?'

Tanner stopped.

'I am glad we have had this talk.'

'Me too, sir,' said Tanner. But now, he thought, it was time to stop worrying about people's feelings and get on with the bloody mission.

That morning, Tanner and Lieutenant Chevannes avoided each other as far as possible. Certainly there was no need for Tanner further to argue his case because, with the men roused, Chevannes stood at the entrance to the barn and outlined the plan exactly as he and Anna Rostad had suggested the previous evening. 'After careful thought,' he told them, 'I have devised a plan that I believe gives us the best chance of success.' They would be crossing the valley that night, he announced, and they were to spend the day resting and getting ready for the continuation of their mission. The three wounded men were to be taken into Tretten, he told them. 'It means they will become prisoners,' he added solemnly, 'but they will also have a chance to live.' Neither did Chevannes object to Tanner's suggestion that he accompany Anna and Erik Rostad part of the way.

'He's hoping you'll get caught, Sarge,' said Sykes.

Tanner grinned. 'You might be right, Stan.'

First, however, Anna Rostad would lead them to the cave, in the woods above the farm, where they would lie up until evening. It proved to be ideal, no more than a quarter of a mile from the farm, approached first through bare grey grassland, then through dense pine forest where there were only patchy drifts of snow, enabling them to reach it without leaving a trail of footprints. The entrance to the cave was further hidden by a jutting rockface.

Tanner left Sykes in charge of the men and his own packs. 'You know the drill, Stan,' he told him. 'And don't let Sandvold out of your sight.' He hoped he would not be seen, but had left his jerkin and tin helmet behind, instead taking the German wind jacket and field cap.

It was an old, creaking cart, led by a plodding mule. Erik Rostad sat up front with his daughter, his foot resting on the flimsy brake pedal, as they stuttered down the track. Saxby was awake and, sitting in the back with the three men, Tanner saw him contort with pain at every jolting stone the cart passed over. 'All right, Sax,' said Tanner. 'Not long now.'

'I don't want to die,' Saxby mumbled. 'I don't want the Jerries to kill me.'

'They won't. They'll look after you. Make you better.' Tanner watched tears run down his face. 'You've got to be strong,' he told him. 'You're a fighter, I know you are. Be brave and you'll get through this. One day you can go home.' He knew he sounded trite. He was sending them to the Germans in the hope that the enemy would show compassion but, really, he had no idea whether they would or not. *Hell*, he thought, and moved away from Saxby's misery to draw alongside Anna and her father. 'Thank you for doing this,' he said.

'I only wish we could have looked after them ourselves,' said Anna. 'I'm training to be a doctor, so I feel bad that I cannot help more.'

'Where are you training, Miss?'

'In Oslo. Or, rather, I was. The war has interrupted my studies. I'm afraid I've rather a long way to go, but in any case, I don't have the equipment or medicines to help these men.' She tucked a loose strand of hair behind her ear, then glanced at Tanner, a wistful expression – and framed by such a lovely face, he thought. It was madness, but he wished he could hold her and tell her all would be well: that her brother Jonny would come home, that the Germans would go away and that one day she would be a doctor. For the first time since the war had broken out, he began to realize what a terrible thing it must be for the Norwegians. He tried to imagine how he would feel if there were Germans swarming across England. It was incomprehensible.

'I'm sorry, Miss,' he said. 'It must be a very difficult time for you.'

'Yes – yes, it is. One minute I feel overcome with grief, for Norway, for me, for Jonny; the next just very angry. It's one of the reasons I want to come with you. I don't want to sit at home feeling sorry for myself and wondering what will become of us all. I want to *do* something.'

'I had a word with Lieutenant Larsen this morning, Miss,' he told her. 'He said he would speak to Lieutenant Chevannes again.' For a brief moment, he held her gaze. *Those eyes*, he thought. 'And for what it's worth,' he added, 'I think you'd be a great help to us.'

She smiled. 'Thank you for saying that.'

Tanner stayed with the cart until they had the first

glimpse of the valley road below. Pasture and forest jostled for space along the lower slopes of the valley, but by weaving his way and keeping within the treeline, Tanner was confident he could remain hidden.

'You won't have to go far along here,' Anna told him. 'You'll soon see Tretten below you.'

Tanner thanked her and wished them luck, then paused to take Saxby's hand. The lad was only nineteen. 'You'll be all right,' Tanner told him. Saxby looked at him, with resentment, deep sadness and resignation, then turned his head away. The cart trundled on, and as Tanner watched it rumble down the track, doubt and guilt flooded over him.

The telephone in his hotel room rang shrilly, shattering the silence in which Reichsamtsleiter Scheidt had been lying for the past three hours. It was Kurz, asking him to come over right away. Scheidt's spirits soared – *at last!* – but then as he replaced the receiver he realized there had been little euphoria in Kurz's voice, and pessimism filled him instead.

He looked at his watch. Seven forty, getting on for twelve hours since news had arrived that Zellner's men had come under attack. Yet there had been good news too: the mountain troops were closing in on Odin, and his capture would surely follow soon.

Scheidt had waited, on tenterhooks, ever since, but the call had never come. It had been a long night of little sleep. A night of too many cigarettes, a half-bottle of brandy, and too much time in the armchair by the window staring out at the cold starry night. With impatient fingers, he put on his NSDAP jacket and cap once more, his long cavalry boots and black breeches. *What could possibly have gone wrong?* He left the room, door slamming behind him, hurried through the hotel out into the crisp sunshine and almost ran to Kurz's office.

The SS major looked up as Scheidt entered, his face grave.

'Good morning,' he said, stubbing out a cigarette in a green marble ashtray. 'We need to go to Tretten. Come on, I've got the car outside.'

'They haven't found Odin?'

'Worse,' said Kurz, brushing past him and heading for the front door.

In the car – a requisitioned black Citroën from Oslo – Kurz gave him the bad news. Hauptmann Zellner and just eight of his men had reached von Poncets' new headquarters in Tretten a short while ago. Stripped to their shirts, underclothes and trousers, mostly wearing British Army boots, they had stumbled into the station house in a terrible state.

'Needless to say,' added Kurz, 'they did not bring Odin.'

For a few moments, Scheidt was unable to speak. He thought of the confidence of von Poncets the day before, the square-jawed youthfulness and apparent professionalism of Hauptmann Zellner. It was impossible to think that a platoon of mountain troops – supposedly élite troops – had failed so spectacularly.

'However,' said Kurz at length, 'Engelbrecht's boys did take Tretten and the bulk of von Poncets' troops performed admirably. The British were crushed yesterday.'

'I don't give a damn about that,' snapped Scheidt. 'As far as I'm concerned they should damn well forget about the rest of the war until Odin has been captured. And no contact?'

Kurz shook his head. 'Not yet, but we'll hear something today, I'm sure.'

'Where the hell are they now?' Scheidt muttered, to himself more than to Kurz.

'I've asked the Luftwaffe for more air reconnaissance.'

'What would you do, Kurz, if you'd seen off your pursuers?'

'I'd try to make as much ground as possible, especially now that the snow's melting.'

'Not on the mountains, it's not.' Scheidt drummed a fist against his leg. 'We have to find him, Kurz. We *have* to find him.'

Tretten was a hive of activity. A small place, like so many of the valley settlements, it now heaved with troops, most of whom, however, were loading up into carts, wagons, trucks and armoured vehicles ready for the advance up the Gudbrandsdal valley. A short way off the road, above the village, Scheidt watched a burial party lining up bodies of German dead in a grey-looking field. By the side of the road the legs of two dead horses pointed stiffly skywards. A burnt-out truck, stripped and skeletal, lay turned over in a ditch, while opposite, a column of dishevelled British and Norwegian prisoners were being ushered into trucks. Kurz drove slowly, weaving through the bottleneck of troops and vehicles, passing bombed-out houses, piles of rubble and charred timber. Even in the close confines of the Citroën, the smell of a recently fought battle was pervasive.

Eventually Kurz turned off the road and down to the station. Two guards presented arms as they entered the building. Inside, clerks and staff officers were busy organizing the next German thrust down the valley. Phones rang, typewriters clattered. Scheidt and Kurz were led upstairs to see Major von Poncets, who greeted them with the affability he had shown the previous day.

'Congratulations, Herr Major,' said Scheidt. 'Another easy victory, just as you predicted.'

'More costly than I'd hoped, but thank you,' he replied. 'And I'm sorry I don't have better news for you regarding Odin. Those men the Norwegians are with clearly have more steel than we had appreciated.'

'Where is Hauptmann Zellner?' asked Scheidt.

'He'll be here any moment. I sent him to get a new uniform.'

'And what now?' asked Scheidt. 'When will you mount another search?'

Von Poncets smiled, and offered both men a cigar, which Kurz accepted and Scheidt declined. 'The Tommies have fallen back a long way, it seems. Our recce boys have been flying up and down the valley since first light and there's little sign of them. It's one thing advancing a few kilometres, but to shift our entire forces any distance takes time. We're moving most of our men out today—'

'So we saw,' said Kurz.

'Yes, well, most will be gone by this evening. Nearly all the men you saw were from the four battalions of the

213

324th and 345th Infantry Regiments, but there is also Artillery Regiment 223 to move, a further machine-gun battalion, a number of panzers and, of course, my own men. Then there are all the accompanying equipment, ammunition, rations and so on, which must be in place before we can attack again. It's easy for the defenders to cover ground quickly because they only take what they can. We have to be better prepared. So.' He clapped his hands together. 'What am I trying to say to you? I'm saying we have something of a respite on our hands.'

'Which means you have time to find Odin?' asked Scheidt.

'Yes, I think so,' smiled von Poncets. 'I'm going to give one of my own companies this particular task. I'm sorry – I thought a platoon would be more than enough. I was wrong.'

'An under-strength platoon,' added Scheidt. 'There was a group missing, if you remember.'

'Yes, well, we won't make that mistake again.'

There was a knock on the door. 'Come,' called out the Major. Zellner entered, freshly shaved and wearing a new uniform. 'Much better, Hauptmann, much better,' said von Poncets, cheerfully.

Zellner saluted. His right eye was swollen and blackened and, Scheidt noticed, much of the swagger of the day before had gone. Zellner began quickly, 'I would like to say, Herr Reichsamtsleiter and Herr Sturmbann-führer, that I apologize unreservedly for failing in my duty yesterday. I underestimated the strength of the enemy and allowed Odin to slip through my grasp, a gross dereliction on my part.'

Scheidt raised a hand to silence him. 'All right, Hauptmann. Now tell me who was there.'

Zellner did so. Yes, he had seen a middle-aged man with spectacles and a moustache. There were two other Norwegians, a few French mountain troops and the rest were British. A French officer seemed to be in charge. 'He's weak, though,' Zellner told them. 'He questioned me and his interrogation was pathetic. Furthermore, he did it in full view of Odin.'

'You told him nothing?' asked Kurz.

'Of course not. He wouldn't touch me – a fellow officer. He's too concerned with behaving honourably.'

'You don't believe in honour?' asked Kurz.

'Only my own, that of my regiment and of Germany. There was a British sergeant there who would have had us killed, I think. The Frenchman – Chevannes is his name – was horrified.'

'So if they are led by this man, how did they defeat you?' Kurz asked.

Zellner bristled. 'The sergeant is good. His name is Tanner. Chevannes does not like him, but he's a clever soldier. He also has a sniper rifle with sights. It was how he ambushed us first. And he has explosives.'

'A good right hook too?' Von Poncets grinned.

Zellner looked down, embarrassed. He regretted having admitted to the major that he had been knocked out cold by the British sergeant. 'Yes, sir.'

'How old is this man?' asked Kurz.

'Young – in his twenties. My age, probably.'

'So, not in the last war.'

'No, quite definitely not. But he has been decorated –

I saw a ribbon on his tunic. I only saw it briefly, but it was striped, blue, white and red.'

'The Military Medal,' said Kurz. 'A gallantry award for men in the ranks.' He turned to von Poncets and Scheidt. 'We've had Poland in which to hone our battle skills, but the British have had their empire. Colonial skirmishes.' He grinned.

'It appears to have done them little good,' said von Poncets. 'Perhaps they were expecting us to attack with spears.' At that even Zellner managed to smile.

'Is there anything else we should know?' Scheidt asked the Hauptmann.

'Two of their men were killed and three wounded. Naturally I made a note of their strength. They are now sixteen strong, not including Odin.'

'Very good, Zellner, you may rejoin your men,' said von Poncets.

'Sir?' said Zellner. Von Poncets looked up. 'Sir, I would like your permission to stay here and help find Odin.'

'Thank you, Hauptmann,' the major replied, 'but that won't be necessary.'

'Wait,' said Scheidt. 'There is logic in continuing to use Hauptmann Zellner and his men, Herr Major. His knowledge of the enemy would be useful, surely.'

Von Poncets drew on his cigar and nodded slowly. 'Very well. Zellner, you may continue the hunt for Odin.'

Zellner thanked them. 'I vowed I would kill Sergeant Tanner, and I will,' he explained. 'And I will also bring you Odin. You have my word.'

'That's enough, Hauptmann,' said von Poncets. 'You've made your position clear.'

'Hauptmann,' added Scheidt, 'I don't care about your personal vendettas, but I cannot stress enough the importance of finding Odin – alive.'

Zellner saluted again and left them.

Zellner walked back towards the village and the troop dressing station where he had left his men. His interview with the *Reichsamtsleiter* and SD *Sturmbannführer* had gone well, he supposed, but the shame of losing so many men and of failing in his mission was hard to bear. Anger and frustration hung over him like a dead weight. *Tanner*, he thought. If it hadn't been for that Tommy sergeant it would have been so different. He had not realized it was possible to hate a man so intensely.

At the dressing station, he moved uneasily through the rows of men. Some were on stretchers, swathed in bloodied bandages, others sitting or squatting on the ground. The air in the tent was putrid. Men groaned and cried out. He spotted three men lying side by side, two Tommies and a Frenchman. He paused beside them, his mind suddenly alert. He peered down at the British men. There was the shoulder tab, 'Yorks Rangers,' on their uniforms. It was the same as he had seen on the men on the mountain. How had they got there? He leant over them. One of the Tommies, wounded in the head and shoulder, was unconscious. The Frenchman, he could see, was dead; he had the blue-grey waxy complexion that he had already learnt to recognize as the mask of death. But the third was awake, his head tilted to one side, staring towards the tent's entrance. Zellner leant closer to him and the Tommy's eyes widened in recognition.

'You!' Zellner said, grabbing the young man's collar. 'Where are they? How did you get here?'

The Tommy looked at him, fear in his eyes, muttering in English.

'Tell me!' shouted Zellner, shaking him. 'Tell me where they are!' Bitter rage consumed him now. 'Speak!' said Zellner in English. 'Where is Tanner?' The Englishman mouthed something, words Zellner could not hear. 'What?' He shook him again. 'What are you saying? Tell me!' Frothy blood appeared from the Tommy's mouth then his eyes became fixed. A faint gasp and a last exhalation came from his mouth. Zellner dropped the lifeless body back on to the stretcher, then raced towards two medics bringing in another stretcher. 'Where did those men come from?' he demanded. 'Those three – the Frenchman and the two Tommies? Who brought them here?' But the medics did not know. No one did.

A hand on his shoulder. Zellner turned and saw a major surgeon standing in front of him. 'That's enough, Hauptmann,' he said. 'We don't concern ourselves with how the wounded get here. Our job is to deal with them as best we can. Now, please, stop making a scene, and let us get on with our job. We have lives to save.'

Chastened, Zellner scowled and left the tent. He wondered what else could go wrong. No British Tommy was going to make a fool of him. Consumed with thoughts of revenge, he stumbled off in search of his men.

11

Not until the afternoon did Tanner return to the safety of
the cave above the Rostad's farmstead, by which time
Anna and her father were safely at home. He had learnt
much, and reported his findings to Lieutenant
Chevannes and the two Norwegian officers. As he had
hoped, Tretten was now far quieter than it had been.
Soldiers had been leaving all day and continued to do so.
A half battalion of mountain troops was still in the village,
as was a tented field dressing station, but a number of the
wounded had already been loaded on to a train south.
The upturned boats that Anna had mentioned were
down by the jetty – the bank jutted out into the river and
there was a shingle beach where they lay. He also
suggested an approach route that would enable them to
stay within the cover of the trees almost to the riverbank.
The only open ground was the last seventy-five yards
across the road to the water's edge.

Chevannes dismissed him without a word, so he went
to find Sykes and the others, who were sitting in a corner

of the cave. Hepworth and Kershaw were on guard duty, McAllister and Erwood asleep, while the corporal, Moran, Bell and Chambers, were playing poker.

Sykes put down his cards when he saw Tanner. 'I've lost a fortune, Sarge.' He grinned. 'IOUs. Mac's cleaning up.'

'I've got to think of my future, Sarge,' said McAllister. 'I see it as a kind of nest-egg for when the war's over. At this rate I reckon I'll be able to move to a big house in Harrogate when I get back.'

Tanner lit two German cigarettes from one of the orange Niderehe packets he had taken from the prisoners the day before, and passed it to Sykes.

'Cheers, Sarge.'

'It's a bit rough, but it's tobacco, isn't it? Better than nothing.'

'Too bloody right.' Sykes inhaled deeply, then said, 'Are we going to be all right, then?'

Tanner nodded. 'It's not going to be much fun crossing the river, but if we hold our nerve . . .'

'Course.' They smoked in silence for a moment, then Sykes said, 'We've been having a gander at some of that Jerry kit. Here.' He picked up a rifle and passed it to Tanner.

Tanner gripped it, weighing it in his hands. 'About the same weight as the SMLE. Eight pounds or so.'

'That's what we thought,' said Sykes.

Tanner lifted it to his shoulder, aimed, then pulled back the bolt. 'Oi, oi,' he said. 'Don't like this much.' He whistled. 'Bloody hell, it comes back a long way, doesn't it? How are you supposed to keep your aim with that bloody great thing knocking your cheek every time?'

'You couldn't fire thirty rounds a minute with it, could you?'

'Not accurately, that's for sure.' He tried a sequence of five blank shots, then passed it back to Sykes. 'I reckon if you fired fifteen properly aimed shots a minute you'd be doing well. I'd rather have my old No.1 Enfield any day. What about the shells?'

'Fractionally larger. Almost nothing in it.'

'But enough. We'd better make sure no one mixes this ammo up.'

'Don't worry, I've warned everyone already. What's the pistol like?'

Tanner took it out of its holster and passed it to him. 'See for yourself. I don't really feel that comfortable with pistols, but useful for clearing a room, I suppose.'

'Close-quarters stuff.'

'Exactly.' Tanner watched as Sykes loaded and unloaded the magazine, cocked and uncocked the pistol, then examined the safety catch. Not far away, the others continued to play cards and sleep. All the Rangers were on the same side of the cave, he noticed, while the French and Norwegians were on the other. There was, he recognized, a cohesion to his men, even though the patrol had originally been brought together by combining two different parts of the platoon. It was strange, he thought, how attached to them he now felt. After all, his background was so completely different; really, he knew very little about any of them, or they about him. They had nothing in common as far as he knew – except shared nationality and the experience of being stuck together, but clearly that was enough.

He hoped he had made the right decision to cross the valley, hoped he wasn't wasting these men's lives. They trusted him, he knew, and trust was so important – but was it justified? Was he leading them to capture – death? Just a few years ago most of them would have been young boys scampering around the backstreets of Leeds, playing football, getting into trouble and bunking off school. Now they were sitting in a damp cave on a mountain in Norway, deep behind enemy lines on a mission of critical importance. *Jesus*, he thought. *How did we all get into this bloody mess?* He looked at Sykes again, still fiddling with the pistol. He barely even knew his corporal, a man he considered in many ways a friend.

'I've been meaning to ask,' he said at length, to Sykes, 'where did you learn how to handle explosives like that? You set that booby trap like an expert.'

'In the Army, of course.'

'In your basic infantry training? Pull the other one.'

'We did a bit of training with grenades. Even live ones.'

'But not handling gelignite.' He stared at Sykes, who smiled sheepishly. 'Come on, Stan. Spit it out.'

Sykes glanced around to check no one else was listening, then leant forward. 'I, um – before I joined the Army – well, I was . . . I got in with a few bad 'uns and, well, I used to rob stuff.'

Tanner raised an eyebrow. *Go on*.

Sykes sighed, took out his tobacco and began rolling a cigarette. 'Yes, you know, houses, offices – I could crack most safes, but they didn't always have combination locks, you see. So that's when I learnt how to use explosives.'

'Christ, Stan,' said Tanner.

'I'm not proud of it. I was the oldest of six kids, my dad was bloody useless – liked the sauce too much – and we needed the money. I'm not excusing it or anything, but when you're doing offices and banks and so on, you persuade yourself they can afford it.'

'When did you join the Army?'

'We was doin' an office in Islington, and we got caught in the act, and before we knew what was going on there was police everywhere. One of the lads pulled out a gun. He didn't hit anyone but it made me think things had gone far enough. Anyway, he was caught but me and the other two got away. I decided there and then that my criminal days was over. I sent my mother all the money I'd saved up and told her I had to leave town for a while and not to try to get in touch. I got on a train to Leeds and joined the Army. That was October 1938. And here I am.'

'And what about the one with the gun?'

'He got banged up but he never said nothing, so I was all right. And I haven't stolen anything since then – except what I nicked from that dump in Lillehammer.' He looked at Tanner. 'I'm not proud of myself, but I did start it with good intentions. You won't say anything, though, will you, Sarge? Not even to the other lads?'

'Course not. You're a good corporal, Stan. I don't care what you did before the war – that's your affair and for your conscience to deal with. It's what happens now that matters.' He paused. 'Anyway, I'm in no position to judge. My past isn't exactly whiter than white.'

They were silent for a moment, Tanner cursing himself for revealing even that, but then Sykes said, 'How come you ended up in the Rangers, Sarge? Where did you say you were from again?'

'Wiltshire,' said Tanner. 'In the south-west.' He was quiet again, toying in his mind with how much to tell the corporal, if anything. Sykes might have been glad to get his past off his chest, but Tanner felt no such compunction. 'My mother died when I was a baby,' he said. He spoke slowly, softly. 'My father was a gamekeeper on an estate.'

'So that's where you learnt to shoot.'

Tanner smiled. 'I reckon I had a rifle in my hands from the age of about five.' There had not been much schooling: his education had been out of doors, accompanying his father, learning about the countryside. He wouldn't have had it any other way.

'So why did you join the Army?'

Tanner looked away. 'My father died. There were . . . complications.' He picked up the German rifle again, pretending to examine it once more. 'I left home and joined the Army as a boy soldier. Straight out to India with the 2nd Battalion.'

'And you saw action out there?'

'A bit.'

Sykes nodded thoughtfully. 'So we're both outsiders, aren't we? Southerners among all these northern bastards.'

Tanner smiled. 'Yes, Corporal, but I think we're licking them into shape.'

* * *

In the offices of the Sicherheitdienst in Lillehammer, Reichsamtsleiter Hans-Wilhelm Scheidt was waiting for news of progress with mounting frustration. Reconnaissance aircraft had reported nothing despite countless sorties up and down the valley. 'Damned Luftwaffe,' he railed at Sturmbannführer Kurz. 'I know they're not really bothering.' He stood up, walked to Kurz's window, overlooking a sunlit street, then strode back to the large, leather-topped desk, snatched the photographs delivered by the Luftwaffe an hour before and peered at them intently.

'I couldn't see anything in those,' said Kurz, sitting back in his chair, his arms behind his head.

'They're taken from too damned high up.' Scheidt smacked the back of his fingers against them, then flung them on to the desk.

Absent-mindedly Kurz picked at a tooth. 'And I suppose the Luftwaffe do have to find the British positions.'

Scheidt glared at him. Kurz ignored him, instead picking up the Luftwaffe's aerial photographs once more. Despite Scheidt's comments, they were both clear and detailed, but even with a magnifying-glass no tracks could be seen in the snow. High on the mountain plateau there was nothing but an undulating whiteness. Then came the treeline, the forest gradually becoming denser as the sides of the valley plunged towards the river and lake below. What was most striking, however, was the rapidity with which the snow was already melting along the lower slopes and valley floor. 'Spring has come,' said

225

Kurz, almost to himself. 'In another week it'll probably be summer.' He looked up at Scheidt, who had sat down again on the other side of the desk. 'Maybe we'll still get a message through.'

'Two days,' muttered Scheidt. 'Two damned days!'

'It happens.' Kurz shrugged. 'Changes in weather patterns. Even small atmospheric fluctuations. It's probably nothing more sinister than that.'

'I'm feeling blind,' said Scheidt. 'Christ, where are they?' He paced the room again, then said, 'I'm going out. I need to think.'

He stepped outside into the cool evening air. Above him the Nazi flag over the door of the SD offices clapped and the rope knocked against the flagpole. A sudden gust swept down the street, throwing up dust. A speck of grit caught in his eye. Scheidt cursed, then looked up to see a sullen Norwegian creaking past in a cart, the mule's head bowed. Scheidt glared at him but the man simply stared back, unmoved and defiant.

Norway. By God, he loathed the place, with its endless mountains and curiously backward people. And what did Lillehammer have to offer? Nothing but a couple of cafés, a few hotels and a population of glowering, resentful inhabitants. He wished he could be back in Berlin, he needed to think. Where were the bars and vitality of Bitte and Friedrichstrasse – places where he could sit with a drink or two, watch the people go by and relax? He was a metropolitan man, born and brought up in the bustle and mass of Munich, and although he had been to university in the country town of Freiburg, in the Black Forest, it had had all the sophistication that could be expected from a centuries-old and highly distinguished university city. Then had come Berlin. How he missed it – a city that had always seemed to him the centre of the civilized world. A city of fine buildings and deep culture that even so seemed always to be moving forward. The beauty of its past sat so comfortably with the daring innovations of the future. He wished he could be there now, just for one night – a drink at the Café Josty to hear the latest gossip followed by dinner at Horcher's. Ah, that would be good.

He walked into his hotel. The reception area was still and quiet, save for the ticking of the pendulum on the clock.

'Brandy,' said Scheidt to the man at the desk, then walked through into the lounge. A couple sat in the corner, speaking in hushed tones and glancing nervously at Scheidt. Ignoring them, he sank into an armchair of deep maroon plush – stale cigarette and cigar smoke had pervaded every fibre of it. Cheap paintings of mountain scenes hung on the walls, while above the fireplace there was an ageing mirror spotted dark where the silver had been damaged. Scheidt ran his hands through his hair, and sighed. His brandy arrived and he took it without a word to the waiter, drank it in one and called for another.

He knew there was a large area in which to search for Odin, but even so, there were practical constraints that limited the opportunities for manoeuvre considerably. He had cursed the Luftwaffe, yet he knew they had flown countless sorties up and down the valley. Von Poncets' men had been trawling it too, yet they had found nothing – not a single clue, even though they were fresh, had trucks at their disposal and could travel further than Odin and his cohorts could possibly have managed on foot. It made no sense.

Then inspiration struck. Suppose they had not been seen because they weren't there? Suppose they had stayed where they were, lying low somewhere, while von Poncets' troops headed north and wasted time hunting for a false trail? He sat up and sipped his second brandy. Yes, he thought, it made perfect sense. Zellner himself had said there were clever, experienced men among them. For God's sake, Odin himself had enough of a brain! He finished his brandy, hurried out of the hotel and back to the SD headquarters.

Rushing into Kurz's office, he said, 'They're going to cross the river!'

Kurz looked at him with utter bewilderment. 'You've lost me, Herr Reichsamtsleiter. Who is?'

'Odin,' said Scheidt, 'and the men with him. We haven't found them because they're still somewhere on the mountain above Tretten. Tonight, when it's dark, they'll try to cross to the other side of the valley. I'm sure of it.'

Kurz looked dubious. 'It seems unlikely. Surely they wouldn't dare.'

'They would because, on the face of it, where's the risk? Who will still be in Tretten tonight? A few reinforcements passing through from the south and that's about it. For God's sake, even von Poncets' company of mountain troops won't be there.'

Kurz still seemed doubtful.

'Listen to me,' said Scheidt. 'They know they can't

travel through the mountains faster than us, and they know the Luftwaffe will be out looking for them. They're stuck on the same side of the valley as the road and the railway line. But what's on the other side? Nothing! If they can get over there, they have a better chance of getting us off their trail. Moreover, the far side of the valley is more densely covered with forest. I know I'm right. Tonight, they'll come down and attempt to cross to the other side.'

Kurz was nodding now. 'Yes,' he said, a smile creeping across his face. 'I think you might be right. It should be easy enough to stop them. The bridge is undamaged. All we have to do is make sure von Poncets' mountain troops are ready and waiting.' He glanced at his watch. 'Ten to nine. Somehow we need to get them back to Tretten – and quickly.' He stood up and slapped Scheidt on the back. 'Smart thinking, Herr Reichsamtsleiter.'

As Kurz disappeared to send a signal to von Poncets, Scheidt leant against the desk and examined the photographs once more. He felt sure he was right. Perhaps, at long last, they really were just hours from snaring their prey. And, if so, it would have been worth the wait.

At a little after half past ten that night, a small column of sixteen French, British and Norwegian troops, with two civilians, began to head down through the trees on the slopes towards the tiny village of Tretten. They were unusually attired. The Tommies, at Tanner's insistence, had put away their tin helmets and greatcoats and replaced them with German field caps and wind jackets. The French, believing their *canadienne* jackets and berets

229

were sufficiently similar to the German mountain-troops uniform, had stuck with their own clothing, while the two Norwegian officers had kept their greatcoats, a similar green-grey to those worn by the enemy, but had replaced their kepis with captured field caps. The idea, Tanner had suggested, was not necessarily to pass themselves off as German troops but, rather, to throw seeds of doubt and even confusion should they be seen silhouetted – however faintly – as they crossed the river. Anything that might chink or make any noise had been removed. It had been impressed upon every man that stealth was of paramount importance to their chance of success.

The sun had set behind the mountains on the far side of the valley, although a faint pink and gold glow crowned the snowy plateau, as though beckoning the fugitives towards a better place. Above, the sky was darkening at last, but there was still enough light with which to navigate through the trees and to warn them of any danger.

Sergeant Tanner, with Anna Rostad beside him and his men behind, led the way, following the route he had worked out earlier that morning. It had been more than twenty-four hours since they had reached the Rostads' farmstead, an entire day in which to rest, recover and rebuild their strength. They had certainly been fortunate to find such willing and accommodating hosts. Even now they were setting off with full stomachs, bread and cold meat in their haversacks. Erik Rostad had told them that most Norwegians in the Gudbrandsdal would share their own antipathy towards the German invaders, and if this was so, Tanner reflected, it would give them an important advantage; they would need such help in the days to come. The thought gave him heart.

They paused on a small crest that gave them a clear view down through the trees towards the beach-like spur that jutted out into the river. Tanner, with his German binoculars, scanned the ground in front of them. He could still see the three upturned dinghies on the shingle but, to his frustration, most of the village and the rapidly narrowing river as it entered the Tretten gorge were hidden beneath the crest and by ever more trees. He glanced at Anna, who bit her bottom lip and stared out into the darkening light with wide, alert eyes.

'It seems quiet,' he whispered.

'But we can't see the bridge or the church from here,' Anna replied.

'Then no one can see us.' He gave her what he hoped was a reassuring smile.

He signalled to them all to crouch and they moved forward again, down the last slope towards the road's edge. A faint brush of air occasionally caressed the trees but otherwise the valley was calm, so although Tanner knew they were moving as quietly as they could, every sound they made seemed jarringly amplified.

Just a hundred yards ahead lay the road. The snow had gone from the ground, replaced by thin, insipid grass, dried and broken twigs and a carpet of russet pine needles. Having paused again, Tanner waved them forward, wincing with every snapping twig, until they reached the edge of the treeline beside the road. There, as birch trees and alder mixed with the pines, long grass returned. A soft bank overlooked the road and beyond, a hundred yards away, was the water's edge.

Tanner lay down in the grass and signalled to the others to fall in beside him. Although it was dark now, the starry canopy above cast a faint glow over the landscape. He could see the mass of the mountains on the far side of the valley, and the inky river ahead, while the road glowed palely below. He tilted his watch to the stars. A quarter past eleven. He took a deep breath – they needed to get a move on.

Chevannes slid beside him. 'It seems quiet, no?'

Tanner nodded, but no sooner had he done so than he heard a rumble coming from the direction of the village. Chevannes heard it too and the two men stared at each other, frozen. In a moment, the noise increased – vehicles accelerating and changing gear. Heavy vehicles. Trucks.

'I knew this was an imbecile idea,' hissed Chevannes.

Tanner could think of no reply. The vehicles were getting closer, winding their way through the village. Then he saw the first, with its faint slits for headlights and dark bulky shape rumbling along the valley road. *Everyone keep still*, he thought. Then, carefully, he pulled up his rifle. They were, he told himself, most likely troops on their way north, but a trickle of sweat ran down the back of his neck and his heart was hammering. The lead truck was now only fifty yards away and, to his horror, he realized it was slowing. Next to him, Chevannes let out a faint groan.

The first truck passed them and stopped just thirty yards beyond. The second in the convoy also ground to a halt – directly opposite and so close Tanner felt he could almost reach out and touch it.

Orders barked, the sound of an engine ticking as it cooled, then troops were jumping out of the back on to the road. Hardly daring to watch, Tanner saw half a dozen men, rifles in their hands, look directly towards him, then cross the road.

His hands tightened round the stock and barrel of his rifle. There were now just a dozen yards between him and the leading enemy rifleman.

12

At his new headquarters in a farmhouse at Heidel, some fifty miles north of Tretten, Brigadier Morgan was bracing himself for General Ruge's visit. Most of 15th Brigade had now landed at Åndalsnes and had been reaching the Gudbrandsdal valley throughout the day, but had brought little relief to the beleaguered brigadier. Their commander, Brigadier Smyth, was junior to Morgan, while Major General Paget, due to take over command of both brigades under the spurious title 'Sickle Force', was not due to reach the front until the following evening. So, Brigadier Morgan was still in charge of the valley's defence. Responsibility for stemming the flow of the German advance was his.

Of course, it was a singular honour to command two brigades and a number of Norwegian units in the field and, as he wrote in a briefly scrawled letter to his wife, he was grateful to have been given the chance to command above his rank. But he felt so tired he could barely stand, let alone think clearly, while the never-ending relay of bad news had made him yearn for someone to lift the burden from his shoulders.

He had been writing a note to Brigadier Smyth when he had felt his eyes close, his head lurch forward and his pen drop from his hand. One of his staff officers had hurried into the room and he had immediately woken, sitting bolt upright in his chair and blinking.

'Sir?' said the young captain. 'Are you all right?'

'Fine, thank you,' muttered Morgan. 'What is it, Grayson?'

'It's the Norwegians, sir.'

'Yes?'

'They're struggling to hold the enemy and are asking for assistance.'

Morgan leant back in his seat and sighed. 'Do they know another battalion is on its way to them?'

'Er, that battalion's already there. They reached them an hour ago.'

Morgan stood up and walked to the window. Outside it was now almost dark. It looked cold out there, cold and clear. He noticed a cobweb in the corner of the window, stretched across the flaking paintwork. A small insect was struggling frantically in the sticky silk as the spider, with all the time in the world, advanced towards it to deliver the death blow. *How appropriate*, he thought.

'Look here, it's nearly dark,' he said. 'Order them to stand firm and then make it absolutely clear to 15th Brigade that they keep up with their deployment at Kvam through the night. If the Norwegians can hold out until the morning, there's every chance they can check the Germans until the middle of the day. Impress upon them the urgent need to remain at Vinstra as long as they can. Every hour they can stand their ground is another hour in which 15th Brigade can strengthen their position at Kvam.'

'Yes, sir.' Captain Grayson wavered, as though he was about to say something else.

'What is it? Come on – spit it out, man.'

'The Norwegians say they've already lost two-thirds of their strength, sir.'

Morgan laughed. 'And how much have we lost, eh, Grayson? About seven-eighths of ours, I'd say, wouldn't you? Tell them to stay where they are. Tell them if they don't, the whole front is likely to collapse.'

Captain Grayson had barely gone, and Brigadier Morgan had hardly had a chance to fill his pipe before General Ruge was announced. The Norwegian Commander-in-Chief strode in, as immaculate as ever, although, Morgan saw, noticeably tired. The past few days had aged them all.

'A present for you, Brigadier,' said Ruge, placing a bottle of whisky on the kitchen table that was now Morgan's desk.

Morgan thanked him, found two tumblers and poured generous measures into each, making sure he kept the chipped glass for himself. Then he spread the map across the table. While Ruge bent over it, Morgan took a large mouthful of whisky, relishing the sharp sensation as it scoured his mouth and throat. *Yes*, he thought. *That feels better.* Beside the general, he pointed out where the Norwegians were attempting to hold the enemy, and where, six miles further back, the newly arrived 15th Brigade were preparing to make a stand.

Ruge nodded thoughtfully. 'And what about 148th Brigade? Should they not help 15th at Kvam?'

'General, there's nothing left. Around four hundred and fifty men and not a single officer of the rank of company commander or above. That's it. Most are at Otta where they're organizing themselves into a reserve, but they've taken even more casualties today, thanks to the Luftwaffe. Is there any news of our air support? Have you heard if it's coming? Because until we have some cover from the air, we're fighting blind and have little or no chance of holding the enemy.'

'Actually, yes,' replied Ruge. 'I thought you had been told. A squadron of Gladiators landed north of Dombas earlier today. They're using a frozen lake as a landing strip.'

Morgan could hardly believe what he was hearing. He stood up straight and walked away from the table, his hand kneading his brow. 'Gladiators,' he muttered, 'but they're biplanes. What good can they do against the Messerschmitts, Junkers and Heinkels? And one squadron! It's risible, General, an abominable disgrace. By God, this is a damned shambles! This whole damned campaign. And 15th Brigade arrived here with just three anti-aircraft guns – three! Needless to say, General, they were all destroyed during the course of today.' Morgan flung his arms into the air in despair. 'I'm sorry – my God, what must you think of us?'

Ruge looked at him, his face grim. 'I do not blame you, Brigadier, or your men. But I do blame London. False promises, lack of appreciation or thought. Completely inadequate planning. It has cost many lives, both British and Norwegian. As it is we are now threatened on our flanks. The Germans are pushing up the Østerdalen with ease. Soon they'll they have the east of the country and will be able to attack Trondheim from the south.'

Morgan sat down again, poured himself another whisky and smoothed back his hair resignedly. 'Your troops at Vinstra will fall back earlier than I'd hoped,' he said wearily, 'but 15th Brigade are building up their positions at Kvam and, God willing, they'll put up a good fight. They're reasonably fresh and well armed – they've got a number of 25mm guns – and they appear to be in good heart. But the hard fact remains, General, that Jerry has the best part of an entire division and as many as nine thousand troops, while we have only around three thousand. And, of course, he's got tanks and armoured vehicles, bigger 4.14s and even 5.9 inch guns, and a frightening amount of air power. From the ground, we have a good position to defend, but from the air you have to face facts: our boys are funnelled into a valley that's never more than a mile wide, with one road and railway line as our only line of communication. The railway, thank goodness, still appears to be in reasonable order but the road is horribly cratered now and anyone travelling down is fearfully exposed to attack from the air. To make matters worse, we've no real way of preventing an outflanking manoeuvre because of the lack of mountain troops.'

'I'm sending you more Norwegian ski troops,' said Ruge. 'We'll put them up in the mountains to watch over our positions.'

Morgan sighed once more. 'Well, that's something.'

'You are tired, Brigadier, I know. But at least it is not your country that is about to fall. At least your king and government are still in London. And in two days' time, General Paget will be here and you can hand over command to him.'

Morgan was chastened. 'Yes, you're quite right, General. I'm sorry.'

Ruge now walked towards the window, tumbler in hand. 'There is one other matter I wish to discuss,' he said, still facing the window. 'This morning I saw the King at Molde.'

'And how was His Majesty?'

'Stoical. Bearing up surprisingly well, all things considered.' Ruge paused, then said, 'But there is one matter that is of great concern to him: the whereabouts of four of His Majesty's Guard.' Under a certain Colonel Gulbrand, Ruge explained, these men had been entrusted by the King personally not only with some priceless Crown Jewels, a number of diamonds included, but also the safe passage of an important scientist, one Professor Hening Sandvold. It was while they were trying to get him safely from Oslo after the invasion that these men became separated from the royal party. The King had not heard a word until two days ago. A message had been intercepted by British Intelligence, indicating that Colonel Gulbrand was dead, but Sandvold and two of His Majesty's Guards were being escorted by a group of British and French troops.

'British and French?' said Morgan, incredulously. 'Really? Where were they?'

'Just south of Tretten. But there's more. Apparently

they defeated an entire platoon of German mountain troops. I have some names too: a Sergeant Tanner and a Lieutenant Chevannes. I have already been informed by the French about him. He's from the 6th Battalion, Chasseurs Alpins.'

'Ah, yes,' said Morgan. 'We had a company of them at Øyer.'

'Chevannes was on a mountain patrol a day earlier when he and his men went missing.'

'Then presumably Sergeant Tanner and his men were doing much the same.' Morgan stroked his chin thoughtfully. 'If you don't mind me asking, apart from the obvious reasons about the jewels, why is the King so particularly concerned about Professor Sandvold?'

'That I cannot say. But I can tell you that it is what this man knows. He would be very valuable to the Germans – and to Norway, eventually. But there are concerns about him. In the early thirties he was a member of the National Party – he was a friend of Quisling's.'

'He *was*, you say?'

'Yes. We're not sure why, but he let his membership drop in 1934, and although he has never been particularly political, he was asked by the government – and, I understand, the King – to leave Oslo the moment the Germans invaded. But he did not, which was why Gulbrand, with the King in Hamar, was sent back to get him and take him to safety. It is a serious matter, Brigadier.'

'You doubt his loyalty?'

'Let us say it would be potentially catastrophic were he to fall into German hands.'

'I see.'

240

'I want you to find out more about this Sergeant Tanner and to keep a lookout for these men. I hate to think what might have happened to them. Gulbrand was under strict orders to kill Sandvold rather than let him fall into enemy hands, so it may be that he is already dead. However, I think it is better to assume he is not. It is one of the reasons I have been able to get ski troops down here for you. The King is determined that they should be found. I am sorry, Morgan – another thing for you to think about, but there it is. I just hope to God they are not already in German hands.'

The leading German soldier walked to barely five yards in front of Sergeant Tanner and Lieutenant Chevannes, then stopped. Tanner held his breath, his mouth as dry as chalk. Then to his amazement, the soldier hoisted his rifle on to his shoulder, fiddled with his fly buttons and began to urinate. Two of his comrades followed suit. By the trucks, soldiers were talking, lighting cigarettes, laughing even.

The German directly in front of Tanner broke wind, grunted, then looked into the inky darkness ahead of him and turned away. *Don't make a sound*, thought Tanner, then felt an overwhelming urge to scratch his chin; a blade of grass was tickling him – or was it an insect? *Keep still*, he told himself. *Ignore it.* He heard a rustle, small but distinct – one of the men moving – and froze. He could hear his heart thumping, and his breathing, however slight, seemed to him to be now strangely amplified. But none of the Germans appeared to hear anything.

Five minutes later orders were barked and the men

were clambering back into the trucks. Engines started, a booming cacophony in the still night, and they were off, a dim column trundling down the road towards the front.

'*Mon dieu*,' whispered Chevannes. 'A lucky escape, Sergeant. And now for the crossing, *non*?' The sound of the column died away, but there was a faint breeze now. Around them the trees rustled. Tanner was relieved: when the air was as still as it had been, sound carried alarmingly. The breeze, however gentle, would help them. Gingerly clambering down the bank to the edge of the road, he reminded each man in turn of the drill: Anna was to lead. Lieutenant Chevannes would wait on the far side of the road while he himself would stay where he was, giving each man the signal to cross.

Everyone was there; everyone was ready. He ran back to Anna and Chevannes.

'All right,' he said. 'Let's go.' His hands were shaking and he felt sick. The enormous risk of what they were about to attempt struck him like a slap in the face. Jesus, what had he been thinking? *It's our only chance*, he reminded himself. He took two deep breaths, patted Anna lightly on the shoulder, saw the fear in her eyes, then watched her disappear into the darkness. Chevannes followed, then his own men and the Norwegians, Larsen, Nielssen and Sandvold, each half crouching, half running across the narrow road and down to the edge of the river. Damn it, they were so loud, he thought. Metal studs on tarmac. He grimaced; he'd not thought of that. *Come on, come on, let's get this over with –* but with every crossing, Tanner winced.

It was the turn of his own men now, and he touched

each man's shoulder as they set off. More noise, jarring, from the river; Tanner tensed. The boats were being righted and taken to the water. Footsteps on the pebbles; someone tripping. Tanner groaned inwardly. 'For God's sake keep quiet!' he whispered. He knew they were trying, but they were heavily laden with their packs and haversacks, and most were carrying not one but two rifles – their own and the captured German Mausers. And, of course, there were those metal-studded boots – brilliant on the mountain, but hopeless for crossing a pebble beach in silence.

With Kershaw across, Tanner followed. Despite the noise from the riverbank, Tretten village itself seemed fast asleep, the teeming mass of men and war matériel that had crowded along the road only that morning now long since vanished, like a dream. He reached the river's edge. Anna and the Norwegians were in the first boat, two French troops rowing them away from the shore. Tanner wiped his mouth anxiously. Six in the boat – six with full kit – and more than the dinghy was designed for. As they moved out unsteadily, the small boat looked worryingly low in the water.

Chevannes, his remaining two Chasseurs, Erwood, Moran and Bell, clambered into the second and pushed off as Tanner, Sykes and the last of the Rangers struggled into the third, the craft tilting and lurching from side to side, water lapping against the wooden hull.

'For God's sake, try to keep it steady,' hissed Tanner. Holding the wobbling dinghy, he was about to clamber in when Sykes whispered, 'Where are the oars?'

'Didn't you pick them up?'

'I couldn't see any.'

Tanner cursed, then glanced around. It was hard to see clearly but the light from the stars cast enough of a glow to show him there were no oars to be found. Tanner could feel himself begin to panic so he closed his eyes and breathed deeply. It worked. 'We'll have to use the Mausers. Everyone get to it. Use them like a canoe paddle.' He took his own from his shoulder and plunged it into the ice-cold water.

From the upstairs dormer window of Tretten station, on the west bank of the Lågen river, Hauptmann Wolf Zellner had a fine view of the bridge below to his right. With the window open, the cold night air wafted across his face. He gazed out, marvelling at the billions of stars, pinpricks of light that gave the land below a faint ethereal shape. He looked at his watch: eleven twenty-three. *Will they come?* he wondered, not for the first time that evening, then lifted his binoculars to his eyes once more.

Despite instructions from Sturmbannführer Kurz to prepare an ambush at Tretten bridge, Zellner had felt there were a number of places where Odin and the fugitives might cross the valley. There was a bridge at Fåvang, for example, just ten kilometres north of Tretten, while six kilometres further on, at Ringebu, the railway crossed back over the river and rejoined the main valley road. True, they had not found the men despite a day of intense search, but Zellner was less convinced than Kurz or Reichsamtsleiter Scheidt that they had remained holed up near Tretten. With this in mind, and hoping to restore both his standing and pride, he had decided, on receiving his orders from the SD Head-quarters in Lillehammer, to deploy his men along the valley not only at Tretten but also at Fåvang and Ringebu. Admittedly, his company was now only three platoons strong, and he was painfully aware that the fugitives had got the better of his men when they had been operating with just one platoon, but he had no doubt that, however skilled the British sergeant might be, the fugitives could not achieve such a victory again. After all, they were now only seventeen strong, and Zellner knew much more about them than he had the day before. Most importantly, he and his men would be ambushing them, not the other way round. So it was that with forty fresh, well-armed men, Hauptmann Zellner had driven back to Tretten that evening confident that he had most possibilities covered and that his men were more than equal to the task.

He had agreed with Kurz that, should the fugitives still be near Tretten, the bridge was the most likely crossing place, simply because it was by far the easiest way for them to get to the other side. He had told his men to keep out of sight: the aim was to encourage the fugitives in their belief that the village was unoccupied.

Time had been tight. On reaching Tretten shortly after ten that evening, they had quickly found a hiding-place for the trucks in a disused barn, then positioned them-selves at either side of the bridge, using bushes and trees as cover, also buildings, both intact and partially destroyed. Zellner had prayed the fugitives would cross here. Playing his moment of triumph over and over in his mind he had begun to believe that Fate would ensure this was so, when a convoy had passed through ripping apart the quiet. How Zellner had cursed, especially when he saw, a kilometre or so beyond the village, that the column had stopped. They had moved on soon enough but in the minutes that followed Zellner had doubted his earlier conviction.

Suddenly he thought he heard something from away to his left – further along the river. He turned to Lieutenant Huber, the platoon commander. 'Did you hear that?'

'What, Hauptmann?' asked Huber.

'Ssh!' said Zellner. 'Listen.' And there it was again, a scraping sound – faint, almost inaudible, but there. 'What *is* that?' He peered through his binoculars towards where the river widened into Lake Losna. He could see the water, smooth as glass, twinkling, the mountains looming behind and beyond, but nothing out of the ordinary.

'Shall I investigate?' Huber asked.

'And give ourselves away? No,' said Zellner. 'Keep listening.'

He continued to stare through his binoculars and, at last, something caught his eye. A faint ripple on the otherwise smooth water. A sensation of intense exhilaration coursed through Zellner and a moment later he saw a boat as it passed in line with the valley and was silhouetted against the sky. Zellner smiled. 'Yes!' he said. 'I think we have them. Quick, Huber. We haven't a moment to waste.'

All six men were paddling with their Mausers and Tanner's boat soon caught up with the one in front

246

and then they passed it. Ahead, the far bank still seemed an interminably long way off. A hundred and fifty metres wide, Anna had said, and from his recce earlier that day he had agreed with her. Now, though, he realized it was more like two hundred yards, if not further.

'Come on, boys, keep at it,' he snapped.

His heart pounded with exertion and raw fear. His whole body was tense, waiting for the sound of shouts and machine-gun fire. He'd never liked being on open water. It made him feel he was no longer in control, that he was exposed and vulnerable.

Closer now. The lead boat was drawing near to the shore. Tanner allowed himself a sigh of relief. Perhaps they would make it, after all.

The sound of an engine shattered the illusion, then another, both from the direction of the village but on opposite sides of the river. The others heard it too, among expletives and panicked paddling. 'Quick, lads, quick!' said Tanner, plunging the Mauser into the water furiously.

Ahead, the first boat was drawing on to the gravel shore. There were splashes as the occupants stumbled out. The beam from the trucks cut across the water. The first lorry had stopped on the side from which they had come. Orders were being barked, and moments later shots rang out, bullets whining over their heads. A warning, thought Tanner. *Don't try to turn back.*

Shapes retreating from the first boat. Where was Sandvold? The lights of the second lorry curving round the river's edge were only a few hundred metres away now. Tanner heard the grinding of gears just as their own boat scraped against the stony shore. 'Get out, quick!' Tanner shouted. 'Cross the railway and head for the trees!' The third boat was closing on the shore too. One of the Frenchmen jumped but the water was deeper than he'd thought, and he flailed trying desperately to free his pack.

'Keep going!' Tanner shouted, kneeling to take aim as the vehicle turned towards them. He fired once, missed, then fired again and hit the windscreen of the lorry, which veered. He fired once more, and heard the ping of a bullet hitting metal. A screech of brakes, and the lorry came to a halt at the side of the road, a hundred yards ahead. A German voice yelled orders, and enemy troops hurried from the back of the truck. The Frenchman in the water was drowning, but Tanner ignored him and grabbed the prow of the dinghy. 'Jump!' he yelled, as Chevannes leapt out. Bullets ricocheted off the stones. Tanner was conscious of someone beside him. 'Go!' he shouted.

'*Non!*' came the reply. '*Mon ami. Vites, Henri, vites!*'

'He's gone, mate,' said Tanner, but the Chasseur stepped into the water to rescue his friend.

'For God's sake,' said Tanner, grabbing him. 'Go! Now!' A machine-gun opened fire, raking the water, tracer arcing towards them. At this, the Chasseur gave up and both men were running for their lives, off the pebble shore, across a grassy verge and over the railway line. The machine-gun had stopped firing but Tanner could hear the footsteps of enemy troops running towards them. He spun round and fired twice, then ran on, up another grassy bank, stumbled, cursed, picked himself up, as more bullets whistled over his head and into the ground at either side of him, then headed for the trees.

Where was everyone? Shouts from below and more shots. He could barely see anything, and hit a thin branch, which whipped back and slashed him across the face. Stinging pain coursed through him, then seared the side of his leg, and he cried out.

'Sarge, is that you?' called a voice.

'Stan!' said Tanner. 'Where the hell is everyone?'

'Up ahead. Are you all right, Sarge?'

'I think so. Thank God for dense forests.'

'A-bloody-men to that.'

Bullets tore into the trees, ripped through branches and smacked into the ground, but the slope was steep and the forest close. Tanner could hear others panting and gasping for breath. Suddenly a machine-gun opened fire again, a long burst spurting bullets up the wooded slopes. Tanner crouched behind a tree as the bullets flew. He saw a flickering torch beam, but it was weak so he stepped out from behind the tree, aimed his rifle towards the light and fired. The reply was another long burst of machine-gun fire, but this time the aim was way off, the bullets cutting through the trees high above their heads.

'Reckon they're angry, Sarge,' said Sykes, from a few yards to Tanner's right.

'Very, I'd say,' Tanner replied. 'Come on, Stan, let's keep going. You sure the others are all ahead?'

'I'm sure.'

The firing lessened as they climbed higher and

eventually, a couple of hundred feet above the lake, they reached a clearing in the trees.

'Hey,' said Tanner, in a loud whisper.

'Sergeant, is that you?'

Larsen. Tanner breathed a sigh of relief. 'Sir,' said Tanner, 'where are you?'

'Up ahead. Keep going, Sergeant.'

Tanner scrambled up the slope and, straining his eyes, peered into the darkness. Above, near the edge of the thickening forest, he could just make out the dark shape of several people crouched together. 'Stan,' he whispered, 'they're up here.' All six from the leading boat – Sandvold included – were still together. *Thank God.*

'We made it, sir,' said Sykes, breathlessly, to Chevannes.

'Yes,' replied the Frenchman. 'A miracle.'

By listening for panting, they were able, one by one, to gather the men together. Most collapsed on the ground, some laughing and whispering animatedly with the release of tension until Chevannes sharply told them to be quiet. 'We're not in the clear yet,' he told them. 'Not by any means.'

A head count showed that two men were missing: Chasseur Bardet and Private Mitch Moran. Both had been in the last boat. 'I'm sorry, sir,' said Tanner to Chevannes, 'but Bardet drowned. He jumped from the boat too early and his pack weighed him down. Chasseur Junot tried to rescue him but it was too late.'

Chevannes nodded. Junot himself was not in a good way. Soaked above the waist, he was shivering. He was also inconsolable at the loss of his friend.

'He needs to change his clothes,' said Tanner, 'or he'll be following his friend pretty soon.' But no one had any spare trousers, only jackets. Neither had they seen Moran. 'Tinker?' he said to Bell. 'You were in the boat with him.'

'We jumped out, Sarge. There were lots of bullets. He might have been hit.'

The valley below was now eerily quiet. Tanner hated to leave Moran behind, but they needed to get going – and quickly. He peered into the trees. Nothing. *Damn you, Mitch, where are you?* he thought. Then, turning to Chevannes, he said, 'Sir? We have to move off.'

'I know, Sergeant,' snapped Chevannes. 'Mademoiselle Rostad,' he said to Anna, 'where should we be heading?'

'Straight up the hill through the trees,' she said. 'At the top there is a track that leads to Svingvoll, a small farming hamlet at the head of a shallow valley. We should head for there, where—' She was cut off by a sharp hiss as a flare shot into the sky, followed swiftly by several more, which burst like crackling fireworks, showering the mountainside with light. A moment later they heard troops below them.

'*Vite!*' whispered Chevannes, the glow from the flares briefly lighting his face. He waved his arm and the men clambered onwards as rifle and machine-gun fire cracked and sputtered behind them. Tanner urged his men, then ducked as a bullet hurtled over him, missing his head by inches. Melting into the trees once more, he paused to fire, then took out a grenade and having pulled the pin, hurled it as hard as he could down the mountain, more in the hope of blinding their pursuers than from any realistic expectation of hitting anyone. A few seconds later, as it exploded, Tanner heard a German cry out. He smiled grimly to himself and clambered on up the slope, through patchy snow, until it seemed that at last the pursuers had given up the chase.

Cresting the hill, Tanner paused. He could only just make out the others, although he could hear them. They had all stopped, and most now stood with hands on hips or knees as they fought for breath. Across the valley, he could see the looming mountains, the formidable mass of rock and snow over which they had struggled the past few days. Now they had made it successfully to the other side. A miracle, Chevannes had called it, and for once Tanner was content to agree with the French lieutenant.

Beneath them, an engine started up. The Germans were back in their truck. Tanner heard the driver revving the engine until it screamed.

'You know what that is, don't you, Sarge?' said Sykes beside him.

'Yes, Stan,' Tanner grinned. 'Jerry's got his wheels stuck.'

13

As Anna had promised there was a track, which wove its way past a number of farmsteads, hidden from the valley floor, but which overlooked the bend in the river as it curved eastwards at the end of the Tretten gorge back towards Øyer. There was snow on the ground, but the track had been well trodden by foot and cart and was compacted in a way that made walking easy. Occasionally a dog barked, but otherwise the same eerie stillness that had accompanied them on the other side of the valley seemed to have descended on the mountains once more. It made Tanner feel that he was not atop some vast expanse of rock, but rather that they were walking through a narrow chasm. Each footstep sounded so clear, his breathing heavy and close.

They reached Svingvoll and skirted the lip of the shallow valley, then joined another track that led across an empty forested plateau of thin snow. Shortly after two in the morning, the first hint of dawn spread pinkly across the horizon behind them. Tanner was glad for the thin light. He had enjoyed the thrill of night as a boy – being out with his father, shooting rabbits and setting traps. Yet that had been on familiar ground; he had known every inch of those woods. Now, though, he was relieved to be able to see in front of him, his surroundings gradually more defined, the men – and Anna – walking in front and behind him.

Anna. She had already more than proved her worth, he thought. And he had been impressed by her cool-headedness: her first time under fire and she had not panicked. He thought of striding ahead and talking to her, but decided against it. Better to wait for the right moment.

Instead he drew alongside Professor Sandvold, the man he had vowed to deliver safely to the Allies. 'How are you, Professor?' he asked.

'Too old for making daring dashes across rivers,' he replied. 'I don't mind telling you, Sergeant, I found the whole experience terrifying. It is one thing being strafed by enemy aircraft because it is all over before you have realized it is happening. But crossing the lake was truly frightening. Tell me there will not be any more episodes like that.'

Tanner smiled. 'I hope not, Professor. I can't say I enjoyed it much either.'

'And all those bullets. Really, how do you keep calm in such situations?'

'I always find that in the heat of the moment there's no time to be frightened.'

Sandvold eyed him sceptically. 'That is why you are a soldier and I am not, Sergeant.'

* * *

Soon after, Junot collapsed. The small column of men stopped and gathered round him as he lay propped against a tree, his teeth chattering, gibbering incoherently. Crouching beside him, Anna felt his brow. 'His temperature's dropped,' she said.

'He's got hypothermia,' said Tanner. 'We need to wrap him in something warm, quickly, or else he'll croak. Here,' he said, taking off his German wind jacket, 'fold this round his legs.' Anna did so, while Tanner retrieved his leather jerkin from his pack. Another makeshift stretcher was assembled using Mausers and greatcoats and the prostrate Junot hoisted on to it. Chevannes' two remaining men took one end, while Sykes ordered Hepworth and Kershaw to take the other.

'He's going to need help,' Anna said, turning to Chevannes.

'And we can't walk all the way to the front with a stretcher,' added the French lieutenant. '*Merde.*' He glanced ahead at the seemingly endless trees, stretching across the plateau. 'How far is it to the valley?'

Anna shrugged. 'Five kilometres, maybe. There's the village of Alstad. We can get help there.'

'Good,' he said, 'Let's keep going.'

It was nearly half past eight on the morning of Thursday, 25 April, when they reached the crest of the mountain plateau and were able to look down over the narrow Jøra valley. On the east-facing slopes, the valley was once again thickly wooded with a blanket of snow still on the ground, but below them, on the west-facing valley sides, the snow had all but gone. On the valley floor, a narrow river wound away to the north-west, silvery in the morning light. Beside it there was a road, little more than a rough track but smooth and free of snow.

Chevannes called a brief halt to change stretcher-bearers. Beneath them lay a settlement of scattered farms and, standing on its own, at the edge of the river, a small church. This was Alstad, Anna told them. Junot was now ghostly white, his lips and ears blue. 'We need to hurry,' she told Chevannes.

They pressed on, clambering down the slopes through open pasture until they reached the first of half a dozen farmsteads. Several dogs ran out into the yard as Anna walked ahead with Larsen, past ageing outhouses with grass-covered roofs. Tanner watched apprehensively, his rifle at the ready.

A few minutes later, Larsen reappeared and signalled to them. The men left their position along a track above the farm, and hurried into the yard, past chickens and geese cackling at the invasion. Old carts and farm machinery, green with lichen, spokes shattered, were piled haphazardly against the sheds. They reached the steps where the farmer stood, watching them approach. His face was weatherbeaten and wrinkled, with a two-day growth of white beard, and he stared at the men suspiciously as they trooped past him into the low-ceilinged kitchen. It was musty, primitive and dark, and with their packs, rifles and equipment, the men crowded it.

The farmer's wife ushered the stretcher-bearers to an armchair by the fire, then barked at her husband, who grudgingly edged his way through the men and began to

256

stoke the fire with more wood. His wife disappeared, but could be heard moving overhead. Soon she returned with a pile of blankets. Junot was then stripped from the waist down, swathed in wool and the woman began vigorously to rub his hands and feet, talking to Anna as she did so.

'She knows how to deal with hypothermia,' Anna said, turning to Tanner and Chevannes. 'Her cousin had it once, but she is worried it is too late for Junot.' The woman now shouted at her husband, who quickly filled a large black pot and hung it above the fire. 'They're making coffee,' Anna explained. 'Sweet coffee. The sugar and hot fluid will help him.'

Suddenly the woman stopped what she was doing and felt Junot's neck. She sat back and looked up at Anna and Chevannes.

'He is dead?' said Chevannes to Anna, disbelief on his face.

Anna nodded. 'I am sorry, Lieutenant. The poor man. It is too terrible.'

Chevannes put his hands to his face. '*Mon Dieu*,' he muttered. '*Mon Dieu*.'

Tanner's first thoughts were about what they should do with the body. They needed to cover not only their own tracks but those of the farmer and his wife. Then they had to consider what they would do next. Chevannes was wavering, he could see, while Nielssen and Larsen were keeping quiet, allowing the French lieutenant to make the decisions. *For God's sake*.

The farmer and his wife were arguing now.

'What are they saying?' asked Chevannes.

'He wants us to take Junot with us,' Anna explained.

'His wife is saying we should carry him to the church – then he can have a proper Christian burial.'

'That's ridiculous,' said Tanner. 'We need to take him up into the trees and bury him there.' He turned to Chevannes. 'Don't you agree, sir?'

'Yes, Sergeant. Yes, we must.' Chevannes seemed distant and distracted.

'Shall I organize it, sir?' Tanner asked.

Chevannes nodded. Tanner gathered his men, told them to ditch their German caps and jackets, put on their old greatcoats, jerkins and tin helmets, then lift Junot. The farmer's wife tried to stop them, but with Anna placating her, the men picked up the dead Chasseur and went back out into the morning light, trudged back through the yard, up the track and into the trees overlooking the farm.

As a shallow grave was dug, Tanner gazed down at the valley below. It looked so peaceful, as though the war could never touch it. There were no charred remains or piles of rubble here. Rather, the only smoke was that which rose in narrow columns from the farms on the lower slopes, their inhabitants up and about, getting ready for another day.

Sykes was standing beside him.

'Do you reckon Jerry knows about our professor, then?' the corporal asked.

'I can't work it out, Stan. The other evening that German patrol seemed to be coming after us for a reason. Why else go to all that trouble just to catch a few soldiers on the run? And last night I could have sworn those men at Tretten were waiting for us, as

258

though they knew we were going to cross the valley.'

'But how could they have done?'

Tanner shook his head. 'I don't know. And there's another thing. Did you notice most of their shooting was high?'

'Was it?'

'Well, not a single one of us was hit, were we? Except maybe Mitch.'

'No, I suppose not.'

'But then again, no one came looking for us yesterday, did they? A few recce planes overhead, but that was all. It doesn't make sense.' He lit a cigarette. 'Maybe I'm imagining things.' He was silent for a moment, then said, 'With any luck they won't come looking for us along here. If we keep our eyes and ears strained for aircraft, we should be all right.'

'We could do with some M/T, Sarge,' added Sykes. 'Perhaps one of these farmers here has got some.'

'Perhaps.'

They gazed at the valley again. 'Just fourteen of us now,' said Tanner.

'A few less to worry about.'

'Yes, that's true.' Tanner sighed. Behind him, the men had finished covering Junot and were putting away their entrenching tools. 'Come on, boys,' said Tanner. 'Let's get back to the farmhouse.'

As they reached the yard, they saw the farmer hurry outside. He glared at them as they passed him.

'Bloody hell, what's the matter with him?' said Hepworth.

'Trouble with the missus?' suggested McAllister.

'She's a tough-looking woman,' said Sykes. 'Had him running around earlier.'

'Maybe he doesn't like having a bunch of soldiers turn up early for breakfast,' said Tanner. They went back inside to find the others putting their packs on their shoulders.

'Have you buried Junot, Sergeant?' Chevannes asked Tanner. 'We need to leave.'

'Er, yes,' Tanner replied, handing him Junot's identity tags. 'He's well hidden up in the trees.'

'Good. We go.'

'The farmer is nervous,' explained Anna. 'He is worried about what the Germans will do if they find out we have been here. Henrik Larsen has tried to reason with him, but I am afraid it is no use.' She looked towards the farmer's wife. 'She is furious with him. She called him a coward and a traitor.'

'Have we asked her whether anyone in the village has any transport?'

'Not yet.' She turned and spoke to the farmer's wife, who replied after a moment's thought, then pointed and gesticulated.

'Uksum Farm,' said Anna. 'A man called Merit Sulheim. She says he has a truck he uses to take livestock to Lillehammer.'

Tanner's spirits rose. 'Perfect,' he said. 'Where is this farm?'

'Not far. About a kilometre north from the church.'

'Good. Let's head there right away.'

As they left the farm and continued down the track towards the valley, they heard the now familiar sound of aero-engines thrumming faintly over the mountains above them. Tanner stopped, and held up an arm. 'Ssh!' he said, cocking his head. There it was, faint but distinct, somewhere over the mountains from which they had just crossed. A little louder, then a Junkers roared into view a few hundred yards ahead as it crested the lip of the mountain plateau and plunged into the valley.

'Everyone, take cover – quick!' shouted Chevannes. They flung themselves onto the track's bushy bank. Tanner watched the aircraft bank and swoop across the valley, then turn, curving, so that its bulbous nose pointed directly towards them.

'It's bloody well coming right for us!' said Sykes, clutching his helmet to his head. Moments later, the Junkers thundered directly over them, the black crosses and pale blue underside startlingly close. They watched as the aircraft flew on, then banked again, arcing lazily across the valley before turning for another run above them.

'Here, Dan!' Tanner called out to Lance Corporal Erwood. 'Have a crack with the Bren, will you?'

'And give away our position?' called Chevannes. 'Are you mad, Sergeant?'

'Sir, he's seen us. The only way we're going to stop him bleating is by shooting the bastard down.'

'No, Sergeant, and that is an order!'

The Junkers was approaching once more, no more than a hundred feet above them. Again it roared overhead, oil streaks from the two radial engines staining the pale underside of the wings. Tanner cursed, then watched as it swung out over the valley and began to bank yet again. 'Sir, he's bloody well seen us!' he shouted. 'Let's have a pop at it. What have we got to lose?' Chevannes said nothing. Tanner smiled, aware that the French lieutenant's silence was the authority he needed. 'Aim off, Dan,' he called to Erwood once more. 'Give yourself plenty of lead.' Erwood glanced at Chevannes, then back at the sergeant. 'Do it, Dan,' said Tanner. He had his own rifle to his shoulder now and saw that the rest of his men had followed his example. He knew a .303 round would probably make little impression on an eight-ton monster such as a Junkers 88, but it was flying so low he reckoned it had to be worth a shot. It was rather like aiming at a high bird, he thought to himself. Admittedly it was travelling at probably a hundred and fifty miles per hour, rather than fifty like a pheasant with a good wind behind it but, he told himself, a Junkers was far bigger.

He watched it straighten and its wings level. At that distance it looked as though it was travelling slower than a pheasant, but all too soon that illusion was dispelled. Tanner pointed his rifle vertically in the air. 'Ready, Dan?' he called. 'Two seconds now. *One, two – fire!*' he yelled, and as bullets pumped into the sky the aircraft swept over them.

Then a miracle happened. The starboard engine spluttered and, as the aircraft banked over the valley, flames appeared, followed by a long trail of smoke. As one, the men on the ground stood up and watched, open-mouthed. The pilot tried to climb and they followed the plane as it headed north up the valley, rose over the mountains, then plunged earthwards. A ball of flame erupted briefly on the far side of the mountains followed by the dull rumble of destruction a few seconds later. For a moment the men were dumbstruck, then raised their rifles and cheered.

It was Dan Erwood who received the most slaps on the back but Tanner knew it could have been any of them, and that in firing together, they had claimed victory together.

'Good shooting, men,' said Chevannes, adjusting his beret on his head. 'Very good shooting.'

'And a very good decision to let us fire, if I might say so, sir,' said Tanner.

'Be careful, Tanner,' said Chevannes. 'My patience is wearing thin.'

'Come on, lads,' said Tanner, ignoring the Frenchman. 'Iggery, all right?'

They walked on quickly, past anxious, startled farmers who had emerged from their houses to see what the commotion was about. Two young boys stood on a gate to watch them pass and several of Tanner's men cheered at them as they did so, the boys grinning back.

'That's enough!' Tanner warned.

'They are like schoolboys,' said Anna, walking beside him. 'It is amazing to see everyone's spirits lift like this.'

'Mine will be even higher if this truck works out,' Tanner replied. He turned and barked at his men: 'Come on, you lot! You can stop congratulating yourselves now and get a bloody move on!'

'We were just saying, Sarge,' said Erwood, hurrying to his side, 'what a shame it is that Mitch isn't with us, him being on my Bren crew an' that. He'd have loved to have seen that Jerry plane come down. I wish I knew he was all right.'

'I'm sure he is.'

'Only I feel bad. One minute he was with us and the next he wasn't. It's not knowing what happened . . .'

'He probably just tripped and fell,' said Tanner. 'Easy to do when it's dark like that. You'll probably find he was picked up by the Jerries.'

'I'm telling you,' mumbled Mitch Moran, 'I don't know anything. We were just trying to get back to our lines.'

Sturmbannführer Kurz sat on the edge of his desk and looked at the pitiful figure in front of him. A swollen and cut eye, so puffed and blackened it had closed, a darkening cheek, cracked and bloodied lips, a line of congealed blood and mucus from nose to mouth. Moran's shirt was torn, but hid the bruising round his cracked ribs, while his feet were bare and also bloody and blackened. With his arms tied behind the back of the chair, his head hung down as though it were too heavy for him now that it had been so badly pummelled.

Kurz sighed. He had been taught torture techniques, but beating someone to within an inch of their life always struck him as crude. And this fellow – well, he was just a simple boy. A few cigarettes, a bit of friendly chat and the Englishman would have been eating out of his hand ages ago. Now it was probably too late. *Ah, well, worth a try.* He ordered the guard at the door to untie Moran's hands, then lit a cigarette.

'A smoke?' he said, and without waiting for an answer, placed the cigarette between Moran's lips. 'Listen, I'm sorry you've been so roughly treated. Hauptmann Zellner was – well, he was a bit frustrated, to put it mildly. I'm sorry he took it out on you.' He saw Moran lift his head a fraction, then shakily raise a hand to the cigarette. Kurz smiled. 'I certainly wouldn't want you thinking we're all like that.' Standing up, he walked towards the window. 'War . . . what a waste of time it is. Killing people, uprooting people from their homes – it is all so futile. You know, I was a teacher before the war. I used to teach English in a small town in the Thüringen. I loved England – I travelled all over when I was still a student. You are from Yorkshire, I believe?'

Moran nodded.

Kurz stood up again and walked to the cabinet behind Moran where he now kept his Baedekers. He picked up the England edition. 'Which part?'

'Knaresborough,' mumbled Moran.

'Knaresborough,' said Kurz, flicking through the pages. 'Near Harrogate, is it not?' He paused, as though lost in the depths of a happy memory. 'Yes, I remember a wonderful English tea at Betty's in Harrogate.' He smiled. 'Do you know it?'

'It's only for nobs and that, really,' Moran mumbled, 'but my grandma took me there for my tenth birthday.'

'I remember it being quite charming,' said Kurz, 'as was all of Yorkshire. One day, when this is all over, I should like to go back.' He sighed, then said, 'And here I am, a soldier of sorts, fighting against a people for whom I have a very great affection. It is damnable, it really is.' He leant closer towards Moran. 'Look, I want to help you. You are just a boy and, I am sure, would much rather be at home in Knaresborough with your family, just as I would rather be at home with my wife and baby daughter in Ludwigsstadt, but there is a war on and that is all there is to it. I cannot get you home tomorrow, but I can get you cleaned up and properly looked after, and I can promise you there will be no more beatings.' He paused, looked at Moran and said, 'Can I get you anything? Some water perhaps?'

'Thank you.'

Kurz went to a cabinet in the corner and poured a glass, then handed it to the Tommy. 'There,' he said, taking the cigarette butt from Moran's lips and handing him the glass. 'I was wondering why you were crossing the river last night. It seems rather a risk.'

'Because you lot were going down the main valley. We thought there'd be less of you about.'

'But difficult to walk through those mountains. There's still plenty of snow up there.'

'Not in the valley beyond.'

Kurz smiled. Really, he thought, this was almost too easy. 'No, I suppose not. So your plan was to head north down the Jøra valley?'

Moran nodded.

'As a matter of interest,' Kurz added, 'what made you cross where you did? It showed extraordinary local knowledge, if you don't mind me saying so.'

'Our sarge had recced the area earlier and found the boats,' said Moran, still almost in a whisper. 'And we had a Norwegian girl showing us the way.'

'Ah,' said Kurz. *Now I understand*. 'Well, I'll let you rest now, Moran. And good luck.' Two guards came over, picked up Moran and took him away.

Reichsamtsleiter Scheidt, who had been sitting silently in a chair in the corner watching Kurz, clapped slowly. 'Bravo, Sturmbannführer. A virtuoso performance.'

Kurz made a mock bow.

'I had no idea you had been a teacher,' Scheidt added. 'You don't strike me as the type.'

'I wasn't.'

'Ah. And you don't have a wife and baby daughter?'

'No, of course not. Nor have I been to England and certainly not Betty's Tea Rooms, whatever they might be. Baedeker's a useful friend.'

Scheidt smiled, but then his expression changed. The British sergeant was proving a thorn in their side. And they had a guide with them. Damn them, he thought. And damn Zellner. Twice he had bungled what should have been a straightforward operation. Worse, last night he had flagrantly disobeyed Kurz's orders and Odin had slipped through their fingers again. He ran a hand wearily through his hair.

'Cheer up, my dear Reichsamtsleiter,' said Kurz. 'We know where they're heading and they've still a long way to go. Patience. We're closing in on them.'

'You keep saying that,' snapped Scheidt, 'yet Odin repeatedly eludes us, and for two days we've heard nothing from our source. The clock is ticking, Sturmbannführer, and if we fail, it won't be only me who falls.'

'Yet we know where they have headed. The Jøra valley is narrow and quite small. Zellner and his men will be able to search it with far greater ease than they could the Gudbrandsdalen.'

'Zellner,' muttered Scheidt. 'Hardly a man to inspire confidence.'

'Don't write him off yet, Herr Reichsamtsleiter. He has excellent credentials and no doubt he'll be anxious to put right his previous attempts to capture Odin.'

'I hope to God you're right, Kurz,' said Scheidt.

At Tretten station, Hauptmann Wolf Zellner was anxiously awaiting a call from the Luftwaffe. At ten o'clock, they had told him, he could expect a report from their morning reconnaissance yet it was now nearly half past and there was still nothing. He glanced at his watch again, drummed his fingers on the desk in the station master's office, then impatiently put a call through to Fornebu. One plane was back, he was told, and had found nothing. The other was late and out of radio contact.

Zellner slammed down the receiver and kicked the door. He cursed Odin and Tanner, every single one of those miserable fugitives – men who were making a fool of him. He still could not believe they had got away. Countless times he had replayed the events of the previous evening over in his mind, and every time, his anger and despair grew.

He could feel the career for which he had worked and trained so hard slipping away from him. As a boy he had wanted to be a soldier, an ambition that had never left him. He had joined the Austrian Army at eighteen, and had cheered when Hitler had marched into Vienna in the spring of 1938. He was proud to be part of what would surely become a great nation – a military nation in which he had a part to play. From that moment on, he had dreamt of great things. Ahead lay a future of endless opportunity in which he would perform great deeds, win a multitude of awards for valour, and in which he would rise steadily but surely to the top of his chosen profession.

Yet now a handful of Tommies, a few Frenchmen and Norwegians threatened to shatter those dreams. It was inconceivable. The sense of humiliation was too great. *Tanner*, he thought. He picked up an old cup from the desk and flung it at the wall.

There was one small consolation. The rest of the division were now further north, engaged in fighting at Kvam. That had meant a reprieve for him and his company. It was not yet too late. If he could successfully capture Odin, all else would be forgotten, and the upward path of his career would continue uninterrupted.

He made a decision. He could not wait for late-returning planes any longer. Odin had to be found. His men were ready and waiting so they would begin the search now, on their own, without the Luftwaffe's help. Kurz had told him they had been heading for the Jøra valley. Well, if that was so, someone somewhere must have seen them. And, that being so, he would make sure they talked.

14

Sergeant Tanner had to remind himself that it didn't pay to allow over-confidence to creep into one's thinking, but nonetheless he couldn't help feeling that things were looking up. Shooting down the Junkers had probably meant their whereabouts would remain secret for a while longer, but had also boosted everyone's spirits. And then they had safely reached Uksum Farm, where Merit Sulheim was considerably more helpful than the nervous farmer they had encountered above Alstad earlier that Thursday morning.

With the men left to keep a close watch from the large barn outside, Tanner, Sandvold, Anna and the officers were ushered into the house. A spry, heavily built man in his thirties, Sulheim had a young family, ran a successful logging business, and also kept cattle, goats, sheep and even pigs, all housed in a number of rambling barns on the farm during winter and on pastures that ran along either side of the Jøra river in summer. Evidently a man of enterprise and zeal, he had, unlike most other farmers of the Gudbrandsdal valley, invested in the latest machinery, including an American Fordson tractor and a large Morris-Commercial truck. Neither was the farmhouse as primitive as some of the others Tanner had seen: rather, it was equipped with electricity, running water, had a modern range in the kitchen and even a radio, on which Sulheim had been carefully following the progress of the war.

It was because of this that the farmer was able to tell them some news as to what was happening in the ongoing battle for Norway. There was fighting to the north of Trondheim, near Namsos; Narvik had also been heavily bombed. In the Gudbrandsdal valley, there was heavy fighting at Kvam, some forty-five miles to the north-east. German-backed radio had reported that they were advancing virtually unopposed up the Glåma valley, east of, but parallel to, the Gudbrandsdal. On hearing this Tanner had glanced at Chevannes. *And you reckoned we could head north in that direction.*

But Sulheim reported something more. That morning an announcement had been broadcast by the German authorities that a dangerous band of British, French and Norwegian troops was at large in the Gudbrandsdalen. There was a reward for any help in securing their capture, but a warning too: anyone offering these men help could expect 'the severest' punishment for doing so. Well, that made one thing clear, thought Tanner. The Germans knew about Sandvold.

The threat of severe punishment did not seem to perturb Sulheim, who explained that he was a patriot and openly professed his desire to help his country against the Nazi oppressor. He had already tried to join up in Lillehammer, but because of his timber business and position as one of the few milk and meat producers in the area, he had been sent home. 'In any case,' he added, in near-perfect English as his wife ladled out bowls of porridge, 'we have seen a few planes, but not a single German soldier yet.' He offered them his truck. Petrol was scarce and there was little in the tank, but he produced two four-litre cans that he told them he had kept to one side. 'You should have enough for maybe fifty kilometres.'

'Then we should leave right away,' Tanner said.

Chevannes shook his head. 'In broad daylight? It would be better to lie up here today, and head off this evening when all is quiet.'

'I agree,' said Larsen. 'Think how far we got last night. If we wait until dark we can drive to here.' He pointed to a spot on Anna's map a few miles west of Vinstra, where the road rejoined the main Gudbrandsdal valley. 'Then we can head over the mountains to Sjoa, west of Kvam, perhaps be there by early next morning.'

Tanner sighed with exasperation. 'Look,' he said, 'it's clear that Jerry knows about the professor. I was already pretty sure of that before I heard about that radio announcement. Think. First we were chased through the mountains. Then last night they were waiting for us to cross at Tretten, and this morning we were given three passes by an enemy reconnaissance plane. Now the Germans have put out a broadcast about us. They're going to be looking for us, and if Sandvold's as precious as I think he is, then they're not going to stop looking

272

until they've found him. We should get going while we've got the chance to keep one step ahead of the bloody Bosches.'

'No,' insisted Chevannes. 'We should lie low until evening, even if that means hiding in the mountains.'

'We should make as much ground now while we have the chance,' Tanner countered. 'Mr Sulheim has offered us his truck. It's sitting there now. Instead of arguing, let's head north, towards the Allies.'

'Sergeant, not for the first time, I would like to remind you that I am the senior officer here, the one in command, not you. And I am ordering us to stay where we are.'

'But this is madness!' said Tanner. 'Do you think those Germans who attacked us last night are going to sit quiet all day? They'll be swarming all over this valley.'

'You were happy enough for us to lie up yesterday,' said Chevannes.

'Yesterday we had no choice. We were exhausted, short of food and had nowhere to go. That's not the case today. We're still reasonably fresh and we have a chance to get a long way north, an option that was not open to us yesterday. Please, sir, I implore you, don't delay. Let's go now, while we have the chance.'

'No,' said Chevannes. 'If the Germans come looking for us today, then fine – we will hide in the mountains and come back down this evening.'

Tanner put a hand to his brow. 'We can't afford to lose another whole day if we don't have to,' he said slowly. 'We have the chance to drive north now, away from the enemy. It's madness.' He turned to Professor Sandvold. 'Professor, surely you see that?'

'How dare you try to undermine me?' shouted Chevannes. 'I have made my decision, Tanner and you will abide by that.'

Sandvold shrugged. 'Both options seem fraught with risk, Sergeant,' he said. 'Please – I am not the one to make such a decision.'

Sulheim now coughed. 'I have a suggestion,' he said. 'I have a *seter* up in the forest. It's quite a climb but no one has used it in years and it's deep in thick forest. You would never be seen from the air and I don't think any German would find you. I can take you there now. Tonight I will come and get you when the coast is clear.'

'That settles it,' said Lieutenant Larsen. 'We stay here today and head out tonight.'

'If we're still able to,' snarled Tanner.

Larsen turned to him. 'Sergeant, this is not about you and the lieutenant. This is about what is best – best for the professor and for all of us. I am sorry – but I agree with Lieutenant Chevannes.'

So, thought Tanner, *that's that*. As they went back outside, Chevannes called everyone together. When the men were gathered round him, he said, 'Today we lie up in the mountains. Tonight we continue our journey north in Monsieur Sulheim's truck. Now, *vite*, we get going.'

Tanner could see the expression on Sykes's face. 'Don't say it,' he growled. 'It's insanity. That man has no brain. Neither does Lieutenant Larsen, for that matter.'

'Isn't it time we left them to it, Sarge?'

'For God's sake, Stan, how can we? Sulheim's not going to lend us his truck without the Norwegians, is he? I tried to persuade the professor but he said it wasn't his place to make a sodding decision. And anyway, I made a solemn vow.'

Sykes nodded doubtfully.

'All right, Stan,' snapped Tanner, 'but what if Sandvold is as important as Gulbrand made out? Think about it. Would these Jerries be after us if he wasn't? It's our bloody duty to do the right thing.' He sighed. 'Look, if you want to try and make a go of it on your own, you and the other lads, I won't stop you. But I've got to stick by him and somehow get him back to our lines, despite that bastard's every effort to stop us. If that means wasting another bloody day, so be it.'

'Don't worry, Sarge, I'm not going to bugger off. I don't like it, mind, but as you say, we have to sweat it out. God knows, though, this place could be swarming by the evening.'

It was largely because Hauptmann Zellner had waited until mid-morning for useless Luftwaffe reconnaissance reports that the fugitives could leave Merit Sulheim's farm safely and make their way across a wooden foot-bridge, over grey pastures and into the dense pine forest that covered the steep western slopes of the valley. By following a mountain brook they hid their progress and were able to reach the heart of the forest without a trail of tracks in the snow. The *seter*, when they reached it, was overgrown with young shoots of alder and pine, the entrance and shuttered window thick with ageing cobwebs. As a place to hide, it was, Tanner admitted, hard to fault. A short distance below, a little clearing that offered a good view of the river, road and the cluster of

275

farmsteads that made up the community of Alstad. It was there that Tanner settled to watch any activity in the valley.

A truckload of German soldiers reached the church just before midday, and Tanner watched as they began their search, one by one, of the farms. Eventually another truck of troops arrived and aircraft flew up and down the valley, then over the mountains but, as Sulheim had predicted, they seemed unable to spot any movement in the thick forest below. Tanner wondered whether that morning's old man had squealed. He could see through his binoculars that soldiers were now searching the place. Sure enough, not long after, a number of troops hurried down the track and made for Sulheim's farm. As they reached it, Tanner hardly dared breathe. He hoped Sulheim held his nerve; hoped he'd be as good as his word and not say anything to the enemy troops now swarming over his house and farm. Then he remembered the truck. Surely the Germans would spot it and requisition it. He cursed once more.

Hauptmann Zellner banged his fist hard on the kitchen table. He was pleased to note that not only did the wife flinch but the farmer too. 'I know they were here, Herr Sulheim,' he said, each word spoken slowly and clearly.

'And so they were,' said Sulheim, eyes wide, 'but they left again. I turned them away.'

Zellner stared at him. 'But why would you? They had your fellow countrymen with them. Are you not a patriot, Herr Sulheim?'

'I – that is we – heard the announcement on the radio.

276

That you were looking for these men. I am a patriot but I love my family more. I didn't want to put them at risk.'

'But you have a truck, do you not?'

'Yes, and they wanted it, but it's not working at the moment.'

'Not working?'

'No – something wrong with the alternator, I think.'

'Did they try to get it to work?'

'They tried but, as I said, it's broken down.'

'Show me.'

Sulheim shot a nervous glance across the room to his wife, then led him out of the house and across the yard to one of the outbuildings where the truck now stood.

'Lift the bonnet,' Zellner ordered. He had no idea how engines worked and called one of his men. In German he asked the soldier to examine the engine bay.

'And where is the alternator now?' he asked, turning back to Sulheim.

'Er, here,' said Sulheim, pointing to a cylindrical block of metal lying on a workbench to the side of the shed.

'And where did they go when they left?'

'Up the road. North,' said Sulheim. 'Whether they stayed on it or not, I couldn't say. I made it pretty clear I didn't want them anywhere near my farm.'

Zellner couldn't decide whether or not the man was lying and wished he had Sturmbannführer Kurz with him, a man more practised in interrogation techniques. The Norwegian's answers certainly seemed plausible, but either he was telling the truth and the fugitives would be further up the valley by now, or he was lying and they would presumably reappear once darkness fell.

He ordered a thorough search of the entire farm. Nothing was found. No hidden troops, no footprints, no dropped cigarette butts. After an hour, he called his men back. He posted half a dozen in the church a few hundred yards to the south of the farm – the bell-tower was to be used as an observation post – then ordered the rest back into the trucks and headed north.

Tanner watched these events carefully. The officers appeared from time to time, but he preferred to trust the task of observation to himself, Sykes and his own men. By taking short cat-naps in the *seter* he was able to catch up on his sleep, then return to watch the valley once more.

During the afternoon more trucks arrived. Planes hummed overhead. On the far side of the valley, he followed a platoon of troops with skis on their backs as they climbed out of Alstad and up into the mountains. But despite these movements, he was painfully aware that the men in the church had remained where they were.

The hours ticked by. The afternoon came and went. As the evening drew on, the shadows lengthened and the sun dipped below the mountains behind them. There was no sign of Sulheim or of the German observers leaving the church.

It was after ten when Chevannes shuffled down the slope beside him.

'They're still there, sir,' said Tanner.

Chevannes peered through his binoculars. '*Merde*,' he said.

'I could go down when it's dark and try to get them.'

Chevannes bit his lip, but before he could answer, a truck arrived at Uskum Farm and men got out.

'I take it we stay here for the time being,' said Tanner.

Chevannes turned away without looking at him. 'Yes, Sergeant,' he snapped. 'For the moment.'

As the brief hours of darkness passed, Tanner's anger and frustration rose. Never had he felt more inclined to throttle the French lieutenant. He could not help thinking about the Allied front line. Was it still at Kvam? Surely not. By now they must have been pushed ever further away. A whole day wasted, and now, perhaps, several more. And it was cold up there among the pines. Not for the first time Tanner wished he had never set eyes on Colonel Gulbrand and his men.

It was with relief that Brigadier Morgan saw Major General Bernard Paget standing before him at his small headquarters at Heidel. He had known him a long time – indeed, they had worked together before the war – and Morgan had always thought the general cut an impressive figure. The fierce, intelligent eyes, the long, aquiline nose and thin lips somehow contained so much authority. Not for nothing had Paget gained a reputation as one of the finest trainers of British soldiers the Army had possessed in many years.

'General, how very good to see you,' said Morgan, stepping forward into the dim light and clasping Paget's hand.

'Harry,' said Paget. 'Good to see you too, although I wish the circumstances might have been different. This is a hell of a bloody mess, isn't it?'

'You've seen General Ruge?'

'Just come from his headquarters south of Dombas.' Paget chuckled mirthlessly. 'And got an earful too. Not very impressed with we Brits, is he?'

'No, sir.'

'And with reason. This is a shambles, Harry, a bloody shambles. Not your fault – you've done jolly well and Ruge is impressed with you. I'm afraid it's the bods back at Whitehall who are to blame. Lack of planning, lack of thought. Not enough kit. Not enough bloody air cover. Anyway.' He sat down in front of Morgan's desk while the brigadier poured two tumblers of whisky from the bottle Ruge had brought the previous evening. It was already nearly finished.

'Tell me what the news is here. Communication seems to be half the problem. No radios, not enough telephones. No reconnaissance. How are 15th Brigade doing?'

'We've held off the enemy so far, General. The narrowness of the valley has worked in our favour and the Gladiators have performed magnificently. I think the sight of them has given heart to the troops.'

'Good,' said Paget, then raised his glass. 'Cheers.'

Morgan raised his in turn, then added, 'But I'm afraid there are only four serviceable aircraft left now, so I'm not sure how much they can achieve tomorrow.'

'And what about tomorrow?'

Morgan took a large gulp of his drink. 'The enemy never seems to attack during the night or early in the morning. A real creature of habit. So I've straightened the line and brought up some reserves, but no doubt by mid-morning they'll come at us heavy again. I hate to say this, General, but I don't think we'll survive another night. Our best hope is to keep the enemy at bay until evening and withdraw overnight. As it is, Brigadier Smyth has been wounded.'

Paget nodded. 'All right, Harry. I'm going to report back to London tonight, if I can, and you should know that I'm going to recommend our withdrawal. Your brigade's already had a savage dusting. I can't see any point in letting the rest of our troops be lambs to the slaughter as well.'

Morgan finished his whisky, then said, 'did General Ruge mention anything to you about a missing patrol of British and French troops?'

'Is this the scientist?'

'Yes, sir. Professor Hening Sandvold.'

'Yes – yes, he did.'

'The King's very anxious they should be found.'

'I know, but we can't hang around here on the off-chance when this fellow might already be dead.'

'I don't think he is, though, sir. London intercepted a radio signal broadcast by the Germans. Apparently they've warned Norwegians to report any sightings and threatened severe punishment for anyone not complying. It seems Jerry's on to them.'

Paget stroked his chin thoughtfully. 'Well,' he said at length, 'we'd better hope they're still out there and that they get to us quickly. I'm sorry, Harry, but the King has to face facts: we can't stay here for much longer. Not for him and certainly not for some errant Norwegian professor.'

15

There had been no movement by the Germans all night, and neither was there as the morning wore on.

Tanner's mood was not good. Not good at all. Nor was it improved by Chevannes, who had joined him and Sykes at the lookout only to pace about, clicking his fingers and grimacing. Trying to ignore him, Tanner watched another German army truck trundle down the valley. An aeroplane droned above.

Chevannes lifted his binoculars and Sykes cried out, 'Sir, no! With respect, sir.'

Chevannes stared at him, then slowly lowered them.

'For God's sake,' muttered Tanner.

'The sun, sir,' added Sykes. 'It could reflect in the lens.'

'Yes, of course,' said Chevannes. 'You are quite right, Corporal.' He pursed his lips, then said, 'Perhaps we should go over the mountains.'

It was something Tanner had thought about as well. Yet behind them there was a range of snow-covered peaks, as much as six thousand feet high. From the map – and Anna had confirmed this – it appeared to be a snow-covered and largely barren wilderness, with no roads and a number of difficult mountain lakes they would be forced to navigate round. Perhaps they could cross them successfully and reach the valley beyond, but there was no knowing how long it might take. 'Sir, I think we should sit tight and hold our nerve,' Tanner said. 'Jerry hasn't taken Sulheim's truck. It's still there. If we trek across the mountains we'll lose more than another day.'

Chevannes was gazing out towards the farm, biting his lip. Then, without another word, he left them and returned to the *seter*.

'A real decisive one there,' said Sykes, once the lieutenant was out of earshot.

'Oh, I don't know, Stan,' said Tanner. 'He was pretty decisive yesterday when he ordered us to stay here. His problem is that he digs his heels in when he shouldn't and not when he should. I've seen his type before. Bloody brilliant officers in peacetime. They can run further than anyone else, they're a damn good shot, they know all the drill, carry out exercises to the letter. They always look spick and span. But when the fighting starts, they're all over the place because the one thing they can't do is lead men in battle. Real fighting isn't like practise fighting. It doesn't follow the training manual. And golden boys, like Xavier bloody Chevannes, find out they're not quite so bloody marvellous as they thought.'

'And they don't like being shown up by NCOs, hey, Sarge?'

'Well, what I am supposed to do? Sit back and let him make disastrous decisions?'

'No, I didn't mean that, Sarge. But it's why he hates you. That's clear enough.'

'Yes,' said Tanner, spitting grit out of his mouth. 'Believe me, Stan, the feeling's mutual.'

The hours rolled by slowly. At around four, the German troops left the farm, yet there was no movement from the church.

'What are they playing at, Sarge?'

'I've been trying to work that one out all day.'

'I mean, we've seen patrols go up into the mountains but they've made no attempt to search the forest.'

'It's strange,' agreed Tanner. 'But I've been thinking about that. I suppose they must be trying to save casualties, but I also think they believe it'll be easier to take Sandvold alive in the open than in dense forest. They're waiting for us to come to them.'

'Yes,' said Sykes, nodding. 'You're right, Sarge.'

'They're assuming we're still somewhere in this valley,' Tanner went on. 'After all, we were seen by a number of Norwegians, and although they've had recce aircraft out in force, they haven't spotted any sign of us crossing the mountains. I suppose they think we'll have to show ourselves soon and are waiting to pounce on us when we do.'

'They've been a bit bloody obvious about it.'

'I suppose they think we won't have seen the men in the church. It's obvious they don't know where we are, just somewhere in the Jøra valley. But put yourselves in their shoes. With every hour that passes with no sign of us, doubt will be creeping into their minds. My hunch is they'll think we'll come down tonight when it's dark.'

'And if we don't?'

'Hopefully they'll give up and bugger off.'

'And if they don't?'

'Don't know, Stan. We think of something else.'

Shortly after six, three trucks of troops pulled into Uksum Farm. The men jumped out and made a show of searching the entire settlement at Alstad once more. A little under three hours later, they loaded up again and, with much revving of engines, drove away in the direction of Lillehammer.

Chevannes appeared at the lookout shortly after.

'So they are leaving,' he said, triumph on his face. 'We set off as soon as it is dark.'

'It's a trap, sir,' said Tanner. 'They've still got men in the church.'

Chevannes' expression changed. 'Are you sure, Sergeant?'

'Yes.' Tanner observed him. The only consolation, he thought, for the enforced frustrating delay was the obvious discomfort it was causing the Frenchman. 'As I said earlier, sir, we need to keep our nerve.'

Chevannes snorted, then sharply turned away.

Not long after, Anna joined them at the lookout. 'I've come in my role as chief medical officer,' she said.

'Is that what you are, Miss?' said Tanner, grinning.

'Yes, and I want to know whether either of you has had any sleep.'

'I have, Miss,' said Sykes. 'Took forty winks earlier this afternoon.'

'Sergeant?'

'Not today,' admitted Tanner.

'Then you must get some,' she told him. 'We need you fresh and alert.'

'Is that an order?'

'It is.' Anna smiled.

'And how about you, Miss?' asked Tanner. 'The lads are minding their manners, I hope?'

'They've been most courteous.'

'What – that lot?' said Sykes. 'I don't believe it.'

'Well,' she said, 'they swear often, but they always apologize afterwards.'

'It's because they're Yorkshiremen, Miss,' said Sykes. 'Me and the sarge are from the south, but those lads are northerners. They're born with filthy mouths. Can't help themselves.'

'I don't mind.' She laughed, then stood up to leave. 'Now remember, Sergeant,' she said, 'sleep. It's very important.'

She was right, Tanner realized, and once she had gone, he lay back, his pack as a pillow, and closed his eyes.

He was asleep in moments, despite the discomfort of his surroundings, and by dawn, he felt refreshed; despite hunger, his head was clear. He watched the sun rise over the mountains on the far side of the valley, casting a golden light over the snow and dazzling him.

It was a little after three when he suddenly saw troop movements at the farm. There were eight men, and soon after he heard the rumble of an engine starting up.

Immediately bringing the binoculars to his eyes, he peered at the farm and watched the troops disappear behind a shed. Soon after, a small truck he had not noticed the day before, emerged and turned right on to the road, heading south.

Tanner reported this to Chevannes. 'It could still be a trap, though, sir.'

'What about the soldiers in the church?'

'That might have been them. But I couldn't say for certain.'

Chevannes nodded. 'We'll wait here a while longer.'

At nearly half past four, Tanner spotted Sulheim emerge from the farmhouse. Constantly glancing around him, he hurried out of the yard, across the river and pastures towards the trees.

When he reached the *setor*, he was short of breath, but his eyes were wide with excitement. 'They have gone,' he told them, then grinned. 'You have been spotted back over on the other side of the mountain. They think you crossed into the Gudbrandsdal valley again.'

'What about the men in the church?' asked Tanner. 'Was that them leaving earlier?'

Sulheim nodded. 'Yes. I did not let them know that I speak German, but the officer was becoming increasingly agitated. He was convinced you would appear when it was dark. I think he was on the point of leaving anyway when he had the signal.'

'How could we have been spotted?' Chevannes asked.

'A Norwegian reported seeing you.' He grinned again. 'You see? We are mostly patriotic countrymen around here.'

They loaded their packs hastily and headed back down the mountain to the valley. Unease dogged Tanner's every step, as though they were heading inexorably into a trap. Yet no shots were fired, neither did enemy troops appear. At the farm, anxious minutes ticked by as Sulheim replaced the alternator in the truck. His wife gave them bread and cold meat, but Tanner's appetite had left him.

At last they were ready to go. It was some time after six o'clock on the morning of Saturday, 27 April.

'What will you say if the Germans return and see the truck gone?' Tanner asked Sulheim.

'That you came back and forced us to hand it over.'

'Perhaps we should tie you up. Otherwise you'd be obliged to contact them the moment we left.'

'All right.'

Shortly after, with the family bound and left in the house, they loaded themselves into the truck. 'I'll drive,' Tanner told Chevannes. 'I know these vehicles. The British Army's got hundreds of them.' It was true, although the military versions were larger, heavier, and of a more basic construction. Nonetheless as Tanner stepped into the cab with Anna and Lieutenant Chevannes beside him, the driving mechanism felt familiar. Turn the ignition key, pull out the choke and press down the starter in the footwell. The engine turned over a couple of times then fired into life, the speedometer and oil pressure gauge flickering. Tanner put his foot down on the deep clutch, pushed the shaking lever into gear, released the handbrake, then eased them out of the yard and on to the road.

* * *

In Lillehammer, Reichsamtsleiter Scheidt had spent another wretched night sleeping little, drinking too much brandy, smoking too many cigarettes and railing against their continued inability to find and capture Odin. With the arrival of morning and his return to the SD offices, his mood had worsened when a signal arrived from Zellner informing him that the night's search had been fruitless and that misinformation from a Norwegian farmer had sent them on a wild-goose chase back to the western side of the Gudbrandsdalen.

'Please stop fretting, Herr Reichsamtsleiter,' Kurz had told him. 'Go out and get some fresh air. Take a walk. But, for God's sake, stop glowering in here.'

Scheidt was contemplating doing as Kurz suggested when a clerk knocked at the door. Kurz looked up.

'A signal, sir. It's just come through.'

Scheidt strode over and snatched the thin transcript paper. As he read it, a smile broke across his face. 'At last,' he said. 'Perhaps your brand of optimism is justified after all, Sturmbannführer.'

'Atmospheric conditions have changed, then?' grinned Kurz.

Scheidt nodded. 'It would seem so, Sturmbannführer.'

A different message was tapped out to Zellner, now back at Tretten after another exhausting night in which he had felt the fear of failure clawing at him. As the clerk brought it to him, he snatched the piece of paper from his hand and read it with mounting excitement.

'Odin located in Jøra valley. They have M/T and are heading north. Stop them. Do not fail. Kurz.'

* * *

Tanner glanced in the mirror. Through the window at the back of the cab, he could see Erwood and Hepworth manning the Bren, its barrel resting on the tailgate. Next to them Larsen was scanning the valley with his binoculars to the south. It was meandering and close, narrowing to no more than a few hundred yards wide, the steep, wooded slopes rising above them. It gave Tanner a claustrophobic feeling, as though the world was closing in on them.

They drove in silence at first, which suited him. He wanted to concentrate and keep a watchful guard on the road ahead without distraction, but at length Chevannes spoke. 'Tell me, Anna,' he said, 'have you always lived here in the Gudbrandsdalen?'

'My family have, yes,' she said, 'but I have been studying in Oslo for the past three years.'

'Studying what?'

'Medicine – at the university.'

'A doctor in the making. You must be very clever.'

Anna looked down, embarrassed. 'Perhaps I will not be able to finish now. I still have another year. Everything has stopped with the war.'

'I am sure it will not go on for ever. In any case, people will still need doctors.'

'I will not become a doctor under the Nazis,' Anna replied, anger in her voice.

'No, no, of course not. Anyway, I am sure we will send them packing. Most of the French forces are in the north. With the British and our joint naval forces we will turn the tide. Lack of proper planning has been the problem here, but that won't be the case on the coast.'

'I hope you're right.' Anna sounded doubtful.

'I am, and let me tell you why. France has the largest army in the world. I know we have all seen pictures of Germans goose-stepping at Nazi rallies, but that is for show. They might have swept aside Poland, but the Polish cavalry was still on horseback. There is nothing so very remarkable about beating Poland. France, on the other hand, has an army of more than two million men, and more tanks and guns than Britain and Germany put together. In any case, we have sent some of our best troops to Norway – the Chasseurs Alpins, of course, but also the Légion Étrangère. So all will be well, you'll see.' He patted her knee.

Tanner felt her flinch. *Shut the hell up, you French bastard*, he thought. This was no time to sweet-talk Anna Rostad.

'Of course,' said Chevannes, after a short pause, 'I never went to university myself, but I did study at St Cyr. That's our national military academy.'

Anna nodded.

'Yes,' he continued, 'it is a fine place. It was established by the emperor himself, Napoleon Bonaparte. Near Versailles. Ah, it was a wonderful time in my life, training to be a soldier – training hard, I should add. It was something I had always wanted to do. And with Paris on our doorstep. I have never been to Oslo, but Paris is a beautiful city. A wonderful city. You must visit one day, Anna. Come to Paris and I will show you around myself.'

'All clear at the back?' yelled Tanner, leaning out of the open window.

'All clear, Sarge,' came Sykes's muffled reply.

'And Versailles is magnificent, of course,' continued Chevannes. 'A stunning palace but also the gardens—'

'Where are we now, sir?' said Tanner.

Chevannes stopped speaking and opened the map on his lap.

'We're leaving the river behind,' added Tanner.

Anna peered over Chevannes' shoulder. 'Yes,' she said. 'We are here.' She pointed a finger. 'We are climbing to the Espedalen where there is a mountain lake.'

Tanner dropped down a gear as they drove out of the valley. The road was now rough and potholed, and the truck laboured as the track steepened. 'Come on,' muttered Tanner, 'you can do it.' The Morris kept going, but more slowly with every yard. 'Are you scanning the skies, Dan, Hep?' he shouted.

'Yes, Sarge,' came the reply.

'Don't worry, Sergeant,' said Anna, 'the road soon levels off again.'

'Good. I don't like going so slowly. Too bloody easy for any passing Jerry aircraft.' He leant forward and tried to look up. A few bulbous white clouds but otherwise the sky was a deep and bright blue. Not good for spotting enemy aircraft.

They inched round a hairpin bend and hit a pothole, which jolted them sideways. Amid groans from the back, Anna was knocked against Chevannes. 'Sorry,' she said.

'Why would I mind having you thrown against me?' Chevannes smiled, and Anna, flustered, brushed her hair off her face. 'I must say,' he continued, 'I do admire you. It was a very brave decision you made, to come with us.'

'I wanted to help my country,' said Anna, quietly.

'Yes, but for us – well, we are soldiers, and we expect—'

'What's that noise?' snapped Tanner.

'I didn't hear anything,' said Chevannes.

Of course not, thought Tanner. *You're bloody yapping too much*. He strained his ears. Yes, there it was again, un-mistakable – an aircraft, maybe two. His body tensed and he bounced up and down in his seat, willing the truck to go faster. 'I can hear an aircraft!' he yelled. 'Can anyone see it?' He turned to Chevannes. 'Sir, can you see anything?'

Chevannes leant from the cab, but as he did so, Hepworth shouted, 'Got them, sir! Two aircraft at five o'clock. Coming up the valley.'

'Get some bloody binoculars on them!' Tanner shouted.

Chevannes turned in his seat and leant out of the window, glasses to his eyes. The truck was gaining momentum once more. Beneath them was a steep, almost sheer, wooded valley. On their right, the mountain continued to climb. An old farmhouse now, perched on a cliff-top; more grass-roofed shacks. Tanner searched ahead for a place to shelter at the side of the road, but there was nothing. Rather, as the road straightened he could see the deep ravine to their left rising towards the long, narrow lake Anna had spoken of. *Christ*. They were even more exposed up here.

'Single engine, Sergeant!' Larsen called out. 'Two.'

'Stukas!' said Chevannes. '*Mon Dieu.*'

Tanner tried to think. *Drive straight on. Keep going. If they know about Sandvold, they're not going to hit us.* He

293

could hear them clearly now, the thrum of their engines. The road was rough, but clear and straight – almost dead straight. He put his foot on the accelerator and watched the needle flicker on the speedometer. Sixty, sixty-five, edging seventy kilometres per hour. What was that? Forty miles an hour? *Come on*, he thought. *Keep going for me.*

'They're right on top of us, Sarge!' said Hepworth. 'Bloody look at them bastards!'

'What are you doing?' said Chevannes, swinging back down into the cab. His face was tense, his eyes wide.

'I'm going to bloody well keep driving. The faster we move the harder it'll be for them to hit us. If I need to swerve off the road, I will.' His hands tightened around the steering-wheel.

The two Stukas flew on, until Tanner could see them, small but distinct. It was hard to know how high they were, but he guessed at least six thousand feet.

'They're flying past us,' said Anna.

'It's not possible,' muttered Chevannes. 'Surely not.'

'They're getting a lead before they dive.'

Sure enough, the aircraft turned 180 degrees on to their backs and dived at about a ninety-degree angle. Sirens wailing, they screamed towards them, the valley resounding to their deafening drone.

'It's such a terrible sound!' Anna closed her eyes and placed her hands over her ears. Then, as the lead Stuka seemed about to plummet straight into them, it levelled out. From its undercarriage they watched as a dark cigar-shaped bomb detached itself from the belly and fell, shrieking its death whistle, seemingly hurtling straight for them. Tanner pushed his foot down harder on the accelerator and ducked. A split second later a deafening explosion behind them rocked the truck. Tanner gripped the steering-wheel and righted it as the second aircraft pulled out of its dive. Another bomb howled towards them, debris from the first raining and clattering across the tarpaulin and metal cab roof. Tanner ducked again, Anna screamed, and there was another explosion, this time ahead.

Tanner felt the brakes lock, and momentarily lost control of the front of the truck, then regained it and straightened the Morris. With a screech of burning rubber, it slid across the stony road and they ground to a halt as a swirling mass of cloud and smoke enveloped them.

'Are you mad?' yelled Chevannes. 'Now we are sitting ducks!'

'Not in this smoke. Anyway, they're not trying to kill us, sir,' Tanner shouted back. 'They're trying to stop us!' He wound up the window, coughing as dust, grit and cordite choked him. Debris – stone, earth, bits of metal – clattered down once more. 'They want Sandvold alive,' Tanner spluttered, eyelids stinging. 'As soon as this clears I'll try to get us going again, but we don't want to fall into any crater.'

As Tanner had suspected, the two Stuka dive-bombers had gone without strafing. It was the confirmation he needed that the capture of Sandvold alive was the enemy objective. Knowing this made no difference to their goal of reaching the Allies, but it meant the Germans had to be careful about how they attacked them. That, he knew, was a useful advantage.

As the clouds of dust dispersed they could see the crater just ahead: a large hole spread across more than three-quarters of the road. The bank on the left, overlooking the lake, had collapsed, while boulders and other rocky debris were scattered twenty yards around it.

'Bollocks,' said Tanner, stepping out of the cab and hurrying to the crater's edge. Chevannes had followed him, and now, from the back of the truck, came Sykes and Lieutenant Larsen.

'Can't help but admire it, can you?' said Sykes, as they stood there regarding the damage.

'Bloody fine marksmanship,' agreed Tanner.

'We'll never get the truck past,' said Larsen.

'Damn you, Tanner,' said Chevannes. 'I knew we should have waited until this evening when we would have been out of sight of the Luftwaffe. Now we're stuck, unless you have any more bright ideas.'

'Well, sir,' he winked at Sykes, then turned back to Chevannes, 'if you'd take your men and keep a good watch out for any trouble, the corporal and I will get us moving again.'

Sykes delved into his bag and produced two cartridges of Polar dynamite. 'See, sir?' Sykes beamed at Chevannes.

'You wish to make another crater?' The Frenchman was clearly appalled.

'No, sir. We're going to blast away a bit of the bank. Then we drive round the crater.'

Tanner hurried back to the truck where Sandvold and the other men were waiting anxiously. Grabbing his pack, he said, 'Get ready with your shovels.

296

We're going to have to do a bit of clearing in a minute.'

'What the bloody hell's going on, Sarge?' asked Erwood.

'Bomb crater in the road. And we need to get past it, pronto.' He hurried back and took out his tin of safety fuse, which Sykes tied round the dynamite and placed in a small hole in the bank that he had already dug.

'How far back, Stan?' said Tanner. 'I've only got about forty foot left here.'

'Forty foot! Blimey, Sarge, we don't need anything like that! A foot or so should be fine. This stuff burns at two foot per minute, so just give me time to get out of the way. You might want to take the truck back a bit, though.'

Tanner nodded, cut the fuse and ran back to the truck. After he had reversed thirty yards, he saw Sykes signal, then put a match to the fuse and run down the road towards him. He turned to Anna, still waiting patiently in the truck. 'Might want to duck your head,' he told her. He kept an eye on his watch, following the seconds ticking by. A breathless Sykes reached him. 'Any moment now, Sarge.'

An ear-splitting crack rent the silence of the valley, the report echoing across the lake, while another cloud of dust briefly obscured the road. Once the rain of rock, stone and grit had settled, Tanner and Sykes hurried back to the crater to see the result of their efforts.

Hallelujah. A six-foot wide chunk of the bank had been blown, most of which appeared to have slumped into the existing crater. The road was a mess of rock, stone and earth, but it would soon be passable once more.

'Stan,' said Tanner, patting his corporal on the back. 'You're a genius.'

'I bloody am an' all.' He grinned.

Tanner returned to the truck, brought it forward, then ordered his men to get out and start clearing. Less than ten minutes later, the road was ready, and with the men standing and watching, Tanner began to inch forward. A scrape of metal as the offside wing ground against the bank. Tanner could feel the resistance of the rock. 'Sorry, Mr Sulheim,' he said to himself, then pressed his foot on the throttle. A painful screech of metal, and the truck lurched forward. A moment later, it was safely on the other side.

'Quick! *Vite!*' shouted Chevannes. The men got back into the truck, Chevannes rejoined Tanner and Anna in the cab and they set off once more. Tanner looked at his watch again: a little over twenty minutes from the start of the attack. A glance at the map, open once more on Chevannes' lap. He wondered how long it would take the Stuka crews to return to their base and warn the ground troops of their position. With the road blocked behind them, he guessed the enemy would be coming from the Gudbrandsdal valley, joining the road at Vinstra. It was a good distance to Vinstra from Tretten, but who was to say whether the troops would come from Tretten or further north up the valley? It was impossible to know. He wiped a hand across his brow. Really, he thought, they might meet Germans at any moment. Perhaps Chevannes had been right, after all. Perhaps they should have waited. *No*, he told himself. *We need to make ground while we can*.

'Are you all right, Sergeant?' asked Anna.

'Yes – thank you, Miss.' Then he said to Chevannes,

'Sir, we need to watch the road ahead like hawks.'

'Yes, *thank you*, Sergeant, but all I can see at the moment is the end of the lake,' said Chevannes, 'so at present there is little I can do.'

'In a couple of kilometres, the road climbs again,' said Anna. 'It follows the lip of the mountain plateau. You can see a long way from up there.'

'What about snow?'

'There will be snow on the mountains but the road will be clear by now. I'm certain of that. There are quite a few farms along it – they will make sure the road can be used.'

'Good,' said Tanner, then took his German binoculars from round his neck and passed them to Anna. 'Here,' he said. 'Do me a favour, will you? Keep a dekko with these.'

'A what, Sergeant?'

Tanner smiled. 'Sorry, Miss. Soldier slang. It means, could you keep a sharp lookout?'

'Of course.' She returned the smile, and Tanner was pleased to see irritation on Chevannes' face.

A mile, then two. Suddenly the end of the lake re-appeared and the climb began. Tanner dropped down a gear, the Morris grinding sluggishly forward. The road was winding, too, so their forward view was never more than a hundred yards at most. Tanner felt a heaviness in his stomach. He tapped his fingers on the steering-wheel, bounced up and down in his seat again, then eventually took out his last remaining packet of German cigarettes, offered one to Chevannes and Anna – who both declined – then fumbled for his matches. The effort of getting at them from under his jerkin, then delving into the right-hand breast pocket on his battle blouse caused him to drive over a pothole and briefly lose control of the wheel.

'Concentrate, Sergeant,' snapped Chevannes. 'We haven't come this far just for you to drive us off the road.'

Tanner ignored him, and as he clutched the steering-wheel, matches now in one hand, Anna said, 'Would you like me to light it for you?'

'Thanks, Miss,' said Tanner, and passed her both matches and cigarette. Having lit it, she carefully placed the cigarette between his lips.

'Thanks,' said Tanner again, inhaling deeply.

'Don't forget to keep watching the road ahead, Anna,' said Chevannes.

'No, of course – sorry,' she said, hastily bringing the binoculars back to her eyes. Tanner smiled to himself – as if they'd be any use on this winding stretch of road. He opened the window and the smoke dissolved through the narrow gap. It felt cooler already, and Tanner felt a shiver run down his back. *Christ! Any moment, just round this corner* ... But then he turned and the road was still empty. He felt a momentary flutter of relief.

'We're nearly there,' said Anna, as they drove round a sharp hairpin. Beneath them, away to their right, there was a deep ravine, dark, forbidding and densely covered with thick forest, but as they crested the brow the road levelled at last. To the left, they saw the snow-covered mountain plateau, to their right the ravine and in front, the long, straight road that hugged the lip for some

300

fifteen miles, almost all the way to Vinstra. 'How far can you see now?' Tanner asked Anna.

'Three or four kilometres at least. It's empty.'

Patches of thin mud-brown snow covered the road, but its surface was clear enough for Tanner to push down hard on the throttle and build up speed. 'See anything at the back?' Tanner yelled.

'Nothing,' came the muffled reply.

Where were they? Tanner wondered. He drummed his fingers, felt the pistol at his hip; his trusted Enfield was wedged between his seat and the door.

Another two miles, and the road veered to the left, round a subsidiary valley to the main ravine, then curved back and straightened once more. As Anna had told them, there were a number of farms along this high mountain route, but not a soul stirred. The road was empty – not a cart, person or animal. Tanner realized he had barely even seen a bird. The place seemed lifeless; it was almost impossible to think a war could be going on. Tanner strained his eyes. One of the eyelids flickered. Fatigue was getting the better of him.

A glint in the distance snapped him out of his reverie. 'There!' he said. 'What was that?'

Both Chevannes and Anna had their binoculars trained. Another glint. 'There it was again!' said Tanner.

'It's them,' said Chevannes. 'A convoy of four trucks.'

Tanner's heart was drumming in his chest, his tiredness forgotten. 'How far?'

'Seven kilometres, maybe eight.'

'What are we going to do?' asked Anna, fear in her voice.

'Stop and head into the mountains,' said Chevannes.

'Here?' said Tanner. 'Where? There's no cover at all.' He glanced at the map. 'Where are we? What's this valley here?' With half an eye on the map, he pointed to a dog-leg in the road.

'It's not far,' said Anna. 'Look, the road turns just ahead.'

'Good. Another valley to skirt round, then we'll be out of view. Ten to one it'll be wooded. We can ditch the truck there and take cover in the trees.'

To his relief, as they turned the corner and lost sight of the enemy, Tanner saw that the landscape was covered with dense forest. To their right a mountain stream was tumbling and cascading down to the ravine. At the corner of the dog-leg, the road crossed the stream and it was here that Tanner stopped.

'Everyone out! Quick!' shouted Chevannes.

Tanner hurried to the back of the truck and grabbed his pack, slinging it on to his shoulders, his mind whirling. 'Five miles at twenty miles an hour,' he mumbled, 'take away five. Ten minutes.' He looked at his watch. Nearly half past ten. Ten minutes to get Sandvold and Anna away and come up with a plan to delay the Germans. *Think, man, think.*

Chevannes was already urging the others to head into the trees. 'Come on!' he shouted. 'Quickly! Get moving!'

'Sir, wait!' Tanner called out. He ran up to him. 'Sir, if you and your men take the professor and Miss Rostad, my men and I will try to hold them off for a while.'

Chevannes paused then said, 'Very well.'

'Miss – Anna,' said Tanner. 'Where will you head for?'

'Here,' she told him. Her finger was shaking as she pointed on the map. 'Skjedalen. There are several mountain *seters* where we can shelter.' She swallowed, her eyes searching Tanner's face for reassurance. 'There are two peaks above us over to the right of where we are now – the Olasfjellet and the Silikampan. Keep those on your right and head almost due north.'

'All right,' he said. 'Now go. Wait for us there.'

Wide-eyed, frightened, she turned and ran.

'Lads, quick,' he said, calling his men to him. 'We need to halt these Jerry bastards. There are four trucks, and by my reckoning that's around seventy men.' The men's faces were ashen. 'Stan, the time has come for us to use up a bit more of our explosive. Can you start rigging the truck? You've got about five minutes. Dan, head up stream a bit, then cut into the trees on the right-hand side. Look for a good view down here, where you can see the road both sides of the bridge. The rest, follow Dan and be ready with your magazines. Find some good cover. The corp and I will join you in a minute. Now get going. Iggery, all right?'

Erwood and the other five hurried off and Sykes was already rigging together four cartons of Nobel's gelignite.

'What have you got, Sarge?' he asked, quick fingers deftly tying a length of fuse round them.

'Five more packets of Nobel's and about ten sticks of Polar. Oh, and half a dozen grenades. Where you going to put them?'

'Round the fuel tank, I thought. And why don't you put one of your cartons of Nobel's in the engine bay?'

'All right. What size bang is this going to make?'

'A big one.' Sykes grinned.

'Good. It needs to be. We've got to blow up as many of those trucks and as many Jerries as possible. How are we going to trigger it?'

'Grenade on the door?'

'Sounds good.' He lifted one side of the bonnet, and placed the carton of gelignite beside the coil.

'Seems a shame to blow her up,' said Sykes, as he opened the driver's side of the cab and leant in to set the booby trap on the passenger door. 'She's a good little runner, this one, and only a year or two old.'

'All for the greater good, Stan.'

'I s'pose. Even so.'

He handed the fuse back to Tanner then said, 'I see Mr Chevannes has buggered off.'

'I told him to. Someone's got to look after the professor and Miss Rostad.'

'He didn't need much persuading.'

'No, the sod. I could read his mind like a bloody book. He was thinking, This might seem a bit cowardly, but there's every chance I'll get rid of that bastard Tanner.' He chuckled. 'Christ, he's a pain in the arse.'

'Well, it's just us now, Sarge.'

'Yes,' said Tanner, 'and I feel happier already. Right. All done?'

Sykes nodded.

'Good. Let's get the hell away from here.' They scrambled off the road and up the side of the stream. 'You in position, Dan?' Tanner called to Erwood.

'Yes, Sarge,' Erwood shouted back, as Tanner and Sykes continued climbing up and away from the road.

'Good cover?'

'Yes, Sarge!'

'Have you sorted out your escape route?'

A pause. 'Think so, Sarge.'

Tanner slipped, cursed, then looked back to see the leading enemy truck turn the last shallow curve in the road a couple of hundred yards behind them. His heart was thumping again. 'Here they come!' Tanner called, and scrambled up through the snow and into the trees, short of breath, chest tight, blood pumping. *Good*, he thought. Erwood, with Hepworth beside him, lay behind a rocky outcrop, a clear field of fire on the road below and the stream beneath them. The other riflemen were nearby, most behind trees but making good use of the undulations on the steep slope rising from the stream. They were learning, thought Tanner. Behind him, he saw the others' tracks disappearing into the trees. The forested slopes, he knew, would be a great help; as the mountain climbed away from them, the dense pines seemed to draw towards one another, so that within about seventy yards from where he now stood he could no longer see any snow-covered ground at all, only the trees. The pines would protect them as they fell back.

'Stan, you stick back on the lip of the ravine,' he told his corporal. He wanted Sykes to be able to make an easy get-away, should it be necessary. 'And here,' he said, taking off his pack and gas-mask bag, 'keep these by your feet, or put them somewhere out of the way.' He now realized how foolhardy he had been in keeping so much high explosive about him during the firefight at the *seter*; he'd been fortunate then, but he didn't want to chance his luck a second time. He grabbed two sticks of Polar dynamite and three grenades, then stuffed them into his haversack, which still hung from his hip, and ran over to Erwood and Hepworth.

'Hep, grab your rifle and move back. I'm going to man the Bren with Dan.'

'Where to, Sarge?' asked Hepworth.

'Up the hill a bit. Where you can get some good shots in and get away quickly. Go! Get a bloody move on!'

Along the road ahead the trucks were drawing near. With shaking hands, Tanner undid the fastenings on his magazine pouches, felt in his haversack for his grenades and .303 ammunition clips, then pulled his rifle into his shoulder. 'Got a couple of tracer rounds, Dan?'

Erwood handed him two. Tanner fed them into an ammunition clip and slotted it into his rifle's magazine.

'Ready?' he asked.

'Sarge.'

'Don't fire until I say.' He took a bead on the truck. The pack of Nobel's strapped to the fuel tank was out of sight, but he had a clear view of the bonnet. His body was tense, heart hammering, as the first enemy truck drew alongside the Morris-Commercial, then slowly pushed on across the bridge. *Damn*, he thought, then saw that the two trucks following had halted alongside Sulheim's wagon. Orders were being barked and troops, most now wearing helmets rather than field caps, were jumping from the back of the lorries. Tanner watched with bated breath as two men approached the Morris. Then, to his annoyance, they stepped round to the far side and opened the door. 'Sod it,' whispered Tanner.

'What is it, Sarge?' mouthed Erwood.

'They've opened the wrong door.' The soldiers were shouting now and pointing wildly. 'They've found the grenade,' muttered Tanner, and pulled back the bolt on his rifle. He knew that the moment he fired the battle would start. Would he survive? Would any of them? *God only knows.* He swallowed hard, took a deep breath and squeezed the trigger.

The first bullet missed, but the men by the truck had had no chance to look up before the second slammed into the bonnet, puncturing the thin metal, tearing into the packet of gelignite and igniting it. Less than a split second later, the explosion in the engine bay provided the spark needed to detonate the two packs of Nobel's that Sykes had tied to the petrol tank. A vast ball of livid orange flame erupted round the Morris, incinerating the men who, a moment before, had been examining the cab, and engulfing the second German truck. Stunned soldiers screamed and fell backwards, some on fire. Now the third truck was aflame, the engine exploding, propelling shards of metal and glass.

'Bloody hell, Sarge!' whistled Erwood.

'Start firing, Dan,' said Tanner. 'We might have destroyed two trucks but that's only half the job.' He fired off several rounds himself as the Bren began to chatter next to him, empty cartridge cases clattering on to the bare rock. Men were falling in disarray at either side of the burning vehicles, too stunned to think clearly or organize themselves, but Tanner knew this advantage would soon pass. Adrenalin had taken over from fear. His mind was alert and clear, and what concerned him now was that the men from the first and last trucks, either side of the carnage, would try to infiltrate round the side of their position. Smoke billowed upwards – thick, black smoke. It covered the road and lead truck too. *Bollocks.* He'd not thought of that, but it gave the enemy from the lead truck perfect cover to make an advance up the slope on the far side of the stream. *We should make what use of it we can too*, thought Tanner.

'We need to fall back, Dan,' he said, with sudden clarity, 'and quick.' A moment later he heard a whistle and twenty yards to his right there was an explosion.

'What was that?' shouted Erwood.

'Mortars! They're firing bloody mortars from behind the smokescreen!' Two more followed in quick succession. Bullets were now zipping through the trees as the enemy troops from the first truck found their composure and their aim. 'Quick, Dan, get off a few rounds towards that first truck! Fire through the smoke!' shouted Tanner. Vague figures flitted in the haze as enemy troops scurried from the direction of the truck and onto the bank beside the road. Blindly, he fired several rounds in succession. A man cried out and a spectral figure fell, but Tanner knew it was now critical that he and his men move back. His mouth was parched with acrid smoke. Tracer now arced luminously through the smoke – a machine-gun: its rapid fire raked the ground around them in short deadly bursts. Even with half the force destroyed or out of action, enemy fire-power was already proving too heavy.

'Come on, Dan, we've got to move.' He pulled out a grenade. 'On three get up and go. One, two, three! Now!'

Erwood stood up, then fell back with a cry. 'Bastard!' he yelled. 'He's got my arm!'

'Think you can still move?'

Grimacing, Erwood nodded.

'Right,' said Tanner. 'Hand over the Bren. I'll cover you.' He rammed another thirty-round magazine into the breech and pulled back the cock. 'Go, Dan!' he shouted, as he opened fire, the butt of the Bren pummelling his shoulder. Tanner glanced back as Erwood slid behind a tree a short way above, then hollered, 'Fall back! Everyone, fall back!' Sykes was still firing at the first truck. More mortar shells fell among them, but the enemy machine-gun was now silent. Had Sykes or one of the others hit the men manning it or had they moved? Tanner couldn't tell. He had to get Sykes's attention above the din of battle. 'Stan!' he yelled. 'Stan!' Out of the corner of his eye, he could see more enemy troops working their way round the lead truck, ghostly figures in the smoke, and opened fire with another burst from the Bren. *Christ, but we've got to get out of here.* The first truck was drawing all their fire, yet he knew the men from the last must be working their way behind them. 'Stan!' he yelled again, and this time the corporal looked across. Frantically, Tanner waved his arm – *fall back!* – and Sykes nodded. First, though, the corporal pulled a stick of Polar dynamite from his haversack. Tanner fired another burst of the Bren, saw Sykes light the dynamite, count, then hurl it across the stream towards the enemy troops now working their way up the slope opposite. More mortar rounds rippled across the slopes, the blast tearing branches and kicking up spurts of snow, rock and mud.

309

Then Sykes's dynamite exploded, and for a moment, the enemy fire from the lead truck stopped.

Tanner snatched his rifle, slung it over his shoulder, grabbed the Bren, stuffed two more magazines into his pouches and scrambled out of his position – to be met by bullets fizzing past his head from the opposite direction. *Damn it!* Frantically Tanner searched the ground above him. He needed cover. Trees ahead and above him and to his left, a fallen trunk. He gasped, lungs straining. More bullets. Something whipped through his trousers. Yards to go. Feet losing their grip. Where were the others? Shouting from behind. Another mortar shell, this time below him, followed by yet another, between him and his attackers from the flank. It was just the cover he needed and as the blast erupted twenty yards away from him, he plunged over the fallen tree, face down, then rolled and lay sideways. He brought the Bren to bear, slammed in another magazine as debris pattered on his tin helmet, cocked it and opened fire.

Men loomed into view ahead. *Bollocks*, he thought. *I've got sodding Jerries either side.* He glanced behind and saw Sykes up ahead, urging him to follow, mouthing something he couldn't hear above the ear-shattering noise of mortars, shouts and small-arms fire. Another shell hit a tree not far from Sykes and exploded. Tanner ducked again, then shot a glance back to his corporal. No one was there.

'No!' yelled Tanner. 'You bastards!' Bullets pinged above him and slapped into the fallen tree-trunk. Blindly he fired another burst of the Bren, then pulled out a grenade and hurled it at his attackers. A whistle as yet another mortar round hurtled towards him, closer this time. Tanner ducked, heard the explosion, then felt the blast knock him back against the tree-trunk.

He was unsure how long he had been unconscious, but when he came to he was aware that the deafening din of battle had gone and then that he was surrounded by half a dozen enemy troops. As his mind cleared and his eyes focused, he realized he was looking up at none other than Hauptmann Zellner.

Tanner rubbed his head. He had a pounding headache, his ears still rang shrilly and his mouth was drier than sand, yet despite his predicament, he had the presence of mind to glance at his watch. *Well, that's something*, he thought. Nearly fifty minutes had passed since Chevannes had led Sandvold into the trees. Fifty minutes was a good head start.

Two men grabbed his arms and pulled him to his feet, so that he was now face to face with Zellner. The German smiled, then rammed his fist into Tanner's belly. The sergeant gasped and doubled over, only to be pulled up again.

'Where is he?' Zellner hissed.

'Who?' said Tanner.

Zellner punched him again, every bit as hard. 'Where is he?' he repeated, as Tanner gasped and retched a second time.

'I couldn't possibly say,' murmured Tanner. 'We're just the holding force – holding you up, that is. And we have. In fact we are. I am, right now. So, let's chat some more.'

'Enough!' said Zellner, and then struck him a third

time, this time on the jaw but the blow was misjudged. Tanner jerked his head back and the blow barely hurt. 'That should wipe the smile off your face. In any case, we do not need to know. We will just follow the tracks,' said Zellner, 'and we will catch him.'

'You won't,' said Tanner. 'Because he'll be shot before you get a chance.'

Zellner pulled out the pistol from Tanner's holster. 'Mine, I think,' he said. He held it, checked the magazine was full, then cocked it and pointed it at the centre of Tanner's forehead. 'I said I would kill you, Tanner, and so I will.'

Tanner smiled. 'You're a fool, Zellner,' he said. 'A stupid Nazi bastard fool.'

Zellner glared back. 'Tanner,' he said slowly, 'you have said your last.'

From the safety of his position among the trees on the slopes above, Sykes crouched, watching his sergeant and wondering what on earth he could do. Having seen Tanner knocked backwards, he had immediately thought to turn his back, follow the others and slip into the trees, but something had made him stop. As he had turned he had seen enemy troops hurry to Tanner and pull him to his feet. Knowing he was alive, Sykes felt compelled to stay and help. But how?

Wincing as the German officer landed repeated punches on his sergeant, he decided that a diversion was his best option. He still had a few packets of Nobel's 808 as well as several sticks of dynamite, and he had Tanner's pack too. Crouching, he glanced to his left in the direction the fourth truck of troops had come from. It was hard to see, so he scampered a short distance forward, climbed a bit higher, then he saw what he was looking for: a jutting outcrop of rock, like a giant boulder. If he could get enough explosives behind it and force it to tumble down the mountainside, he might help Tanner escape or, at worst, give the enemy a further headache.

He took a deep breath, then glanced back at Tanner and the enemy troops around him. He froze. The sergeant was now obscured from view by another of the German troops but the officer had his arm extended with a pistol pointing at Tanner's head. 'No!' mouthed Sykes, under his breath. He turned his head, not daring to look.

Then came the sound of a single pistol shot.

16

Tanner had eyed the men gathered round Hauptmann Zellner. There were six, with more milling about in the trees beyond and, he knew, others on the far side of the shallow ravine behind him. But it was the seven men in front of him that he needed to worry about first. Three had their rifles slung on their shoulders, two clutched them loosely with one arm, while a sixth had a machine-gun slung by his side from a strap that ran over his shoulder. Tanner was not familiar with the different types of German machine-gun, but it looked to him to be a similar if somewhat more sophisticated weapon than those he had seen after the firefight at the *seter*. It had a similar air-cooled perforated barrel jacket, with ribbed and rounded side magazines. The cock, he noticed, was on the right of the breech. The crux of the matter, he realized, was whether or not the magazine was empty. Surely no machine-gunner would wander around with an unloaded weapon while the battle still had a chance of continuing. In any case, it was his only hope of getting out of his current predicament alive.

Tanner was glad he had kept Zellner talking long enough to take all of this in, but accepted that the moment had arrived to act. Holding Zellner's stare, he brought up his left hand quickly and knocked away the German's arm. Zellner fired harmlessly into the air as Tanner rammed his stronger right fist straight into the man's mouth and nose. As the unconscious Zellner fell backwards, blood spraying in a mist round his head, Tanner lunged for the machine-gun and slid it down the stunned soldier's arm. Pulling back the breech, he fired.

The recoil of the machine-gun nearly knocked him backwards – it was heavier than the Bren – but a rapid burst of bullets emerged from the barrel at a rate of fifteen rounds per second, neatly scything through the six men so that only Zellner, who had slumped backwards, escaped being nearly sliced in two. Seconds – that was all he had. Firing another quick burst at the startled men behind, he grabbed a rack of two-drum magazines, then spotted his rifle lying on the ground a few yards above him. He snatched it and raced for the trees. Act decisively, act quickly, his first sergeant had told him some years before. It was an adage Tanner had not forgotten.

It took the shocked German troops a few seconds more to recover their composure, take their weapons from their shoulders and fire after him. Bullets pinged and zipped either side of him, smacking into trees and kicking up snow, but although one passed clean through a loose part of his trousers, the trees were closing protectively round him.

On he ran, heart pumping furiously, driven by instinct alone, until an explosion shook the ground and made him stop, lungs almost bursting. Below and away to his left, he could hear the blast of rock. Screams followed and as he stared wild-eyed, uncomprehending, through the pines he heard someone call: 'Sarge! Sarge!'

Startled, he swung round and saw Corporal Sykes scrambling towards him.

'Stan, you're alive!' Tanner grinned and held out a hand, which was shaken gratefully. 'I thought you'd been killed back there.'

'And me you!'

They hurried on without any more talk, preserving what energy they had for their climb. At last the gradient began to ease and as they reached the plateau and the edge of the treeline, they emerged into a wide expanse of snow.

'Look!' said Sykes. 'The others! All of them! We made it!'

Away to their right, a peak emerged magisterially from the snow. 'Olasfjellet,' said Tanner. 'That's the first of two that Anna mentioned. Christ, we need to watch our backs up here. It's bloody exposed, Stan.'

'And bloody hard going.'

'You're not wrong.'

One of the others turned and waved. Moments later Tanner and Sykes had caught up with them.

'Come on, lads, get a bloody move on,' said Tanner, as he reached them. 'Dan, what's the damage?'

'It just nicked me, Sarge. Took a bit of my forearm out, but didn't break anything.'

316

'Good,' said Tanner. 'Any sign of the others?'

'Only tracks. Easy enough to follow,' said McAllister. 'Do you think Jerry's coming after us, Sarge?'

'I don't know. We need to catch up with the rest, then get the hell out of this snow.'

'I'm about done in,' said Hepworth.

'Me too,' said Bell. 'Tell me it's not much further, Sarge.'

'Stop bloody bellyaching,' said Tanner. 'We're all sodding tired, but we've got two, maybe three miles of this, and then we should be among the trees again, so it's not far. Come on, boys, keep fighting. We've done the hard part – seen off those Jerries. We can't let ourselves down now.'

He said this for his own benefit as much as his men's, for exhaustion had swamped him too. Fighting was tiring, especially when it was followed by a steep running climb weighed down by a leaden load. The instinctive desire to survive seemed to make part of his brain shut down so that an adrenalin-fuelled primal capacity to keep going took over. Once the immediate danger was past, though, his mind returned to normal and told him he was physically and mentally all but spent.

The snow was crisp and hard, so walking on it was not as difficult as it had been, but even so, each footstep seemed ever harder. On his shoulders, he still carried his rifle and the German machine-gun, as well as the drum magazines, his pack, gas-mask case and haversack. The weight now seemed agonizingly oppressive. *Keep going. Keep bloody going.*

And what of the enemy? There was still no sign. He

thought of Zellner and reckoned he'd judged the punch about right. A broken nose, probably a broken jaw, and it would take him a while to wake up. Whether they followed now or regrouped depended, he guessed, on whether other officers and NCOs were present and still fit. By God, he was tired. He now realized he was hungry and thirsty too. He leant over to pick up some snow and stumbled, falling to his knees. McAllister was now beside him, grabbing his arm, but Tanner shook him off. 'I tripped,' he snarled.

'Only trying to help, Sarge.'

Tanner got to his feet again, using his rifle as a staff, and put the snow in his mouth. Numbingly cold, it offered some relief from the cloying dryness. He fumbled in his pack and found a piece of bread the Sulheims had given him. Slowly chewing it, he tramped onwards, his men following. At least, he thought, it was nearly May. These mountains would be deadly during the depths of winter, but with a high, warm sun, they presented less danger and although it was cold, it was not debilitatingly so. In any case, he now felt well dressed for the task in hand. His stout German boots were warm, his clothes dry. The leather jerkin, with his belt and packs binding it to his body, offered perfect insulation, while the snow goggles protected his eyes from the worst of the glare; the rim of his helmet worked well as a sun visor. No one would succumb to exposure.

Exhaustion was their main enemy now, but already Tanner could see the second peak Anna had mentioned and then he heard – they all heard – the distant boom of guns. His spirits rose. The battle at Kvam – the Allies were still there! New reserves of energy found their way into his legs. 'Lads!' he said, grinning. 'Hear those guns? We're nearly there. We've nearly bloody well gone and made it!'

McAllister cheered. 'Hoo-bloody-ray, Sarge!' he exclaimed. 'Come on, boys, let's get a move on. What's that you say, Sarge? Iggery!'

Tanner glanced back: still no sign of the enemy, but they had to remain watchful. The horizon behind them was shortening now that they had crested the highest point of the mountain ridge and had begun to climb down the reverse slope of the plateau. Ahead, he could see the treeline, still masking the view beyond, but marking the crest of the valley sides.

Ahead, a figure emerged from the darkness of the trees. *Bloody hell*, thought Tanner, those pines offered good cover – the man could not be seen until he was well clear and standing in the snow. Tanner put his binoculars to his eyes. 'Lieutenant Nielssen,' he said, and waved.

'You made it!' said Nielssen, grinning as they reached him. Over the past few days his beard had grown, and without his kepi, his flaxen hair was tousled and unkempt.

'They don't seem to be following us,' said Tanner. 'Where are the others?'

'Sheltering in a *seter*, but we wanted to be below the snowline, so I've been waiting, keeping watch, to guide you there.' He patted Tanner's back. 'It's good to see you safe.'

He led them through a finger of dense pine until they emerged into open snow once more, then reached the crest of the next valley. When they came into a small clearing a vast view stood before them.

'The Gudbrandsdalen once again,' said Nielssen.

Guns were booming dully, shells still exploding, and away to the right beneath them, a thick pall of smoke hid the valley and the Lågen river. Above, they heard the faint drone of aircraft.

'Heavy fighting, Sarge,' said Hepworth.

'That's not just from shells and bombs, Hep. Look.' He took a few steps forward and away to the east. Through the smoke he could see a hazy orange glow. 'That's a sodding great fire. They've set the forest alight.' His heartbeat had quickened again and the blood drained from his face. *Christ*, he thought. *That's all we bloody well need*. He turned to Nielssen. 'How much further, sir? We need to hurry.'

'Not far, Sergeant.'

Tanner turned to his men. 'Come on, boys. Keep going. I know it's been bloody hard, but we're nearly there.'

The *seter* stood beneath the crest of the valley, hidden by trees but with a view of the village of Sjoa and the curve of the river. Stretching away to the west from the Gudbrandsdal valley was a smaller, lesser valley.

'You're alive!' said Anna, smiling as Tanner entered the hut.

'Just about,' he said. 'And you? Are you all right?'

'Yes – I'm fine, thank you.' Tanner saw her shoot a glance at Chevannes.

'What happened?' said the Frenchman.

'We destroyed two of their trucks and killed a number

320

of them, I'm not sure how many. They don't seem to have followed us. One of our men is slightly wounded.'

'Your Bren?'

'Lost,' admitted Tanner. 'But I found this Spandau.' He tapped the German machine-gun. 'And a couple of magazines. Look, sir, we need to hurry.'

'The battle is still raging, Sergeant.'

'Yes, sir, but not for much longer, I fancy. We need to keep going.'

Chevannes gave orders for them to move.

'There's a bridge across the river Sjoa about a kilometre west of the village,' said Anna. 'We can cross there and then get over Lågen at the village itself.'

'Very well,' said Chevannes.

They stumbled down the steep valley sides. Tanner disliked walking down mountains more than he did climbing them, and now his knees felt particularly weak, as though his legs might buckle at any moment. They headed diagonally across the valley, in a north-westerly direction, until they reached a rough track. As they tramped across the undulating slopes, the valley ahead was lost from view then reappeared, but although Tanner paused repeatedly to peer through his binoculars, the sounds of battle had now all but died away. The shellfire was nothing more than desultory, the small-arms had almost petered out, while enemy bombers continued to drone overhead, appearing through the thick pall that had now risen high into the sky. Bitter disappointment swept over him, yet part of his brain refused to accept what his eyes and ears were telling him. 'Come on!' he urged his men. 'Keep going!'

By seven o'clock they were standing above the bridge over the Sjoa and now all could see that the bombers were dropping their loads further north. For a moment, no one spoke. Tanner scanned the valley. Clearly the main Allied effort had fallen back, although from the edge of the mass of smoke, on the far side of the valley, it appeared that some British troops were still fighting. His spirits rose momentarily, but then he spotted enemy forces blocking the road south of Sjoa. They had evidently outflanked them over the mountain and come in behind, cutting off any further Allied retreat. He lowered his binoculars and breathed deeply. *No*, he thought. *This is too much.* He wanted to crumple to the ground, fling away his weapons, to scream with anger. Instead he stood silent, numbed by the knowledge that again they had missed their chance of freedom by a sliver.

'We've missed them.' It was Sandvold, and Tanner turned to him. Defeat and despair clouded his face. 'They're bombing them as they retreat.'

Tanner glared at Chevannes, who continued to stare through his binoculars. *You stupid bastard*, he thought. He blamed Chevannes for this – Chevannes and Larsen. Thwarted for want of a few hours. Time that should have been theirs.

'What can you see?' said Anna, anxiety in her voice.

'Have a look,' said Tanner, passing her his glasses.

'Germans,' she said quietly.

'Bastard bloody hell!' McAllister kicked the ground.

Kershaw began to sob.

Tanner looked at the disappointment on their faces,

the bloodless cheeks and dark rings round their eyes; the sheer exhaustion. He wondered whether he himself had the strength to keep going. He could feel the dirt and dried blood on his face, and his uniform filthy and torn. 'A couple of hours earlier and we'd have been safe,' he growled. 'A couple of sodding hours! Jesus Christ!' He was uncertain that he could control his anger any longer. His desire to thrust his fist into Chevannes' face was almost overwhelming.

'I did what I thought was best for all of us,' said Chevannes. 'Lieutenant Larsen agreed with me. So did Professor Sandvold.'

'For pity's sake, man,' snarled Tanner, 'you're in charge. It's your decision, not theirs, and it's your fault we've missed the chance yet again to rejoin the Allies.' For a moment no one said anything. Tanner walked away a few yards. He took another deep breath. *Calm down*, he told himself. *This is not helping.* They were too late. That was all there was to it. He had to think clearly and rationally. 'We must work out a new plan,' he said. 'What do you suggest, sir?'

'The map,' said Chevannes, icily. 'We must look at it.'

A rough track followed the southern side of the Sjoa valley as it ran north-west. There were no villages of note, but scattered farmsteads all the way to Heidel, some ten miles on. A couple of miles south of the village there was a bridge where they could cross. If they kept going now, Tanner suggested, they could cross when it was dark, then try to find a farm to rest for a few hours before heading into the next ridge of mountains. 'Jerry won't be coming down here tonight. He's just been fighting a two-day battle, and if the jokers that were after us earlier haven't followed us across the mountain, they're not going to get us now. We should be able to make good progress.' Beyond the next range lay the Otta valley and the town of Vågåmo. 'Look,' he said, pointing to the map, 'there's a road leading north. It bypasses Dombas and joins the Åndalsnes road further north – here. What's that? Forty or fifty miles? And it means we keep well away from the main German axis of advance but we still run parallel to it.'

'What if the enemy is already past Dombas by then?' asked Larsen.

Tanner shrugged. 'Do you have a better idea, sir? Perhaps we'll find some more transport. Maybe in Vågåmo.'

'Good,' said Chevannes. 'This is what we'll do. First, we rest for a short while, eat what food we have left and drink something. Then we head for the bridge.'

Tanner's men gazed at Chevannes with contempt, then delved into their packs and squatted on the ground. A cool spring breeze blew across the valley, bringing with it the smell of woodsmoke, which blended with the strong scent of pine. Even though it was hardly cold, Tanner saw that Bell and Kershaw were shivering. 'Listen, boys,' he said, to all his men, 'this is a blow, I know, but we've got to put it out of our minds. It's in the past. We need to look forward now. Come on, I know we can do it.' Tanner watched the resigned nods, the faces blank with exhaustion and renewed despair.

He wandered away from them, and leant against a tree, then let his back slide down the trunk until he was squatting on the damp, needle-strewn ground at its base. Taking off his helmet, he ran his hands through his hair and took several deep breaths. Christ, his words had seemed fatuous. 'Chin up, lads, it's not all bad!' *Jesus. Hardly inspiring.* He wondered how long they would be content to follow him. What reserves of strength were left in the tank? A man's will to survive was only so strong. At some point it would break – sooner rather than later, if there were any more soul-destroying setbacks.

The crack of a twig made him turn.

'I'm sorry to disturb you, Sergeant,' said Sandvold, 'but I wondered whether I might talk to you a moment.'

Tanner began to get to his feet.

'Please,' said the Professor. 'You rest where you are.'

'What is it?' asked Tanner.

Sandvold kneaded his hands together. He now wore a full beard, grey at the chin. It made him seem older, more venerable. 'I want to apologize,' he said.

'For what?'

'I should have backed you up at the farm. If I had we might have persuaded Lieutenant Chevannes. Then we would have reached the Allies before it was too late. I—' He cleared his throat. 'It was weak of me, but I thought I should not get involved in military decisions.'

'What's done is done, Professor,' said Tanner, 'but we've still got a long way to go. There will be other difficult decisions to make. But if you're prepared to trust me, you could back me up. If we work together, we'll have a better chance of succeeding.'

Sandvold nodded thoughtfully. 'All right, Sergeant,' he said. 'I will do my best.'

Soon after, Chevannes gave the order to move off. Tanner tried again to rouse his men. 'We'll still make it, boys,' he told them, slapping their backs as they got to their feet. 'We will. Don't lose heart.'

'It's easy to say that, Sarge,' said McAllister, 'but I felt knackered before and I'm even more done in now.'

'Listen, Mac,' said Tanner, grasping his shoulder, 'you either give up now, and at best spend the rest of the war in prison, or you keep going. I know what I'm going to do and it would be terrific if you'd keep me company. We're not high on a mountain now, we're on a decent track. We'll be at the bridge by nightfall and once we've got across we can have a rest. It's not far. You can do it.'

They were strung out in a patrol line. Of the enemy there was still no sign. The track passed through dense forest that ran almost all the way to the river's edge, giving them good cover.

'Don't worry, Sarge,' said Sykes, drawing alongside him. 'They're good lads. They'll be all right.'

'You think so?'

'Course. We were a bit low back then, but you adjust. We've got a bit of grub inside us now. That helps.'

'Perhaps.'

''Ere, Sarge,' said Sykes, after they had walked on in silence for a short while, 'I've been wanting to ask all afternoon. How the hell did you get away from those Jerries? I saw that officer pointing his pistol straight at your bloody head and the next minute I heard a shot. I thought you was a goner.'

Tanner smiled. 'He made a mistake. I brought my arm up quickly and simply knocked the gun to the side of my head. By the time he'd pressed the trigger the shot was already wide.'

Sykes whistled. 'Blimey.'

'He couldn't react quicker than the speed of my arm. No one can because the eyes don't pick up the movement fast enough – not at that distance. If he'd been standing a few feet away and pointing that pistol, I really would have been in trouble. So, anyway, before he knew what was happening, I'd given him a right hook to remember me by. The men around him weren't quick enough either, so I grabbed the machine-gun and fired before they could do anything. You've got to remember they weren't expecting it. They'd relaxed, rifles on their shoulders, and were enjoying watching their commander get his own back. But I was lucky after that. Got a bullet through my trouser. Another inch and, well—'

'Did you kill him? The officer, that is?'

'Zellner? I don't think so. Broke his nose. Possibly his jaw.' He grinned. 'Any explosives left after your little diversion? I haven't even looked in my pack yet.'

'Not much. A carton of Nobel's and a few sticks of Polar. It seemed the right thing to do at the time.'

'Damn right, Stan. It's thanks to you those bastards aren't at our backs now. You did well.'

'But we don't know when we might need some more.'

'We'll cross that path if and when.' They were silent for a moment, then Tanner said, 'You don't have any beadies left, do you? I could murder a smoke.'

'I'll roll you one.'

Sykes pulled out the tobacco and papers he had taken from the captured Germans a few days before. 'Sarge?'

he said eventually, passing the cigarette to Tanner. He eyed him furtively as he did so.

'What?' said Tanner, pausing to light his cigarette.

'It's probably nothing, and I don't want you to take this the wrong way—'

'What, Stan?'

'It's just that, well – nah, it's nothing.'

'Spit it out.'

'Well, I'd just like to know how those Stukas knew it was us. And how did those trucks know where we'd be?'

'They've had aerial reconnaissance buzzing over nearly non-stop in case you hadn't noticed.'

'Yes, but not first thing this morning. We didn't see anything before them Stukas turned up, did we?'

'What are you saying?'

Sykes made sure no one was listening, then said, in a hushed voice, 'I'm hoping we haven't got a spy among us.'

'A spy?' Tanner gaped at him. 'Are you joking, Stan? Who?'

'I don't know, do I?'

'And, more to the point, how? Don't you think we'd have noticed by now? I mean, how on earth would anyone be contacting the enemy? We've been together pretty much all the time.'

'Yes, but not *all* the time. There've been times when we've been kipping, when we've wandered off to – you know ... and so on. We don't know what those Norwegians are carrying in their rucksacks. Perhaps they've got a radio or something.'

'But wireless sets are pretty big. And how could they use it without anyone else seeing?'

'I don't know. All I'm saying is that this whole thing seems fishy to me. I keep thinking about how those Jerries keep dogging our every move and that makes me think someone's tipping them the wink. That's all.'

Tanner was quiet.

'Look, Sarge,' Sykes added, 'I don't claim to know much about this sort of thing but you have to admit it's a bit strange. I mean, you yourself thought those Jerries were waiting for us in Tretten. For that matter, how did that mountain patrol know to come after us back on the other side of the valley?'

'That could have been because of air reconnaissance. At Tretten, they might simply have worked it out. I don't know. You don't think maybe we're becoming overly suspicious?'

'I don't know. I still think those Stukas arriving was odd. No buzzing around beforehand. They came straight over. Knew exactly who we was and where . . . Sarge?'

'I'm thinking, Stan, if any one of us could have had the time to make some kind of signal.'

Sykes shrugged.

Tanner said, 'I suppose someone could. Unlikely, but possible.'

'So?'

'We keep this to ourselves and watch everyone – the Norwegians at any rate.' They walked on in silence, Tanner deep in thought. It seemed so fantastical, yet there was no denying that the enemy did seem to have been second-guessing their movements. A result of logical thought processes and aerial reconnaissance, or a more sinister source of intelligence? *My God*. It hardly bore thinking about.

The sun had disappeared, casting the valley in deep shadow. A shiver ran down Tanner's back, whether from the cold or the suspicion that the corporal might be right, he couldn't say.

17

They reached the bridge safely. A sliver of moon appeared, but the valley was dark and still. Although an occasional light twinkled from the farms and houses round about, not a soul stirred. Once again, Tanner was struck by how far away the war seemed, yet only a dozen or so miles to the south-east a two-day battle had been fought. He could still smell the whiff of woodsmoke on the night breeze, but he knew that was as likely to be from a home fire as the blazing forest near Kvam.

They crossed the bridge, Tanner cringing at the sound of the studded boots on the wooden struts. They were bunched up now, walking together so they didn't lose one another. 'Keep together, boys,' Tanner told his men, and to Sykes he added, 'Don't take your eyes off those Norwegians. No matter how dark, keep within arm's reach.'

They walked in silence along the soft verge that ran close to the northern bank of the Sjoa river to deaden the sound of their footsteps. Even so, Tanner sensed they were dragging their feet; he was too. Every step seemed harder. His shoulders ached, his knees hurt, his calves burnt. In the faint creamy night light, he could see that Sandvold was almost falling asleep as he stumbled on.

'Sir,' he said to Chevannes, 'we should stop soon.'

Chevannes snorted. 'And this from the man who never thinks we should rest at all.'

'I need to rest,' muttered Sandvold. 'I cannot go much further.'

Chevannes lit a match and squinted at Anna's map. 'We're near Heidel, I think.'

'Yes,' agreed Anna. 'It's not much, a few houses and farms, that's all.'

'Very well,' said Chevannes, 'we will look for some-where to rest for a few hours. A hut, a farmhouse, a barn. We can try to find food in the morning.'

For once Tanner found himself agreeing with the Frenchman and only a short distance further on a farm-house loomed, set back from the road. It was dark, with no light showing, but in the drive and the yard there were signs of vehicle tracks.

'Larsen, go and have a look round,' said Chevannes, as they clustered at the open gate. Larsen, with Nielssen accompanying him, walked forward cautiously. Tanner glanced round his men, dark shadows all, leaning against the gate, most so tired they could barely stand.

When the Norwegians returned, the news was good. 'It's empty,' said Larsen. 'Someone's been here recently, though.'

'Sergeant,' said Chevannes to Tanner, 'organize guards. The rest, follow me into the house.'

'Hep, you can take first watch with me,' said Tanner.

Hepworth groaned. 'Sarge, why's it have to be me?'

'Would you rather be woken up in an hour? This way you get it over and done with.' He leant his machine-gun against the gate. 'Now, stay here and watch the road.'

'Where are you going, Sarge?'

'For a nose round. I won't be long.'

Tanner watched the others head into the house, then walked quietly towards the farm. There were two barns and several other outbuildings, while to the back a shallow field rose steadily towards the patchily wooded valley sides. The house, he noticed, was shuttered, and effectively so – only the faintest light could be seen from within.

The smell of woodsmoke again. A wisp now floated from the chimney. *Good*, he thought. *They've found some scoff.* His stomach groaned.

Back at the gate he found Hepworth leaning against it, his head in his arms.

'Hep,' he said, 'wake up.'

'Hm?' said Hepworth. 'Sorry, Sarge . . .'

Tanner left him and, taking his machine-gun, walked across the road. There was only one way the Germans could come, he reasoned, and that was from Sjoa. He had his rifle and the MG set up on its bipod. The night was so quiet that if any vehicles approached he knew he would hear them a long way off.

Satisfied that should there be any sign of the enemy he could raise the alarm and get everyone hidden in the woods behind the farm, he sat down on the bank, listening to the water hurrying over the rocks in the river below and thinking of what Sykes had said earlier. He felt sure it couldn't be Sandvold, yet the professor had been in Oslo during the first days of the occupation and had admitted to him that he had been reluctant to leave. Perhaps the story of his mother was a lie. Perhaps he was working for the Nazis after all. Then he considered Larsen and Nielssen. Again, it was possible, but seemed so unlikely. If one was a spy, he could surely have killed the other two and taken Sandvold to the Germans long before they ever reached the Balberkamp.

He thought about Anna. In truth, he'd thought about her quite a lot over the past two days, although it troubled him that he should even consider her as a spy. Yet there was no denying that she had been very keen to help them – perhaps overly so. But if she was a traitor, how was she passing on information? She carried a rucksack, but was it big enough for a wireless? Tanner wasn't sure. And what was her motive? He shook his head. It didn't make sense.

And, of course, there was Chevannes. No one, in his view, had done more to hinder them at every turn. And yet it couldn't be the Frenchman – of that he was sure. Maybe it really was just paranoia.

Sleep. That was what he needed. Sleep and food. Perhaps he'd be able to see the situation more clearly after that.

An hour later Sykes and Bell relieved him and Hepworth.

'Go on, Sarge. Get inside,' Sykes told him. 'We found a whole load of tins of Maconochie's and a few bottles of vino too. There's no doubt about it, some of our boys were here not so long ago.'

334

'Probably till this afternoon,' muttered Tanner. He shook Hepworth awake. 'Wakey, wakey, Hep, you useless sod. Time for some food.' Hepworth grunted then staggered after him.

Inside, Tanner found Chevannes and Nielssen sitting at the table, one empty and a further half-drunk bottle of wine between them.

'Where's the professor?' he asked.

'Upstairs,' said Chevannes, pointing above his head. 'Don't worry – he's safe, and sound asleep.' His eyes were glassy, his words somewhat slurred.

'For God's sake,' mumbled Tanner.

'What?' said Chevannes. 'What was that you said, Sergeant? *Parlez haut.*'

'Nothing, sir. I'll just get something for me and Hepworth to eat. I hear there's some stew about.'

'*Oui, oui.* Heat up another tin. And have some wine.' While Tanner found two tins of stew and vegetables, Chevannes poured out a chipped tumbler of wine, spilling some. 'A toast, Sergeant,' he said, pushing the tumbler in Tanner's direction. 'A toast to surviving so far.'

Give me strength, thought Tanner. He scowled at the Frenchman, said, 'No bloody thanks to you,' then picked up the tumbler and drank, slamming the glass down only when he had finished it all.

'What did you say, Sergeant?' slurred Chevannes.

'You heard,' Tanner retorted. He went back to heating his tins of stew over the fire.

'How dare you?'

'How dare I what?' said Tanner, turning on him. 'If it wasn't for you, we wouldn't be sitting in this

335

God-forsaken hole. Now, get drunk if you want to but in a few hours' time we'll be off again and I'm not bloody well waiting for you.' Tanner grabbed the tins and stormed out of the room.

'Sergeant!' Chevannes called after him. 'Come back here!'

Tanner ignored him. He found Hepworth almost asleep on the stairs, then entered another room on the ground floor in which McAllister and Kershaw were already asleep. He lit a match and saw a half-burnt candle on a desk, which stood before a fireplace. Lighting it, he looked around, eating his stew as he did so. It was not warmed through, but he didn't care. It was food, and he'd eaten a lot worse. An empty whisky bottle stood on the table, while in the grate he found the remains of a number of papers. Tanner picked up the top of a sheet entitled, 'War Diary or Intelligence Summary', beside which had been scrawled in pencil, '148 Inf Bde.' What remained of the writing underneath had been scribbled out. So, this had been Brigadier Morgan's headquarters, he thought. Missed by hours.

Tanner lay down on the floor by the fireplace and, using his captured jacket as a pillow, closed his eyes and slept.

He was being shaken roughly. 'Sarge! Sarge!'

'What?' he said. He had been sleeping deeply and his eyes, reluctantly opening, strained in the dark to see who was standing over him.

'Sarge, it's me, Bell. You need to come. The corp sent me.'

Rubbing his eyes, Tanner got wearily to his feet, grabbed his rifle and stumbled outside. Sykes was by the gate. 'What is it?' Tanner asked.

'Someone came out the house, Sarge,' Sykes whispered. 'I couldn't see who it was, but they went into the barn. Whoever it is, they're still there.'

'All right,' he said. 'Let's go over and have a look.'

They crept towards the barn. The door on the ground was ajar and they paused beside it. Tanner's heart was hammering again; he hated creeping round buildings at any time of day but especially in the dark. 'Cover me,' he whispered, then pushed open the door and went in.

A sudden scratching made his heart leap and he flinched, then realized it was only rats or mice. He listened intently but could hear nothing. Sykes and Bell were now behind him. He felt in his trouser pocket for his matches, took out the box and lit one.

The flame gave only a little light, but it was enough to show a row of animal stalls in front of them. Nearly burning his fingers, he pinched out the match, lit another and walked slowly along the stalls.

The match died and he lit a third. As the flare subsided, he reached the last stall and there, asleep on a pile of hay, was the mystery person.

'Miss!' said Tanner.

She woke with a start. 'Sergeant,' she said, blinking, 'what's the matter?' She sat up, propping herself on her elbows.

'We heard someone leave the house,' said Tanner. Suddenly he felt rather foolish. 'We weren't sure who it was...' Sykes lit another match. There was

337

nothing beside her: no rucksack, and certainly no radio.

'I'm sorry,' she said. 'It was the lieutenant. He was drunk.'

'What did the bastard do?'

'Nothing, really.' She made to stand up and Tanner stepped forward to offer her a hand. 'He – well, he was drunk and making a nuisance of himself.' She smiled uncertainly at Tanner, then took his hand. Her fingers were cold, but gripped his tightly. 'I didn't want to make a scene.' The match went out again, but her hand stayed in his.

'I'm sorry,' she said. 'I didn't mean to alarm you. I just thought it would be quiet out here. Although, actually, I should have known there would be rats.'

With his heart still hammering, but now for a different reason, he said, 'It would be safer if you came back inside, you know. If anything should happen . . .'

'Don't worry, Miss,' said Sykes. 'I'm sure the lieutenant will be sound asleep by now.'

'Yes, of course,' she said. 'I understand.'

Back outside the barn, Tanner turned his watch to the light of the moon. 'Just gone one,' he said. 'Stan, you and Tinker are on until half past, then get Mac and Kershaw out for an hour and they can get me again. I'll get Chevannes' man, Dérigaux, to join me. We want to be away by half three. All right?'

'Got it, Sarge.'

'Night, Sarge,' added Bell. 'And night, Miss.'

Tanner led Anna back into a silent and sleeping house. 'In here,' he whispered, showing her to the office. McAllister and Kershaw were still asleep on the floor, their slow, rhythmic breathing clearly audible in the close atmosphere of the room. In the dark, he bumped into her, apologized, then whispered, 'Over here.' Having found his pack and wind jacket, he crouched and heard her settle next to him. 'Would you like my jacket?' he asked.

'No, no – I'm fine. Thank you. I've got my own.'

'Try to get back to sleep, then,' he said. He closed his eyes, then felt her hand stretch out and take his, squeezing it. Was she genuine, or playing a part? *To hell with it*, he thought. In less than two hours he had to be awake again. For now, the soft warmth of her touch was a much-needed comfort.

He had been in a deep sleep when McAllister woke him but this time was alert in an instant. Deciding to let Dérigaux be, he went out to watch the road alone. Not for the first time since arriving in Norway ten days before, he watched the dawn rise, creeping over the mountains to the east and sweeping over the narrow valley, bathing it in a rich golden light.

Soon after three, he hurried back into the house, woke Sykes and ordered him out to watch the road, then stoked the fire and roused Anna. 'I need your help,' he said. 'Can you heat some more tins of stew for me?'

She nodded sleepily.

'Are you all right?' he asked, as she stretched and yawned.

'Yes, I think so. This is harder than I thought it would be. I am used to tramping over the mountains, but I had not realized we would get so little sleep.'

He smiled, and touched her cheek lightly. 'It's an occupational hazard, I'm afraid.'

'I know.' She looked up at him. 'Jack – do you think we'll make it?'

'Of course. We have to.' He smiled again, then went to wake the others.

One by one, the men stumbled into the kitchen, stretching and yawning. Chevannes was the last to appear, eyes narrow and puffy, cracked lips stained with wine. Tanner chuckled to himself, then noticed Sandvold standing alone in a corner, rocking gently, eyes glazed. 'Professor?' he asked.

Sandvold jumped.

'How are you feeling? How are the legs?' Tanner asked.

'My legs – well, they are still here. I feel my age, Sergeant. How far do you think we must go today?'

'Perhaps a dozen miles – seventeen kilometres.'

Sandvold nodded gloomily. 'We still have such a long way to go.' He paused, then said, 'Ignore me. I have these moments of depression.'

While the others ate the remaining tins of Maconochie's, Tanner spread Anna's map on the stone floor. 'Anna,' he said, 'do you know this stretch of mountains?'

'I know Bringsfjellet. It's the peak above Vågåmo, and I've been to the town before.'

'Good, but what about here?' He pointed to a narrow, steep-sided valley that ran north from Heidel.

'No,' she admitted. 'I've not been up there.'

'Do you think it will be wooded?'

'Almost certainly.'

340

'And it looks as though there's a track through it. What's more, it's mostly south-west facing so with luck there won't be much snow.' He rubbed his chin thoughtfully. 'I think we should head down there.'

'Excuse me interrupting,' said Chevannes, his voice laden with sarcasm, 'but it is not up to you, Sergeant, to decide.' He leant over, stale wine fumes heavy on his breath, and snatched the map. He examined it briefly, then said, 'We should find some transport. The men are still exhausted. I have noticed that the welfare of yours is not of paramount concern to you, Sergeant.'

Tanner took a deep breath. 'I agree that if we see something we should take it, but I don't think we should waste time looking for it. It's no more than a day's march to Vågåmo where we'd have to ditch any M/T we had anyway.'

'And the fact that the men are exhausted?' said Chevannes. 'We should find a vehicle.'

'We need to get going while it's still safe, sir. We're by a main valley road, and it's not long before Jerry will be down here. I've had a look at the sky. It was clear three-quarters of an hour ago, but the cloud's building and it looks like rain. We need to get away and under the cover of the forest as soon as possible. We can rest up later. Better to do so where we can post proper sentries and prepare a decent escape route. We should aim to get to the mountains above Vågåmo. Anna knows those peaks.'

'There are good views of the river Otta, the Vågåvnet lake and the town from the Bringsfjellet,' added Anna.

'So from there,' Tanner continued, 'we can look down on the town. It may even be that we'll get there before the Germans do, in which case we'll be fine. If not, we can work out how to join the road north of the town. I agree, we will need some M/T then, but we don't have time to look for transport now.'

'The track we take this morning should be fairly easy going,' said Anna.

Chevannes turned sharply to face her. 'Oh, I see,' he said. 'You two, you have – how shall I put this? – a little understanding. It seems as though you have it all planned.'

Tanner reddened.

'That is charming,' continued Chevannes, 'but, Sergeant, you must not let your feelings for Miss Rostad cloud your judgement.'

Something inside Tanner snapped. He prided himself on being able to keep a cool, calm head, no matter how testing the circumstances, but at several moments in his life uncontrollable rage had got the better of him. He had reached one such moment now.

Without further thought he clenched his fist and swung his right arm at Chevannes. The movement was so quick, and executed with such lightning precision, that the Frenchman had no time to react. The force of the punch knocked him backwards in an unconscious heap against McAllister and Bell, who caught him clumsily, thus saving him from further injury.

For a moment, no one said a word.

Damn, damn, damn, thought Tanner.

'Sergeant,' said Larsen, eventually. His face showed incredulity. 'What did you think you were doing?'

'He pushed me too far.' He glared at the Norwegian.

342

Hoisted upright by the two Rangers, Chevannes groaned, then came round. Blinking wildly, he suddenly focused on his assailant. 'Tanner,' he hissed, 'you struck an officer!'

'You insulted me and Miss Rostad, sir.'

'You struck an officer,' Chevannes repeated. 'I have never seen anything so disgraceful in my life.'

'Jesus Christ,' muttered Tanner.

'You had better apologize, Sergeant,' said Larsen.

'For God's sake,' said Tanner. He wasn't sure how to react. *You bloody fool*, he thought.

'Sergeant, it would be better if you just apologized,' said Larsen again, his voice firm and measured.

'You most certainly will apologize, Sergeant!' shouted Chevannes. 'Now!'

Tanner sighed, then said to Chevannes, 'Sir, I apologize for hitting you. And now can we get the hell out of here?'

'Just a minute,' said Chevannes, cheek muscles twitching with anger, 'don't think that's the end of it, because when we get back to our lines, Sergeant, I'm going to report you, and you will be court-martialled. I'm going to make sure your career is finished for what you have just done.'

'Enough!'

The Professor had stepped forward. 'Enough of this,' he said again. 'Lieutenant – please. Ask everyone to wait outside. You, Sergeant, and you, Henrik Larsen and Nielssen, stay here.'

Chevannes was plainly surprised by the professor's intervention. 'Yes, all right,' he said. 'Everyone – out. Now!'

'Listen to me,' said Sandvold, once the men had gone

and the door had closed. 'I'm not interested in your petty squabbles and, with the greatest respect, no one else is either. What I *am* interested in is successfully reaching the Allies, and it is your task to help me. If you want to bring charges against the sergeant once this is over, that is up to you, but for now you must put aside your differences, because if I may say so, Lieutenant, your desire to undermine Sergeant Tanner is, to my mind, undermining our chances.'

Tanner smiled to himself. *Good lad*, he thought.

'Now, Sergeant Tanner has clearly studied the land carefully and it strikes me his plan is the right one.'

Chevannes sniffed. 'And with the greatest respect to you, Professor,' he said slowly, 'you are not a military man. You should be leaving any such decisions to me.'

'No,' said Sandvold. 'I am not under your orders, Lieutenant. I am a civilian. I have already been dragged from my home and I have come this far without complaint or protest, partly because His Majesty the King has requested that I do so, and also because I have no desire to become a prisoner of the Germans. Sergeant Tanner is surely right. We must stop bickering and leave now.'

Chevannes was silent, then glanced at Larsen and Nielssen, hoping for support, but found none.

'Maybe there's something in what he says,' said Nielssen.

Chevannes clenched his fists, then smacked his right hand hard and flat against the wall. 'Very well,' he said stiffly. 'We leave now.'

18

Reichsamtsleiter Scheidt could hardly believe it was only six days since he had last stood in this corridor at the Bristol Hotel; somehow, it seemed like a lifetime ago. As he waited to see the Reichskommissar, he bit his finger-nails and paced uneasily. Coming back to Oslo was a gamble – a horrible one – and he was uncertain how Terboven would react. By the door, the two SS guards stared ahead implacably, unmoved by Scheidt's agitation.

At last the door opened and an Allgemeine-SS officer in a pale grey uniform appeared and ushered him into the same top-floor suite where he and Quisling had first seen Terboven, then discreetly slipped away.

Although it was now morning, the room was still one of refined and subtle light. The Reichskommisar, behind his desk, was every bit as immaculate, not a hair out of place, his face smooth as glass. Already Scheidt felt inferior. He had driven through much of the night to reach the city. His suit was now creased, he had not shaved in eighteen hours and his right eyelid was flickering with fatigue. Damn you, thought Scheidt.

Terboven was writing at his desk and did not look up as Scheidt entered and stood before him. At one point, he paused, glanced at the wall to his right, apparently deep in thought, then continued scribbling. The silence in the room was so complete that Scheidt could hear the nib scratching the paper.

It was an old trick to impose oneself and one's authority by keeping a subordinate waiting in agonizing silence. Nonetheless, Scheidt reflected, it was still an effective one. *The bastard.* He could feel the greasy sweat on his palms. A further minute or more passed, then Terboven stopped writing, carefully replaced the lid of his pen, laid it on his desk and said, with a hint of a smile, 'Ah, Reichsamtsleiter Scheidt – you are the bearer of good news, I hope?'

Scheidt's heart sank, but he looked Terboven directly in the eye. 'No, I'm afraid not.'

Terboven leant back in his chair, fingers together, and raised an eyebrow. *Oh yes?*

'We have located Odin several times and have been within a hair's breadth of capturing him but, alas, he has always eluded us.'

'You had my authority to use whatever troops you needed. How can this be possible?'

'General Engelbrecht has had his hands tied fighting the British and Norwegians. The most he could spare was a reconnaissance company of Gebirgsjäger. These troops were lightly armed and met stiff resistance from a mixed company of British and French troops who have joined Odin and his Norwegian guardians. Killing them all has not been the difficulty; killing them and rescuing

Odin unscathed has, however, proved more challenging.'

Terboven nodded. 'And what about your "source"?'

'The information has been crucial, but sporadic. It is the nature of intelligence.'

Terboven leant towards his desk calendar. 'You have until tomorrow, Herr Reichsamtsleiter, until our deal is over. I don't mind telling you I'm rather surprised to see you here. I'd have thought that in the circumstances your time could have been used more profitably.'

'I'd like your help, Herr Reichskommissar.' He said it flatly and, he hoped, without any trace of panic or fear.

'I thought I'd already given you that.'

'You have, Herr Reichskommissar, but I'm here to ask you to speak with General Engelbrecht. The company of Gebirgsjäger that he gave us – well, they have suffered heavy casualties over the past few days. Yet he refuses to give us more troops or equipment. I showed him your letter, but he insisted he had no more men to spare.'

'He has a battle to fight.'

'A battle he has all but won. His forces far outweigh those of the enemy. He can readily spare some men and equipment.'

Terboven brought his hands to his chin, and pursed his lips. 'My difficulty, Herr Reichsamtsleiter, is this. You are asking me to order a general in the field to redirect some of his forces at a time when he is engaged in heavy fighting – albeit a battle he is winning – but without my being able to give him much reason. Now, yes, I am Reichskommissar here, but there is nothing to stop General Engelbrecht from contacting the OKW in Berlin and complaining vociferously about such interfering.

When the OKW demands an explanation, I will have to tell them that I can't give them one but that Reichsamtsleiter Scheidt has assured me these troops are needed for a very good yet unspecified cause. "Yes, my Führer," I will say, "Reichsamtsleiter Scheidt did work with Bräuer, the disgraced ambassador."' He smiled. 'So you see, Scheidt, I think the time has come to stop the games and little subterfuges.' He leant forward, his elbows on the desk and eyed Scheidt carefully. 'My answer to you is therefore this: before I speak with General Engelbrecht, I want to know who this Odin is and why you think he is of such enormous importance.'

Scheidt swallowed. *Of course he was going to demand this.* 'I understand your position, Herr Reichskommissar,' he said, 'yet—'

Terboven cut him off. 'My dear Reichsamtsleiter, you have no other hand to play. But let me reassure you. If this man is as important as you say and if he does indeed fall into our hands, there may yet be a role for you here. At the very least, you will not suffer the fate of Bräuer. You could return to Berlin with your career and reputation intact, if not enhanced.' Terboven took his spectacles from his nose and, with a silk handkerchief, began to polish them. 'So, no more games. Let's hear it. My patience is not inexhaustible.' Having replaced his spectacles, he stood up. 'Come, let's sit more comfortably,' he said, motioning Scheidt to the Louis XIV chairs in which they had sat six days before.

Of course, the Reichskommissar was right, Scheidt realized. Was there any truth in what Terboven had said about his future career? Really, Scheidt knew, that was

348

irrelevant. He was now cornered and would have to play his hand. Odin's secret would be his no more. He sat, smoothed his tie and said, 'Very well. Odin, Herr Reichskommissar, is a scientist . . .'

Tanner's prediction about the rain had been correct. That morning it poured, soaking the men and turning the track through the valley to mud. But with the rain came low cloud. Above them, the mountains were invisible. Ahead, wisps of seemingly stray cloud hovered among the trees. Aero-engines could briefly be heard droning across the sky, but they never saw the planes. More importantly, as Tanner was well aware, the aircraft could not see them.

It was small consolation, and had done nothing to improve his dark mood. The humiliation he had suffered at the hands of Chevannes still preyed on his mind. How dare that bastard talk about him and Anna in front of his men? He hated people knowing his business and the thought of the others looking knowingly at him and Anna infuriated him. He had avoided her since. After all, what were they going to do? Walk through the mountains hand in hand? He could not deny that he found her attractive, or that he liked her, but now was not the time to be distracted. They had a mission to complete.

The valley climbed gently and, with the rain, the snow was receding almost before their eyes. Tanner pushed back his helmet and turned up the collar of his battle blouse, but still water dripped down his back, while the rain pattered noisily on his helmet. And while his jerkin was resisting the rain, his battle dress, so warm in cold, dry weather, was now heavy and sodden. His trousers clung to his legs. He stopped and, under the shelter of a pine tree, wrapped his remaining three packets of Nobel's and sticks of dynamite tightly in the German wind jacket and stuffed them back into his pack. The heavy canvas of their webbing protected the remaining rounds of ammunition, but the possibility of losing it to the wet was another thing to worry about.

So too was professor Sandvold's condition. As Tanner rejoined the column, he saw Anna and Larsen speaking with him, and Larsen put a hand on his shoulder. Alarm bells rang in Tanner's mind. After the professor's unexpected outburst at the farmhouse, Tanner had seen him put a hand to the wall to steady himself. He had pushed aside the first stab of concern as he had watched Sandvold set off from the farmhouse with a steady step.

Now Tanner hurried along the wet track, splattering his boots and legs with mud. 'What's the matter?' he said, as he reached them.

'Nothing – really,' said Sandvold.

'He's got a temperature,' said Anna. 'Feel his brow.'

'A slight one, perhaps,' said Sandvold, but his teeth were chattering.

Tanner closed his eyes briefly. *What next?* he thought. 'Are you wet through yet?' he asked.

Sandvold shook his head. 'No. The Norwegian Army's greatcoats are first class.' He smiled thinly.

'How much have you drunk?' asked Anna.

'Enough, I think. I don't feel thirsty.'

'Water helps to bring a temperature down,' she said. 'I'll get some from the stream.' The others had gathered round them.

'What's going on?' demanded Chevannes.

'Nothing – please, I'll be all right,' said Sandvold. 'Let's keep walking.'

'He needs rest,' said Anna. 'We should look out for a *seter* or other shelter.'

Chevannes glared at Tanner, his implication clear: *I told you we needed more rest.* 'Very well,' he said. 'We'll keep going for now, but let's hope we find somewhere to rest soon.'

Luck was with them. They pushed on, more slowly now, but soon the western side of the valley folded away to reveal a mountain lake and an isolated farmhouse on a thin plateau of pasture between it and the stream.

Thank God, thought Tanner, then prayed they might find refuge there. Chevannes halted them and sent Larsen, with Anna, towards the farm. As they waited, Tanner walked away from the others and signalled to Sykes to join him. 'If one of them is a spy,' he said, hushed, 'this will give them another opportunity to make contact. We need to keep a close watch, Stan.'

'Why not talk to the others?'

'I don't want to frighten them.'

'Better that than Jerry turns up.'

Tanner thought for a moment. 'No, Stan. You know what they'll be like. They'll chatter among themselves. Mac or Hepworth will say something. I don't want to arouse suspicion. If there is a spy – and, let's face it, we don't have enough evidence yet to come out and accuse anyone – we want to catch them, not put them on their guard.' He patted Sykes's shoulder. 'No – you and I are going to have to take responsibility here.'

'All right, Sarge. You're the boss.'

Larsen returned. 'The farmer has gone to fight, but his wife is there with two small children and her father-in-law. He's out and about on the farm, but she says we can come in. Astrid Madsen is her name. Her father-in-law is called Claus Madsen.' He smiled wistfully. 'Two girls, they have. Beautiful children.'

Tanner and Nielssen helped the professor to his feet, but he staggered, so Nielssen took his arm and placed it round his shoulders. Tanner caught a glance from Anna: there was fear in her eyes, but what could he say? The professor was ill, and for the moment they could go no further.

Hurrying back to the Gudbrandsdal valley in Kurz's black Citroën, Reichsamtsleiter Hans-Wilhelm Scheidt had instructions to report to Generalmajor Engelbrecht's headquarters at Vinstra. The general, Terboven had assured him, would be far more compliant this time; the Reichskommissar had made it clear that he was to give every assistance to Scheidt and the SD in their quest to capture Odin. 'You will have the men and equipment you need,' Terboven had told him. 'Odin will not escape for lack of resources.' The Reichskommissar had spoken with General Geisler, the commander of the Luftwaffe in Norway, too. 'If you have any problems, Scheidt,' Terboven had told him, 'any problems at all, let me know. Understand?'

Now he looked out at the passing countryside through the rain-streaked window. The snow was melting in the valley, leaving ever more drab fields, grey-yellow from lack of sun. His gamble, he supposed, had paid off, but although he now had the support he had gone to Oslo to ask for, he felt no sense of elation. Rather, he could not stop thinking about what would become of him once the hunt for Odin was over. It was as though he had reached the endgame, not only for Odin but for himself.

In Lillehammer, he stopped at SD Headquarters, picked up Kurz and together they drove on to Vinstra. The signs of battle were obvious. Shell-holes littered the route. In places, the road had been only roughly repaired. Tretten was a pitiful sight: a collection of burnt and collapsed buildings, with rows of fresh graves dug in the fields leading away from the road. The scenes of destruction were similar in Fåvang and Ringebu, villages unfortunate enough to have played host to bitter fighting. Burnt-out vehicles and dead horses could be seen at every mile. In places, wide swathes of forest had been in flames. The smell of scorched timber hung in the valley, in places mingling with the stench of decomposing flesh, invading even the car as they swept through.

They found the commander of the 163rd Infantry Division in a large, ornate building a few hundred yards south of the railway station. He was in conference with several of his commanders, including Major von Poncets, and insisted they be ushered into his planning room, where a large map of the Gudbrandsdal valley had been hung on one wall.

He cut an impressive figure, Scheidt thought, immaculate in his field grey and glistening black cavalry boots, with a strong, square, youthful face and shaved head. He spoke clearly and crisply. Reconnaissance reports earlier that morning had suggested the British would be making a stand in battalion strength only. The first attack had been made a few hours earlier, but repulsed with heavy casualties.

'I had hoped we would force a way through quickly,' said Engelbrecht, 'but we must now wait and deploy in strength.'

'It's always easier for the defender to get away quickly, General,' said one of his commanders. 'The road between Sjoa and Otta is badly damaged. It's been a long night trying to get my guns in place. The rain hasn't helped either.'

'The engineers are working flat-out,' said another officer.

Engelbrecht nodded. 'Don't worry. Your artillery is now in place, is it not, Oberst?'

The colonel nodded.

'And, Major,' continued Engelbrecht, 'when will your two battalions be ready?'

'Any moment, Herr Generalmajor.'

'Good,' said Engelbrecht, rubbing his hands together. 'The Luftwaffe will bomb the British positions once more, followed by a short but concentrated barrage. Then Infantry Regiment 307 will attack on a wide front with von Poncets' men sweeping around the eastern flanks.' He smiled. 'That should do the trick. But I want everyone else to continue bringing their troops forward towards Otta. There must be no let-up.'

He dismissed his commanders, then turned to Scheidt and Kurz. 'Forgive me, gentlemen,' he said, shaking their hands and leading them into another room, which he had established as his office. 'Sit,' he said, pointing to two chairs in front of his desk. After offering them both a cigarette, he sat down. 'Now,' he said, 'I've spoken with the Reichskommissar and I assured him I will do what I can to help. So where do you think this elusive fellow is?'

'We're not sure, General,' said Kurz. 'We had contact yesterday to the west of Vinstra, then received a signal that they were heading for Sjoa.'

Engelbrecht laughed. 'Then I'm sorry to say they've most probably reached the British.'

Kurz shook his head. 'I don't think so, General. Yesterday evening we intercepted a message from the British Brigade headquarters in Otta to their HQ in Dombas informing them that they still had no news of Odin. Another intercept this morning confirmed they still have not made contact. They are as in the dark as we are.'

'And your intelligence is reliable?' Engelbrecht asked.

'I'm certain. It was picked up from an insecure civilian telephone line. The British have few radios – and what communication equipment they do have is far from secure.'

'Even so,' said Engelbrecht, 'you may have to accept that this fellow has already reached safety.'

'It's possible, yes,' admitted Kurz.

'The point, however, General,' said Scheidt, 'is that we must be ready to strike if and when we do hear news. Assume Odin is still at large and that there is much to be gained by his safe capture.'

'Yes, yes,' said Engelbrecht. 'Herr Reichsamtsleiter, I've heard all this from Terboven. Of course we will do what we can. But my forces are engaged in a battle at

Otta. This afternoon, or perhaps this evening, we will have beaten the British once more and the town will be in our hands. Thereafter, I will be in a better position to help, not least because, as you heard, most of my division will have caught up with the vanguard.' He smiled again. 'So it might be better for you if Odin is not only still at large but that he waits for us to clean up at Otta before making his whereabouts known again.'

As it happened, Odin was no more than twenty-five miles as the crow flew from Engelbrecht's headquarters. He was lying in a dark, shuttered room, with a perilously high temperature and a crushing migraine. He had vomited repeatedly, although now could only retch bile.

In the barn, the men had been fed – boiled eggs, chicken, bread and stewed apple. The old man and his daughter-in-law had been generous hosts. They had rested too, and the straw in the barn had helped dry their clothes. Above, the rain clattered on the red tin roof.

Tanner leant against some straw, carving a small aircraft from an old piece of wood with his bayonet and clasp-knife, watched by the two little girls, who sat beside him, cross-legged, their chins in their hands.

Larsen wandered over. 'You're a natural, Sergeant.'

'It's something to do. Anyway, you should have seen Corporal Sykes earlier. Had them captivated with his coin tricks.'

Larsen spoke to the children, then smiled. 'They want to know which will have the plane. Perhaps you should make two.'

It was nearly three o'clock, Tanner saw. He smiled

ruefully. 'I've nothing better to do.' He had already checked his weapons, stripped and cleaned his rifle, then examined the working parts of the Spandau.

'You do not have children yourself, Sergeant?' Larsen asked.

'No, sir.'

'I have two girls, a little younger than these.' He sighed. 'I do not mind telling you, Sergeant, that I miss them terribly. This war . . .' He shook his head. 'It is a terrible thing.'

'But you're a soldier, sir. One of the few Norwegian professionals.'

'Yes – you are right. And I should not say this, but if I am honest, I never expected to fight. I thought I would remain a member of His Majesty's Guard in Oslo, but not that Norway would find itself at war. We are neutrals, Sergeant.'

'Yes,' said Tanner, 'you're not the first to say so. We British are a bit more used to it. There's not a year goes by without a bit of fighting, war or no war.'

Tanner finished the first model and gave it to the elder child. He had just begun a second when their mother entered the barn and spoke with Larsen. She was, he guessed, perhaps thirty, with a thin, kind face. The fear in her eyes that had been so evident when they had first descended on the farm had gone, soothed by the soldiers' apparent harmlessness and by the reassuring return of her father-in-law. But the anxiety was still there. Tanner could hardly blame her. It was brave to take in Allied soldiers with the Germans only a short way off.

She looked at her daughters and the model Tanner had made, smiled, then spoke with Larsen.

'What news?' Tanner asked him, once she had left them.

'Not much. The professor's asleep. Anna has put her medical training to good use.'

On their arrival at the farm, Chevannes had ordered Tanner to organize guards, so he had. One was stationed in the attic at the top of the house from which there was a clear view of the valley they had walked up earlier, while the other stood guard outside Sandvold's room. Each man did two hours on, four hours off; only the officers were exempt. Later, when Tanner and McAllister went into the farmhouse to relieve Kershaw and Erwood, he had a chance to talk to Anna.

She looked tired, Tanner thought, as they sat on the wooden floorboards of the second-floor landing. 'You must get some rest too, you know,' he told her.

'I will.' She leant her head against his shoulder. 'I could fall asleep now.'

'Why don't you? I can listen for you.'

For a moment there was silence between them. Downstairs, they could hear chairs scraping, the children talking. In the hall at the bottom of the staircase, an old grandfather clock ticked methodically.

'At least he's going to be all right,' said Anna at length.

'He is?'

'Yes. It's exhaustion more than anything. He's twenty-five years older than most of us, not a young man. Ten days he's been on the run now, tramping over mountains, across rivers and lakes without proper sleep or food.'

'And he's been shot at, strafed and bombed.'

'Yes. It creates a great strain, physically and mentally. And the professor's a scientist, a city-dweller. It's not surprising that his body is rebelling. Oh, and he has migraines. I pity anyone who does – a terrible affliction. If you get a bad one, you can do nothing except lie in a dark room until it passes.'

'And your prognosis, Doctor?'

'The migraine should have passed by the morning. I expect the fever will subside too.'

'Will he be able to walk?'

'He'll be a bit weak, but possibly.'

'We could always make a stretcher.' Tanner sighed. 'I know this can't be helped, but the moment he can move again, we must leave. God knows where the front is now, but one thing is for certain: our forces are only going backwards. To have any hope of catching them up again, we can't afford to stay here too long.'

'Let's pray he sleeps well tonight, then.'

'You too, Anna. If we get going tomorrow, we all need to be rested.' Her face was truly lovely, he thought. The eyes, the gentle arc of her eyebrows, the curve of her lips. She moved her head, her eyes turned to his. Leaning down, he kissed her. Suddenly it seemed the most obvious and natural thing in the world.

A long night and an even longer morning. The rain had passed, and so had the professor's fever, but the head-shattering migraine was proving more stubborn. The men were restless; so, too, were Astrid Madsen and her

359

father-in-law. It was clear they had had enough of sheltering a disparate bunch of soldiers.

And that damned clock, ticking away the seconds, the minutes, the hours. Tanner had taken over guard duty again outside Sandvold's room at around noon, and all the time he waited there he could hear it, reminding him that time, a precious commodity, was passing. He had felt more at ease on the mountain at Uksum Farm, where at least he could see the valley spread before them and watch the enemy's movement. Here they were hidden; the view back down the valley was not a long one – and it had occurred to him that they might now just as likely see German troops approaching from the north.

At one, Anna checked on the professor again, clasping Tanner's hand as she passed him. Reappearing a few minutes later, she said, 'The migraine has subsided. We can leave.'

Tanner breathed out heavily. *At last.*

The old farmer helped make a stretcher from two lengths of wood and an old piece of tarpaulin. The professor protested half-heartedly that he was capable of walking, but after nearly collapsing down the stairs that led from the farmhouse, he acquiesced. He looked ill, Tanner thought, his eyes dark hollows and his skin sallow.

'Are you sure he's fit to travel?' Tanner asked Anna.

'He is weak, but if he is on a stretcher he will be fine. It is no worse for him than lying on a bed. He needs rest, that is all.'

At least the others were now refreshed, Tanner thought. With the exception of Nielssen, who had kept his beard, the men were now cleanshaven once more, the sloping shoulders and foot-dragging of the previous morning replaced by a renewed vigour that was clear from the moment they set off.

They skirted the lake, then turned north-west, back under the protection of the forest and beneath the snow-capped peak of the Bringsfjellet. There was birdsong: the first Tanner had heard since he'd arrived in Norway. Among the pines and silver birch he could pick out a missel-thrush, a lark, and even a woodpecker. His mood lightened.

Aircraft appeared occasionally in the sky and at one point a Messerschmitt 110 had swept by close enough to make them take cover, but otherwise they had not seen a soul. By evening they were approaching the Otta valley, only a few miles from Vågåmo, the small town that Tanner hoped would provide the gateway for their continued escape north.

They found a boarded-up *seter* among the trees beside a mountain brook, shielded behind a wooded outcrop. It was, Tanner knew with satisfaction, a good place to base themselves while they prepared the crossing. Hidden from the air by the dense covering of surrounding birch, alder and pine, it was also shielded from the valley below. On the other hand, the outcrop, climbing sharply half a mile beyond, would provide an ideal observation post from which they could watch the town and the lake.

He had barely spoken a word to Chevannes since he had hit the man the day before, so he turned now to Larsen and the professor. 'We need to have a look round,' he said, 'perhaps from this knoll.'

361

As he had hoped, Larsen suggested this to Chevannes, who silently concurred. Leaving the others at the *seter*, Tanner climbed through the trees, scrambling over patches of bare rock, until he reached the summit. From there the view stretched far and wide, the valley before them and the mountains on the far side in sharply defined clarity. With his naked eye, Tanner spotted the bridge crossing the mouth of the river, and the road along which he hoped they could escape, snaking through a valley to the north-west of the town. Now he peered through his binoculars. The bridge was of iron construction with wooden boarding across it, seventy to a hundred feet wide, he guessed. The town itself was set back from the river and, he now realized, spread more round a small, lesser river coming down from the valley beyond. He cursed; he'd not noticed that on Anna's map. Dark timber-framed buildings lined the main road and there was a wooden church, with what looked like a separate bell-tower next to it. And, yes, trucks and German military vehicles parked round an open area beside the church.

'The enemy is here,' said Chevannes, also looking through his binoculars. 'We will never get across.'

'Not in daytime,' said Tanner.

'What should we do?' asked Larsen.

Chevannes said nothing, so Tanner went on, 'Sir, with your permission I'd like to carry out a reconnaissance tonight.'

'What are you thinking? Crossing further east down the river?' said Larsen.

'No. I was considering crossing the lake. Look.' He

362

pointed westwards. 'See that spur jutting out? And there's another on the other side. What's that? Two miles from Vågåmo? The crossing would be quite narrow there. Jerry'll be pretty thick along the river between the town and Otta, but there's no need for him to go further west. There's nothing on the road west of Vågåmo at all. I reckon we can get across there tomorrow night when it's dark, then double back and cross into the valley beyond, bypassing the town altogether. With any luck we'll pick up some M/T along there.'

'It means another long delay,' said Larsen.

'We need that road beyond,' Tanner said. 'It's the only clear route to Åndalsnes. I admit it's a risk, but what alternative is there? One thing's for sure, we're not going to get through Vågåmo with all those Jerries there.'

'You have a point, Sergeant,' agreed Larsen

Chevannes nodded. 'Very well. Do your reconnaissance tonight, Sergeant, and then we will decide.'

Tanner smiled to himself. A plan had already formulated in his head. A plan to solve all of their problems.

19

''Ere, Sarge,' said Sykes, after Chevannes had told them
they would be remaining at the *seter* for the time being.
'What's going on?'

'You and I are going out on a recce tonight.' He walked
away from the hut and crouched on a rock beside the
stream.

'Both of us?'

Tanner nodded. 'I need you with me.'

'But what about keeping an eye on the
Norwegians?'

'Don't worry about that.' He winked.

Sykes looked at him suspiciously. 'What you up to,
Sarge?'

'All in good time, Stan. All in good time.' He took off
his pack and gas-mask case and put them on the ground.
'Right,' he said. 'What explosives have we got left? I've
got two packets of Nobel's and four sticks of Polar, plus
three Mills bombs.'

Sykes delved into his own pack. 'Two packets of

Nobel's and two sticks of Polar. You got some fuse left, Sarge?'

'Yes – I've got the tin here.' He took it from his pack and held it up, then put everything back and rubbed his hands together thoughtfully.

'We can still do some damage with this lot,' said Sykes.

Sandvold was walking towards them.

'Good to see you up and about, Professor,' Tanner said. 'How are you feeling?'

'An honest answer? Not so good, but better than I was.' He cleared his throat. 'I must apologize to you both, holding you up like that. I feel we have done more to stop ourselves reaching the Allies than the Germans have. I am as anxious to get north as you are, but not sorry to have this opportunity to build up my strength a little.'

'My old mum used to get migraines,' said Sykes. 'Couldn't do nothing while they were going on. Terrible they were.'

'Yes – well, hopefully the Allies are not yet out of reach.' He shuffled his feet, then said, 'I wonder, Corporal, would you mind if I had a word with Sergeant Tanner alone?'

'Not at all, sir.' He picked up his pack and stood up. 'I'll be in the *seter*, Sarge.'

When the corporal had gone inside, Tanner said, 'What is it, sir?'

The professor glanced around him. 'Perhaps we could wander a little further away.'

'Of course,' said Tanner, and picked up his pack with his rifle.

Sandvold walked along the stream until they were

almost out of sight of the *seter*. 'Sergeant, I've been think-ing,' he said at length. 'You and your men – Chevannes and the Chasseurs too, for that matter – have sacrificed much to help me get away. A lot has been expected of you but you have kept your promise to Colonel Gulbrand without complaint and without once thinking to save yourselves first. I am very grateful.'

'I hope it proves worthwhile.'

'Yet you have no idea what it is all about.'

'One day I'll get to the bottom of it.'

'Actually, Sergeant, I would like to tell you now.'

Tanner was surprised. 'You don't have to, you know. Perhaps it's better you don't.'

'No,' said Sandvold. 'It's better I do. In any case, you have earned my trust, Sergeant. It is only fair that you know why you have put your lives at risk on my behalf.' Sandvold glanced around him again. 'Do you know what modern armed forces need most to fight a war?'

Tanner shrugged. 'Men. Weapons. Machinery. I don't know – tanks, trucks, aircraft. Lots of aircraft.'

'In a way, yes. But what is it that enables those machines to work? What do they run on?'

'Fuel?'

'Exactly. And what is fuel?'

'Petrol.'

'Which is?'

'Oil?'

The professor smiled. 'Yes! Black gold, it is sometimes called, and so it is to anyone wanting to wage war. Now, I do not expect you to know much about the natural

366

resources of Greater Germany, but please trust me when I say that the country lacks its own oil. And without it Hitler will be unable to continue the war. Think of all the aircraft we have been so impressed by. How will they fly without it? How will his tanks run? How will factories work? How will even a machine-gun fire without that most precious liquid? They can't. That is the simple truth.' He continued, 'It is true that I am a scientist, Sergeant Tanner, but my field is geology. So far, man has tapped only a fraction of the world's oil resources, but the difficulty is that most of it lies underground and, more specifically, under the sea. The problem is how to find it and how then to get to it. My career so far has been dedicated to solving these problems.'

'And you've been successful?'

'More so than I could possibly have hoped. I shall not bore you with the details of how I reached my conclusions but, suffice to say, study led me to believe there are large oil fields waiting to be mined on the Norwegian continental shelf.' Sandvold smiled. 'You look confused. The point, Sergeant, is that on the continental shelf, the sea is shallow – at least, shallow compared to the ocean. And in the North Sea off the coast of Norway it is only around a hundred metres deep, sometimes less.' He clapped his hands. 'So. The question is, how to get the oil up and out across the sea?'

'How?'

'Ha!' said Sandvold, wagging a finger. 'It is not an easy matter, but I have worked out a way to do it. The answer is by making a drilling platform. The principle is the same as a land-based oil-drilling station. You make a platform and its accompanying legs on land, tow them out to sea and embed them in the sea floor. Then you begin drilling.'

'But surely, Professor, you would then need legs for this platform of more than a hundred yards?'

'Yes, but that is not so very long. There are ships longer than that.'

'And you think this is possible? What about the oil? What happens to it once it is drilled?'

'Siphoned into waiting tankers. And, yes, I do certainly believe it is possible.'

'And you are the only person who knows how to do it?'

Sandvold nodded. 'Exactly, but only because no one else has thought to do it. There are better engineers than me in the world. But there is no one else who knows where this oil is. Last year I applied for a royal grant, which was awarded.'

'Which is why the King has taken such a personal interest.'

'Yes. He realized the implications. Norway could become a very rich country. But he also appreciated, as did I, that war was coming to Europe and that these discoveries, these inventions, could be a cause of potential trouble for Norway should Germany – and, I might add, Britain – find out about them.'

'How did they?'

'That I cannot say.'

'You can't or you won't?'

'I do not know. I work mostly alone. Only I have the blue papers. But the King knows, and presumably so do some of his advisers and ministers. When the war is over and we are left in peace once more, Norway will become rich, very rich indeed. But now ... That is why the Germans want me. They want my knowledge.'

'And your plans.'

'Yes, so I can help them produce the oil they will so badly need if this war goes on for any great length of time.'

'Why don't you just burn the blue papers?'

Sandvold laughed. 'Do you have any idea how much work has gone into them? It is not something I simply have stored in my head. What I have told you is how it can be done in its most simplified form. Believe me, Sergeant Tanner, reaching a stage where oil might actually be extracted from below the seabed has taken literally years of work. If it comes to it, I will burn them, but I have been hoping that with your help it will not.'

'Yet you didn't leave Oslo as the King ordered you to.'

'Because I thought that without the King in Oslo, I could be anonymous, forgotten. The arrival of Gulbrand made me realize otherwise. The experiences of the past week have confirmed my worst fears.'

Tanner ran his hands through his hair. *So*, he thought. *It's all about oil.* 'Tell me one last thing, Professor,' he said. 'Wouldn't such a platform be vulnerable to attack from the air and the sea?'

'You surround it with thick and deep minefields, and it would be within easy reach of land. In any case, you're forgetting, Sergeant, that the Nazis fully expect to control all of Europe. Or, at least, they expect all of Europe will be compliant with their designs. And after the way in which they have invaded our country, who is to stop them? Not the British.'

'We're being defeated here, I know,' said Tanner, 'but that doesn't mean we'll lose the entire war.'

'Maybe you won't *lose*. But can you defeat the Nazis? No. Not at the moment, at any rate. But I think Hitler is looking beyond Europe.'

'What do you mean by that?'

'I mean America and Russia.'

'But they're allied with the Russians and America isn't even in the war.'

'Not yet, but it is only a matter of time. And when that day comes Germany will need vast amounts of oil – which the Soviet Union and the United States have in abundance.'

Tanner shook his head. 'What happens next month, next year, is beyond me, Professor. All I want to think about at the moment is getting us out of here. Getting you to safety.'

'But you see now why that is so important?'

'Yes – and thank you, Professor.' He shook his head again. 'Oil – I would never have guessed. I thought it must be some secret weapon.'

Sandvold chuckled. 'In a way it is. But take heart, Sergeant. Without oil, the Nazis won't win. Not in the long term.'

In the dank confines of the *seter*, Tanner and Sykes prepared for their reconnaissance mission. It was nearly half past ten. From their packs they took out the German uniforms they had captured several days earlier, and put on the tunics, wind jackets and field caps. Both men had lost their Mauser rifles at Tretten, but they took two from

370

the Norwegians, as well as several rounds of ammunition. Their own uniforms and packs – including the explosives – they left with Lance Corporal Erwood and their men.

'*Heil, mein Führer!*' said McAllister, standing up and performing a mock Nazi salute, one finger pressed above his lip.

Tanner laughed, then turned to Chevannes and the Norwegians. 'We'll be off, then, sir,' he said. 'We'll have a good look at the town, but then we'll head west down the lake and try to find a good crossing-place.'

'Yes,' said Chevannes. 'Now go.'

In the darkening light, they headed towards the valley, Tanner explaining his plan. It was nearly dark by the time they reached the lower slopes directly above the bridge into Vågåmo, but there was still just light enough for them to study it sufficiently. Two stone pillars jutted out from the banks at either side, and across it there was a simple iron construction much like the bridges they had already seen in the Gudbrandsdal valley.

'What do you think, Stan?' said Tanner, from their position among the trees.

'It can be as strong as it likes,' he replied, 'but if it's got a wooden roadbed, we're going to be able to put it out of action. Simple as that.'

There were, they noted, just two guards on the bridge, both on the southern side. 'That'll make life easier,' said Tanner.

'What I want to know, Sarge, is why Jerry's here anyway.'

'Because of that road, I should think,' said Tanner. 'It

gives them another line of advance north towards Åndalsnes. And it might also be because they're hoping to catch us. But it's clear they're not using it yet. I've not seen any movement north.'

With the light now all but gone, they moved quietly away through the trees until they were a safe distance from the bridge, then dropped down on to the valley road. The night sky was clear. Millions of stars twinkled above, reflected in the inky darkness of the lake. A thin crescent moon stood high over the valley and, with the stars, cast a pale creamy light across the landscape, enabling the two men to see the shape of the road, the lake, the mountains.

A few miles to the west the road forked.

'Where's that lead?' whispered Sykes.

'I'm pretty sure back to Heidel and Sjoa,' said Tanner. 'It's quite a long way round, though.' He paused to study its approach, then the valley. He could no longer see the knoll in front of the *seter*.

They walked on a short way through the silence, the air cool and crisp, until they reached the small headland that projected into the lake. There was a farmstead, but a small wooden jetty too – and, as Tanner had hoped, a number of small boats.

It was a little after midnight. The dawn of a new day – and the last, he realized, of the month. Twelve days they'd been in Norway. It felt like eternity.

With the first streaks of dawn, the *seter* stirred into life. The dusty floor was hard and uncomfortable, and although the soldiers were used to sleeping wherever they had to, most had had enough rest over the past twenty-four hours to ensure they now slept only lightly. As they woke, they stumbled outside, some to urinate nearby, others to wander somewhat further. Since Anna had joined them they had been more careful about such things.

One of their number, an agent of the *Sicherheitsdienst* wandered away from the hut, safe in the knowledge that it was possible to break away from the others for a few minutes without arousing any suspicion whatsoever. At least, it was now that Sergeant Tanner and Corporal Sykes were away. It had been difficult during the past couple of days with them watching every move; they suspected someone, that was certain. *But not me*, the agent had decided. At any rate, with them out of the way for the time being, there was now a clear chance for him to send another signal.

Passing within clear sight of the sentry, the agent smiled – morning ablutions – and then headed into the woodland until the *seter* was out of sight. Finding as wide a tree as possible, the traitor squatted and took two small metal boxes from a haversack, both no more than five and a half inches long, four and a half wide. One was a transmitter, the other the accumulator. From a pocket, three leads were produced, each with crocodile clips. The agent attached the two boxes together, then turned a small black knob at the front of the transmitter until it clicked, causing a faint light within the box to glow. From another pocket, a long length of wire was produced, which was then connected to the back of the box with trembling fingers. This done, the person took the weighted end and threw it high into the tree above. With a hammering heart, the agent glanced round, even though it would have been possible to hear anyone approaching. Then a quick look back down at the transmitter. The light was glowing brighter now, as the valves warmed up. *Half a minute more.*

The agent prayed this message would get through. Instructions had been to send as many as was possible without jeopardizing the mission. The transmitter that was to be used was just that – a device for sending Morse signals – not a receiver. There was no way of telling whether the messages that had been sent had been read or not. Until the Stukas had arrived two days before, the agent had begun to think that the transmitter could not be working at all: a specific message from the Rostads' farm had been sent and several from the Jøra valley, yet despite troops arriving at Uksum Farm, they had made no attempt to act on his information.

'No one will suspect you,' Kurz had said, 'because we will swoop down and whisk Odin away before anyone has the chance.' Perhaps that would have been so, had it not been for Tanner and his men turning up. *Tanner.* The agent cursed him. Despite repeated efforts, the sergeant was still alive, still jeopardizing the mission. Thanks to Tanner, several golden opportunities for Odin to be captured had been foiled. Now perhaps all would be well. For once, the sergeant appeared to have let down his guard.

The agent leant back against the tree, eyes briefly closed, then checked the time once more. *Nearly there*, he thought. *Just a few more seconds.*

374

As soon as a minute had passed, the agent turned the middle knob to number seven, tuning the oscillator of the transmitter frequency, and then adjusted the aerial load, the last of the three knobs at the front of the tiny S108/10 transmitter, until the light was at its brightest. Taking a deep breath, the crouching figure held a still quavering finger above the Morse button and began to transmit.

Less than a minute later, the message was completed. Having rolled up the wire and put the boxes back into his pack, the agent stood up and walked steadily towards the *seter*.

20

Reichsamtsleiter Scheidt was shaken awake, and rolled over to find Sturmbannführer Kurz leaning over him.

'What the devil is it?' he croaked.

'A message – good news!'

Scheidt sat up now, the remnants of sleep gone. He snatched the typex from Kurz and read: *'In mountains above Vågåmo. Crossing planned over lake west of town when dark 30 April. More details later.'*

Scheidt's face broke into a grin. 'Excellent,' he said. He looked at his watch. It was only half past four, but he knew there could be no more thought of sleep. 'Well done, Kurz,' he said. 'We've got him this time.'

Soon after, having shaved and dressed, he hurried downstairs to the conference room of Generalmajor Engelbrecht's spacious headquarters in Vinstra. Three men were standing by the map pinned to the wall – Major von Poncets, Sturmbannführer Kurz and Hauptmann Zellner.

'Ah, good morning, Herr Reichsamtsleiter,' said von Poncets. 'Good to see you again.'

Scheidt nodded, then looked at Zellner. A white bandage had been strapped across his nose, his cheek had blackened, while his eye, purple last time Scheidt had seen him, had turned yellow. 'Hauptmann Zellner,' he said, 'what are you doing here? Shouldn't you be in hospital?'

'I'm well enough, thank you, Herr Reichsamtsleiter,' he replied.

Scheidt stared at him with contempt. 'You have come off worst against those men no less than three times, which should have put paid to your chances of taking any further part in the operation. However, far be it from me to make such decisions.'

'We suspect the men will be wearing German uniforms,' said von Poncets. 'The Hauptmann will be of help in identifying them.'

'I suppose there's something in that. And what forces has the general given us for this?'

'There's a company of the 324th Infantry Regiment,' said von Poncets, 'and two companies from my own battalion of Gebirgsjäger.' He pointed to the map. 'The 324th boys are already based at Vågåmo. They moved in two days ago after the fall of Otta. They were hoping to catch any British troops retreating that way, but as it happened the Tommies hadn't used that route.'

'As you know,' put in Kurz, 'the general agreed to leave them there in case there was any sign of Odin.'

Scheidt nodded. 'Will that be enough?'

'More than enough.' Von Poncets smiled.

'I only ask because I recall that we had the same conversation some days ago, Herr Major, and it seems both

377

you and the Hauptmann underestimated the enemy.'

Von Poncets took out a cigarette, and tapped the end against his silver case. 'We're talking about the best part of five hundred men being available for this operation, which is far more than we either need or will use. Numbers are not the issue here. Execution is what counts.'

'Which, so far, has left much to be desired.'

Von Poncets paused to light his cigarette. 'We have been unfortunate, but this time we have firm intelligence. It is no longer a guessing game.' He drew on his cigarette, then said, 'Herr Reichsamtsleiter, with the greatest respect, let's not dwell on what has already happened. Let's concentrate on making sure we get Odin this time.'

'Quite so, Herr Oberstleutnant,' said Kurz. 'My team are, of course, on standby waiting for any further signal. They'll send through anything they receive the moment it arrives.'

'Yes, Kurz, we know that,' said Scheidt. He felt annoyed that the operation appeared to have been left to von Poncets and Zellner, of all people, men who had lost his respect. He wished General Engelbrecht would join them. It was as though no one but he truly understood the importance of capturing Odin. Turning back to the major, he said, 'So, what are your thoughts?'

Sunlight was already pouring through the window, highlighting the thousands of dust particles suspended in the air. Von Poncets exhaled again, sending a cloud of tobacco smoke swirling in front of the map.

'We have to assume,' he said, pointing airily to the

mountains south of Vågåmo, 'that they will be able to observe the town at the very least.'

'Is there a case, then,' said Scheidt, 'for attacking up through the mountain rather than waiting until tonight?'

'No,' said von Poncets, his tone emphatic. 'None at all. We don't know precisely where they are, and attacking uphill makes little tactical sense. Fighting in dense forest offers many hazards and leads to confusion. Experience, I think, has shown us that it would be difficult to capture Odin alive in such circumstances. No, we must wait for them to come to us.'

'So the difficulty,' said Scheidt, 'is laying the trap without the enemy spotting it first.'

'Exactly,' said von Poncets, 'which is why a large number of troops is not necessarily the key.'

'So have you had thoughts about this?' asked Scheidt.

'Yes. Of course, I need to confer with the general and also with Hauptmann Frick in Vågåmo, but I suggest we use this route – here.' He pointed to a road that ran west of Sjoa, linked with another that ran roughly north–south until it joined the valley road several miles west of Vågåmo. 'They can approach by truck and debouch in the valley out of sight of the town or of anyone in the mountains, for that matter. We won't have reconnaissance pictures for a few hours yet, I'm afraid, but a request has been made. Assuming there's good cover, I see no reason why this movement should be seen at all.'

'And what about the troops in Vågåmo?'

'It's important the enemy believe it's still strongly held, so I propose we leave most of the company there.'

'Isn't that rather a waste of these men?'

'I don't think so, but don't worry, Herr Reichs-amtsleiter, we shall show the plans to the general. And in any case, we may receive another signal.'

They did, just after ten o'clock that morning. *'Still above Vågåmo. Crossing tonight at midnight 6 kms west of town after fork in road.'* Scheidt's spirits rose, and he was invigorated by the activity at Engelbrecht's headquarters. Outside, soldiers arrived in trucks, awaiting the order to pull out. Just before midday, a Luftwaffe despatch rider hurried into the building and deposited the morning's recon-naissance photographs. Poring over them in the briefing room with von Poncets and Engelbrecht's divisional staff, Scheidt had shared the mounting excitement when the pictures showed, as von Poncets had suggested they would, that the proposed approach for the ambush was indeed densely forested.

A brief conference followed, attended by company and platoon commanders of both von Poncets' battalion but also from the 324th Infantry who had been called back to Vinstra for the briefing. The mood in the room was buoyant, a haze of cigarette smoke rising to the rafters, the officers laughing and joking. And why wouldn't they be? thought Scheidt. Flush with victory, ahead lay another operation that would end successfully. Through the windows, the sun continued to shine. The greatcoats and jackets had gone; summer was on its way. *This time*, thought Scheidt. It had to be.

When the general arrived, the assembled officers stood up, scraping chairs across the wooden floor. He strode in, movements crisp, back erect, then casually waved at them to sit down, as though this was not a time to stand on ceremony. Then he, too, was seated, his head smooth and gleaming, the red and gold tabs of his general's collar and thick red stripe down either side of his breeches standing out vividly in the room of field grey. Scheidt was struck by his effortless air of authority.

Von Poncets stood to explain his plan, first pointing out key features each officer should memorize. They would be leaving directly after the briefing and would disembark from their trucks three kilometres south of the junction. They would then make their way to lying-up positions. Scouts would be sent forward to reconnoitre their ambush positions, and to mark where they would place spotlights. The men would move into these positions at 2300 hours.

Hauptmann Dostler of the 324th Infantry stood up. One platoon was to drive along the opposite bank of the lake. A potential problem was that the area to the west of Vågåmo was well cultivated and the road could easily be seen from the mountains opposite. They were thus to drive beyond the crossing-point, after which the road was hidden by forest. They would then leave the trucks and head back through the trees, close to the crossing-point where they would set up another spotlight. The remaining three platoons would remain in Vågåmo to give the impression that the town was still heavily occupied.

At this point, Scheidt raised his hand. 'Surely, Herr Hauptmann,' he said, 'the town will be heavily occupied if there are three whole platoons there?'

'Not particularly,' said Dostler. 'We've been fighting

up through the Gudbrandsdalen and all our units are now under strength. There will be about sixty men.'

The general cut in. 'Which is more than enough, Herr Reichsamtsleiter. Don't forget there will be vehicles, artillery pieces and other equipment in the town as well. Let's get on with the briefing.'

Chastened, Scheidt said no more, and after Kurz and Zellner had briefed the room about Odin and the accompanying fugitives, Engelbrecht stood up and addressed them. 'I can't stress enough, gentlemen,' he said, 'how important it is to capture Odin alive. The fear, of course, is that they will shoot him before you can get to him, which is why it is essential that none of you makes a move until they are almost in the boats. They will have travelled through the darkness and their eyes will be used to it. That, gentlemen, is where the lights come in. Caught in the beams, these fugitives will be momentarily blinded. That is the time to strike. The men must be killed and Odin left standing. Major von Poncets will brief you further, but remember: do not give away your positions until after the signal.' He eyed the officers in turn. 'Understand? Good.' He clapped his hands together. 'Right, gentlemen, off you go. And good luck.'

More scraping of chairs, and the men were on their way out. Scheidt followed them, watching them get into the trucks and other vehicles waiting in the streets outside. The sun still bore down between large white summery clouds; the snow had now gone from the valley. Scheidt put his hand on the balustrade outside the house and found it warm. A bark of orders, and engines rumbled into life.

Kurz paused beside him and offered a hand, which Scheidt took.

'Exciting, isn't it?' He grinned. 'If only we'd had this kind of intelligence and preparation five days ago.'

Scheidt smiled thinly.

'See you later,' added Kurz. 'With Odin, of course.' He waved, then trotted down the steps and along the road to von Poncets' waiting Kübelwagen.

Scheidt took out a cigarette. Exciting? He supposed so, although he did not share Kurz's obvious relish; he would save that until Odin was sitting before him. He struck a match, brought the cigarette to his lips and realized his hands were shaking. 'It's out of my control now,' he muttered, then sighed. Ahead lay long hours of waiting.

Sergeant Tanner was no less apprehensive as he watched the hours tick by. He had left Sykes alone on a ridge overlooking the road from the south with instructions to return only if he spotted any German troops, and had then waited on the lower slopes observing the town before he returned to the *seter* around seven that morning.

Chevannes had accepted his story without question. Even when he explained that he had left Sykes on guard above the bridge, the lieutenant had merely nodded. 'Did you have a chance to see whether there were enough oars this time?' he had asked.

'Yes, sir – there are.'

'Good.' Chevannes had ordered him to organize look-outs on the knoll and dismissed him.

Tanner had spent most of the morning there himself, and was still there, keeping watch with Lieutenant Larsen, when at around three a staff car arrived from the direction of Otta. He followed it as it drove to the centre of the town and stopped opposite the church. Four men got out. There was no further movement of vehicles until after four when two trucks headed west along the far shore of the lake. A couple of miles later, they disappeared. Tanner was puzzled, yet relieved to see troop movement at last from the town. He counted the remaining vehicles: five troop-carrying trucks, five medium guns, two further lorries and two staff cars.

Shortly after, Hepworth arrived with Anna in tow. Tanner was glad to see her. It was now nearly half past four and he wished Sykes would reappear. The distraction would be good.

'Have you come to relieve me, Hepworth?' asked Larsen.

'Yes, sir,' said Hepworth.

'Cleaned your rifle, Hep?' asked Tanner, then grinned at Anna.

'Yes, Sarge.'

'Checked your kit?'

'Yes, Sarge.'

'Here,' said Larsen, handing Hepworth his binoculars. 'Look after them.' He got up, patted his sides, then picked up his rucksack and said, 'Let's hope the town stays as quiet as this, Sergeant.'

'Here's hoping, sir,' Tanner replied, then turned back to Hepworth. 'Get the far side of the knoll, Hep,' he said. 'Make sure you've cover behind you, that you're clear of direct sunlight, then try to work out where those troops are.'

With Hepworth gone he and Anna were alone. 'Everything all right at the *seter*?' he asked.

'The resting has done the professor good.'

'Is he up and about?'

'He's shaved off his beard in the stream.'

'He's not going to need the stretcher then?'

'No. And he's been eating too.'

Tanner continued to peer through his binoculars. Anna sat behind him on a loose rock. A cool breeze drifted over the knoll but it was warm, even there. A few small patches of snow remained, but otherwise tufty grey grass now sprouted between the pines and birches.

'And Chevannes?' said Tanner at length.

'He's been quiet. Barks orders occasionally, but that's all.'

'As long as he doesn't get in my way, I'm not bothered,' said Tanner. 'He's done enough damage.'

'It's since the professor spoke up on your behalf. That undermined his authority. He doesn't want to say anything now that might lead to another clash.'

'Hm,' said Tanner. 'I'll still need to watch him tonight.'

They were silent for a while, then Anna said, 'Jack, do you think it'll be all right? The crossing? We were lucky last time. I wonder whether we will be again.'

'We'll be fine.'

'Good God,' she said, exasperation in her voice. 'Don't you ever get frightened? How can you be so calm all the time?'

'It's just a front,' he said. 'But we will be fine, I promise.' It was a promise he knew he was in no position to make. Where the hell was Sykes? Over the years, he had learnt to trust his intuition but with Sykes missing he was beginning to wonder if it had let him down. He looked back at the town. Nothing stirred. How many troops were down there? It was hard to say. Fifty? Eighty? More? So long as the enemy weren't expecting them there, and so long as no more troops arrived in the meantime, all would be well. But there was no Plan B. It was the town or nothing. He trained his binoculars on the trucks parked next to the church, and in them he saw their chance for freedom. Whatever happened, they had to take one. It was as simple as that.

'Trust me,' he said. 'It'll be fine.'

By six o'clock, Tanner was finding it increasingly difficult to maintain his outward *sangfroid*, although he knew that to betray his mounting anxiety would be a grave mistake. Having returned to the *seter*, he now busied himself cleaning his rifle and the Spandau once more, and hoping the others did not notice his near-constant checking of his watch.

At around twenty past six, his corporal finally appeared.

'Well?' said Tanner, hurrying to him.

Sykes grinned. 'They're there. A company, maybe two, of mountain troops.'

'Ha!' said Tanner, laughing. 'We were bloody right, Stan!'

'*You* were right, Sarge.'

'Good work, Stan. Bloody good work. And you weren't seen?'

'No. Zellner's with them, though. And they've got searchlights – small ones, but lights all the same. Brought accumulator packs and everything.'

Tanner grinned. 'Perfect. And *you* were right all along,' he whispered. 'There is a spy.'

'I've got the nose for it, Sarge. I tell you what, you watch my back and I'll watch yours. Cos together, I reckon, we make a good team, you and me.'

Tanner slapped the side of the corporal's arm. 'You've done well. I owe you.'

The final hours were interminable. At half past nine, accompanied by Chevannes and Larsen, Tanner left the knoll for the last time. The town was as quiet as ever, the troops, it seemed, billeted in the town's houses and the trucks still parked next to the church.

'It looks calm,' muttered Chevannes. 'And you've seen nothing, Sergeant, to make you think they're up to anything?'

'No, sir. Apart from the truck and staff car earlier, there's been no movement.'

'I saw nothing, either,' said Larsen, 'and the crossing is nearly six kilometres away. No one from the town will hear or see us rowing across from that distance.'

'Jerry doesn't seem to have bothered pushing further west, sir.'

'Apart from the truck you saw earlier, Sergeant.'

Tanner shrugged. 'Probably just reconnaissance.'

Chevannes nodded. '*Bon*.'

They walked in silence back to the *seter*, where the rest of the men were waiting outside, wearing German tunics, field caps and black-leather webbing. Tanner followed quickly, rolling his jerkin and battle blouse into the bottom of his pack. He had already transferred most of his explosives into his haversack and gas-mask bag. Having wedged his tin helmet into his pack, he placed the last two packs of Nobel's 808 on top.

When they were ready, Chevannes looked at his watch. 'Three minutes past ten,' he said. 'Let's go.'

Tanner, heart pounding, glanced at Sykes. 'Actually, sir, I'd like to say something.'

A flash of irritation crossed Chevannes' face. 'What, Sergeant? Be quick about it.'

'I don't think we should cross the lake after all.'

Chevannes and the Norwegians looked equally aghast. 'What?' said Chevannes, angry now.

'I don't think we should cross the lake,' Tanner repeated. 'I think we should go through the town.'

'Have you gone mad, Tanner?' said Chevannes.

'No, sir.' *Say this right*, he told himself. *Don't muck it up now*. 'I'm sorry, sir. It's just that there are only about fifty or so men in the town. They're not expecting us. We can climb down to a spot above the bridge and watch for an hour or so. I reckon we can take out the guards quietly enough, then march up to those trucks. You speak good German, sir, and so do the lieutenants here. At night, when all is quiet, they wouldn't suspect a thing.' He could see some of his men nodding now.

'Except that every German soldier for a hundred miles seems to know about us.'

'I'm sorry, sir. I hadn't considered it before, but as we were walking back from the knoll . . .' Chevannes was rubbing his chin. *Good. Indecision again.* 'The thing is, sir,' Tanner continued, 'it's the far side of the lake that's bothering me. We're going to have to climb up and over the mountain, which will take time. I don't suppose we'll be followed again, but those trucks are just sitting there. This time tomorrow we could be in Åndalsnes.'

Chevannes bit his bottom lip and glanced at Larsen and Nielssen.

'I think there's something in what Tanner says, sir,' said Nielssen. 'I've had a look down on the town today and I'm certain they're not expecting us. I think it's a risk worth taking.'

'I'm not so sure,' Larsen said. 'We know the coast is clear at the crossing. Going through the town seems to me too big a risk.'

'We need M/T straight away,' said Tanner. 'The crossing will hold us up. For all we know our boys might be about to evacuate. The more I think about it the more I'm convinced we should head straight down the hill and go through the town. In any case, they wouldn't think we'd have the nerve. That's precisely why we should do it. Fortune favours the brave, sir.'

'I could walk ahead,' said Anna. 'See whether the coast is clear.'

'That's not a good idea,' said Larsen. 'There's bound to be a curfew.'

'I think we should do it, Henrik,' Nielssen said to Larsen.

'Me too,' said Tanner. 'Come on, sir,' he said to

389

Chevannes. 'We can do this. Those trucks are just sitting there. It'll be dark, we're wearing German uniforms – it'll work, I know it will.' *Come on, Chevannes.*

'Let me think—' said the Frenchman.

'No,' said Larsen. 'We should stick to the original plan.'

Now, Tanner thought. 'Why, sir?' he said, stepping towards Larsen. 'Do you know something we don't?'

'What do you mean?' Larsen's eyes darted briefly, almost imperceptibly, to either side of him. But Tanner saw.

'Exactly that, sir. Are you hiding something from us?'

Larsen shifted his feet. 'No – of course not. Whatever do you mean, Tanner?'

'What the hell are you talking about, Sergeant?' Chevannes frowned.

'I'm just wondering, sir, if he can explain why the best part of two hundred German mountain troops are lying in wait for us in the trees beside the crossing-point.'

'*What?*' Chevannes was incredulous. So were the others, but Larsen simply stood where he was, the colour draining from his face.

'No!' said Nielssen, shock and anger in his voice. 'No, Henrik! Say it is not true!'

'I–I do not know what you are talking about.'

The professor stumbled forward and tugged at Larsen's arm. 'Henrik?'

'Lieutenant?' It was Chevannes' turn, utter incomprehension on his face.

'You – you are wrong,' stammered Larsen, 'I know nothing about it. You are lying, Sergeant. How dare you?'

'The only one lying is you,' said Tanner. 'Someone has betrayed us. Those Stukas didn't come from nowhere. Neither did those trucks on the pass. But this confirms it.'

'It was a set-up,' mumbled Larsen.

'Yes,' said Tanner. 'We'd suspected it for a while, but when those Jerries turned up this afternoon we knew for certain. The only thing I didn't know was who.'

'Men!' called out Chevannes. 'Hold him!' But Larsen already had his pistol in his hand. He grabbed Sandvold and pulled him towards him, the gun thrust towards the professor's stomach.

'You traitor!' said Anna, tears in her eyes. 'How could you?'

'Get back! Get back, all of you!' said Larsen, dragging Sandvold towards the *seter*.

The professor gasped. 'Stop this madness, Henrik!'

'Quiet! Now get back – or I will shoot!'

Tanner took a step towards him. 'Sir, put the gun down.'

'Get back, Sergeant!'

Tanner took another step towards him. 'Sir, put down the pistol.' He was now just three yards away.

'Sergeant! Not a step closer!'

'Tanner, don't be a damned fool!' There was panic in Chevannes' voice.

'Don't worry, sir. He won't shoot. Not the professor anyway. The Germans want Professor Sandvold alive, not dead. If all the lieutenant can offer them is a body they'll not thank him. Not after all this effort.' He took another step forward. 'It's over, sir.' Larsen's eyes

391

flickered wildly. 'Sir,' Tanner said once more, 'put down the pistol.'

Larsen pressed its muzzle harder into Sandvold's side, then suddenly pushed him forward so that he staggered and fell. 'You were right, Sergeant,' he said, trickles of sweat running down his face, 'I wouldn't shoot the professor, but I will kill you.'

Tanner took another step forward so that he was now only a few feet away.

'Sergeant, this is your last chance,' said Larsen. His eyes were still darting from one man to another and his outstretched hand quivered.

Tanner continued to stare at him. His mind was clear; the nerves he had felt earlier were gone. Timing was everything, and although he was fairly sure no shot would be heard in the town, it was a risk he would rather avoid.

Then Nielssen stepped forward. 'Why, Henrik?' he said, and for a fraction of a second Larsen turned his head towards him.

Tanner grabbed Larsen's wrist and pushed the lieutenant's arm backwards, both quickly and hard. The pistol fell from his hand, and Tanner drove his left fist into the Norwegian's head with a punishingly hard jab. Larsen's eyes rolled back and he toppled over, unconscious.

For a moment no one spoke. Then Tanner picked up the pistol, stood over him and said, 'Treacherous bastard. And to think I liked him.'

'Have you killed him, Sergeant?' asked the professor.

'No,' he said, wiping the back of his hand across his mouth. 'He'll come round in a minute.' The others gathered round the prostrate figure. Tanner felt Anna take his hand. Tears ran down her face.

'I cannot believe it,' she said. 'I just cannot believe it.'

Larsen groaned and Nielssen squatted beside him. 'Why?' he said. 'Why, Henrik?'

Larsen mumbled in Norwegian.

'What?' said Chevannes. 'What is he saying?' But Larsen continued to speak in his own language, not to Sandvold or to the others but to Nielssen.

Tanner walked back to where he had placed the Spandau, lifted it and hoisted it on to his shoulder. It was twenty past ten, and he was anxious to leave so that they could reach a position above the bridge before dark. And there was another reason: the guards changed every two hours at half past the hour and the next changeover was due at eleven thirty. Tanner reckoned eleven o'clock was the right time to deal with them – when their alertness was diminishing but well before the fresh shift arrived.

He was about to ask Chevannes what they should do with the traitor when he heard a strangled cry. He pushed through his men and saw Larsen dead on the ground. Nielssen was cleaning his short bayonet grimly on Larsen's tunic, then put it back in its sheath. 'I had no choice,' he said.

Tanner nodded. 'How did he do it?'

Nielssen rolled the dead man over and took off his pack. First he pulled out a small cloth bag, then a sheaf of papers and two metal boxes with a length of wire.

'Christ,' said Tanner. 'What the hell are they?'

Nielssen looked at them. 'I'm not certain, but from

these dials, I'd suggest this one must be a transmitter of some kind. It's tiny.'

Tanner turned to Chevannes. 'Sir?'

Chevannes swallowed hard. 'I still cannot believe it, Sergeant.'

'Sir, we need to go.'

'Yes, yes, of course,' he said. 'Right, men, we will go through the town. We must now forget about this traitor. We need to clear our minds and concentrate on the task ahead; successfully getting into Vågåmo, and taking one of those trucks.'

As they finally set off from the *seter*, Tanner did not glance back: his mind had already turned to what lay before them. Larsen's body was left where it lay: unburied on a patch of hard ground among the trees, high on an empty mountainside.

21

From the upstairs window of the newly requisitioned farmhouse beside the lake, Hauptmann Wolf Zellner had a grandstand view of the headland that jutted out into the water, and the boats lying roped to the short wooden jetty. Beside him were Sturmbannführer Kurz and Major von Poncets. Next to them, a field telephone had been rigged up, linking them to the men crouching in the trees round the farm and along the shore for a hundred metres and more. His nose still throbbed, his cheek still throbbed, and the pain of being cheated by the British sergeant a third time hurt him most of all, yet the prospect of Tanner's imminent death had improved his mood. The last light of the day was fading in the west. He looked at his watch. *An hour – that's all*, he thought.

Next to him, Kurz was telling them about their source. 'We pinned him down at Hamar, the day after the invasion,' he said. 'He was with the King and the rest of the government. He didn't need much persuading, I must say, although we did mention that we knew where his family was. He's got a charming wife and two small girls in Oslo. I'm not sure how much it had to do with it but we did mention that we might not be able to guarantee their safety should he decline our offer.' He chuckled. 'Not that I *would* have done anything to them. But a man like that, with a young family and everything, it's what they hold most dear, isn't it?'

'Yes,' said von Poncets. 'It is. I'm certainly not doing this for Hitler.'

'Actually,' said Kurz, scratching his cheek, 'I must give Scheidt some credit. He's a bit of an old woman, you know, but he's sharp. He's been over here since last year, grooming that buffoon Quisling on the say-so of the Führer. But he's also been working all sorts of other people in preparation for the invasion. I think it was Quisling's men who put him on to Larsen. Apparently he was a secret National Party man.'

'So he was primed,' said von Poncets.

'Primed – yes, exactly. And then with a bit of gentle persuasion we had our spy. A massive stroke of luck, of course, that he was chosen to go back and fetch Odin. Initially, we thought we would use him to get to the King and the gold.'

'Why didn't he lead you to Odin in Oslo, then?' asked Zellner.

'He didn't know. It wasn't until later. We ransacked Odin's offices and interrogated his mother. We didn't find any blue papers but we found enough to know what he was trying to do. Trust me, if this fellow can truly get oil from under the seabed, we'll have the eternal gratitude of the Führer.'

The thought cheered Zellner even more. Well, it wouldn't be long now. This time nothing had been left to chance. He was certain they could not fail again.

It was mindless work, patrolling a bridge. One man walked one way, one the other, up and down, back and forth. Schütze Pieter Greiger was tired. It had been a gruelling two weeks, and although they had successfully hammered their way northwards, victory helped keep you going only so far. The fighting at Dombas had been gruelling for his company and they had lost several men. Half his platoon had been killed or wounded. One of the dead had been a good friend, Dieter Manser; they had known each other since boyhood. He'd tried hard to put his loss out of his mind and found that so long as he was busy it was quite easy to do. But sentry duty gave him too much time to think about Dieter's bloodied body, the life draining from him . . . He reached the north side of the bridge, then began to walk back, the rhythmic clump of his boots loud on the thick wooden planking.

He had passed Reitmann when a sound pulled him from his reverie. Clasping the strap of his rifle more tightly, he listened. Then, a short distance ahead, he saw a column of men emerge from the shadows of the mountain, silhouetted against the pale dirt of the road. The men were marching towards the bridge and, seeing the outline of their field caps, he relaxed. He called to Reitmann and they strode towards the southern end of the bridge.

'Halt!' said Greiger, as the men approached. The officer brought his men to a standstill and waited as

Greiger, with Reitmann beside him, walked towards them.

'Good evening,' said the officer. 'We've come from the crossing-point. We've been ordered to help man the bridge.'

Greiger stared at him but it was hard to see much in the darkness. Then he noticed the white *Edelweiss* on the side of the cap, standing out starkly in the gloom.

'Gebirgsjäger?' he asked. The officer nodded. 'May I see your orders, sir?'

The officer said, 'Of course,' then made for a leather satchel at his waist. Instead of producing papers, though, the officer pulled out a short bayonet and thrust it hard into Greiger's side, under his ribs, through his liver and into his kidney. The pain was so extreme, Greiger had only a quarter-second of intense agony, then his body shut down. His heart seized and the signals to his brain were severed. It was as though a switch had been turned off. Pieter Greiger's short life was over.

At the same moment Nielssen was ending the life of the second man he had despatched within an hour, Sergeant Tanner, beside him, had used his right fist to knock the second sentry out cold before the German could so much as pull back the bolt on his Mauser.

'Quick,' whispered Tanner to his men, as he grabbed the first man's Mauser. 'Get the rest of their weapons, ammo and helmets and drag them off the bridge. 'Mac and Hep, put these helmets on and take over sentry duty.'

Chevannes was now standing beside him.

'Good work, Nielssen,' said Chevannes to the Norwegian. 'Now for the truck.'

'Sir?' said Tanner.

'What now, Sergeant?'

'Sykes and I are going to blow the bridge – prevent any of those mountain boys coming after us.'

'You don't think it might alert the enemy?' His voice was heavy with sarcasm.

'We'll set a delay with the safety fuse.'

He dithered, then said, 'Well, be quick about it.'

'Yes, sir. If you and the men wait off the road, sir, I'll put up two sentries.'

'Yes, yes, all right. Get a move on.'

Tanner called over McAllister and Hepworth. 'Put those Jerry helmets on you two,' he said, 'then start walking up and down the bridge.' He hurried over to Sykes, who was already delving in his pack, took out a packet of Nobel's from his gas-mask case and passed it to him.

'Sarge, open it, take out two cartridges and tie them together with a small length of fuse.'

'You think that'll be enough?' He could just see that Sykes was doing the same with another packet.

'Yes.'

Tanner nodded. His heart was thumping in his chest again, his brittle fingers tearing at the thin cardboard. Taking out two cartridges, he put the remainder of the packet back into his gas-mask case, then took out the tin of fuses. With his clasp knife, he cut a strip and tied the two cartridges together. 'Done,' he said.

'Good,' said Sykes, fumbling with the detonators. 'How long do we want to wait?'

'Six hundred yards to the church,' he muttered to himself, 'but we need to get in the truck and start it. On the other hand, the distraction of the blast might be useful. Ten minutes? No – let's say eight.'

'Sure?'

'Yes, eight minutes.'

'All right – cut me a sixteen-foot length.'

Using his forearm as a measure, Tanner did so, then passed one end to Sykes who managed to crimp the fuse to the detonators with his teeth.

'And another length the same, Sarge,' whispered Sykes.

Suddenly Chevannes was beside them. 'Have you finished?' he hissed.

'Almost, sir,' said Sykes.

'Hurry.' He disappeared back down the bridge as Tanner measured another length of fuse. This time he had only counted thirteen feet when he reached the end of the tin. 'I've run out, Stan. I'm three foot short.'

'Bollocks,' said Sykes, then scratched his head. 'All right, here's what we do: we tie the explosives each side of the bridge rather than at either end and run a length of fuse from one on to the main fuse. Here, give it me.' He took one end, crimped it to the detonator, then hurried across to the other side of the bridge. Lying down and straining over the side, he used another short length of fuse to tie it to one of the girders. That done, he ran back to the other side, feeding the fuse through his hands, and tied it to the longer length. Grabbing the second batch of cartridges, he lay down again, head and arms disappearing over the side of the bridge.

A few moments later he stood up, dusted off his hands and said, 'All set, Sarge.'

In a loud whisper, Tanner called to McAllister and Hepworth, then Sykes lit the fuse.

'About time,' whispered Chevannes, as they rejoined the others. 'Same marching order, all right?'

'Sir,' said Tanner. He held the face of his watch to the sky. He could just make out the hands. Fourteen minutes past eleven. *Christ!* he thought. *This'll be close.*

A couple of minutes later they had still not reached the first houses of the town and had gone less than two hundred yards. Frantically trying to perform mental arithmetic, he realized they needed to increase their pace if they were going to reach the truck before the gelignite detonated.

'Sir,' he whispered to Nielssen, 'we need to speed up.'

Nielssen nodded and a couple of minutes later they reached the edge of the town. Ahead, the wooden spire of the church was silhouetted against the sky.

Two figures emerged in front of them. Tanner felt himself tense, but as the two men passed, they merely saluted. *Replacement sentries*, thought Tanner. *Poor bastards.* Part of him wanted to warn them of what they were walking towards.

23.20 hours. Six minutes gone. Either side of the road, sleeping houses, the night as still as ever. The church getting closer. Tanner struggled with the overwhelming desire to run. His heart continued to pound. Two minutes until the shooting started. Would they make it? Or was he now facing the final moments of his life? *Stop thinking like that.*

401

He held up his watch to the night sky again. *23.21.* *Seven minutes.* And there they were, two trucks parked together, a third the far side of the church. Nielssen halted them.

'Sir, we might as well take both these trucks,' whispered Tanner to Chevannes, standing directly behind him. 'More fuel and in case anything happens.'

'*D'accord*,' said Chevannes.

Suddenly figures appeared before them, calling out. *Christ, sentries*, thought Tanner. Nielssen spoke to them. How many? Tanner couldn't see but he had his rifle off his shoulder and felt in his haversack for a grenade.

'Lads, get ready,' he hissed.

A German soldier stepped forward, his tone aggressive, angry even. The moon now drifted clear of a cloud. It did not have much light to offer but it was enough for Tanner to see half a dozen men round the trucks. He glanced at his watch. *23.22. Eight minutes.* Where the hell was the explosion? Had the fuse gone out? Had he miscounted? A bead of sweat ran down his back but he felt a chill at the nape of his neck. *Come on, come on.*

The German NCO pointed to the rest of them and walked towards Tanner. He was looking at Tanner's rifle and the Mauser slung on his other shoulder. *Damn it*, thought Tanner. Now just a few feet away, the German addressed him directly, ignoring Nielssen. Again he pointed angrily to the rifle Tanner held and the other on his shoulder. What was he saying? Why have you got two? Where did you get that Tommy rifle? Tanner had no idea.

Sod it, he thought. 'I'm sorry, mate, I don't understand

402

a word you're saying,' he said, as he drew back the bolt on his rifle, pushed it forward, clicked it back into place, and squeezed the trigger. The report echoed round the church and surrounding buildings, the German crumpled to the ground, and at that moment, the bridge blew. Tanner started, but so did the enemy soldiers, who ducked involuntarily and looked south towards the bridge as an orange ball of flame mushroomed into the night sky. Seeing his chance, Tanner sprinted towards them. Pull the bolt back and forward, fire. Another man fell. A third fumbled at his rifle as Tanner swung the butt of his own into the man's head. The soldier cried out as Tanner kicked a fourth to the ground, all before one had fired a shot.

Shouts now from the surrounding houses. Tanner yelled, 'Into the trucks, quick!' Pistol shots – Nielssen and Chevannes. Screams from another man. Tanner grabbed Lance Corporal Erwood's shoulder. 'Get into the second truck and fire that bloody Spandau from the tailgate!' He searched frantically for Anna and the professor. 'Get in! Get in!' he yelled, when he saw them running, crouching, towards the first truck.

'Sir,' he shouted to Nielssen, 'drive the second truck!' Nielssen nodded, Tanner grabbed Anna's arm, shoved her towards the cab of the first and hastily jumped in beside her, shoving his two rifles between them. Of course, it was dark in the cab and the German Opel was unfamiliar. He hadn't thought of that. 'Jesus Christ!' he muttered. 'How do you start this bloody thing?' He fumbled around with his feet in the pitch-dark footwell, hitting pedals but there was no starter knob on the floor.

Frantically, he slapped his hand against the dashboard, finding what felt like a button, but although he pressed hard, nothing happened. Chevannes now clambered in next to Anna.

'Come on, Sergeant!' shouted Chevannes as Tanner inadvertently switched on the wipers. *Merde!* Get us out of here!'

Troops were now running out of the surrounding houses, shots cracking apart the night. Another button on the far right of the dashboard. What was it? The choke? From the back of the truck, their own men were firing and then, behind, an engine roared into life and the truck drew alongside.

'I can't get it started!' he yelled across to Nielssen.

'Isn't there a key?' Nielssen shouted back.

'No, nothing!'

'Use a piece of wire, or a screwdriver – it's above the ignition button.'

Tanner's mind raced as bullets smacked into the side of the truck, then feeling into his haversack he fumbled for his tool wallet and found what he was searching for – a set of five different-sized reamers. The first he tried was too large for the hole. 'Bloody hell,' he muttered, his heart hammering, then felt the second slide into the ignition. Immediately a small red light came on, revealing a sign that said 'ANLASSER' and what had to be the ignition button. Pulling what he hoped was the choke on the far side of the dashboard, he then pressed the button and the engine coughed into life. Yanking the reamer hard upwards to keep it in place, he shouted across to Nielssen, 'Tell Erwood to spray the other vehicles, sir!'

A bullet cracked through the windscreen. Anna screamed, and Tanner thrust the truck into gear, released the handbrake and the Opel lurched forward. 'Professor?' he shouted. 'Professor, are you there?'

'Yes! Just go!'

Chevannes fired his pistol through the window. More bullets rang out. Another thumped into the door and died. Tanner found the headlights, switched them on. Slits, just slivers of light, but enough. Out of the church square. Ahead, troops kneeling in the road. Tanner stamped on the throttle. Another bullet cracked through the top of the windscreen, and ripped through the metal roof, and Anna screamed again. Tanner charged at the men. Figures scattered but he felt a thump as he hit one, heard a scream. Feeling in his pocket he passed a grenade to Anna. 'Here!' he said. 'Pull the pin and throw it out the window. Can you do that?'

Anna nodded, pulled the pin and tossed it away. It hit the framework round the door and rebounded on to Tanner's lap. 'Jack, I'm so sorry!' she cried. Half looking ahead, half fumbling in his lap he found it and hurled it out as hard as he could.

Behind him the men were still firing. He was conscious of the Spandau's short, clattering bursts. Ahead the second bridge. *No time to blow that.* He dropped a gear, turned, rumbled across the short expanse, then drove left towards the valley road that led north. More shooting ahead, and Tanner ducked every time a bullet pinged nearby. From the back someone yelled. 'Keep going, Tanner, faster!' screamed Chevannes, then leant across Anna, grabbed

Tanner's Mauser and fired off five rounds in quick succession.

Changing up a gear, Tanner pushed down again on the accelerator as they reached the edge of town. He was vaguely aware of Chevannes reloading the Mauser and preparing to fire, then suddenly realized what the lieutenant had done. 'No, sir, don't fire!' he shouted.

With a loud crack, the rifle jerked upwards, Chevannes screamed and his head and shoulders were flung backwards. Anna cried out as Chevannes threw his hands to his face, howling wildly. Even in the faint moonlight, Tanner could see blood on the windscreen.

'Sir!' shouted Tanner. 'How bad is it? How bad is it, sir? Anna, try to calm him down. See if you can find out what he's done. I can't stop now.' He dropped down a gear once more, pressed hard on the throttle to bring up both revs and speed, then changed up. The town was now behind them, the shooting receding. From behind him he could hear desultory shots, and an occasional second-long burst from the Spandau.

Chevannes groaned.

'Keep still,' said Anna, her voice calm once more. 'Rest your head on my lap.' She took his shoulders and straightened him. 'Try to bring your legs up.' Slowly, he did so until he was lying across half the seat and her. 'There's a lot of blood,' she said. 'He needs dressings as soon as possible.'

Tanner hitched his pack and webbing from his back and waist as he drove, shoved them on to his lap, then began taking off his German tunic. 'Here,' he said, 'have this. I'll stop as soon as I can.' Then he called, 'How are you in the back?'

'Tinker's hit, Sarge,' McAllister yelled, 'but I don't think it's serious.'

'Yes, it bloody is!' called Bell. 'My arm's agony!'

Almost too late, Tanner saw the road ahead fork. 'Which way?' he said, bringing the truck to a halt.

'I can't get to my map,' said Anna.

'Hold on,' said Tanner. With the engine still running, he jumped out of the cab and ran towards the other truck.

'What's happened?' asked Nielssen.

'We don't know which way – left or right? Do you have your map, sir?'

'A moment, Sergeant.'

'Any casualties?'

'I'm afraid so – one.'

'Who?'

'Your lance corporal. Erwood. Shot in the head.'

'Dead?'

Nielssen nodded.

'Damn,' said Tanner. 'He was a good man. Is he still in the back?'

'No, he was hit as he was trying to get in. Hepworth's been on the Spandau. What about you, Sergeant?'

'The lieutenant's hit in the face. He needs dressings and attention soon. And Bell – not serious.'

Nielssen looked at the map and passed it on. 'We need to turn right. We've a bit of a climb, then in thirty kilometres we reach the main road to Åndalsnes. How much fuel do you have?'

'About a quarter of a tank. Not enough.'

Nielssen grinned. 'We've some spare cans in the back and the gauge is reading over half a tank. And that is enough.'

'Let's keep going,' said Tanner. 'It would be good to be on the main road by first light.' He paused to get some field dressings, then hurried back to the cab. Passing the bandages to Anna, he pushed the stick into gear and rolled forward.

Hauptmann Wolf Zellner had seen the explosion before he heard it: a bright orange glow lighting the sky to the east. A moment later, the report. Then a sickening feeling swept over him. An almost speechless von Poncets had immediately sent a signal to Vinstra. A quarter of an hour later the truth was revealed: around fifteen men, dressed in German uniforms, had infiltrated the town and stolen two troop carriers. And the bridge had been blown to pieces.

On hearing this news rage gripped him, rage he feared he would not be able to control. Staggering outside, he walked to the water's edge, picked up a large rock and hurled it at one of the moored dinghies. The boat sank, until all that remained was a length of rope disappearing beneath the water.

Zellner watched it. His rage had abated slightly but he was now overcome by the oppressive weight of despair. *Tanner*, he thought, and hurled another rock into the lake. Somehow he would have his revenge. 'I swear it.'

22

May Day, 1940 – Wednesday – and as the dawn rose to their right, the sun gleaming over the mountains amid a cloudless sky, the signs were that summer had indeed arrived.

'Damn it,' said Tanner. 'What we want is a bit of rain and low cloud.' The speed with which winter seemed to have passed had surprised him. 'What happened to spring?' he asked Anna.

She laughed. 'We don't have one. Winter then summer. Now it's summer.'

Tanner glanced down at Chevannes' bloodied head, wrapped in an assortment of stained bandages and torn strips of lining from a German tunic. 'Stupid bugger,' he said.

Chevannes moaned.

'What happened to him, Jack?' Anna asked him, the Frenchman's head still resting in her lap. 'Was there something wrong with the rifle?'

'He put a clip of French ammunition into a German

breech. The French rifles use a fractionally smaller cartridge than the German ones – but it's enough to bugger up the firing mechanism. When he fired, the bolt sprang back and hit him in the face. He should have known, but in the heat of the moment – well, he'll have a whopping scar to remind him not to make that mistake again.'

They had emerged into a deep, narrow valley, with mountains towering steeply at either side. Tanner whistled as he craned his neck to admire one of the most breathtaking stretches of scenery he had ever seen. Then, glancing at his petrol gauge, he saw the tank was almost empty.

Chevannes moaned again, louder this time.

'Jack,' said Anna, 'we need to stop. He needs attention.'

'We'll pull in at a farm. Perhaps we can find out what's happening.'

They reached a settlement called Lia, another collection of farmsteads nestling beside the river. The grey, tired fields of a week earlier had already been replaced by lush green pasture. Approaching a brightly coloured red farmhouse with clean white wooden fencing, Tanner slowed. 'This looks smarter than most.'

'You think they will have a wireless?'

'That's what I'm hoping.'

The farmer and his family had been asleep but they seemed untroubled to be roused prematurely by two trucks of fugitive troops pulling into their yard. As the men soon gathered, they had not been the first to arrive there over the past couple of days: since the fighting at

410

Otta had ended, troops had been streaming past, most by train, but a fair number in trucks and even on foot. And while the farmer had a radio set, he made it clear that the news announced on the wireless had told him nothing he couldn't see with his own eyes; the British were evacuating. 'You're the last,' he told Nielssen. 'You'd better hurry.'

The farmer and his wife brewed coffee and gave them bread while Anna examined Bell and Chevannes. Bell's wound was clean enough – a bullet had gone through his upper arm, but no bones had been broken. Chevannes' head, however, was a mess. His right cheekbone had been smashed, and a large gash had been torn in the side of his face, leaving the eyeball to hang loose. As Anna removed the bandages he screamed again. 'He needs pain relief,' she said.

'I don't have any,' said Tanner.

Neither did the farmer – not morphine at any rate – but he did have whisky. 'Take it,' he told Anna. 'Get him drunk.'

They made a bed of sorts for the lieutenant and laid him in the back of the first truck, then poured one of the five-gallon fuel cans into the tank. 'Change back into your own uniforms,' Tanner told his men.

When they continued on their way north, Tanner and Anna were alone in the cab. She yawned and leant her head on his shoulder. He could feel the warmth of her body against his. If they managed to reach Åndalsnes, he wondered whether she would come with them to Britain. He hoped so.

'How are you feeling?' he asked.

411

'I don't know. Tired. I can't stop thinking about last night – getting through the town. And about Larsen. It seems so incredible.'

'Yes . . . yes, it does.'

'I thought he was going to shoot you.'

'No,' said Tanner. 'He didn't have it in him. He liked us too much. In any case, it's one thing shooting someone from a distance – they're not real people, just objects – but quite another killing someone when you're face to face. It's not impersonal then. I suppose it was a bit of a gamble, but I was pretty certain he wasn't going to fire.'

She smiled at this. 'Always so rational.'

'What was he saying to Nielssen at the end?'

'Larsen? He said he'd had to do it. That they had threatened his family. And then he kept saying, "I should have turned you in at Økset, but I was trying to protect Stig." Then Nielssen said, "Some protection that was." And that's when he killed him.'

'What did he mean by that?'

'I asked Nielssen a moment ago. Apparently they had been hiding at a farm in a village called Økset, north of Elverum. It had belonged to Larsen's cousin. The Germans had turned up and searched for them. They had even been led by the same officer – Zellner?'

'Zellner? Bloody hell.'

'Yes, him,' Anna continued. 'Nielssen hadn't seen him, but Larsen did and recognized him when you first captured him in the fight above our farm. Anyway, although Larsen had the perfect opportunity to betray them there and then, he hadn't wanted to get his cousin into trouble and kept quiet while Zellner and his men searched the place. After the Germans had gone, they took his cousin's truck, crossed the river and headed north. But at that point Larsen realized the Germans would have seen them from the other side of the river.'

'And put two and two together,' said Tanner.

'Exactly. And since then he worried not only about the fate of his wife and daughters but also his cousin and his cousin's family.'

'Christ,' said Tanner. 'What a bloody mess.'

'Enemy aircraft!' A shout from behind.

'Damn, damn, damn!' cursed Tanner. Pasture still stretched a hundred yards or more to their right, while on their left the ground sloped down towards the river. They were hopelessly exposed. He felt Anna's hand grip his arm. 'There's no cover,' he said, 'We've got to hope for the best.' He pressed his foot on the throttle. 'Can you see them, Mac?' he shouted.

'Yes, Sarge. Four of them coming up behind, straight down the valley!'

'Can you tell what they are?'

A pause, then Bell said, 'They're bloody Messerschmitts, Sarge, 110s.'

'Christ, this is bloody suicide,' he muttered. The four planes were upon them now. Tanner looked through the side of the cab to see two lines of bullets kicking up the ground to their left. The bullets of the second aircraft raked the ground in front of them, while those of the third were way too wide. But those of the fourth cut a swathe across the road from right to left, clattering and pinging into the bonnet of the truck. Anna ducked, Tanner swerved, then righted the truck, but the

Opel was spluttering, steam hissing from the radiator.

Ahead, the four aircraft hurtled onwards down the valley until they became dots, then disappeared from view.

'Will they come back, Jack?' asked Anna.

Her hands were shaking, Tanner noticed, as she moved a strand of hair from her face. 'Doubt it,' he said. 'They would have started turning back towards us by now. They've probably gone on to attack Åndalsnes.'

With the engine coughing, he rolled the truck off the road and brought it to a standstill. 'Bollocks!' he said, smacking the steering-wheel.

He jumped out of the cab and ran to the other.

'We are all right,' Nielssen called out. 'They missed us entirely.'

'That's something,' said Tanner. 'Our truck's had it.'

'Get into this one quickly,' said Nielssen.

Tanner ordered McAllister and Chambers to take the spare wheel from the ruined Opel, while he and Dérigaux lifted out Chevannes.

Within ten minutes they were on their way again, Tanner and Anna now beside Nielssen in the cab. 'How much further is it?' Tanner asked Anna. To their left, the river had developed into a narrow lake.

'About sixty kilometres,' said Anna.

'We can't stop,' said Nielssen. 'We've got to risk it.'

'Those bastards'll be back, though.' Tanner sighed heavily, tapped his fingers on his knees, then sighed again, this time even louder. 'Jesus,' he said. 'This is going to be close. Damned close.' They passed a small column of shattered and burnt-out vehicles left beside the road. Several blackened corpses lay spreadeagled to either side.

'As if we needed reminding,' said Nielssen.

A few more miles slipped by, then a few more. Tanner struggled to sit still. He wished he was driving; at least it would have given him something to do. The valley no longer seemed beautiful; rather, Tanner saw it as little more than a death-trap – a single road and a railway line, with only intermittent cover. At any moment more enemy aircraft would be upon them. So long as they had the truck they could outrun any pursuit on the ground, but if they lost this vehicle as well . . . 'This is torture,' he said at last. 'Absolute bloody torture.'

They passed a settlement called Brude. 'How far now?' he asked Anna.

'About forty kilometres, I think.'

'Aircraft!' yelled Sykes from the back. 'Bloody hell, and there're lots of them!'

Tanner groaned, and leant out of the window. They were only specks on the horizon, but he could see two distinct formations, one higher than the other. The valley had narrowed again, and with it the stretch of pasture off the road. A hundred yards ahead the road curved and beside it the forest reached the road's edge.

'Can we make the curve of the road?' A thought, but said aloud. Leaning out of the window, he saw the lower formation swooping downwards towards them.

'Now!' he said. They were close enough to the bend. 'Sir, get the truck to the side of the road, and let's get out! Out, everyone, quick, and into the trees!' He leapt from the cab, hurried round to the back and, with Sykes, grabbed Chevannes' legs, hoisted him on to his shoulder and sprinted to the trees. He had barely stepped away from the road when the first line of bullets spat a line behind him. Laying Chevannes roughly on the ground, he crouched behind a tree, aircraft roaring overhead, seemingly only just above the canopy. Bullets hurtled through the branches and along the road. A line pinged across the truck. A moment later there was a loud boom and the vehicle was engulfed in flames, the canvas cover and wooden rear crackling loudly.

It was over in moments, the six aircraft thundering onwards. A miracle: no one had been hurt, although as Tanner lifted Chevannes to his feet, the Frenchman groaned with pain.

Twenty miles, thought Tanner, *give or take*. They could walk it, but would the enemy catch up before they reached safety? He rubbed his eyes, rubbed his cheeks, wished he had a cigarette.

They made another stretcher, this time for Chevannes, and on they went. For a while no one spoke and all that could be heard was the tramp of boots. They had come so far . . . Tanner cursed.

'Come on, boys,' he said at length. 'Let's lift our heads. We're nearly there. We can bloody do this. Just a few hours' hard march, that's all, and we've done that plenty of times.'

'Sarge!' said Sykes, suddenly. 'Look!'

They followed his outstretched finger and there, a few hundred yards ahead, they saw the unmistakable sign of a roadblock. Hastily, Tanner brought his binoculars to his eyes.

British troops.

'They're ours, lads!' he said. 'They're bloody well ours!' And he began to run towards them.

The roadblock was manned by a small detachment of Royal Navy Marines, whose commander stepped forward as Tanner stood gasping, his hands on his knees.

Immediately he straightened and saluted. 'Sergeant Tanner, sir, of the King's Own Yorkshire Rangers, and Lieutenant Nielssen of His Majesty the King's Guard.'

'Lieutenant Lindsay,' the Marines officer replied. 'Where in God's name have you come from?'

At Lieutenant Lindsay's command post – a roughly built sangar made from stones and branches among the pines – Tanner gave a brief account of their journey from the Balberkamp, and stressed the importance of getting the professor away as quickly as possible.

Lieutenant Lindsay, a thin-faced Scotsman of about thirty, stroked his moustache thoughtfully as he listened, then said, 'We have a dilemma, though, Sergeant. Although the port is only eighteen miles up the track, it would be suicide to attempt the journey now. You know what it's like – you've suffered two close calls yourself. A mile behind us, though, there's a small village and a four-hundred-and-eighty-yard tunnel. To be honest, that tunnel's the main reason we're here. Most of our forces are already at Åndalsnes, but what's left are in the tunnel. We're the last outpost here. We've been ordered to cover them should Jerry push on through.'

'How many are up there, sir?' Tanner asked.

'Rather more than one company of Green Howards,

plus various other loose strands, so to speak,' Lindsay told him. 'The aim is to hold off the enemy here, then slip away tonight. The chaps in the tunnel are going by train – it's in there, ready and waiting to go – and we've got seven trucks hidden here. There are ships coming for us tonight – assuming they haven't been sunk.' He paused. 'I'm sorry, it's pretty grim, I'm afraid.'

Tanner took off his helmet and turned to Nielssen. 'What do you think, sir?'

'We should wait until this evening. If we are caught out in the open we could be in big trouble.'

Tanner nodded, then walked a few steps away.

'Sarge?' It was Sykes. 'What are you thinking?'

'I'm thinking a handful of Marines won't stop a concerted effort by the Germans.'

'We've still got a few explosives. Could always put them to good use.'

'You're right.' He turned back to Nielssen and Lindsay. 'Sir,' he said to Nielssen, 'why don't you go with the professor, Chevannes and Dérigaux, and take cover in the tunnel?' Then, to Lieutenant Lindsay, he said, 'If we can help here, sir, we'll stay with you. We've got some explosive left we could use.'

Lieutenant Lindsay smiled. 'Yes, I'm sure you could, Sergeant. I'm afraid demolitions aren't really my line.'

'And if you don't mind me asking, sir, what ammo have you got left? We're almost out.'

'Enough. We've got a two-inch mortar, one Lewis gun and two Brens, plus an assortment of rifles and a fair amount of ammo for those. There is an ammunition train as well in the tunnel, though, so you can get some more if you need it.'

At this news Tanner's spirits rose. He thought quickly. 'With your permission, sir, I'd like to take one of the trucks to the tunnel, leave Lieutenant Nielssen and the professor, then load up with a few supplies.'

'Good idea,' said the captain. 'I'll get a couple of my men to help you.'

The tunnel had been blasted through the steep valley side. It was dark and narrow, the air close; there was a strong musty smell of urine and soot. Although most of the waiting troops were already on the train, a number were milling about at the tunnel's entrance. They were clearly exhausted, faces and uniforms filthy. Tanner asked a Green Howards corporal if there was an RAP.

'Aye,' he replied, pointing into the tunnel. 'On the train in the tunnel. Just follow the screams.'

They found the RAP and woke a medical orderly who was asleep on the carriage steps. 'All right,' said the medic, yawning, 'bring him in.' Tanner and Dérigaux hoisted Chevannes aboard. The stench of medicines and putrid flesh was overwhelming.

'What are you bringing me?' said a doctor, his overalls covered with blood.

'A smashed cheek,' said Tanner.

'All right, put him there,' said the doctor, pointing to a space in the corridor.

At long last, thought Tanner, as he helped lay down the lieutenant.

The dank and fetid air of the tunnel was a relief after

the RAP carriage. They pushed on alongside the dimly lit train until they found the adjutant of the Green Howards. After a brief explanation, the Norwegians' names had been added to his list.

'You take the train when it leaves,' Tanner told them.

'Thank you, Sergeant,' said Nielssen, 'for everything.'

'What about you?' asked Anna.

'We're going to help the Marines,' he replied. 'We've got to make sure that that train can get you to the port.'

'But you'll be able to escape in time?'

'I hope so, yes. We'll find you at Åndalsnes.'

She looked up at him, biting her lip. 'Good luck, Jack.' She kissed him, then stepped up on to the train.

He walked back slowly towards the others.

'Cheer up, Sarge,' said Sykes. 'At least you've still got us.'

'Yes, give us a kiss, Sarge,' said McAllister.

'I'll give you a bloody sore gob, if you're not careful, Mac.'

The ammunition train was further towards the tunnel entrance, and although the quartermaster in charge seemed reluctant to let them on board, when Tanner produced Lieutenant Lindsay's note of authorization, he relented. Twenty minutes later, they were back at the waiting truck, clutching a wooden crate of gelignite, another of grenades, four tins of safety fuse and another of detonators. Their pouches were stuffed with clips of .303 rounds.

'You took your bloody time,' muttered the Marines' driver. 'Come on, load up and let's get the hell out of here.'

In the back of the truck, Sykes said, 'He's a bit jumpy, isn't he?' No sooner had he said that than half a dozen Stukas appeared over the valley and dived down behind them, sirens screaming.

'That's why, Stan,' said Tanner. 'Bastards are trying to block the tunnel. Better pray they don't succeed.'

'Better pray Jerry doesn't catch up with us on the ground neither,' said McAllister.

Sykes grinned. 'If he does he'll have a hell of a headache after getting through this lot.' He delved into his bag. 'Anyway, I've got something for you.' He produced a dozen packets of cigarettes.

'Stan, you genius, where did you get those?' asked Tanner.

'Saw a box of 'em on the ammo train and half-inched a load.'

The packets were torn open, matches lit and the truck filled with tobacco smoke. Tanner leant back and exhaled. 'I've missed this,' he said, then winked at Sykes. 'I'm ready for action again now.'

At the Marines' position they unloaded and reported to Lieutenant Lindsay.

'A successful trip, Sergeant?'

'Very, sir, thank you,' Tanner replied.

'Now, what had you in mind? The Luftwaffe have had another crack at that tunnel, I see. Mercifully, it's been quiet enough here, but how long that will last, God only knows.'

'We need to get a move on, sir, that's for sure. Perhaps you could show me round.'

'Of course, Sergeant. Follow me.'

It was, Tanner recognized, a naturally strong position. The sides of the valley were steep and rose sharply from the river's edge on both sides. Just behind them, a smaller river cascaded down the mountain sides to join the Lågen, while the valley road and the railway line, the latter lying above the former, had been cut away from the mountain. To the north of the railway, thick forest covered the slopes. For an attacking force, there was only one way any vehicle could pass and that was by either road or rail. Otherwise, the position could be turned only by infantry.

Tanner was reluctant to be too critical of the captain's dispositions. He could see the northern side of the valley and the Lågen, which ran wide and fast, full of melted snow. The mortar team and heavy and light machine-gun crews were dug in behind hastily built sangars, while the rest of the men had made good use of what cover there was.

The tour over, Tanner gathered his men. 'What are your thoughts, Stan?'

'Well, Sarge,' said Sykes, 'we should blow the road in a couple of places, then set up a few booby traps – wires between trees, that sort of thing. As soon as they come we want a fairly clear field of fire, but also to leave ourselves enough time to scarper if it comes to it.'

'So, how far down the track?'

Sykes shrugged. 'Six hundred yards?'

Tanner agreed. 'That should do it. Iggery, lads. Let's be quick about it.'

* * *

422

In Vinstra, Reichsamtsleiter Scheidt was having one of the worst days of his life. Woken for the second morning running in the early hours, he had received the shattering news that Odin had eluded them again. Only as the morning progressed did the extent of their failure become apparent. First, Henrik Larsen's body had been found, then reports had arrived from General Geisler's Luftwaffe headquarters that two German Opel trucks had been spotted and strafed heading northwards. Either Odin was already dead, or he had surely made it to Allied lines.

Having badgered Engelbrecht's staff all morning, he was finally granted an interview shortly after noon.

'General, about time, I—'

The general put up a hand to silence him. 'A moment, Herr Reichsamtsleiter,' he said, put a lit cigar into his mouth, stood up, walked round his desk, and led Scheidt into the briefing room.

At the map on the wall he paused, took a puff of his cigar, then pointed to the map. 'Herr Reichsamtsleiter,' he said coolly, 'this is our difficulty. There are three blown bridges here, at Dombas, and here –' He pointed to a small village a few miles further north '– at Hauge. This has considerably slowed our advance.'

'So when do you think your troops will be through?'

Engelbrecht sighed. 'Soon. They'll reach Verma around seven o'clock this evening, I should think. The Luftwaffe are harrying their positions continually and bombing Åndalsnes too.'

'But what about Odin? How are we going to capture him now?'

'Odin is no longer my concern, Scheidt.'

'General, do you have any idea how important this man is? You must make another attempt to—'

Engelbrecht turned on him. 'We're not going to do anything about Odin,' he said, taking his cigar from his mouth and jabbing it at Scheidt. 'I don't give a damn about him. I'm sick of him. I'm sick of you! I've already wasted enough time and men on this, running around as you asked me when I've got a battle to manage. And what do I discover? That your intelligence is about as reliable as snow in a desert! Now let me tell you, the enemy are evacuating and it's my task to make sure that as few as possible get away. So, please, leave this head-quarters. Go back to Lillehammer or Oslo or wherever you want to go, but stop bothering me.'

'You can't speak to me like that!' Scheidt retorted. He was taller than the general by a couple of inches yet somehow felt as though he was looking up at him. 'I'm going to speak to Terboven about this. I'm sure he'll be delighted to hear about your attitude.'

'Save yourself the bother, Herr Reichsamtsleiter. I've already spoken with him.'

'You have?' Scheidt was incredulous.

'Yes, and believe me, Herr Reichsamtsleiter, he's not very happy. Not very happy at all. Now get out! Go on! Get out of my sight!'

Scheidt was speechless. He turned, twisting his foot as he did so, then hobbled from the room.

23

Sergeant Tanner and his men, under Sykes's imperturbable supervision, had blown the road and the railway line three times with fifty yards between each crater. They had also felled a series of trees and linked a web of booby traps among them so that the moment anyone tried to move the barriers one or more cartridges of Nobel's finest No. 808 desensitized gelignite would explode in their faces. In addition, they made liberal use of grenades and safety fuse, preparing a variety of trip-wires between trees further up the slopes away from the road.

Since midday, two more waves of bombers had headed over, dropping loads at either end of the tunnel, then going on to paste Åndalsnes, but the tunnel had not been blocked, Lieutenant Lindsay had confirmed, and the tiny port was still open for business. A number of Junkers 88s had swept low down the valley, half-heartedly strafing the Marines' position, but no one had been injured; men dug in and spread out were a far harder target than a lone convoy on a narrow road.

There had been no sign of the enemy on the ground, which had given Tanner and his men the chance to put some finishing touches to their devil's nest of explosives and booby traps. At well-spaced intervals, they were now placing single cartridges of gelignite, some propped up on rocks, others wedged atop mounds of earth and pebbles. All, however, were visible from a number of vantage-points along the Marines' positions.

'A bloody good idea of yours, this, Sarge,' said Sykes, as he handed over his last cartridge.

'Waste not, want not, Stan. Got the box?'

Sykes handed it to him.

'I can't resist this.' Tanner grinned. He upended the wooden box in the middle of the road, then placed the last cartridge on top. 'Now, where's Hep? I need some tracer rounds. Hep?'

Hepworth hurried over from one of the other jelly-mounds – as the men had christened them – and gave him a handful. Placing them in his haversack on his hip, Tanner strode forward and, binoculars to his eyes, gazed down the valley.

Sun glinting on glass, a few miles away. 'They're coming,' he muttered, under his breath, and glanced at his watch: *19.35*. His heart began to beat faster, but this time with exhilaration rather than fear. 'They're coming!' he yelled. He felt in his haversack, took out his Aldis scope, unravelled the cloth in which it was wrapped and screwed it on to his rifle.

Sykes hurried over to him. 'How many, Sarge?'

Tanner peered through his binoculars again. 'Eight trucks – company strength, I suppose.' He watched as the trail of vehicles drew ever closer. Then, when he judged them to be a little over four hundred yards away, he pulled back the bolt of his rifle, pushed it into place and said to Sykes, 'Right, Stan. Keep still.' Resting the rifle on Sykes's shoulder he took careful aim, inhaled gently, held his breath and squeezed the trigger.

Five rounds slammed into the leading truck, which swerved off the road, rolled down the side of the hill and crashed into the river. Tanner's men cheered. They could hear the screams of the enemy troops. Raising his binoculars once more, Tanner watched men pour out of the remaining trucks and spread out in a wide arc.

'Time to go,' said Tanner.

They ran back to the Marines' lines and watched as the enemy cautiously approached. Germans shouted as they reached the gaps in the road, then pressed on, spreading out through the trees. Soon after, as Tanner and his men wove their way through the Marines' positions, they heard a small explosion and another scream.

McAllister grinned. 'That's one trip they didn't notice.'

Crouching beside one of the Marines' Bren crews, Tanner took a bead on one of the jelly-mounds. A short distance beyond he could make out some enemy troops darting from tree to tree. 'Come on, Jerry,' he muttered, 'a bit closer.' *Now.* As he squeezed the trigger, the tracer round hurtled down the rifle's barrel at a little under two and a half thousand feet per second, smacked straight into the cartridge of gelignite and exploded instantly. Several men disintegrated with the blast, while others were flung through the air, limbs torn from them. A half-minute later, Tanner had detonated a second. Trees caught fire, enemy troops cried out and then, as the first Germans came into range of the Marines' Lewis and Bren guns, the chatter of small-arms rang out around the valley.

A tank was now squeaking and scraping its way forward, trundling at a steep angle round the side of the trucks. It was huge, larger than any Tanner had seen before. Pausing to watch, he followed it as it edged its way towards the first of the fallen trees.

'Come on, my lovely,' said Tanner. 'A bit closer.' He glanced round and saw that his men were crouching beside him, watching too.

The tank drew within twenty yards of the first of the felled trees, then opened fire at point-blank range. Immediately a huge ball of flame erupted into the sky followed by a second explosion as the tank's magazine detonated. The dark shape of the turret was silhouetted against the flames as it was propelled into the air. Thick black smoke engulfed the road and railway line and swept across the river, and then, as indistinct figures emerged through the smoke, the machine guns opened fire again. But the enemy infantry pressed on. Half a dozen ran straight down the road towards them, shouting as they came.

'The mad bastards,' said Tanner, carefully drawing his rifle to his shoulder and taking aim at the lone gelignite box now directly in front of the advancing soldiers. He fired, the gelignite exploded, and when the smoke cleared, the six men were gone. So, too, were the rest of the attackers, who had slipped back behind the cover of the smoke.

The attack had been stopped dead.

The small band of Marines and Rangers now waited. Pacing up and down through the trees, Tanner peered ahead through the smoke and haze, straining his eyes for any sign of the enemy. The tank still burned, thick black smoke pitching high into the valley. 'Where are those bastards?' he muttered. An eerie quiet had descended across the valley. A cough from someone beside him, a chink of metal, but no one spoke. He saw the exhausted and tense expressions on the faces of his men and on those of the Marines nearby.

Minutes ticked past. Sykes passed round a packet of cigarettes. Tanner smoked, looked at his watch for the twentieth time in as many minutes, then said, 'Damn it,' and strode towards Lieutenant Lindsay's sangar.

'Any news, sir?' he asked.

'None, Sergeant, I'm afraid. Perhaps Jerry's called it off for the night.'

'Maybe,' said Tanner. 'I just wish that damned train would leave.' He looked at his watch: *20.21*. He walked back to his men, and as he approached Sykes, he stopped suddenly and cocked his ear.

'What is it, Sarge?' asked Sykes.

'Listen.' The faint, but increasingly distinct sound of engines. Aero-engines.

They could all hear them now, the sound rising to deafening roar. *Jesus*, thought Tanner, *how many is that?* A dozen at least. The aircraft were above them now, and through the trees and the thinning smoke, he saw a formation of Stukas high above them. As he craned his neck, the first flipped over on to its back and dived, siren howling, then the next, and the next, and the one after that, until the air was rent by the crescendo wail of their diving scream. Tanner lay flat on the ground, his hands clasping his tin helmet to his head as bombs hurtled towards them.

Explosions, an ear-splitting clatter, one after another. Tanner heard the scream of one man, then was lifted clean off the ground and smacked back down again, the air knocked clean from his lungs. He gasped, debris and grit tinkling on to his hands and helmet, and pattering through the branches above. Suddenly he noticed he could no longer hear. He could feel the pulse of the bombs rippling through the ground, could see the flash of orange and thick clouds of smoke, but there was no sound. Daring to look up he saw two Marines crouching in their sangar not forty yards from him as another falling bomb seemed to detonate right on top of them. Tanner ducked again as debris sprayed him. When he raised his head and the smoke cleared, he saw the men had gone, their sangar replaced by a large hole in the ground. There was something wet on his hand – a glob of gore. 'Christ,' he said to himself, and wiped it off. Five yards ahead the bloodied face of one of the Marines lay among the dried pine needles. Of the rest of the head and body, there was no sign.

His ears began to ring, a high, piercing whine, then sound returned. The sirens of the Stukas had gone but, he realized, shells were now ranging in towards them from the south. 'Rangers!' he shouted, and began to run between the trees. He found Hepworth vomiting, then saw Sykes and McAllister. Another artillery shell fizzed over and exploded behind them. 'Where are the others?' he yelled.

Sykes pointed to Bell and Chambers, taking cover a short distance behind, then spotted Kershaw half running, half crouching, towards him. 'Keep looking out for the infantry,' he shouted.

A glance at his watch: *20.42. Bloody hell*, he thought. Artillery shells continued to smash through the trees and along the valley, and there were mortars, too, popping down, almost with no warning, blasting deadly shards of shredded metal.

'We can't hold out here much longer, Sarge,' said Sykes.

'No,' agreed Tanner, 'I just hope to Christ that train's gone now the Stukas have buggered off.'

A shrill single whistle blast rang out, and as one the Marines moved from their positions and hurried backwards.

'Rangers!' shouted Tanner again, at a second whistle blast. 'Fall back!'

A shell screamed above them and now the burp of a Spandau and the crack of rifle fire could be heard. As Tanner began to run, he turned to see shadowy figures emerging through the smoke. 'They're coming,' he yelled, then a flash of orange and more screams as another trip-wire was detonated. He paused briefly, squatting on his haunches, and using his scope, aimed at one of the remaining jelly-mounds. Bullets whiffled through the air, zapping through branches and slapping into the ground around him. Spotting the stick of gelignite, he aimed his rifle as troops materialized through the smoke. Tanner squeezed the trigger, watching the tracer trail slice through the air and hit the explosive. A ball of flame erupted. He turned and ran, more bullets hissing and slicing around him.

A searing pain scorched his neck and he stumbled, crashing to the ground. Gasping he put up a hand. It came back red with blood. Someone grabbed his shoulders and yanked him to his feet. Sykes and Hepworth were beside him.

'Can you still run, Sarge?' yelled Sykes.

Tanner nodded.

'Then run!'

The three sprinted through the trees until at last the bullets were no longer following them. Ahead was a clearing and Tanner groggily saw trucks pulling out.

He stumbled again. A hand grabbed his collar and urged him forward. 'Come on, Sarge, nearly there!' *Sykes*. Tanner's neck stung like hell, his chest was so tight he thought it would burst, and his legs felt as though they had turned to jelly. A shell whistled over, and another landed a hundred yards to the right. The trucks were leaving. *One left*. Men leaning out, arms outstretched. Tanner cried out, then sped towards it. Suddenly his hand was clutching the wood of the tailgate and he was being pulled aboard.

He collapsed on to his back as the truck rattled away out of the clearing and sped on to the road, away from the carnage and turmoil of battle. Grimacing he clutched his neck. Sykes and Lieutenant Lindsay were staring down at him.

'The trains? Have they gone?' he asked.

The captain nodded. 'Yes, Sergeant. They have.'

Tanner closed his eyes briefly. 'Thank God for that.'

'Here, Sarge,' said Sykes, handing him a field dressing. Tanner sat up and, still short of breath, hoisted himself on to the wooden bench. As he pressed the bandage to his neck he saw that all six of his men were among the Marines. *Thank Christ.*

'Let's have a look at you, Sarge,' said Sykes. He pushed Tanner's head forward. 'It's just grazed you. You'll live. Here, let me wrap that bandage round it.'

As he began to breathe more easily, Tanner felt his composure return. His neck hurt, but his mind had cleared. His legs no longer felt weak. As Sykes bandaged him, Tanner gazed at his men: Hepworth and Kershaw, McAllister, Bell and Chambers. McAllister and Hepworth were by the tailgate, scanning the skies for aircraft; he'd not even asked them to do that. They were becoming soldiers, he thought. Not kids any more.

'You did damned well there,' said Lieutenant Lindsay, sitting opposite him, 'you and your men. If it hadn't been for your pyrotechnics, I'm not so sure we'd have held them off.'

'Thank you, sir.'

'And it was a pretty close-run thing.'

'But you know for certain that the trains went, sir?'

The Captain smiled. 'Yes, Sergeant. I had a clear line throughout. They left after the Stukas went. And we

433

haven't had any more visits from the Luftwaffe, so they'll be there already.'

They fell into silence as the truck rumbled on. They had left the Germans and the enemy artillery behind, and were within touching distance of safety, yet just one enemy attack from the air could end their chances. Tanner smoked almost continuously, until his throat, already sore from the thick smoke of battle, was so dry he could barely speak. He tapped his feet and drummed his fingers, patted the wound on his neck and stowed his father's old scope in his haversack. But the truck would not go any faster, however much he might wish otherwise.

At last, after nearly an hour, they emerged from the valley, and there, nestling at the water's edge beneath a thick pall of smoke, stood the tiny port of Åndalsnes.

The town was a wreck, hardly any houses standing; most had been reduced to little more than charred, blackened remains. Thick, cloying smoke hung heavy on the air. The harbour teemed with exhausted troops, but there was no sign of the ships. Tanner and his men jumped down from the truck.

'Thank you, sir,' he said, offering his hand to Lieutenant Lindsay, 'but we must leave you here. We need to find the Norwegians.'

Lieutenant Lindsay shook his hand. 'I hope our paths cross again, Sergeant. Good luck.'

They left the Marines and headed down a rubble-strewn road towards the quayside. 'Stick close to me, boys, and keep your eyes peeled. We've got to find them.'

'Why, Sarge?' said McAllister. 'They'll be here some-where.'

Tanner turned on him. 'I'll tell you why, Mac. Because we've lost good men for that professor. We've hacked over mountains and across lakes, been strafed, bombed and shot at, and I'm damned if I'm going to leave this God-forsaken place without knowing that they're here and safely on a ship.'

His head throbbed and now that he was on his legs once more, the depth of his post-battle fatigue weighed down on him. Ahead, as they reached the quayside, all he could see was a sea of men. *Jesus*, he thought, *how are we ever going to find them?* They pushed their way through amid angry cries from equally exhausted and irritable men. 'We're looking for three Norwegians,' he said. 'Two men and a girl? Anyone seen them?' It was hopeless asking, he knew.

'There are lots,' said one wag. 'Have a look the other side of those mountains.'

They pushed on, but the light was fading, and then ahead, inching its way towards them, a ship – a destroyer. As it sounded its horn, the entire throng let out a massed cheer.

'Blimey, Sarge, it's like bloody Elland Road around here,' grinned Hepworth.

Tanner looked up at the skies. The light was fading.

'Another ten or fifteen minutes,' said Sykes, 'and then it'll be too dark.'

'I know, Stan,' said Tanner. 'That's what worries me.' He craned his neck. 'Come on, come on,' he muttered, 'where are you?'

'I didn't mean that, Sarge,' said Sykes. 'I meant it'll be too late for the Luftwaffe.'

They reached the end of the quay, but there was no sign of them. 'Where the bloody hell are they?' said Tanner. 'Come on, back we go. Let's have another look.' Doubts were creeping into his mind. What if they had never got aboard that train, after all? Perhaps they had been turned away. The destroyer was pulling into the quay. And it was getting darker by the minute.

They pushed their way through the mass of soldiers, but still nothing: no blue-grey greatcoat; no fair-haired girl in a long blue coat; no middle-aged professor. As the destroyer berthed and a gangway was pushed out on to the quay, Tanner lurched forward, forcing his way through the throng. 'I've got to get to the gangway!' he called out frantically. 'I've got to get to the gangway.'

The crowd of increasingly annoyed soldiers closed in on him.

'You don't understand,' pleaded Tanner, 'I've got to make sure someone gets on that ship.'

'Sarge! Sarge!' Tanner felt a hand on his shoulder and turned to see Sykes and the others behind him. Then Hepworth and McAllister parted and Tanner turned to see Professor Sandvold, Lieutenant Nielssen and Anna standing before him.

For a moment, he felt as though he had seen a ghost, and then he was laughing.

'He's been getting in a right flap,' Sykes told them. 'Worrying 'is pretty head that you got left behind.'

'You need not have done, Sergeant,' said Professor

Sandvold. 'We have been here for over an hour and a half, quite safe.'

'We were worried about you, though,' said Nielssen. 'We heard there was heavy fighting.'

Tanner looked at Anna and pushed his way towards her.

'You're wounded,' she said, reaching out to him.

'A nick, that's all. I was lucky.' He squeezed her hand. 'Anna, I'm very glad to see you.'

She smiled, but then he saw a wistful expression cross her face – the same he had seen on the morning they had headed towards Tretten together.

'Will you come with us?' he asked, but he knew what her answer would be.

'I cannot leave my family, Jack. I have to find my brother. If I went with you, I would feel as though I am running away. Deserting my country.'

Tanner nodded. He took both her hands in his. They were nearing the gangway, the throng pushing them towards it. 'What will you do?' he asked.

'I don't know. Try to get home. Continue the fight.' She looked at him. 'The war will not go on for ever. One day . . .'

They had almost reached the gangway. Professor Sandvold was now walking up it on to the ship. Tanner glanced at him, then turned back to her.

'I'll miss you,' she said.

'And me you.'

'Sarge?' said Sykes.

'You must go,' said Anna. She kissed him, her lips lingering a moment on his. 'Goodbye, Jack.'

Tanner swallowed hard and felt her fingers let go of his. Someone pushed into him and then he was walking up the gangway, looking back towards her. He stumbled, steadied himself and then, as he was about to step aboard, he looked back once more. She had gone.

As the destroyer pulled away to ferry the men to the waiting cruiser, Tanner leant on the railings and gazed at the black outline of the mountains. It was little short of a miracle, he thought, but they had made it. He took out a cigarette, cupped his hands and lit it, inhaling deeply. Sandvold was safe. He and six of his men were safe. But far too many men – good men – had been left behind.

'Cheer up, Sarge,' said Sykes, beside him. 'We're going home.'

Tanner smiled. 'Yes, Stan.' He patted Sykes on the back. 'I suppose we are.'

THE END

HISTORICAL NOTE

The Norwegian campaign, sadly, was not Britain's finest hour and, indeed, directly led to the resignation of the Prime Minister, Neville Chamberlain, on 10 May 1940 – a day that saw Winston Churchill take on the mantle in his stead and marked the start of the German blitzkrieg in the west.

The events in the Gudbrandsdal valley occurred largely as written. 148th Brigade, under Brigadier Morgan was deployed south to Lillehammer and destroyed at a series of engagements in much the way I have described it. They were short of artillery, transport, aircraft and just about everything else; and although it was not Morgan or even General Ruge's fault – and certainly not the fault of the men who fought there – the British effort in the Gudbrandsdal was an utter shambles. By the time Major General Paget and 15th Brigade arrived, there was little that could be done to stop the rot. Fortunately, the eventual evacuation at Molde and Åndalsnes was one of the best pieces of organization of the entire central

Norway campaign, enabling a number of men to survive.

Further north, the war in Norway continued for another month, but the writing had been on the wall almost from the outset. On 8 June, the last Allied troops were evacuated. King Håkon VII and his son, Crown Prince Olav, were among those to be shipped to Britain, where they remained until Norway was liberated at the end of the war. In their absence, Norway was left under German occupation, although Norwegian resistance remained a thorny problem for the Germans. I would like to think that Anna Rostad would have been among their number.

Reichsamtsleiter Scheidt was a real person, but I could find out very little about him after his time in Norway came to an abrupt end at the beginning of May 1940. However, he resurfaced later in the war. By 1942, he was working for one of his pre-war Nazi Party champions, the notorious Reichsleiter Alfred Rosenberg, one of the architects of the Final Solution. Equally real were Reichskommissar Terboven and Generalmajor Erwin Engelbrecht, the latter of whom won the Knight's Cross for his performance in the Norwegian campaign.

Professor Sandvold was not a real person, however, and neither is his claim to have discovered oil off the coast of Norway. I'm afraid that didn't happen until the early 1960s, and the first oil-rig didn't start pumping out oil until 1971. Since then it has made Norway a rich country. However, it is certainly true that had the Germans had a whiff of there being extractable oil off the Norwegian coast they would have been very determined indeed to get at it. Oil was a commodity that Germany never had quite enough of during the war, and its shortage was one of the factors in her eventual defeat. Also true is the detail about the Norwegian gold reserves, which were successfully smuggled to Britain.

Soldier's slang and the liberal use of acronyms are as much a part of military life now as they were before and during the war. The words that Tanner uses were mostly of Indian origin, and became part of his normal vocabulary during his time in India before the war.

For those unfamiliar with them, however, here is a guide:

Basha	shelter, house
Bunduck	rifle
Croaker	dying person, someone severely wounded
Cushy	easy
Dekko	to take a look
Iggery, jaldi	get a move on

And here is a further glossary of the military terms used:

HE	high explosive
M/T	motor transport
RAP	Regimental Aid Post
Sangar	a small defensive position above ground (usually built when the ground is unsuitable for excavation)
SMLE	Short Magazine Lee Enfield

To those unfamiliar with military jargon and terminology,

the complexities of structure and organization may be hard to grasp. An army of the Second World War – British, American, German or Italian – was divided into corps, divisions, brigades, regiments and battalions. A force could be designated an 'army' if it consisted of two or more corps. A corps had no great significance but was a contained force within an army, usually comprising at least two divisions, i.e., no less than thirty thousand men. Next down the scale was a division. This was still a major tactical and administrative unit of an army, and within its structure contained all the various forms of arms and services necessary for sustained combat. However, different divisions had different emphases: the fighting core of an infantry division was an infantry brigade, and could, as was the case in Norway, be deployed on its own. An infantry brigade was made up of two or more infantry battalions, plus attached artillery, engineers and other units. The battalion was the basic infantry unit, usually made up of four companies of, in total, between seven hundred and nine hundred men of all ranks. A company was divided into platoons of thirty-six men, which in turn were split into three ten-man sections. The remaining six men would be the platoon commander, the platoon sergeant, and four other ranks. The size of an infantry brigade could vary enormously, but a three-battalion brigade plus additional units would be between four and six thousand men strong. An infantry division – at full establishment – usually included around seventeen thousand men.

The Norwegian campaign showed Britain that she had a lot to do if she was to keep the Germans at bay. Too many of her tactics were out of date. There was no concept of co-ordinated air power, for example, or even all-arms tactics, whereby infantry, tanks and artillery were trained and employed together. Britain would have to learn the hard way and suffer numerous bitter disappointments before the tide began to turn.

For the men of the Yorks Rangers, the end of their part in the Norway campaign marked only the beginning of their war. There was much work for them still to do over the long years to come. Jack Tanner and Stan Sykes were needed again all too soon.

I owe thanks to the following: Oliver Barnham, Robert Boyle, Dr Peter Caddick-Adams, Trevor Chaytor-Norris, Rob Dinsdale, Richard Dixon, Professor Rick Hillum, Steve Lamonby, Peta Nightingale, Hazel Orme, Dr Hugh Pelly, Michael Ridpath, Bill Scott-Kerr and everyone at Transworld, Jake Smith-Bosanquet, Lt-Col. John Starling, Patrick Walsh, Guy Walters, Susan Watt, Rowland White, Major Steve White, Bro, Rachel, Ned and Daisy. Thank you.

Jack Tanner returns in

DARKEST HOUR

Dunkirk, 1940. With the British Army in full retreat,
someone must stand against the Nazi tide.

Here's the first chapter as a taster . . .

1

A little after half past ten in the morning, Thursday, 9 May 1940. Already it was a warm day, one of blue skies and large, white cumulus clouds; a perfect early summer's day, in fact. It was also quite warm inside the tight confines of the Hurricane's cockpit, even fifteen thousand feet above the English Channel; Squadron Leader Charlie Lyell was beginning to wish he hadn't worn his thick sheepskin Irvin over his RAF tunic, yet the air had seemed fresh and crisp when he walked across the dew-sodden grass to his plane just over half an hour before. As he now led his flight of three in a wide arc to begin the return leg of their patrol line, the sun gleamed through the Perspex of his canopy, and its strong warmth through the clear plastic felt hot upon his head. A line of sweat ran from his left temple and under the elastic at the edge of his flying goggles.

Nonetheless, it was, he thought, the perfect day for flying. The air was so clear. He could see for a hundred miles and more. As they completed the turn and began heading southwards again, there stretching away from them was the mouth of the Medway, shipping heading both towards and out of London. Southern England – Kent and Sussex – lay unfolded like a rug from his starboard side, a soft, green and undulating patchwork, while there, away to his port, was the Pas de Calais and the immensity of France. Somewhere down there were the massed French armies and the lads of the BEF. He smiled to himself. Rather you than me.

Lyell glanced at his altimeter, fuel gauge, and oil pressure. All fine, and still well over half a tank of fuel left. The air speed indicator showed they were maintaining a steady 240 miles per hour cruising speed. Then he turned his head to check the skies were clear behind him before glancing to see that Robson and Walker were still tight in either side of him, tucked in behind his wings. *Good*, he thought.

Something away to his right suddenly caught his eye – a flash of sunlight on metal – and at the same moment he heard Robson, on his starboard wing, exclaim through the VHF headset.

'Down there look! Sorry, sir, I mean, this is Blue Two, Bandit at two o'clock.'

'Yes, all right, Blue Two,' said Lyell. He hoped he sounded calm, a hint of a reprimand in his voice, even though he was conscious his heart had begun to race and that his body had tensed. He peered down – and yes! – there it was, some five thousand feet below, he guessed, and perhaps a mile or so ahead. It was typical of Robson to immediately assume it was an enemy plane – they all wanted the squadron's first kill – but the plain truth was that most aircraft buzzing around the English coast were British, not German. *Even so.*

'This is Red One,' he called over the R/T, 'We'll close in.' At least the sun, already high in the sky, was behind them, shielding them as they investigated. Lyell pushed open the throttle and watched the altimeter begin to fall. His body was pushed back against the seat, and he involuntarily tightened his hand around the grip of the control column. A few seconds later and he could already see the aircraft ahead more clearly. It appeared to have twin tail fins, but then so did a Whitley or a Hampden. The brightness was too great to see the details of the paint scheme or symbols on the wings and fuselage.

Ahead loomed a huge tower of white cloud and together they shaved the edge of it, so that Lyell fleetingly lost sight of the plane before it appeared again and then, in a moment when the aircraft ahead hung in the shadow of the cloud, he saw the unmistakable black crosses and felt his heart lurch. *Christ*, he thought, *this is bloody well it.*

Pushing open the throttle even wider, he closed in on what he could now see was a Dornier. It appeared not to have seen them yet, but as he was only around seven hundred yards behind and a thousand feet above, Lyell checked that Robson and Walker were still close to him and then said, 'Line astern – go!' Still the enemy plane continued on its way, oblivious to the danger behind it. Lyell quickly turned his head to see Robson and Walker now directly behind him. Taking a deep breath, he flicked the firing button to 'on' for the first time ever in a real combat situation and said into his mouthpiece,

'Number One Attack – go!' Opening the throttle wide he dived down on the Dornier. As it grew bigger by the second, he pressed his thumb down hard on the gun button and felt the Hurricane judder as his eight machine guns opened fire. Lines of tracer and wavy threads of smoke hurtled through the sky, but to his frustration he could see they were falling short of the enemy plane. Cursing to himself he pulled back on the stick, but already he knew he had misjudged his attack. Seconds, that was all it had taken, but now the Dornier seemed to be filling his screen and he knew that if he did not take avoiding action immediately, the two would collide. Pushing the stick to his left, the Hurricane instantly flipped onto its side, the horizon lurching as it did so, and scythed past the port wing of the Dornier, just as a rip of fire cut across him. He could hear machine guns clattering, Robson and Walker shouting through the airwaves – all radio discipline gone – and saw tracer fizzing through the sky, and then in a moment he was away, circling and climbing and scanning the skies trying to pinpoint the enemy once more.

Lyell cursed then heard a rasp of static and Robson's voice.

'Bastard's hit me!' he said.

'Are you all right, Red Two?' Lyell asked, desperately peering around the sky for the Dornier and conscious that several enemy bullets had torn into his own fuselage.

'Yes, but my Hurri's not. I'm losing altitude.'

'I've got you, Robbo.' Walker this time.

Damn, damn, damn, thought Lyell, then spotted

the Dornier again, a mile or so ahead, flying south-west once more. 'The bloody nerve,' muttered Lyell.

'Red Two, turn straight back for Manston. Red Three, you guide him in.'

'What about you, sir?' asked Walker.

'I'm going after Jerry. Over.' *Damn him. Damn them all*, thought Lyell. He glanced again at his instruments. Everything looked all right; the plane was still flying well enough – it was as though he had not been hit at all. But the fuel gauge showed he was less than half full now – it was a shock to see how much he had used in that brief burst of action. *Well, bollocks to him*, Lyell thought. He was damned if some Bosche bomber was going to make a fool out of him or his squadron. Applying an extra six pounds of boost he climbed five hundred feet and turned towards the Dornier once more.

He soon began to catch up, and making sure the sun was behind him again, waited until the German plane began to fill his gunsight, and then, at a little over four hundred yards distance, pressed down on the gun button. Again, the Hurricane juddered with the recoil and Lyell felt himself jolted in his seat despite the tightness of his harness. Lines of tracer and smoke snaked ahead, but the bullets were dropping away beneath the Dornier, so Lyell pulled back slightly on the stick and continued pressing down hard on the gun button. Still his machine guns blazed, and his tracer lines looked to be hitting the German plane perfectly, but still it flew on. It was as though his bullets were having no effect at all.

'Bloody die, will you!' muttered Lyell, and then tracer was curling towards him in turn, from the Dornier's rear-gunner, seemingly slowly at first and then accelerating past him, whizzing across his port wing.

'For God's sake,' said Lyell, involuntarily ducking his head as he did so.

Then suddenly the Dornier wobbled, belched smoke and turned, before diving out of Lyell's line of fire. 'Got you!' said Lyell out loud, then pushed the stick to his left and followed the enemy down. Not far below and away from them was a larger bank of cloud. So that was the enemy's plan – to hide. In moments, the Dornier was beginning to flit between puffs of outlying cloud, all signs of black smoke gone, but Lyell was rapidly gaining once more, the Merlin engine screaming, the airframe shaking, as he hurtled towards the enemy and opened fire again.

And then, just as the lines of tracer began to converge on the German machine, Lyell's machine guns stopped. For a moment, he could not understand it – could all eight really have jammed? But then it dawned on him. He had used his ammunition up. Fifteen seconds' worth. Gone. More than two and a half thousand bullets pumped out and still that bloody Dornier was flying. Lyell cursed and watched the German disappear into the bank of cloud. Following him in, he then banked and reluctantly turned towards home, a strange bright and creamy whiteness surrounding him, the airframe buffeted by the turbulence. Suddenly, the whiteness thinned, whisping either side of him and over his wings and moments later he was out into bright sunshine once more, the Kent coast ahead of him. Trickles of sweat ran down his back and from beneath his leather helmet, tickling his face.

Having throttled back, for a moment he closed his eyes, lifted his goggles on to his forehead and rubbed his eyes. A sickening feeling filled his stomach, not from being thrown about the sky, he knew, but from bitter disappointment. The squadron's first kill! It should have been his – a sitting duck if ever there was one! And yet, somehow, it had got away.

From the corner of his eye he suddenly noticed feathery lines of grey between his cockpit and his starboard wing. Urgently glancing up at his mirror, he saw the glass filled by the enemy plane. Swivelling his head he could see the machine bearing down on him, pumping bullets, its great ugly Perspex nose horribly close.

Christ almighty, thought Lyell, momentarily stunned. Something in his brain then clicked and he remembered that a Hurricane could supposedly out-turn most aircraft – and certainly a lumbering twin-engine Dornier, so jamming the Hurricane to its full throttle, he turned the stick, added a large amount of rudder and then opened the emergency override to increase boost. The Hurricane seemed to jump forward with the sudden and dramatic increase in power. With the horizon split between sky and land and sea, Lyell grimaced, his body pressed back into his seat.

In no more than half a circle, he could see he was not only getting away from the enemy, he was already creeping up on the Dornier's rear. Again, the German rear-gunner opened fire. *Jesus*, thought Lyell, *how much ammunition do these people have?* The two aircraft were now circling together in a vertical bank. Lyell wondered how he was going to get away without the German rear-gunner hitting him, but a moment later the firing ceased, so pushing the stick to starboard, he flipped the Hurricane over and reversed the turn, breaking free of the circle and heading out of the Dornier's range as he did so.

Although certain the enemy aircraft had neither the speed nor agility to follow, Lyell nonetheless glanced back to make sure the German pilot was not coming after him. The Dornier was banking away from the circle too, levelling out to return home. And as he straightened, he waggled his wings.

'Bloody nerve!' exclaimed Lyell. Was the enemy pilot saluting or sticking two fingers up at him? Either way, Lyell knew the German had out-foxed three RAF fighter aircraft – out-thought, out-flown, and out-gunned them.

About thirty miles away, a Bedford fifteen hundred-weight truck turned off the Ramsgate road that ran through Manston village, almost doubling back on itself as it entered the main camp at the airfield. The driver swore as he ground down through the gears, then the truck spluttered, jerked, and slowly rumbled forward, past two hangars on the right and then towards several rows of one-storey wooden huts. Turning off the road, the driver brought the truck to halt, and letting the engine idle, said to the sergeant sitting beside him, 'Hold on a minute. Let me find out where they want you.' Then he jumped down from the cab, and strode to what appeared to be an office building.

Sergeant Jack Tanner stepped down from the cab as well and wandered round to the back of the lorry.

'All right, boys?' he said to the five men sitting in the canvas covered back, then pulled out a packet of cigarettes from the breast pocket of his serge battle blouse.

'It's certainly a nice day for it, Sarge,' said Corporal Sykes. 'Not a bad spot up here, is it? I've always had a soft spot for Kent. Used to come here as a boy.'

'Really?' said Tanner, flicking away his match.

'Hop picking in the summer. Quite enjoyed it.'

Tanner made no reply, instead turning his gaze towards the open grassland of the airfield in front of him. A number of aircraft were standing in front of the hangars to their right, bulky-looking twin-engined machines, their noses pointing up towards the sky. Further away to his left, he saw several smaller, single-engine aircraft that he recognized as Hurricanes. A light breeze drifted across the field. Above, skylarks twittered busily.

'It's all right round here,' said one of the men, a young looking lad called McAllister. 'But give me Yorkshire any day.'

'Nah,' said Sykes, 'it's always bloody raining up there. Every time I go to HQ it bloody pours. Half my kit's still damp. And the air's a lot cleaner here than Leeds too.' He breathed in deeply and sighed.

'I meant the Dales, Stan,' said McAllister. 'The Dales are grand, ain't that right Tinker?' He nudged another of the men, a short, fair-haired boy.

'Don't know really,' said Bell. 'I suppose. I like our farm well enough.'

Tanner smiled, took a drag of his cigarette and then a faint hum caught his attention and he turned, looking

455

back towards the coast. In a moment the sound grew louder and he stepped away from the truck, his hand to his forehead to shield his eyes, and looked to the deep blue sky.

'Sarge?' said Sykes.

'Aircraft,' he said. 'Sounds like one in trouble.'

Sykes immediately leapt down from the truck and on to the road beside Tanner, and together they scanned the skies.

'There,' said Tanner after a few moments. Hepworth and McAllister were out of the truck now too. Approaching the north end of the airfield were two Hurricanes, one above and seemingly gliding towards the grass strip effortlessly, the other belching dark smoke, a grey trail following behind. The engine of the stricken aircraft groaned and thrummed irregularly, the airframe slewing and dipping, the port wing sagging.

The men watched in silence as the crippled plane cleared some buildings the far side of the 'drome, suddenly dropped what seemed like fifty feet, recovered briefly, gave a last belch of smoke then crashed into the ground, the port wing hitting the soft earth first, the undercarriage collapsing and the plane ploughing in an ugly arc through the grass, the propeller snapping and the fuselage buckling as it did so.

'Come on, get out you stupid sod,' muttered Sykes. For a moment there was silence, then they saw the pilot heave himself out of the cockpit, jump onto the wing and sprint for all he was worth away from the scene. He had not gone thirty yards when there was an explosion and the broken Hurricane was enveloped by a ball of angry

456

orange flame and billowing black smoke. Tanner and the others flinched at the sound, saw the pilot fling himself flat on the ground then watched the fire wagon, bells ringing, speed out from the watch tower ahead of them and hurry to the scene.

'Look, 'e's getting up again,' said Sykes, who had taken it upon himself to be the commentator for them all.

'Good lad,' said Tanner, then turned to see the other Hurricane safely touch down behind them.

The driver now returned and said, 'One's still not back. The CO an' all. Station Commander's not at all happy.' He clicked his teeth and indicated to them to get back into the truck. 'You're just down here,' he added, as Tanner clambered back into the cab beside him, 'the other side of the parade ground.'

He took them to the last of a long row of long wooden huts. 'Here,' he said, coming to a halt. 'Make yourselves at home. The CSM will be along shortly.'

Tanner undid the tailgate, waited for his men to jump down and then grabbed his kitbag and rifle. Like all British rifles, it was a Short Magazine Lee Enfield, a No.1 Mk III model, and although the newer No. 4 version was now coming into use, Tanner had no intention of surrendering this personal weapon. The son of a gamekeeper from south Wiltshire, Tanner had learned to shoot almost as soon as he could walk and with it had come the well-drummed lesson of looking after a gun, whether it were an air rifle, twelve bore, or Lee Enfield rifle. But more than that, Tanner had made an important modification to his. It was something he had done almost the moment he had returned to the

457

Regimental Headquarters in Leeds back in February after nearly eight years' overseas service. Having been issued with new kit, he had gone straight to the Royal Armoury and had had a gunsmith mill and fit two mounts and pads for an Aldis telescopic site. These were discreet enough and few people had ever noticed; no-one in authority, at any rate, not that he imagined they would say much about it even if they did. The scope had been his father's during the last war and Tanner had carried it with him throughout his army career; and although he had never attempted to become an army sniper, he had certainly sniped on occasion. He could think of several occasions when the Aldis had proved a godsend. Slinging the rifle and his kitbag on his shoulder, he followed the others into the hut.

Jack Tanner was twenty-four, although his weather-worn and slightly battered face made him appear a bit older. He was tall – more than six foot – with dark hair and pale, almost grey eyes and a nose that was slightly askew. He had spent almost his entire army career in India and then the Middle East with the 2nd Battalion, the King's Own Yorkshire Rangers – despite being a born and bred Wiltshireman. This last Christmas, he had finally returned to England. Home leave it had been called, not that he had a home to return to any more. Four weeks later, he had presented himself back at Regimental Headquarters in Leeds and been told, to his great dismay, that he would not be going back out to Palestine. Instead, he had been posted to bolster the fledgling territorial 5th Battalion as they prepared for war. In Norway the Territorials had been decimated;

Tanner and his five men, along with a few others were all that remained of the 5th Battalion. A fair number were dead, but most were now in either German hospitals or on their way to prison camp.

Tanner had hoped he might be allowed back to the 2nd Battalion after all, but the regimental adjutant had had other ideas. The 1st Battalion were with the British Expeditionary Force in France; new recruits were being hurried through training and sent south to guard the coast. Men of his experience had an important part to play: all the veterans of Norway did. The 2nd Battalion would have to do without him for a while longer. Forty-eight hours' leave. That's all they'd had. The others had gone home, to their families in Leeds and Bradford, or in Bell's case to his family farm near Pateley Bridge, while Tanner and Sykes had got drunk for one day, and had recovered the next.

The hut was more than half empty. Just ten narrow Macdonald iron beds and paliasses were laid out along one wall. Tape had been criss-crossed over each of the windows, but otherwise it was completely bare. Tanner slung his kitbag beside the bed nearest the door then lay down and took out another cigarette.

'What are we supposed to do now, Sarge?' asked Hepworth.

'Put our feet up until someone turns up and tells where we're supposed to go,' Tanner replied. He lit his cigarette then closed his eyes. He was conscious of another Hurricane landing – that sound of the engine was so distinctive. *Bloody airfield and coastal guard duty*, he thought. *Jesus*. Part of him told himself to be thankful for it. They had escaped from Norway by the skin of their teeth; a soft job would do him and the others good. In any case, the war was not going to be over any time soon, that much was clear. Their time would come soon enough. Yet another part of him still yearned to rejoin his old mates in Palestine. For him, England was an alien place now; he had spent too long overseas, amongst the heat and dust and monsoon rains of India, and the arid desert of the Middle East. Before that, he had only ever known one small part of England, and that was the village of Alvesdon and the valley of his childhood. He still missed it, even after all these years. Often when he closed his eyes, he would remember: the ridges of chalk, the woods on the farm, and the clear trout stream, the houses of thatch and cob and flint. But both his parents were gone, and dark events from his past ensured there could be no going back.

He sighed. Long ago, he had resigned himself to his exile, but it still saddened him. That long train journey south from Leeds: too much time to think; to remember. Tanner rubbed his eyes and silently chided himself. *No point in getting bloody maudlin.* What he needed was a distraction. Activity. It was, he realized, barely a week since they had returned from Norway and yet already it felt as though he had been kicking his heels for too long.

Soon after, he dozed off, the chatter of the others a soporific background noise that helped lull him to sleep. He was awake again, however, the moment his subconscious brain heard a new voice arrive in the hut – a distinct voice; a deep, yet softened Yorkshire accent that was strangely familiar to him.

'Morning, gents,' Tanner heard, followed by a squeak of springs and clatter of boots on the wooden floor as the men quickly stood to attention. Tanner opened his eyes, and swung his legs off the bed.

'All right, lads,' said the newcomer. 'As you were.'

Tanner looked up and his eyes widened in shock. A big, stocky man of nearly his own height stood in the doorway. The bright sun behind cast the man's face in shadow, but Tanner would have known him anywhere. Blackstone, he thought. Jesus. That was all he needed.

Blackstone looked down at him, stared at him for a moment, and then winked, before turning back at the others. Tanner groaned inwardly.

'Welcome to Manston, lads,' he said, 'and to T Company of the 1st Battalion.' He had a lean face, with deep lines running across his brow and between his nose and mouth. He was in his mid thirties, with thick sandy hair that showed beneath his field cap.

'My name is CSM Blackstone,' he said. 'Captain Barclay is the officer commanding this training company, but as far as you lot are concerned, I'm the one that runs this show. So if I were you, I'd try and keep in my good books. It's better that way isn't it Sergeant? Then everything can be nice and harmonious.' He looked at Tanner and grinned. 'Now,' he continued, 'I'm going to take Sergeant Tanner here away with me for a bit, and then later on you'll meet your platoon commander and be shown about the place. For the moment, though, stay here and get your kit together. All right?' He smiled at them again, pointed the way to Tanner and said, 'See you all later, boys.'

Outside the hut, Blackstone said, 'Well, well – my old friend Jack Tanner. Fancy us ending up here like this.'

'Fancy,' muttered Tanner. 'You recovered then.'

'Oh yes, Jack. You can't keep a good man like me down for long.' He chuckled. 'I'm taking you to see the CO, Captain Barclay.' Blackstone took out a packet of Woodbines and offered one to Tanner. 'Smoke?'

'No thanks, sir.'

'Don't tell me you've given up the beadies, Jack.'

'I just don't want one at the moment.'

'You mean you don't want one of mine.' Blackstone sighed. 'Jack, can't you tell I'm trying to be friendly? Come on – let's not have any hard feelings. It was a long time ago now. Let bygones be bygones, eh?'

Tanner still said nothing. Blackstone stopped and offered him his packet of cigarettes again. 'Come on, Jack. Have a smoke. Water under the bridge, eh?'

They were now at the parade ground. A platoon of men were being drilled on the far side, the sergeant barking orders. Tanner looked at Blackstone and to the packet of cigarettes now being held out towards him. For a moment, he considered taking one.

'Look here, Jack.' said Blackstone. 'We're at war now. We can't be at each other's throats.'

'Agreed,' said Tanner. 'But that doesn't mean I have to like you.'

The smile fell from Blackstone's face.

'A few pleasantries and the offer of a smoke,' Tanner continued, 'and you think I'll roll over. But I was never that easily bought, Sergeant-Major. Trust and respect have to be earned. You prove to me that you're different

462

from the bastard I knew in India and then I'll gladly take your bloody cigarette and shake your hand.'

Blackstone stared back at Tanner for a moment, his jaw set. 'Listen to you!' he said. 'Who the hell do you think you are? I offer you a bloody olive branch and you have the nerve to spit in my face.'

'Don't give me that crap. What the hell did you expect? You listen to me. Whether we like it not, we're both here and for the sake of the company I'll work with you, but don't expect me to like you, and don't expect me to trust you. Not until you've proved to me that you've changed. Now, I thought you were taking me to see the CO, so let's bloody get on with it.'

Blackstone chuckled mirthlessly. 'Oh dear,' he said, shaking his head. 'You always were an obstinate bastard. I can promise this much, though, Jack. It's really not worth getting on the wrong side of me. It wasn't back then, and it certainly isn't now.'

'Just as I thought,' snarled Tanner. 'You haven't changed a bit.'

'You're making a big mistake, Jack,' said Blackstone slowly. 'Believe me – a very big mistake.'

Darkest Hour

By James Holland

MAY 1940. SERGEANT JACK TANNER has been posted to a training company on the south-east coast of England. But all is not well in the camp. The mysterious death of two Polish refugees leads Tanner to believe there has been foul play. When he and his corporal, Stan Sykes, are nearly killed, Tanner finds his suspicions directed at an old comrade from his early days in the army.

As the Germans launch their Blitzkrieg in Europe, training is abandoned and the entire company are sent to join the battle to stop Hitler's drive across the Low Countries. Almost immediately, they are thrust into the thick of the action and cut off from the rest of the battalion. Trapped behind the enemy advance, Tanner must use all his ingenuity to get his men back to Allied lines.

Soon enmeshed in the long withdrawal to the French coast, Tanner, Sykes and his new platoon commander, Lieutenant John Peploe, find themselves pitted against not only the die-hard Nazis of the SS 'Death's Head' Division but also the great panzer commander himself, General Rommel.

Even then, in the chaos of retreat, Tanner must deal with the corrosive treachery bubbling within the company's ranks – and an enemy more deadly than the Germans – if he and his men are to have any hope of surviving the mayhem of Dunkirk . . .

9780593058367